This Book Will Save Your Life

OAC

~~tttft~~

MGT

WITHDRAWN

Books should be returned or renewed by the
last date stamped above

_____

_____

_____

This Book Will Save Your Life

A. M. Homes

W F HOWES LTD

This large print edition published in 2007 by
W F Howes Ltd
Unit 4, Rearsby Business Park, Gaddesby Lane,
Rearsby, Leicester LE7 4YH

1 3 5 7 9 10 8 6 4 2

First published in the United Kingdom in 2006
by Granta Books

A CIP catalogue record for this book is available
from the British Library

ISBN 978 1 40740 249 9

Typeset by Palimpsest Book Production Limited,
Grangemouth, Stirlingshire
Printed and bound in Great Britain
by Antony Rowe Ltd, Chippenham, Wilts.

For Juliet

He stands at the glass looking out. The city spreads below him, blanketed in foggy slumber. Low pressure. Clouds roll over the hills, seeping out of cracks and crevices as if the geography itself is sending smoke signals.

Below him, far down the hill, a woman swims, her long brown hair floating through the water. Her suit is a beautiful bright-red dot, a rare tropical bird in a pool of unnatural blue. Every morning she swims – crawls like an Olympian. He takes comfort in her swimming, in her determination, rhythm, routine, in the fact that she is awake when he is awake. There is urgency in her stroke; she cannot *not* swim. She is his confidante, his muse, his mermaid.

He is at the glass; usually he is not here, not now. Usually he gets up and gets on his machine – he runs while she swims. He runs watching the electronic ticker tape go by, trading from a keyboard strapped to the treadmill, typing as he trots, placing his bets, going long and short, seeing how far up or down he can go, riding an invisible electronic wave.

Usually he, he usually. Everything today is not the same, and yet it is exactly the same and it can never be the same again.

He stands at the glass. The mechanical sounds of the house catch him off guard. Ice tumbles into the freezer bin, the coffeepot begins to fill with water, air whooshes out of the vent, billowing up the leg of his pants. He shudders.

'Hello?' he calls. 'Anybody home?'

Usually he doesn't hear it. He hears nothing, feels nothing, he makes sure of that. He wakes up, puts on his noise-canceling headset, goes to the glass, looks at the woman swimming, and gets on his machine.

He is in a vacuum of silence – life canceled.

He didn't even know the coffeemaker was automatic – he doesn't drink coffee; it is brewing for Cecelia, the housekeeper, who comes between seven-thirty and eight. He breathes deeply – nice, the smell of coffee.

After years of making sure that he is left alone, he is suddenly afraid to be alone, afraid not to hear, not to feel, not to notice. He presses his ear to the glass. Music. Up the hill men are installing a lawn where there would otherwise be nothing – scrub. They have built a bulkhead, a frame for the grass, and are rolling out sod. They are making a small putting green – one hole.

Above and below, a chain of houses climbs the canyon wall: a social chain, an economic chain, a food chain. The goal is to be on top, king of the hill – to win. Each person looks down on the next, thinking they somehow have it better, but there is always someone else either pressing up from below or looking down from above. There is no way to win.

He stands at the point of the house, where two thick panes of glass meet, a sharp corner jutting out over the hill like the prow of a ship. He stands – captain, lord, master, prisoner of his own making.

Ahead, in the distance, there is something orange and smoky; it takes him a moment to decide – brush fire or simply dawn in Los Angeles?

Yesterday seems realer than real, a dream, an accident, like some sort of seizure or suspension. Did something happen?

There is a depression in the earth, a large soft circular indentation that he doesn't remember from the day before. He looks at it, mentally measuring – approximately eight feet in diameter, about fifty feet from the house. Where did it come from? How long has it been there? How would he describe it? Like the mark made by the back of an enormous ladle pressed into the earth. Do things like that happen overnight?

On the floor of the living room, on the glass-topped coffee table, near the sofa, in the otherwise ordered world, there is debris, little bits of things, plastic nubbins, a piece of tubing, ripped paper, a single piece of bloody gauze – proof.

He is thinking about the pain. It started as a knotty cramp in his back, a strange tightening from his gut up into his chest. The lentil soup he had for lunch? He waited. He took an antacid. It got worse, spreading, searing knifelike down the leg, pressing up into his jaw, a rock-hard ache, a long sharp knitting needle poking into his arm, pain trickling into his fingers – were they numb? His whole body splitting like an ax cutting through fresh wood, a spasm pulling his shoulder blades back like a bow arching, bending him forward, curling him into a cramped crushing 'c,' a hard, violent spasm that could crack a man in two. He didn't think to call anyone, didn't know who to call, what to say, exactly where was the pain? It was everywhere, staggering, sweaty, dizzy-making.

Early on, while he still could, he went into the bedroom, put on a nice pair of pants, a belt, a casual sweater, shoes and socks. He dressed as if he were going out with friends, to a dinner party, to some low-key event, muted colors, soft fabrics. He dressed thinking he might have to get himself down the hill, to a doctor's office, not realizing that it was already late, already past the hour when anyone would still be there.

He lay on the sofa, something he'd never done before; it was against the rules – the private, personal rules we all have for ourselves – no lying down except in bed and never during the day.

He lay on the sofa trying to get comfortable. Was it something he'd done with the trainer, some wrong twist or turn? Or maybe he was getting a bug, cold or flu? The pain continued. How had it come upon him? Had the pain just started, or was it always there and he was just now noticing?

He got up, took some ibuprofen, and stood at the glass looking out over the city, at cars on the boulevard below making the turn, climbing into the hills. The sky was starting to fade, headlights were on, houses were glowing with life. The coyotes howled. The city in the distance was both so large and small.

He was standing at the glass – overcome by pain. Collapsing, every blood vessel, every nerve, every fiber in his body folded in on itself, as though starved, parched. He was standing at the glass in pain, and the strangest thing was he didn't know where it hurt, he couldn't feel anything.

He began to cry. He cried without making a sound, and when he realized he was crying, the very fact of crying, or the fear of it, told him that something was very wrong. And he cried harder.

Was this 'It'? Was this how 'It' happens? Was there something before this, something he should have noticed, a warning? Or was this the warning? Either this was the warning or this was IT.

He dialed 911.
'Police, fire, ambulance.'
'Doctor,' he said.
'Police, fire, ambulance.'
'Rescue,' he said.

'Police, fire, ambulance.' It was a recording.

'Ambulance,' he said.

'One moment please.'

He waited to be connected, and in the moment of silence, the pain left. The pain passed, and then he began to think it was all a nightmare, a daydream, a lousy lunch gone down wrong.

Just as he was going to hang up, a woman came on the line. 'What is the emergency?' she asked, and the pain returned, reminding him.

'Pain,' he said. 'Incredible pain.'

'Where is the pain?'

'I think this is IT,' he said.

'Sir, where are you feeling the pain?'

'Everywhere.'

'Have you sustained an injury – a gunshot wound, fall, snake bite, bow and arrow?'

'No,' he said. 'No. I'm home, I've been home all day. It's seeping through me, it's like I'm soaking in pain.'

'How long have you been in pain?'

'I don't know.'

'Minutes, hours, days?'

'Hours at least.' But it could be days or years – he had no idea.

'On a scale of one to ten, how much pain are you in?'

'Ten.'

'How would you describe the pain – sharp, throbbing, stabbing, dull?'

'Yes.'

'Which of those best describes how you're feeling right now?'

'All of them.'

'Do you have a history of heart attack, stroke, or seizure?'

'No.'

'How old are you?'

'Fifty-five.'

'Are you home alone?'

Inexplicably, this question terrified him. 'I'm divorced.'

'Is anyone there with you?'

'No.'

'Have you ever had this pain before?'

'I never noticed it, until today.' He was becoming increasingly anxious. It felt like a test – too many questions. Was she going to send help or just talk to him all night?

'Are you short of breath?'

The idea of a heart attack or a stroke hadn't exactly occurred to him. It had occurred to him that this was IT, but not that he was having a heart attack.

'Can you cough for me? Take a deep breath and give me a couple of good strong coughs.'

He did the best he could.

'Can you confirm your name for me and your address?'

'You can call me Rick,' he said.

'Is that your real name?'

'What are you getting at?'

'Do you own your home?'

'Yes.'

'Is there any other name that your phone or property would be listed under?'

'Richard,' he said.

'Thank you, Mr Novak,' the operator said.

'How do you know who I am?'

'Our system is enhanced. Help is on the way. As part of a pilot program which helps train crisis counselors, I can transfer you to a counselor who will remain on the line with you until help arrives.'

'Are you trying to sell me something?'

'No, sir, there is no additional charge. It's a service you qualify for because you fit the profile?'

'Profile?'

'You're in the right ZIP code with a potentially life-threatening crisis. With your permission I'm going to transfer you to a counselor; her name is Patty.'

'Is she real or automatic?'

'She's right here; one moment.'

'Hi, Richard, my name is Patty.'

'Hi, Patty,' he said.

'What are you doing, Richard?' He didn't know how to answer that.

'I'm dying.'

'What are you dying from?'

'Pain.' A rupture, an explosion, a slow, tortured death.

'Where in your body is the pain? Can you close your eyes and go into it?'

There are men who keel over at lunch, who are having lunch at the most wonderful, delicious, most expensive restaurant in town and – boom – they just fall over and die. Kaboom. He could be one of those. He could go just like that – out like a light, his aunt used to say. He could step outside, fall down dead in his driveway, and be eaten by wolves, picked apart by vultures. There was no difference between his body and the pain – his body was the pain.

'Richard, what was the last movie you saw?'

It was one of those 'only in L.A.' questions – even as you were dying people were talking about the movies.

'I have no idea,' he struggled to think back. He remembered seeing *Bonnie and Clyde* at the Wellfleet, Massachusetts, drive-in a million years ago.

'Do you have any hobbies? Do you play golf?'

'I like to swim,' he said, surprising himself.

'Where do you swim – do you have a swimming pool?'

'No.'

'When did you last go swimming?'

'About five years ago. At a hotel in Miami; I took a woman there for a long weekend. It ended badly.' He paused. 'I think I'd rather not talk right now. It's very distracting to try and have a conversation.'

'What would you rather do?'

He imagined old people with the 'I've fallen and

9

I can't get up' transmitters around their necks. He imagined them lying on the floor, talking to the transmitters, while help was on the way, just grateful that someone would come and pick them up.

'Patty,' he said, 'where are you from?'

'Minnesota,' she said.

'I thought so,' he said. 'You sound like someone from Minnesota or Modesto.' He was sitting on the sofa, staring at the glass. 'That's OK, you don't have to keep talking to me. I think I'd like to just be quiet so I can concentrate.'

'Are you able to sit, stand, or walk?'

'I'm in pain,' he repeated as though that meant something.

'They'll be there soon,' she said.

He wondered if he had enough cash to pay them – he wondered where that thought came from – he didn't have to pay them, he already paid them, that's what taxes were for. When he was married and living in New York City, he once ordered Chinese food and was still on the phone with the restaurant when the order arrived. They used to joke that the restaurant had a satellite kitchen in the building's basement. He and his wife always kept cash in the apartment to pay them – they were always paying someone, deliverymen, doormen, handymen.

'Are you there?' she asked.

He heard sirens in the distance, the rumble of engines, trucks climbing the hill, the siren grinding to a stop outside his house. He could see the reflection of the red flashing lights in the glass. He knew they were out there.

There was a knock at the door.

He lay on the sofa, thinking he should get up.

'Richard,' Patty said, 'the firemen are at the door; can you let them in?'

'I don't know,' he said, scared, like all of this was a bad idea, like he never should have called.

He watched. He saw them walking around the side of the house, coming down the hill, their flash-lights bouncing, their heavy coats, like branded elephant skins, with iridescent numbers glowing. He heard their radios squawking.

They announced his name over a megaphone in a way that compelled him to surrender.

'Richard Novak, can you hear me, can you open the door?'

'Is there a key hidden somewhere?' Patty asked.

'The garage is open.'

'Good luck, Richard,' Patty said, hanging up.

They came in carrying bags, their coats smelling like fire.

'I'm on the sofa,' he said. 'I'm crying.'

There was no fire.

They were surrounding him, kneeling in front of him, talking to him. 'We're going to take your pressure and give you a little bit of oxygen.'

He nodded.

'Are you in pain right now?'

'I don't know,' he said, speaking into the plastic

11

mask. His voice sounded muffled, distant. 'I don't remember anything.'

A police officer arrived. Were they going to arrest him for making a crank call, for crying wolf, wasting public services, pulling a false alarm?

'Are you home alone?' the cop asked.

He nodded again – why were they so obsessed about who was home?

The house was filling with people – calling him by name, talking to him very loudly. The paramedics arrived and opened boxes – hard cases, like tackle trays. They set up the machine he'd seen on TV, the defibrillator. He prayed they weren't going to use it on him. He was conscious, wasn't he? On TV the medics call out 'All clear' and 'Stand back' and then shock the hell out of the person. The machine was sitting there, ready, green light – go.

'That's a nice de Kooning,' one of the paramedics said.

They took off his shirt, put leads on his chest, swapped the oxygen mask for the small tubes that go up your nose.

'It's a pinched nerve,' he said, looking for a way out.

'And I really like your Rothko. I saw that one once at MOCA.'

'It was on loan,' Richard says.

'Oh yeah,' one of the firemen said. 'I thought that looked familiar. That's by the guy they made the movie about, Ed Harris.'

The paramedic shook his head. 'Ed Harris played Jackson Pollock, those were action paintings, drips. This is Mark Rothko, darker, more serious.'

'Are you paramedics or art experts?'

'I was premed and art history at Harvard. Do you take any medications?'

'Vitamins and some spray for my nose, bad sinuses.'

'Sir,' the paramedic said, 'we're going to send an EKG into the hospital, and from there they'll advise us about further treatment. While we're waiting, I'm going to start an IV.'

The seriousness with which they treated him made him nervous. It was no joke; they acted as though they were saving his life.

'Are you allergic to aspirin?'

'No,' Richard said.

The paramedic put two tiny baby aspirin in his hand.

He chewed. The pills made a paste, a dry, pink, powdery paste that tasted like childhood.

'It's nice you're here,' he said to no one in particular.

'Base to field number four, the strip looks good, you're clear to transport.'

They lifted him onto the stretcher, and as they lifted he cried out; he didn't know why. There were firemen, paramedics, and policemen all around him, carrying him – no one had carried him in years. He tried to help them, to make himself light.

A cop asked where his house keys were – in a

silver bowl on the kitchen counter. They locked the door and handed him the key.

As they wheeled him out, the ride, the bumpy rocking, made him sleepy.

'Does everyone feel sleepy?' Richard asked.

No one answered.

They wheeled him into the night – the red lights of their trucks ricocheting off the house. He breathed deeply – oxygen.

They drove him down, winding round and round the canyon. The farther they went, the riding backwards, the siren's dampened wail, the stop and start of the meat wagon's wobbly waddling, all conspired to make him disoriented, nauseated, lost. He could almost see it coming; as they backed up into the hospital bay, he closed his eyes, dropped his jaw, and puked. Widescreen, he vomited everywhere, spraying the back of the ambulance with black BB pellets of lentils, spraying the faces of the men as they hurried to free him. They threw the sheet over his face to protect themselves, to absorb. As the stretcher was pulled out, as the wheels dropped to the ground, he passed out.

And as fast as he was unconscious, he was conscious again, fully alert, as if launched from a cannon. Had they given him something, a little picker-upper, a shot of the secret sauce?

'Mr Novak, can you hear me?'

He was afraid to speak, to open his mouth, but he nodded.

'Do you know where you are?'

He nodded again.

They lifted him off the gurney, onto a bed, and wiped his face.

'I'm sorry,' he said when it felt safe to talk.

'No need to apologize,' someone said, which prompted him to repeat, 'I'm sorry.'

His mind raced; he was no longer sleepy, he was awake, very awake. His thoughts skipped: Were his papers in order? Who did he leave the Rothko to – MOCA or MoMA? Should he have done things differently? If he died, would his lawyer even know? For comfort he added up his money – how much was in each account, how much was enough?

Had they given him something, a drug that made him speedy? Should he say something, should he tell them that everything was happening too fast? He watched the second hand of the clock – slow, so slow.

'Take a deep breath. Just keep taking those deep breaths. I need you to relax. You're in good hands, Mr Novak, very good hands.'

They were poking him, drawing blood, checking and rechecking his pressure, his pupils, looking at the endless EKG. With cheap ballpoint pens, they wrote on his clean white sheet.

An impossibly skinny woman came to the side of the bed, a twig, a lifeless tree. 'Do you have your insurance card? Who do you want us to locate if . . .' Her bones were sticking out, elbow, wrist, collar, every bone was practically bare, picked clean. 'We need a name and number.' She was like a contact from the other side, booking passage. He expected her next question to be: Do you have any dead relatives that you'd like to have dinner with? I could make you a reservation.

He gave her his lawyer's name. 'I don't know his number.'

It was all so surreal. The fluorescent lights were so harsh, he kept thinking that at any moment they would overwhelm him, bleach out everything; at any moment he'd be going towards the euphemistic white light.

'How did it start?' A resident stood at his knees with his chart in hand.

He couldn't remember, couldn't remember when he could remember, he had no sensation of suddenly not remembering, no one thing or another slipping his mind, but more the sensation that there was nothing. He was searching and seeing nothing, no pictures, no memories, no idea where he'd been.

'Mr Novak, do you understand what I'm asking? When did the pain begin?'

'I'm not sure,' he said. 'Not sure if it just started or if I just noticed it. The more attention I paid, the worse it got. Is Patty here?'

'Who's Patty?'

'I talked with her earlier, the woman on the phone.'

'I don't know anyone named Patty,' the resident said, annoyed.

'My sister's name is Patty,' a nurse said.

'She's very nice, Patty from Minnesota or Mendocino,' he said.

The resident walked away.

'I can offer you this,' the nurse said, handing him a portable phone. 'Is there anyone you'd like to call?'

He shook his head.

'Sometimes people feel better if they talk to someone.'

'Are you a pink lady or a nurse?'

'Nurse. I retired twenty years ago, but now I'm back. It's my second act.'

'What brought you back?'

'My husband died and, truth is, I can't bear to be home alone at night. I wasn't sleeping, and so I thought, why not work nights, it keeps me off the streets and out of the bin.

'There's no one you want to call?' the nurse asked again.

Who would he call?

He parents were snowbirds, still somewhere in Florida – where? His brother in Massachusetts? The nutritionist who suggested the lentil soup that may have been the culprit? His housekeeper, the only one who would actually notice that he wasn't home when she arrived tomorrow morning? His trainer was also coming in the morning, and his masseur was due in the afternoon, and at some point the decorator was going to stop by and tell him what color the guest bedroom should be – if he had their numbers he'd call them all and tell them to forget it, cancel everything.

He lay there realizing how thoroughly he'd removed himself from the world or obligations, how stupidly independent he'd become: he needed no one, knew no one, was not a part of anyone's life. He'd so thoroughly removed himself from the world of dependencies and obligations, he wasn't sure he still existed.

'There has to be someone,' the nurse said.

'You're nice,' he said.

'I'm old,' she said.

'Do you mind if we . . .' Someone pulled the curtain around his cubicle closed.

Who would he call if he was never going to call anyone again, who would he want to speak to just once more – his son, Ben? He wouldn't do that to the kid, they didn't have that kind of relationship. Hi, Ben, it's your dad calling from the emergency room; just wanted to check in, see how your life is going, wanted to wish you BOL – best-of-luck. Hope you do better than me, kid, hope you get what you want, what you deserve and then some. Remember, son, this is IT.

His ex-wife. She left a message on his machine yesterday, or maybe it was a few weeks ago. He never called back – he didn't know why.

'Think about it,' the nurse said.

His ex-wife runs a company that publishes lifestyle and self-improvement books, books that tell you how to live – what to do based on what sign, blood type, or color you are, coffee-table books on living simply and how to find time if you have

18

no time and what to do if none of the above applies.

Over the two-way radio he heard the paramedics communicating with the hospital, calling in a Code Orange.

'What's Orange?'

'Celebrity,' the nurse said. 'They let us know so we can be on the lookout for photographers – sometimes the photo guys get here before the patient. The worst is a dead celeb, that's the money shot. Any photo of a celeb covered in blood is worth thousands.'

'Field to base, Orange is female, mid-, late seventies, auto accident, possible head injury, vitals stable. We've got her in a collar and strapped to a board – we're on our way in.'

'When do you find out who it is?'

'Sometimes we start guessing. We know the approximate age of the patient, where the incident occurred, and we start making bets – was it the Viper Room, up in the hills, in a store on Rodeo Drive, at the hairdresser's? You can get a stroke from tilting your head back in those hair-wash sinks and no one notices, until they try to sit up – we've had a couple of those – celebs are always having their hair done.'

The resident yanked his curtain open. 'They're coming to get you. I ordered a brain scan, want to make sure it's not an aneurysm, that you're not about to spring a leak, pop a berry.' The aspiring doctor laughed at his own joke.

'I don't know where they find them these days,' the nurse said, excusing herself as a pair of state troopers wheeled in a boy tied to a desk chair with yellow nylon rope, like he'd been lassoed.

'I'm God,' the boy announced loudly.

'Hi, God, I'm the emergency-room nurse – can you tell me what you took?'

'Don't fuck with me,' the boy said. 'Don't fuck with God. Because I know, God knows. And I'm God, I can fly, I'm free. I'm God,' he screams, 'I'm God, I'm God, I'm God,' each scream progressively louder than the last.

A doctor shined a light into the boy's eyes. 'Tell me about yourself – what was your name before you were God?'

'I'm God, I'm Jesus, I'm nailed to the stake, that's why I can't move my arms. I'm God, God is a dog,' he barked.

'OK, God, we're going to give you a shot that will help you come down off the mountain.'

'I'm flying,' he shouted. 'And I'm free.' He started wiggling inside the ropes. 'Free me, I order you to free me.'

Meanwhile, the Code Orange auto accident arrived and was wheeled into the cubicle next to him, curtains pulled around her.

The old actress was moaning. From what he overheard, he knew she had some sort of scalp laceration.

He ran through a mental list of names – who could it be? – old actresses? Most of the ones he thought of were already dead – Lucille Ball, Bette Davis, Garbo.

'Let's go ahead and cut it off, I need to see what's under there,' someone said. 'Pass me a scissors.'

'Don't cut,' the actress said.

And then – plunk – through a crack in the curtain he saw something bloody smacked down on the metal tray table.

'Gauze,' someone called out. 'Apply pressure. How deep is it? Any foreign matter?'

He was terrified that her scalp had come off. He couldn't help staring at the metal tray – what was he looking at? – hair, flesh, blood, a bloody scalp.

A nurse grimly stepped out from behind the curtain.

'Did she lose her head?' he asked.

'We don't give out patient information.'

Whatever he'd seen was sufficiently terrifying that it drove him to dial. He called his ex-wife. It was the one number he'd memorized – it was his old number.

Before he could say anything she said, 'I just got home, I'm exhausted. I was in meetings all day. I'm crazed. Can we talk tomorrow?'

'I'm in the hospital. They said I should call someone.'

'What can I do for you from here? It's after midnight.'

'I was in pain and it just kept getting worse. I dialed 911. I'm at Cedars-Sinai with electrodes on my chest and an IV in my arm. They keep asking if I have a history of heart disease.'

'Why don't you call your son?'

'It doesn't seem like the best time to call Ben.'

'I'm exhausted, Richard. Will you be home tomorrow? I'll call you tomorrow.' She hung up before he could speak.

It didn't occur to him to say, This might be the last time we ever speak, this might be IT – don't you get it? He couldn't believe he'd called her – was she always so mean? He shouldn't have called her – he must have been crazy to think he should call, he shouldn't have called anyone – he should have kept it to himself.

As the thought crossed his mind, pain sliced through him like lightning. Why not just die? He didn't want to die. He couldn't die. He hadn't even lived yet.

'I'm scared,' he said to no one. 'And the woman next to me has lost her head.'

The nurse was speaking to the man across the way, talking loudly, like she was making an announcement. 'Mr Rosenberg, you have a broken hip. Your daughter is on her way. Do you know where you are?'

'Of course I know where I am, I'm at the movies, this is all a movie,' he said. 'I wish it were. I'm at the home, the home where I live, or I should say where they put me – waiting to die. Cold storage, that's where I am. I may be old, but I'm not senile.'

'You're in the hospital, Mr Rosenberg. You fell, and they brought you here. Do you know who the president is, Mr Rosenberg?'

'What does it matter? They're all thieves.'

'Mr Novak?' An escort in yellow scrubs appeared at the foot of his bed. 'I've come to take you away.' His gurney was wheeled, IV flapping, down antiseptic corridors and into the bowels of the institution.

CAUTION-RADIATION. A technician appeared with a big syringe. 'Are you allergic to seafood, shellfish, iodine?'

'Not that I know of.'

'Are you claustrophobic?'

'I never thought so.'

The big syringe, and then a smaller syringe: the contrast and a little something to peel the edges back, to sedate him.

'The scan takes about forty-five minutes; it's important that you don't move – we don't have time to start again, we're squeezing you in.'

He felt the squeeze. He felt lentil bile rise in his throat.

The contrast sloshed through him like cold radioactive jelly. His mind was strange. He remembered the ambulance door opening, the feeling of relief that he'd made it there. And then the almost simultaneous rush up from his gut, the sensation of bringing up everything, vomiting up himself, so that in the end he was entirely raw, inside out, exposed. The nurse had wiped the vomit off his

23

mouth with a paper towel; that was nice. If she'd said his name, if she'd smiled at him, if she'd had a damp washcloth, if she'd been a little more gentle, it would have been perfect. It was all a little too matter-of-fact but he was glad they were there, standing by.

The test: it was like test-driving a coffin, as though they were scanning him to make a 3-D model – a virtual death. He could imagine them scanning him and then taking him back upstairs and showing him a PowerPoint presentation of how he would look in a variety of coffins: coffins with different fabrics, head pillows, some with embroidered quotes, a monogram on the lid.

He lay on the narrow, flat bed of the scanner, eyes open, the ceiling two inches from his nose, and all he could think of was his ex-wife.

Back to the beginning, that seemed to be where he'd left off. She was going to be a journalist and he was going to be an economist, an intellectual, a policy man. They met in college – Barnard and Columbia – lost their virginities to each other – or at least he did. And they got married – got an apartment first on the Upper East Side, in a new but nondescript building on Lexington Avenue. From the beginning she made it clear that that wasn't good enough – she wanted Fifth Avenue, overlooking the park. And the whole thing started with a feeling of failure. What should have been an up, a moment celebrating two young people starting a life together, became a theme of nothing being quite good enough. She threw herself into work – determined that, one way or another, she would get exactly what she wanted – and he quickly felt left out. In an effort to do good, to get her attention, he too threw himself into work, and it became all about the money, making enough to impress her and then enough to protect himself, and then just raking it in, making money from money. There was so much money out there, money that could be his for just having an opinion, a point of view, making a good guess. It was the game of money, the fun of money, it was addictive, and he kept winning. He'd tell himself that he'd won two million dollars, he'd won a big bonus, he'd won the admiration of all of those around him who took it to heart, who took it seriously, who got eaten up by it. It's a game, he told everyone – it doesn't mean you don't want to win, but you have to be willing to lose, you have to not take it personally. It's only paper.

'You can afford to say that,' they would say.

After a while, he could. He got up every morning and went home every night without worrying. Was that true? Was that possible? Or was that just the story he told himself?

'We're almost done,' a mechanical voice droned through the speaker in his coffin, interrupting the flow of thoughts.

He lay on the flat bed of the scanner thinking about his ex-wife. Why had he called her? Because it was late in New York City and he knew she'd be home? Because she was the mother of his child? Because, despite how amazingly self-centered she was, he still loved her? Why?

The hum of the machine shifted and he changed the subject. When was he last in a hospital? He looked into the tiny mirror over his head. When was he last in a hospital, ankle twist, tennis injury, bad flu?

Ben. The birth of Ben. How did they manage to have a child? What were they thinking? Did they even want children? Or were they just doing what couples do? Was it like people who buy a puppy for Christmas – it looks cute with the bow on, but who's going to walk it in the middle of the night?

He remembers Ben being born. When he stops to think about it, he remembers everything: the hospital room, the vending machines in the basement, the burned, stale coffee. One thing opens into the next, he can put himself back in time, the big moment, his wife cursing at him, the nurses telling him not to take it personally – 'she's in transition.'

Ben with his eyes closed, thin skin, transparent, not ready for any of it yet. Ben asleep, resting after a long trip, protecting himself. Ben, who always loved his sleep – who slept through the night from eight weeks. Richard would come home from work and check on Ben. He'd stand over the crib in the dark, listening for his breath, touching him, and sometimes a tiny hand would grab his finger – holding on.

'It took longer than I thought,' the technician

said. Lying on the gurney, looking up, Richard was lost in time.

Back in the emergency room, a very young doctor pulled the curtains and sat on a small chair close to his bed. For the first time in his life, Richard didn't even feel middle-aged – he felt OLD.

'When you reach a certain age, we take everything all the more seriously,' the young doctor said. 'Personally, I don't think you had a heart attack – your EKG was fine, your enzymes look good. How do you feel now?'

'Who can tell?' he said.

'Are you still in pain?'

'I don't know.'

'That's rather unusual, the not knowing. That was your presenting complaint, yes, pain?'

'Unbelievable pain.'

'And now?'

'There's a moment when you can't tell if it's better or worse, come or gone, when you don't feel anything.'

Not knowing what to say, never having heard of such a thing, the young doctor looked down at the chart. 'As I said, your CAT scan was fine. EKG looks good – there was no fall, no blow to the head?'

'Nothing,' he said. 'There was nothing.'

'Any travel to unusual places?'

'I never go anywhere.'

'Are you drinking enough water? Dehydration is more of a factor than people realize.'

'I drink water.'

'We have a couple of choices. We can send you up to the unit for twenty-four hours and see how you do, or we can send you home.'

'What kind of a unit?' he asked.

'Step-down. We'd put you on a monitor.' He paused. 'My personal opinion is that it was just one of those things – but what do I know? Lots of things happen, things we can't document. I'm not saying nothing happened. But it may have been an isolated incident, something that passed.'

'Is this the nice way of saying I'm crazy?' He was under a thin sheet, in a crappy gown.

'It's difficult to know how to think of these things – what do we call them? – events. Don't overthink it – accept it. Something happened, we just don't know what.' He paused and forced a smile. 'For the moment, you're not dying, so that's good, that's what's important. You have time. None of us know when they're going to blow the whistle and pull us out of the game. Until then, consider everything useful information.'

'So – I should be glad I'm alive.'

'We all should.'

'The pain was excruciating.'

'In my opinion, you're good to go, but you're the customer, so, if you want me to send you upstairs, I can check and see if there's room at the inn. We can do more tests, we can always do more tests.'

He didn't want to make a decision; he wanted the doctor to tell him what to do. He was distracted, shaken, medicated, bleary from having been up all night. 'Is there Musak in here? I'm hearing Peter, Paul and Mary. "Dawn is breaking, it's early morn . . ."' He sang along.

'Are you staying or going?' the doctor asked, impatiently.

'No heroic efforts,' he said, thinking he was making a joke; the doctor didn't laugh. 'I'll go home,' he said, as if asked to choose between doors number 1, 2, and 3.

'Something happened, don't ignore it. Just because I can't tell you what it was, doesn't mean it wasn't real. Follow up, see your internist – maybe he'll have something interesting to say. And start taking a couple of baby aspirin every day, make that part of your routine, and, besides, they taste good – like Flintstones or Chocks.'

'Like what?'

'Vitamins I used to take when I was a kid – still do.' He pulled a bottle of Flintstones vitamins out of his pocket. 'I pop 'em like candy; Wilma's my favorite, an orange Wilma; second to that is a blue Barney, and a red Dino, I love Dino. I'd offer you one but I can't – against the rules.'

It was a little hard to take the Flintstones doctor seriously – he reminded Richard of someone he once knew who had a job dressing as a Planters Peanut.

'I'm God,' the boy in the cubicle next door mumbled. 'I'm God.'

'I have to ask you something,' Richard said,

leaning forward, whispering. 'It may seem un-related, but in the next cubby – did she lose her head? I saw something.'

The doctor didn't know what he was talking about. 'I'm just the cardiac fellow. So take care, and hope-fully we won't see each other again any too soon.'

When he was gone, the curtain between the cubicles opened. She was there – he knew who she was, sort of; she was that funny kind of familiar, a long-lost aunt, someone who lived next door, part of the family.

'I heard it too,' she said. 'The song.'

'Someone must have a radio.'

There was a bandage wrapped around her head like a turban, and a visible makeup line.

'I was here when they brought you in,' he said. 'I saw something . . .'

'My head.' She reached into the trash can. 'This is what you saw – my wig. "Blond, bloody, a hundred percent human hair. I don't think it can be cleaned. I've got another one at home, but someone's got to get it – that's what the delay is all about. I'm waiting for a fresh head."

The nurse interrupted – 'It's my job to discharge you,' she told him. 'I hope you had a pleasant flight.' She smiled. 'The current time is three-twenty a.m., and the temperature outside is fifty-five degrees. It's going to be another beautiful Los Angeles day.' She pulled the IV needle out of his hand. '"X" marks the spot.' When she was unhooking the EKG, she lifted

30

the leads from his chest before turning the machine off – for a minute there was a flat line. 'Scared you, right?'

He nodded.

'I'm not supposed to do it that way – but I do, it keeps everyone on their toes. What are they going to do, fire me? Seriously, though, here's the plan: you're to continue on the baby aspirin, follow up with your regular doctor, and if your symptoms return we're here twenty-four hours a day, seven days a week – open all night.'

He sat up and was about to swing his legs over the edge. 'I think I'll take a little walk before heading home.'

'Oh no,' the nurse said, 'you can't just walk out of here. Either someone picks you up, or you wait until eight a.m. and we can have the hospital's VIP car take you home. We offer free pickup and delivery, but not before eight. Do you have a friend?'

He looked bewildered.

'Let us call you a taxi.'

He drew the curtain closed, found his clothing in a plastic bag at the foot of the bed, pulled on his sweater – speckled with vomit – and patted his hair back into place. He stuck his head out into the room. 'Do you have a toothbrush or some mouthwash, something I could rinse with? I have a foul taste . . .'

The nurse handed him a stick of gum. 'Enjoy.'

He sat on the gurney, chewing gum, waiting for the taxi.

31

'Do you ever eat?' he asked the skinny overnight clerk.

'Batteries,' she said. 'I run on batteries, triple A.' And he believed her.

Released into the custody of the Beverly Hills Cab Company, Richard stepped into the Los Angeles night. There was an evanescent glow to the sky as light seeped back into the atmosphere, hinting at the day to come. He sat in the back, with the windows down, his head into the breeze like a dog. The driver babbled like a bad bartender, talking about everything, anything, nothing. 'So – what was it, too much to drink, hit by a car, stepped on a nail, kidney stone, pistol-whipped?'

He didn't answer; the last thing he wanted was a confessional conversation with the cab driver.

'Fine, keep it a secret, see if I care. Everyone thinks they're entitled to keep it to themselves. What do they know? That's how you get sick, really sick – ulcers, colitis, cancer. I tell people everything, what do I need to keep secrets for? Ask me anything.'

Richard didn't respond. He didn't ask.

'OK, well, let me tell you a couple of things about this little trip we're on – people with problems, that's who's on the road at this hour; it's either hardworking guys like myself trying to make a living, or maniacs who've been up all night doing Christ knows what.'

He heard the echo of the emergency-room kid's voice in his head – I'm God.

'This time of day, the traffic goes two ways, and I don't mean two directions. You've got your early birds and your night owls, couldn't be two more different species, crossing paths. You got the gals going to the gym and the freaks just coming home.'

Ahead of them, like slow-motion, a car sped through the intersection, just missing another car, spun a half-circle, and sped off. For the flash of a second Richard made eye contact with the driver who was almost creamed; the man glanced at him, dumbfounded, shaking his head in a repetitious, palsied kind of way.

'Musician – had to be. They're like that, can't drive. Musicians and Mexicans don't belong behind the wheel. That and the old people – the old people should be taken off the road. And women, women are the worst drivers . . .'

He watched as buildings passed by: low, flat buildings, tan, brown, green, earthy red, the colors of camouflage, of ground cover. One after another, mile after mile of car shops, yoga studios, cell-phone stores, wig outlets, car washes, hairdressers, furniture outlets.

They passed a store with an orange neon sign – 'Donuts.' A buttery warm glow emanated from the window. They passed the store, and when it was gone, Richard wished they'd stopped. He couldn't go home, not yet, not so fast. He needed a minute to clear his mind, to put the events in order.

'In fact,' the driver continued, 'most people

33

shouldn't ever get behind the wheel. Driving should be left to professionals.'

He leaned forward. 'I need to go back.'

The driver ignored him.

'I just realized I forgot something.'

Still no response.

'Excuse me,' he said. 'I want to go back.'

'To the hospital?'

'No, to the donut shop we passed about ten blocks ago.'

The man continued to drive. 'You want me to turn around?'

'Yes,' he said.

'So you don't want me to go up Sunset?'

'No, I want to go back to that donut shop.'

'Are you just running in, or am I dropping you there?'

'I don't know, why?'

'I'm just wondering if I'm dropping you or waiting. I'm supposed to take you home – that's why they call us, to take people home.'

'I'm hungry, and there's no one at home, so unless I'm under arrest or something I think I'm allowed to get out at a donut shop.'

The driver made the U-turn. 'You're not, like, a suicidal diabetic or anything, are you?'

He didn't answer.

'OK, so let me know. I mean, let me know if you're just running in.'

'Do you want something? If I run in is there something that you want?'

'No, I don't think so,' the driver said. 'Well, maybe a cup of coffee, and, you know, if they have something not too sweet, a plain donut, a couple of plain donuts, that's all. Or if they have the glazed ones, the high puffy ones with chocolate on top. I'll take two of those.'

As they pulled up to the donut shop, Richard said, 'I think I'll just get off here. If you'd just drop me off – that would be great.'

'Does that mean you're not getting me a cup of coffee?'

'No, I'll still get you yours. I'll run in, get you yours, and I'll be right back.' He got out of the car. 'Shouldn't you turn the meter off?'

'When you come back, we'll settle up.'

'So, basically, I'm paying you for the privilege of buying you a coffee?'

'Look,' the driver said, 'let's not start the day on the wrong foot.'

The donut shop was empty. The man behind the counter smiled.

'I need something for that man out there – a coffee and two raised, glazed chocolate donuts.'

'Anhil,' the man said, extending his hand.

'Richard,' he said, shaking the man's hand, surprised by the physicality of the welcome.

'Milk and sugar?'

'Why not.' He took out his wallet.

Anhil shook his head. 'After.'

Richard brought the donuts out to the driver. The meter was still running. 'How much do I owe you?'

35

The man sipped the coffee; the meter ran higher. The fare on the meter was nine dollars and twenty cents. 'Let's call it ten,' the driver said.

'Should I deduct the cost of the donut and coffee?'

'Figure it's part of the tip.'

The sky was a whitewashed charcoal-gray.

'What can I make you?' Anhil asked when Richard came back into the shop.

Richard stood at the window, looking out at the taxi parked at the curb, the driver eating his donuts, and – what? – waiting for him? Was he just sitting there to be annoying, or was he so dim that he was sitting there without a clue?

'Your mind is outside. Come in, sit down, have coffee,' Anhil said.

'I don't get it. Why is he sitting there? He didn't want to stop, and now he's just sitting there, eating donuts.' Richard suddenly wanted to kill the guy, wanted to go rushing out and pound on his car – 'Don't you understand, you're making it worse, you're making everything so ordinary and boring. Why are you just sitting here?'

'Donuts are like that. What can I get you?'

Richard sat on a stool and looked at Anhil. 'Coffee.'

'No donut?' Anhil asked.

'OK, donut.'

'What kind?'

'Your best donut.'

Anhil poured the coffee and placed a donut in front of Richard with the simplest of ceremony. 'It's warm,' Anhil said, proudly.

Something about Anhil prompted Richard to surrender his annoyance at the driver. There was a purity to the donut shop; the wood-paneled interior was genuinely old, the lighting had a dim yellow glow, the display cases were heavy glass. All of it was as it must have been in the 1940s.

Anhil's coffee was hot, dark, full-flavored, perfect chasing the equally well-turned donut: golden brown, dense without being leaden, not too sweet.

Richard closed his eyes and took a breath.

'What do you think?'

'Heaven,' he said, opening his eyes. 'I didn't have dinner last night.'

'Would you like me to make you some eggs?'

'I don't see eggs on your menu.'

'That doesn't mean I can't make eggs. Why didn't you have dinner?'

Without intending to, he spilled the story of last night: 'I was in incredible pain, I went to the hospital, they thought I was having a heart attack.' He spoke too loudly, the way you do when talking to someone whose first language is not English. He tapped his chest as if Anhil might not know where the heart was.

'I thought I was going to die,' he said. 'I called my ex-wife, she lives in New York.'

Anhil laughed.

'What's funny?'

'Everything. You lived, and now you're eating a donut. That's not Mr Healthy.'

'I never eat donuts – that's why I wanted one. I am Mr Healthy. I eat cereal that the nutritionist makes for me; it tastes like wood chips. I drink Lactaid milk. I never break the rules.'

'Let me make you some breakfast,' Anhil said, going into the kitchen. He continued to talk to him through a hole in the wall. 'This used to be a kosher bakery, used to be this area was Jewish, now it's immigrants like me and old men with curls. This is the land of money – every man can have his own store, look how many stores there are.' He cracked the eggs. 'When I first got here, I worked in a garage, fixing cars. In my country I was a car salesman. What do you drive?'

'I have a Mercedes, but I don't drive a lot.' Richard smelled the eggs cooking.

'Of course you drive a lot, you live in Los Angeles. Just to go to work in the morning you drive a lot.' Anhil poured him a glass of orange juice. Richard couldn't bring himself to tell Anhil that he didn't go to work, that he hadn't gone to work in years, that he had no idea of what work was anymore.

'What kind of cars did you sell?'

'Other people's cars. All kinds, Ford, Chevrolet, strong cars from the 1970s. "Pre-owned," they call them here. I like making donuts better. And here my wife can work for me, my brother can work. I employ everybody. So what did they say, what is wrong with your heart?'

'They don't know.'

'For smart people, Americans are very stupid.' Richard nodded.

'In America everybody is somebody. They have so much and they all want more. In my country we are all nobodies; it's easier. Here they are always trying to be somebody else. They go to the doctor and get a new nose, they get bigger chests – why aren't they happy to have a nose that works and weather that is always good?' He spoke as though all of this were so obvious, so funny.

'It's always about the weather, isn't it?' Richard said, making small talk. 'We stay for the weather.'

'Where are you from?' Anhil asked.

'New York City.'

'Me too,' Anhil said, excitedly. 'I was born at Lenox Hill Hospital. My mother was visiting. I arrived early. In my own country I might have died. I stayed one month in hospital and then went home. I am forty-one years old. I came back to America four years ago to make myself into something.' Anhil leaned forward. 'Explain, why does everyone in America pretend to be blind? They practice not seeing. They get into the car and they call someone on the cell phone. They are afraid to be alone but they don't see the people around them. See your plate?'

Richard looked down; his eggs were on a nice old plate.

'You didn't see it until I said to look.' Anhil laughed. 'I buy them at the flea market in Pasadena.

I like it when people sit down, when they stay. Everybody wants everything to go. Go, go, go. If someone sits down, I give them a nice plate and a good cup. If they stay, I give them free refills. If they go, they like the paper cups that say "Always a Pleasure to Serve You." When I first opened, I had Kevin Costner paper cups, I got them on sale. People started coming in and asking for a cup of Costner to go. But now, if a woman came in, if a woman ordered tea, I'd have the right cup for her. Women don't eat donuts,' he said, disappointed. 'But that's better for me – I like women. My wife would be very angry if my shop was filled with women.' Something about the way he said it prompted Richard to imagine a group of women, like the Dallas Cowboy Cheerleaders, filling up the place.

Anhil spread his assortment of dishes across the counter. 'People should pay more attention. Everyone wants attention, but no one wants to give attention.' He finished arranging the dishes. 'What do you think?'

'Nice,' Richard said, picturing the immigrant donut-maker walking up and down the aisles at the flea market, bargaining for dishes.

'Try this,' Anhil said, putting a coconut-topped chocolate donut on a small plate in front of Richard. He looked at Richard and the donut with great intensity, as if this were the donut that would fix Richard, as if there were certain donuts that were better for certain ailments, as if a donut could have curative powers.

Richard bit into the donut, sweet rich cream squirted out the side, he licked his fingers. 'Delicious. What is it?'

'Almond-flavored cream on the inside, chocolate icing and coconut on the outside – my own invention. I call it a Cream-Filled Mons – from the candy bars Almond Joy and Mounds.'

'Mons. You might have to change that.'

Anhil looked at him, confused.

Richard pointed to his crotch. 'On a woman, this is a mons.'

'And the coconut gets stuck in your teeth like private hair,' Anhil said, laughing. 'They're very popular, especially with the policemen.' Anhil laughed even harder, and at that point even Richard had to laugh. 'That's my audience – police, landscaper, taxi. I came to California to make somebody. The first week after I opened the shop, I got robbed by someone from television. I looked at him – I said, I know you; you're from TV. Go away, come another day – buy donuts.'

'Did he leave?'

'He hit me with his gun and took the dollar bill off my wall.'

'He took your first dollar?'

Anhil nodded.

'That's bad.' He finished the breakfast. 'You're a good cook – you should have a restaurant, not just a donut shop.'

'I am a good donut-maker,' Anhil said. 'Mr Dunkin' doesn't even think of me, but I know my donut is better. Mine is the real donut, the human donut. I am not going to get rich making donuts – donuts are not gold records, donuts are not box office – but every morning I make a donut and I am happy.' He laughed again. 'I count my donuts. I feel very lucky.'

'You work very hard.'

'Sometimes I don't go home. I call my wife and tell her good night and I sleep here. When you came, I wasn't open. But I saw you and couldn't turn you away.'

'Aren't you afraid at night?'

'I sleep with the light on.'

They were silent for a few minutes. Outside, the sky was getting lighter; traffic was picking up. Someone came in and got a cup of coffee and some donuts to go.

'I should call a taxi,' Richard said.

'No need to call; they'll come soon. When the shift changes, they meet in the parking lot.'

And, sure enough, about ten minutes later, the shop was filled with taxi drivers tanking up.

Before Richard left, Anhil filled a big box with donuts. Richard pulled out his wallet, but Anhil wouldn't take any money.

'You're a lousy businessman if you don't let me pay you.'

'It's not about money.'

'I know that now; please, take some. I can't go home unless you take my money; that's the rule in America, you must take my money.'

'You are hurting my feelings,' Anhil said. 'I thought we were friends.'

'Yours is the human donut,' Richard said, putting money on the counter.

'You may think you're rich because you have a lot of money, but there's always someone with more. I'm rich because I have my heart in the donut shop.' He pushes the money away.

Richard could see that he was hurting Anhil's feelings; he took the money back. 'Fine, then, let me do something for you.'

'I will drive your car,' Anhil said. 'I have never driven a Mercedes.'

Richard nodded.

'See you tomorrow,' Anhil said, and Richard didn't know if it was a joke or not.

'See you,' he said, leaving the donut shop filled with possibility, with breakfast, with his spare collection of donuts in a box on the seat next to him. He felt good, buoyant.

Did he get lucky? Did he survive something? He had the sense of having traveled a great distance, of time having been suspended. Maybe this was IT, this was luck, it was all supposed to happen this way. Maybe that's what he was supposed to think – how lucky he was – he had a nose that worked, the weather was good, who could want more? Maybe everyone was lucky and didn't notice – was it foolish to think that even when everything fell apart it was luck?

He belched – the full flavors of coffee, eggs,

donuts repeated, and he thought of Anhil. He smiled.

'Nice being up in the morning, isn't it?' the driver said, catching his smile in the rearview mirror. 'I used to work the night shift. I felt like a creep, a vampire. And talk about coffee, I drank so much coffee, even after working a twelve-hour shift I couldn't sleep. I'd go home and shake.'

Richard nodded. The taxi climbed up the hill. As they got closer, it was harder to think forward. The donut-and-coffee combo was turning into a bad mix, the acid, the sugar, the high becoming sugar confusion, a cold hard crash. He didn't want to go back – he couldn't go back. Filled with dread, he was tempted to tell the driver to keep going, he'd made a mistake, he didn't want to get off.

The taxi stopped in front of the house. And he was out, standing at the curb with the box of donuts in hand.

He could stand outside and wait until Cecelia came, and pretend that he didn't have his key, that he was locked out. He could sit on the front step and admit he was afraid to be home.

'I'm afraid,' he would call out to anyone looking out a window. 'I'm afraid,' he would announce to the paperboy tossing the morning news out the window of a station wagon while his father coasted downhill in neutral.

He forced himself to walk to the front door. The grass was damp, tickling his ankles – he hadn't put his socks back on in the ER, they had vomit on them and he'd just left them there. Brown socks. He didn't want to wear brown socks ever again; he didn't want to wear any socks. Shoes without socks, blisters and raw skin – who cared? He couldn't cover everything up anymore, he needed to feel everything as it was.

'Morning,' he called, opening the door. 'Morning,' he called as if expecting someone to answer.

The brushed stainless-steel kitchen gave off a modern, reflectionless, dull shine. Everything was in order, perfectly placed, perfectly clean. To the left was the living room, matching white sofas, an Eames chair, glass-topped coffee table, handmade Belgian shaggy rug. Each item chosen for its beauty, its perfection. These were the things he wanted: controlled, precise, ordered. He had bought them when he moved here. On the walls were paintings, important paintings, paintings that museums wanted. It was part of his plan when he moved to Los Angeles. He told himself he was setting up a new life, a good life, and he wanted beautiful/important things to be a part of it. He told himself that he'd worked hard and should surround himself with proof of his hard work, his assets. He should surround himself with art, so that in some way he himself would become art.

The house was still, pulled tight as though holding its breath, motionless, trying not to be. He breathed deeply – nonscent. The house had no smell at all except that it smelled clean, almost lemony and crisp.

The comfort of the familiar had become uncomfortable; it was too comfortable and not comfortable at all.

He put the donuts down, flipped the box open. If he ate one, maybe he'd feel good again. Eeny, meeny, miney, mo – which one to pick, which one would do the trick? Plain cake. 'Classic,' Anhil called it.

Richard glanced at the clock on the microwave – 5:37 – almost twelve hours, almost one half-day since he'd dialed 911.

In the living room there were scraps, scattered debris of the incident, spare parts from the IV kit, the semicircular peel-off backing from the electrodes they put on his chest, a cotton ball with a large red bloody dot on it.

What had happened?

He took off his shirt and touched his chest; there was goo in the hair.

The whole thing might have been a weird dream, a hallucination – except that he had proof, the debris, the sticky stuff. Like an alien abduction, he'd been taken, probed, and returned, wondering what the hell had happened. Would he ever feel like himself again? And what did he feel like in the first place? He had no memory.

He was standing at the point of the house, where two thick panes of glass meet, a sharp corner jutting out over the hill like the prow of a ship.

Below him to the left was the dent, the depression.

He almost thought it was growing as he watched it – wider, deeper.

'Something happened, don't ignore it,' the doctor had said.

Ahead are rooftops, Spanish tile roofs, flat modern roofs, peaked slate roofs. Between the houses is lush, vibrant greenery, purple and yellow flowers, roses, orange trees, dashes of color like specks of hot pepper, something is always blooming.

And she is there, down below, in her humming-bird-red suit, crawling through the blue water, with strength and purpose. She gets to the wall, flips, pushes off, stroke, stroke, her head turning and lifting for air. He is usually on the treadmill, he is usually running while she is swimming, but now he is afraid of exercise, afraid for his heart. He imagines himself underwater, out of air, suffocating. As he imagines it, he feels it.

She stops swimming, pulls off the goggles, and looks up.

To the woman down below, he is simply the man up above, staring.

Accidentally he touches the glass. It is cool. He presses his cheek, his nose, his mouth to the glass. He takes a deep breath and exhales long and slow, fogging the glass, and for a moment everything, even the swimmer, is gone.

He is standing at the glass waiting for his life to begin.

⋆　　⋆　　⋆

'You all right?' Cecelia the housekeeper asks.

'Yeah, why?'

'You're just standing there, staring. I've been here fifteen minutes and you haven't moved. You're not wearing your morning clothes, and you don't have those headphones on. You sure you're all right?'

He can't decide whether to say anything, whether to tell her about last night. He decides to act normal, to act like nothing happened.

'Fine,' he says.

'Where'd the donuts come from? Fund-raiser? Kids going door to door?'

'On my way home; help yourself.'

She looks at the address on the box. 'What were you doing all the way down there?'

'I was starving.'

She looks insulted. 'You know if you need something I always bring it to you – you just call me and I'll bring it with me. I do a good job taking care of you – don't I fill your fridge with good, healthy foods? This kind of thing isn't for people like you.'

'I had a craving.'

'I could take them home with me,' she says, 'save you from them, but then I'd eat 'em myself. I should resist that temptation.' She picks up the box and dumps it in the trash. 'Nothing worse than eating other people's garbage. Now, are you ready for breakfast?'

'I was thinking I'd shower first,' he says.

'All I can say is, I hope you got lucky, because

this is so not you, not the man I know, and I just want there to be a good reason for it.'

In the shower he opens the retractable skylight; steam rises like smoke. He imagines he can use his washcloth to send signals, messages, up the canyon. Covered with the creepy crawl of the emergency room, he scrubs himself, washing off the night. There are a couple of electrodes still attached. The Band-Aid on his hand slides off and is sucked down the drain.

He is trying to put it behind him, and yet it plays in his head – the lights, the people, the pickling disinfectant smell, the God boy coming down.

He pictures the nurse getting home in the morning, glad to have missed a long night alone. 'As long as my knees hold out,' she'd said, 'I'll keep doing it.' She was a good nurse, a damned good nurse. He pictures her house, the kitchen filled with crocheted pot-holders, knitted afghans, hens and chicks on the windowsill. She was a nice lady who had loved her husband. He pictures her making herself a cup of tea and then, without taking her nurse's scrubs off, lying down on the sofa. She can't go into the bedroom, can't put her nightgown on. She can't pretend.

Dressing, he can't help glancing at the ticker tape going by. The night in the ER didn't cost him so much; in fact, he might even be up a little bit. Footage of the actress's crashed car comes up on CNN, they report that the eighty-seven-year-old actress is in serious but stable condition.

Could she really be eighty-seven? He thinks he might call her, she'd remember him, they had an official moment. Hi, it's me. How's your head – is it on straight, is it a good fit?

Glancing at the clock, he sees he's off schedule. He hates it when the day unfolds other than as expected. He picks up the phone. It's still morning in NYC. What is he going to say? Hi, Ben, is this a good time? I didn't catch you in the middle of something, did I? I thought we could talk. Ben, this is your father. Ben, I think it would be nice if we had some sort of relationship. Ben, is your mother home? Is she still sleeping with her trainer? Is your mother just mean to me or is she like that with everyone? Have you noticed? Ben, can I call you that, can I call you Ben?

A groggy voice picks up. 'Hello?'

'Ben.' He pauses. 'Ben, it's your father.'

'What's wrong?'

'Nothing's wrong.'

'What happened?'

'Did your mother mention anything?'

'I haven't seen her; I'm in my room. I slept late. She might have left a note, she leaves notes in the kitchen.'

'I tried calling her last night. I didn't feel well, I was in pain, knotted up like a pretzel. I went to the hospital, and while I was there I realized that the last time I'd been in the hospital was when you were born.'

50

'That's weird. Pain from what?'

'I don't know –it may have been there for a long time. I was remembering, when you were born your mother was calm. I stood next to her – sweating profusely.'

'I was born during a heat wave, broke all the records, it's never been as hot.'

'Who told you that? I don't remember the heat.'

'Your brother – Uncle Ted. He gave me the *New York Times* from the day I was born. Record heat, stopped everything on the East Coast; there was almost a blackout in New York.'

'Well, I don't want to keep you.'

'You're not going to die, are you?'

'No, not now, not today.'

His breakfast is waiting. The newspapers are laid out on the table the way he likes them, one atop another: *Financial Times, Wall Street Journal, New York Times, Los Angeles Times.* He should cancel one and see how it goes. Maybe he should cancel two; what does anyone do with four papers?

Cecelia makes his special shake – frozen organic blueberries; two powders, one muscle-building, one protein; half a banana; a half-cup yogurt – whipped into a frenzy. And then there's his special bowl of cereal and the Lactaid milk. And his drink, a hot herbal infusion that tastes like Lemon Pledge. He has taught himself to drink it, to like the waxy aftertaste, the chemical tinge.

He eats breakfast, not telling Cecelia that he has

already eaten. He does what he always does, because it's easier.

Sitting at the dining-room table, trying to seem casual, he calls his brother. The phone is answered and dropped. 'Sorry,' his brother says.

'It's Richard.'

'Are you all right?'

'I'm all right, I just wanted to be in touch. What's the weather like?' he asks, not because he cares, but because he doesn't know what else to say. Before this, if you'd asked Richard about his brother, he would have said they were 'pretty close,' but the truth is he can't recall when they last spoke.

'Nice,' the brother says. 'The weather is very nice.'

'It's raining.' Richard hears Meredith, his brother's wife, in the background. She takes the phone. 'It's been raining all week,' she says. 'He never notices anything. Is everything OK?'

I didn't feel well. I was in pain, knotted up. I went to the hospital. 'Fine,' he says.

The brother takes the phone again. 'I spoke to Mom and Dad last week; they're great. I can't get over how much they're doing, they seem to have found themselves a whole new life.'

'I took a chicken out of the freezer,' Meredith announces to no one in particular.

'Listen, I'm just on my way out the door, running late – can I call you this afternoon, from the office, or how about tonight –can I call you tonight?'

'Yeah, sure, that's fine.'

Meredith takes the phone again. 'We'd love to

see you. Why don't you come and spend a few days with us?'

'Well, that's part of why I'm calling,' Richard lies. 'I have some business in Boston, and I wanted to see if you were free for dinner . . .'

'Free for dinner? You'll stay with us.'

'A hotel is fine. I'm not exactly sure when it will be.'

'We're still in the same place,' she says. 'Two-eighty-nine Chestnut Street in Brookline.'

Online, he searches for an e-mail his parents sent – he was one of thirty-two people copied. He finds it – a perky message about their travel plans. 'Almost time for our annual migration. We're just back from Las Vegas, so lively. And last summer we took a wonderful cruise to Alaska. It was delicious,' she writes, as though they'd eaten a glacier. 'We're looking forward to seeing all of you. Come visit – golf, tennis, aqua aerobics, sun – what's a few more wrinkles when you've gotten this far.'

He calls the number listed under contact info at the bottom of the screen. His mother answers. 'It's a beautiful day down here, we just had lunch, and now we're going to play golf. Well, I don't play, because of my knee and my back, but I drive the cart. And tonight we have art appreciation, a beautiful young man from the museum is talking about the M's – Manet, Monet, and Marden. Have you heard of them?'

She talks as though he could be anyone. He waits for a pause and then identifies himself again.

'I know who it is,' she says. 'What am I supposed to say, long time no see?'

'I just wanted to say hello.'

'We're not sure we believe you,' his mother says, invoking the plural power of the couple. 'Have you spoken to your brother lately?'

'Do you believe him more?'

'We know him better – he calls every Saturday. We like having a schedule. We're very busy. Your father makes a lot of friends, we're always seeing this one or that one. And you, what are you doing?' she asks, implying that she's expecting something big – world peace, a cure for cancer. 'Are you working?'

'I'm retired.'

'It's a shame.'

He feels himself getting angry – he doesn't say anything.

'We moved,' she says. 'We're in a place that didn't exist before. A community. We don't have to do anything unless we want to. If we don't want to make dinner, we pick up the phone and they deliver it. If we need a bulb changed, they come running. I've never seen people work so hard. They'll even bring a snack in the middle of the night. And we have friends, we talk about the grandchildren who call once a year – Hi, Grandma, did you remember my birthday? We all know what that means . . .'

Cecelia is vacuuming. He walks towards her on purpose. She tries to get away. She tugs on the hose and the motor unit scurries across the floor,

54

like an electric puppy. He's chasing her, and she's running with the vacuum.

'Where are you, it's so noisy? It sounds like a train station.'

'Talk to you soon,' he says, lying.

When he gets off the phone, Cecelia is shaking her head and clucking. 'People don't make those calls during the week – only nights and weekends.'

He looks puzzled.

'Free nights and weekends,' Cecelia says.

The phone rings. 'I'll get it,' he calls.

Cecelia already has it. She has picked it up behind his back, literally. 'Yes,' Cecelia says. 'There's always someone here. Thank you.' She hangs up.

'Who was that?'

'The florist, wanting to know if there's someone home to receive a delivery. They tried to deliver to the hospital, but you weren't there. Is there something you want to tell me? Whatever it is, I'm not surprised. I figured something was going to happen to you – you didn't leave the house for almost a month.'

'Is that true?'

Cecelia nods. 'Twenty-four days, I counted. I was going to say something and then I figured it wasn't my place. You sat in front of that computer for so long, I thought you'd start glowing in the dark.'

She is spraying the counters with Fantastik.

'Do you clean every day?'

'Different things on different days, there's always something to do.'

'And what do I normally do?'

'You sit at your computer with those things on your head. Sometimes people come to see you, sometimes people you used to work with, sometimes those art people trying to sell you things, they show you pictures of paintings.'

He nods. 'And then?'

'You don't buy anything. You used to, but you haven't bought anything in years.'

From the bedroom, with the door closed, he calls to make his doctor appointment.

'I can put you in with Dr Anderson two weeks from tomorrow, at eleven a.m.'

'I don't think I'll last that long.'

'If it's an emergency, you should go to the emergency room.'

'I just came home from the emergency room – they told me to call my doctor as soon as possible.'

'Why didn't you say so? I can put you in with the new fellow, Dr Lusardi, this afternoon.'

'The new fellow is fine; he's a doctor, right?'

'Oh, he's more than a doctor – he's everything. We'll see you at three-thirty. Be sure to get a parking ticket so we can validate you.'

He changes his clothes and goes into the exercise room. The trainer is already there. That's how it goes, they don't keep you waiting, it's all about convenience, your schedule – you.

'How are you?' she asks as he lies down on the mat.

'I didn't do the treadmill this morning,' he says. It is probably the first morning in years that he hasn't been on the treadmill.

'It's OK to take a day off,' the trainer says.

'I didn't take a day off, I missed a day,' he says. 'It's different.'

She lifts his leg. 'How does that feel? Am I getting to you?'

He nods.

'Where are you feeling it, hamstring?'

'More in the calf.'

'How about now?' She adjusts the leg.

They have a strange conversation, about the minutiae of muscles, about the feelings in his quads, in the glutes, if the sinuses are clear. The conversation is at once intimate and incredibly distant, it is not about *his* body but about *the* body.

'You have a big bruise on *the* hand,' she says.

'It's from last night,' he says, nonspecifically.

Halfway through, as she's bending his leg up over his head, he begins to feel it again – the pain.

'You're sweating,' she says. 'A lot.'

Is he sweating? He's crying. Soundless tears are running down his face.

'Oh no,' she says. 'What's wrong, did I hurt you?'

Only when she says that – Did I hurt you? – does it turn to a choking kind of cry. As someone who never cries, he never knew he had so many different kinds of cries in him.

He is crying and she is patting him on the back like she is burping him. 'Are you all right? Maybe

57

we loosened up something that was trapped in there – maybe it's a good thing.'

He is still crying.

'Do you need a hug?'

He shakes his head no and stops crying.

'Let's do something different. Can you lie on your stomach?'

He is happy to turn away, to lie facedown. 'I didn't feel well last night,' he confesses. 'I went to the hospital. I guess I'm not over it.'

'You should have called me,' she says. 'We could have rescheduled.'

'I didn't want to cancel,' he says. 'I wanted to keep everything the same as always, except I can't.'

'It's OK,' she says. The same small words they said last night as they lifted the stretcher into the ambulance. He was glad they were there, that group of men, an impromptu pow-wow, taking him seriously, not telling him to snap out of it, pull himself together, keep marching.

She rolls him over onto his back. 'Give yourself over to it,' she says. 'It's OK. Sometimes it just has to come out.'

The flowers arrive while the trainer is there. The flowers of death, lilies, enormous smelly lilies, sickly sweet. Cecelia brings them in to show him, and then takes them away to find a vase. After the session he goes into the living room. They are on the coffee table, looking large, grotesque, out of place.

He is standing at the glass, looking out, and doesn't

see it coming until it's too late. A bird dive-bombs. They are eye to eye, and then, with a thick thud, it hits the glass. Right in front of him – 100 percent living – it hits the glass, and – 100 percent dead – it falls to the ground. He goes into the kitchen, finds a big spoon, goes outside, digs a hole, and buries the bird. He goes back into the house, gets the flowers, and puts them on the grave.

Later, she calls. 'I only have a minute,' she says. 'You really are something. I got no sleep last night. You always were a hypochondriac: your neck, your back, your headaches.'

'That's not what they said at the hospital – no one called me a hypochondriac.'

'They were being polite,' she says.

'I talked to Ben this morning.'

'Did he tell you about the trip?'

'What trip?'

He's going to drive cross-country, like *On the Road*. Ben and Barth, the first cousins, together for the summer. I told them they could use my car.'

'The Porsche?'

'No, I sold that long ago – a Volvo wagon.'

Sounds like fun.'

They're planning to spend the summer in California.'

There is silence; Ben didn't mention it to him; maybe Ben doesn't want him to know. Ben in California: it's thrilling, it's terrifying. Now's his chance, and he feels like he's already blown it.

'Thanks for the flowers,' he says. 'I already used them.'

'Did I send flowers? That was nice of me.'

'Nice to know you have feelings for me.'

'I have feelings, Richard, I just never have time.'

After lunch, the woman comes to talk about the color of the guest room. She moves through the space, touching the walls, getting a feel for things. 'Did you decide what this room is for? We need a purpose before we can give it a personality.'

It was supposed to be Ben's room. Thirteen years ago, when Richard bought the house, he excitedly went shopping for the stuff of a boy's room: a bed shaped like a car, a carpet that had a road woven into it, trucks to push around, things a young little boy would like. It would be ready by Christmas, and then he would fly to New York and pick up Ben, who was still too young to fly alone, and come back out for a couple of weeks. But then she got an invitation to go somewhere; wherever it was sounded better than what he could offer – he'd be selfish if he said no.

'You'll have him another time,' she had said. 'There are a lot of Christmases to come.'

And he put a temporary stop on the furniture order. And then it was spring vacation, and Ben had a cold and couldn't fly, and then it was summer, and there was another reason. And what was supposed to be a visit every month became every two or three, and Richard would go to New York for a week or so and come back feeling worse, and once or twice Ben came to L.A., but it never felt right, never felt like home. And now it was just a room, a plain room with a bed. Cecelia stayed there for a week during the riots, and every now and then, when she and her husband were having a bad time, she spent a night.

'It's a guest room,' Richard says.

'Twin beds, two doubles, or a king? You tell me.'

'One double and a desk,' he says.

The decorator attaches paint chips to an unfolding aluminum ruler and waves them around the room – picking up the light. She opens her kits, does a little mixing, and paints swatches of four different colors on the walls. She waits a few minutes – to see what hums – and then decides on a purplish white. 'It's clean,' she says. 'Bright but not aggressive, which is important. I can have the painter here by the end of the week.'

'Good. Let's do it right away – before things change.'

'I'm leaving,' he tells Cecelia, 'I have an appointment.'

As he's pulling out of the driveway, he can see the depression, the dip, like a lunar crater, almost perfectly round, and about ten feet across. The perfection of the circle makes him nervous, he thinks of signs he's seen pinned to telephone poles near the bottom of the hill. UFO? You Are Not Alone . . . Talk to Me.

'Would you like me to validate you in advance?' the receptionist asks.

'Sure.'

'You look very nice today.' The receptionist smiles as he hands her his parking ticket. 'I like your shirt. One time I was in Neiman Marcus and I went up to the counter and slapped my ticket down and said to the girl, 'Violate me.' Scared the hell out of both of us.' She laughs, licks a couple of square stamps, and presses them onto the ticket. 'You're valid, for one hour,' she says, handing the ticket back. 'Follow me.' She leads him into a room, weighs him, takes his blood pressure and temperature, and tells him to hop up onto the table. 'Go ahead and make yourself comfortable. Would you like a magazine?'

'I'm OK,' he says.

'I know you are.' She winks. 'The doctor will be right with you.'

'What can I do for you?' Dr Lusardi asks, sweeping into the room, his white coat following him.

'I was in pain, incredible pain. They took me to the hospital, they thought I was having a heart attack.'

'And how are you feeling now?'

'Fine. I feel fine, and then I remember the pain. I'm not sure if I'm remembering the pain or am still in pain.'

Lusardi flips through his chart. 'You were last seen seven years ago for pneumonia.' The doctor gestures, for him to take off his shirt. 'What's your life like? Everything under control? What's a typical day?'

'Up early,' Richard says. 'On the treadmill, trainer comes to the house, nutritionist a couple of times a week, maybe a massage. I try to stay healthy. I read four newspapers. I never go out.'

'That's one way to avoid things,' Lusardi says. 'I want to get an EKG, even though I'm sure you had one last night.' With his foot, he drags the machine towards Richard, peels open a package of electrodes, and puts them on Richard's chest.

The EKG feels like a lie-detector test: it's running while the guy is quizzing him. It's distracting, difficult to perfect his heart rhythm while Lusardi is asking him questions.

'Were you suddenly in pain, or did it creep up on you?'

'I don't know; it was as though I'd been in pain and then, sort of, suddenly, it was too much.'

'Describe it.'

'Deep, unending, a root with tentacles spreading out from the center, a hard knot through my shoulders down my hands.'

The EKG is flickering. Lusardi wiggles the machine; it stops.

'How far does it go?'

'All the way down.'

'Married, divorced, kids, custody?'

He's never had a doctor ask him such personal questions. 'A son, in New York, with my wife.'

The doctor nods. He sits and crosses his legs. 'Just rest for a minute, and let's see what the tape looks like.'

'It hurt so much I cried. And I cried again this morning. I never cry.'

'Any trauma or abuse as a child?'

'Just my parents – they're Jewish,' he says. 'I spoke with my mother this morning, and she thinks I'm a failure because I'm retired.'

'Depression mentality.'

'Do you think that's it, depression? Is depression physically painful?'

'I meant that your parents were children of the Depression. I'm going to draw some blood. I want to look at everything.'

Something about Lusardi is unusual. He has more hair than most men, he looks like a guy who has to shave a couple of times a day, a heavy beard, a thick head of hair, almost like a helmet protecting his head. And he seems too young.

'What kind of doctor are you?'

'Psychological internist – it's new. They realized that people want to be not just examined but listened to. So – they made it a specialty, there's a fellowship at Yale. I was in the first group; there are eight of us in the country, four in New York, three in Los Angeles, and one in Florida.'

'Do you have a particular point of view – a

way of life, something you want others to do as well?'

'It changes all the time.'

'I need to know that I'm not just making it up.'

'What do you mean, "making it up"? That you invented the idea of being in pain? You're not "making it up."'

'Why am I in so much pain?'

'I don't know – we just met. Would you like to come back and see me again?'

'Do I need to?'

'It's up to you.'

'Do you see something? Something I should know? Is there something wrong?'

'You're in pain.'

'What should I do in the meantime?'

'Live.'

He leaves, feeling uncomfortable; he both liked Lusardi and felt taken advantage of, all at once. In his mind, he calls him Lizard. After the visit with the lizard, he drives without knowing where he's going, just that he can't go home – not yet.

He drives back down the hill, down Sunset; he will take himself out for a drink, for dinner.

At the Four Seasons, he gives his car to the valet and heads for the bar.

'What can I get for you?'

What did he used to drink? 'Vodka martini,' he says.

'How would you like it – dry, dirty, twist, olives, onions, atomic mushroom cap?'

'Neat,' he says, 'neat and clean, nothing floating in it. No debris.'

'And what kind of vodka?'

Now he's wishing he'd just said something simple – like beer.

'I've got Ketel One, Grey Goose, Absolut, Stoli, a potato vodka, a new electric vodka, which has energized particles.'

'You pick,' he says. 'Bartender's choice.'

The man nods as if charged with enormous responsibility. While he's waiting, Richard pops a nervous handful of salted nuts into his mouth. The drink arrives, strong, like rocket fuel. He sips, he picks through the nut dish, now eating them one at a time, cashew, hazelnut, walnut, pecan, peanut, filbert. The nuts are greasy, salty, and quickly gone. As it gets to be close to the same time as it was yesterday when the trouble began, Richard worries: will the pain come back, will it be as bad as before, more than he can handle?

'A glass of water, please.'

'Bottled or tap?'

So many questions. He looks around at the businessmen having meetings, the d-girls chatting up screenwriters, the movie star and his entourage. The rocket fuel is sending him on a loopy ride. He is getting drunk. The mixed nuts are gone, and he doesn't want to ask for more. He puts down ten dollars, picks up his glass, and heads for the dining room.

The bartender runs after him. 'Sir, the drink is sixteen dollars.'

'Really?' He is embarrassed, annoyed – whoever heard of a drink costing sixteen dollars? He takes out a five and a few ones and slaps them into the man's hand. 'Let's call it even.'

'Party of one?' the dining-room hostess asks.

'That's an old joke if there ever was one.'

'Just one?' the hostess asks again.

He nods.

'This way,' she says, leading him into the empty dining room.

Someone hands him a menu, someone else pours him a glass of water, another puts a dinner roll on his bread plate and some butter beside it. He immediately eats the roll. He hasn't been eating bread – it's not part of his program. The roll is warm, yeasty sourdough. He eats it with cold butter – he closes his eyes – good. It cleans his palate, clears the salt, the sting of the alcohol. He eats the roll, and the bread man comes around again and offers him another, which he eats.

And then – as though he's just woken up – he looks around the room, realizes that he's in a restaurant by himself. He can't do it. He's got to get out.

'My cell is by the pool,' he tells no one in particular and hurries out of the dining room.

Richard gives the car jockey his ticket and hopes the car comes before they discover he's stolen the dinner rolls. Stolen the dinner rolls? Not only did he eat the ones they put on his plate, but on his way out he passed the unattended basket and couldn't help dipping his hand in and, in a broad grip, grabbing a few like they were tennis balls. He's got a pocketful of warm dinner rolls.

A little drunk, he drives until something called the Bodhi Tree catches his eye – he assumes it's the same bookstore that the trainer and the nutritionist talk about. Inside, tall reedy men with unusual hairstyles – too much, too little, all of it in the wrong places – and women with almost no hair, women who look like men, peek out from behind the stacks, giving him furtive glances like they're trying to make contact. There are books on everything from the margins to the middle – UFOs, philosophy, cookbooks, fifty volumes on miracles. A huge stack of 'the book that Elvis loved most next to the Bible' is piled up by the register. From the title it sounds as though the book is relevant – somehow about him – *The Impersonal Life*. Richard picks up a copy; his stomach is growling. The martini is wearing off. He makes a plan – pay for the book and walk down the block to the grocery store, buy some food, go home, eat, read, and call it a night.

Outside, a blind woman is bent over, picking up dog shit. She's patting the ground, trying to find it. 'To the right,' someone says.

'Thanks.'

He takes a turn and – boom – is hit by a car. Someone pulling out of a parking lot accelerates into him, and he goes down like a sandbagged punching clown. The woman who hit him leans out of her car and yells, 'What, are you crazy?'

People gather. 'Is anything broken?' someone asks.

He's struggling to get up.

'Don't move him,' someone says.

'He's moving himself.'

'Let's call the police,' someone says.

'Oh, great, thanks a lot,' the woman who hit him says, getting out of her car.

'Do you want the number of my chiropractor? She's really great, she can release anything.' A girl scribbles a number on a piece of paper and gives it to him.

'Oh, please, I hardly tapped him.'

'Show some compassion,' one of the tall guys from the Bodhi Tree says.

'What were you doing? How would you expect me to see you, just one little man, one line of a person walking?'

'I was going to the grocery store.'

'Why didn't you just drive, like a normal person?'

'You ran me down,' he says.

'You ruined my day,' she says.

'Well, lucky for you, it's already late.'

She is on her cell phone calling a friend. She

turns away from the crowd. 'Oh, hi, I had an acci-dent. I was pulling out and I hit some guy. No, not his car, his person, I struck his person. He's really giving me a hard time. I hate men – if I'd run over a woman, you can bet she'd be apolo-gizing to me.' She interrupts herself to ask him, 'Do I have to wait until the police come? Because I have things to do.'

A man from the gas station across the street comes with a big bag of ice and puts it on his leg at the point of impact. He winces. The gas-station man uses a roll of gray duct tape to bind the ice to his leg. 'I was a medic,' he says, 'in the Reserves.'

'What do I owe you?' Richard asks the man.

'You don't owe me anything.'

He forces himself to stand; the crowd applauds as he crawls to his feet. 'Thank you. Thank you very much.'

In the grocery store, overcome by hunger, he starts eating in the aisles. He peels a banana and pushes his cart forward with one hand. The banana will protect him, it will keep him from fainting, and the cart acts like a walker, he can lean on it. He needs food. At the end of a row, he grabs a bag of sunflower seeds, tears it open with his teeth, and throws a handful into his mouth. He's still got the martini in him and the dinner rolls, but he needs some protein. He stares at the BBQ chickens going around on the rotisserie. He tosses more seeds into his mouth. He's trying to skip over the fact that he just got hit by a car, but every step he takes hurts more. His shoulder hurts, his head hurts, his leg hurts; he's in pain, real pain. He finds the 'Care of the Self' aisle, picks up a bottle of baby aspirin, puts a few in his mouth; they sit on his tongue like buttons, sensors, strangely perfumed dinner mints – puffing up as they dissolve. He tosses a bottle of Flintstones with extra C into the cart for good measure. He cruises the aisles, a somnambulist in a strange dream landscape. Where did all this stuff come from? Who thought it up? Is there a reason we need graham crackers in assorted shapes, flavors, and colors? Twenty-two varieties of orange juice?

There is a crying woman in the produce section, distracting him from his reverie. He sees her between the lettuce and tomatoes. He watches, wondering if it is just a problem with the onions, an allergy of sorts, or if she is really weeping. She blots her eyes and sniffles as she's putting cucumbers and peppers into her cart. He intersects her at the carrots.

'Are you OK?'

'Don't talk to me,' she says, not even looking at him.

'Sorry, I just noticed you crying between the lettuce and tomatoes.'

'You're a freak,' she says, still not looking up.

'No, I'm not,' he says, surprised.

'What are you, like the Mr Whipple of Ralph's, spying on people – "Don't squeeze the Charmin"?'

She looks him up and down and goes back to feeling the tomatoes. 'And you're leaking. You're a freak. The sight of a crying woman made you wet your pants.'

'What are you talking about?'

She points at his pants.

There's a huge wet spot on his thigh. 'I was hit by a car,' he says, 'And that's an ice pack, my ice pack is sweating.'

'Maybe you need to go to the emergency room,' she says, looking at him more closely.

'I was just there yesterday, it seems too soon to go back,' he says. A wave sweeps over him, nausea, fatigue, the pain. 'I'm really not feeling well,' he says. 'I need to sit down. Do you want to get a cup of coffee? They have tables and chairs over there.' He points across the store.

'That's appealing,' she says. 'A drippy freak, who got hit by a car and doesn't feel good, wants me to have coffee. Sure, why not, what do I care – chop me into a thousand pieces. Clearly, I'm not doing so well myself.'

They push their carts over towards the 'Marketplace' section of the store.

'I hope you asked for money,' she says.

'Why does everything have a price tag on it? What were you crying about?'

'I was thinking about my salad,' she says. 'Every day I buy things to make a nice salad for dinner, and no one notices. I put in two kinds of lettuce, contrasting colors of peppers, sometimes I throw in chickpeas, or crumbled blue cheese, and they just wolf it all down like it's one big trough, like no thought went into it whatsoever.'

They sit in the 'Marketplace' section, which despite the hour is still filled with strollers and nannies feeding what look like breadcrumbs to their infant charges – turns out it's free samples of day-old cake.

'How come you have time to have coffee?' she asks. 'Shouldn't you be at work or on your way home to your family? How do I know you're not some kind of a freak?'

'I hope you don't take it the wrong way, but do you think crying, depressed women appeal to most freaks?'

'What are you, then?'

'A person having a kind of crisis of my own.'

'Are you weird?'

'No, I'm self-employed.'

'Like Charlie Manson?'

'I'm rich, if you must know.'

'Why would a rich guy go to the grocery store? He'd have someone who shops for him.'

'I do. Why are you so negative?'

'I don't know,' she says. 'I have no business being anything. I've got a husband and two kids who don't talk to me, so I can't imagine why some rich guy in the grocery store would chat me up. I'm nonexistent, I'm like a floor lamp.'

He starts to notice that she's very pretty – was

it there before, does she notice it? She's pretty, she's funny, and she's smart.

'What does your husband do?'

'What do all men do? He runs a company for some other guy.'

'Did you two ever go for counseling?'

'Are you some sort of shrink, a religious nut? I get it, you're a Scientologist, and you're recruiting me.'

'No, I just always wondered, in retrospect, if my ex-wife and I should have talked to someone before we separated, would it have made a difference.'

She is staring at his leg. 'It looks bad,' she says. 'The leaking doesn't stop.'

'Fortunately, it isn't as bad as it looks.'

'That's the problem – people think what they see is real.'

He rolls up his pants leg and tugs at the tape. 'I can't get it off.'

She goes over to the deli counter, takes a handful of plastic knives, and starts sawing at the tape.

'Hey, Patty,' someone walking by calls out, 'Patty Hearst, why don't you take him out in the parking lot and detonate him.'

'Thanks,' Richard calls after the guy. 'That's very helpful. Is your name Patty?'

'Do I look like a Patty?'

The first knife breaks, gouging his skin. 'I'm sure if you ask for the butcher he probably has a hatchet somewhere in back, and you could just chop my leg off.'

She laughs. 'Cynthia. My name is Cynthia.'

The second knife saws through the tape; the melting ice pack drops to the floor.

'Is that all you're getting?' She glances into his cart.

He reaches behind him and throws a package of butter cookies towards the cart – they miss, land on the ground; the cookies crumble.

She laughs.

'Don't you need ice cream? Whenever something happens to me, I need ice cream.'

When did he last need ice cream? He'd completely forgotten about ice cream.

'Want me to get you some?' she asks.

'Sure.'

'What kind?'

He has no idea. 'Whatever kind you like – your favorite. I want to try your favorite.' While she's gone, he puts the cookies back – too much carbo-hydrate.

Cynthia comes back with a Carvel ice-cream cake. 'It's my favorite.'

'It's so cheerful,' he says. The cake is white, decorated with multicolored confetti. 'I pictured you more with a spoon and a pint of Häagen-Dazs chocolate.'

'Oh, I do that all the time, but this is for special occasions.'

'What am I celebrating?'

'You survived,' she says. 'You got hit by a car.'

'Do you want me to eat this now?'

'No, take it with you.' She hands him a huge jar of bath salts. 'And when you get home, put a cup of this in a hot tub and soak. I better go – if I'm not home, I'll get in trouble. On the one hand, they don't notice me; on the other, I'm on a very short leash. Good luck with your injury.'

Using a grease pencil from the bakery counter, he scrawls his number on a white bakery bag.

She shakes her head. 'If Andy finds a number in my pocket it's only going to make things worse.'

'Tell him I'm a cleaning lady. Just take it; if things get really bad, if you need a place to go, a day off from your life, call me.'

'What are you – a run-over Good Samaritan?'

'I'm just someone who's trying.'

'OK, well, don't try too hard – you might get yourself killed.'

He gets in the checkout line. He's been so distracted that he didn't really buy anything – all he's got is the open bottle of baby aspirin, the Flintstones vitamins, a banana peel, the sunflower seeds (which have been sprinkling themselves across the floor, leaving a long trail), and the ice-cream cake.

'On a roll?' the girl asks as she's ringing him up.

'Huh?'

'Looks like you're on a binge, like a raccoon has been tearing through here. All of your packages are open. Did you eat anything else along the way?'

He holds up the banana peel.

'Should we call it fifty cents?'

What is it going to take for him to break out of himself, dancing in the aisles of the grocery store, screaming at the top of his lungs, starting a program to help small businessmen like Anhil open donut stores? He wants to be more, do more. And he wants to feel better. He wants to be heroic, larger than life – rescue people from burning buildings, leap over rooftops. And he wants people to notice him. He catches his reflection in the chrome dairy case. How does a middle-aged Joe become anything, much less a superhero?

It is Night; he is going home in the dark. A car passes with a lighted pizza box on top. He sees the box and unconsciously chants the number to himself the whole way home. He goes in through the garage door, calling 'ollie ollie oxen free,' half expecting to greet himself. He goes into the kitchen with his small bag of goods, opens the fridge, and visits his dinner – an orangey slab of poached salmon, green beans, roasted-tomato-and-fennel salad with pink plastic wrap over the top.

He dials from memory. 'Pizza Palace, our pies are made to please.'

'I'd like to arrange for a delivery.'

'What do you want on it? One for three, three for five, five for ten. We got mushroom, pepperoni, onions, peppers, garlic, regular cheese, smoked mozzarella, feta, goat, cheddar, Swiss, fresh garlic, sun-dried tomato, fresh tomato, avocado, broccoli,

broccoli rabe, spinach, pineapple, sausage, turkey sausage, tofu, red peppers, green peppers, green olives, black olives . . .'

While he's listening to the recitation of the toppings, he takes an ice pack out of the freezer and holds it against his leg.

'Regular,' he says to the guy. 'Plain cheese, and maybe broccoli, some turkey sausage, and throw a few mushrooms on there.'

He pulls down his pants and looks at his leg; it's pink from the ice, red from the adhesive, and a kind of bluish green from the huge bruise that's forming. He presses deeper, harder, examining.

'Thirty-five, forty minutes. Cash only, twenty-seven eighty-eight. You need anything else with that?'

'Like what?' He goes to the window, looks out. The exterior lights that go on automatically at dusk are lighting up the hill. The hole is definitely bigger.

'You tell me.'

'I'm fine.' He pauses. 'Hey, who do you call when there's a sinkhole, when the land is moving – any idea?'

'Buddy, it's a pizza parlor, not the Department of the Interior.'

He hangs up and dials 911 – this time much more casually, not sure it's really an emergency. If he hadn't called last night, he certainly wouldn't be calling tonight. Is he trying to live the whole thing over again – staging a dramatic reenactment?

'Police, fire, ambulance.'

'Police,' he says, clearly.

'Is this an emergency? All nonemergency calls should be directed to your local precinct. If this is a police emergency, please stay on the line.'

Someone comes on the line. 'Police. What's the nature of your problem?'

'There's a hole outside of my house; it started as a dent and it's getting bigger and deeper. It looks like one of those places where a UFO might have landed, if you believe in things like that.'

There is a pause. 'And when you look into the hole, do you see anything coming out of it, like little green men? Look, buddy, give it a rest – spare me the paperwork.'

'This is not a crank call, if there's some other number I should call, then say so, but it needs to be reported.'

'You say it's a hole?'

'Yes.'

'And who dug the hole?'

'No one dug the hole, it's just forming. It's a public safety issue – the earth is sinking. I've been watching it all day.'

'Well, it's dark now; why don't we wait until morning and see if it's still there.'

'Aren't you supposed to be helpful? What's your name?'

'What are you going to do, tell on me? Grow up, Richard. Don't abuse the system.'

There is silence. 'If you know who I am, then you must know where the hole is.'

'Look, Dick, our fellas stick to the Joe Friday stuff – holdups, missing children, domestic disputes, the body with a bashed-in head. Give the Highway Department a call, and don't mention the bit about the UFO and "if you believe in things like that."'

'Have you got a number for them?'

'That would be a 411, not a 911.'

He hangs up, gets the number, and dials.

'Highway,' the man says.

He tells him about the hole – leaving out the UFO. 'It just keeps getting bigger.'

'Is it on private property, in the middle of a road, or on a public right-of-way?'

'It's on a hill.'

'Have you seen any water, heard any gushing sounds? Is there anything bubbling or seeping out of the hole? Have you felt any land movement or earthquakelike activity? Was there a previous incident, or lack of stability in your neighborhood?'

'Not that I know of.'

'Let me check and see if we have any activity in your area.'

On hold, he hears a calming woman's voice, discussing what to do in case of an earthquake. '. . . have your earthquake kit readily accessible. Don't forget to include water, dried foods, snacks, medications, and emergency supplies for your pets. In the event of an earthquake . . .'

The guy comes back on the line. 'I don't see any notes in the computer, but I can send a man out. Will you be there?'

'You're sending someone now?'

'Yes, sir. He should be there fairly soon; it's an otherwise quiet night in Tinseltown.'

Richard waits. He paces the house, looking out the window, the city beyond, glittering like a million ships at sea. An hour and change later, the pizza delivery boy calls from his car, panicked. 'I keep thinking I'm close and then I lose it,' he says. 'I've been circling for thirty minutes.'

'Where are you now?'

'I'm driving, I just keep driving. At one point I ended up on Mulholland, I went for, like, ten miles, I almost fell off the edge. I couldn't even call anyone, I lost signal.'

'Where now? What are you looking at?'

'Trees, houses, street signs; here's the one that says Shadow Hill Way. I've been here before, I just keep going around and around.'

'You're right here – stay to the left and come up the hill.'

'Don't hang up on me, man, not now; bring me in, can you bring me in?'

He takes the phone with him out the front door. 'Blow your horn.'

The horn echoes up the hill in the phone. 'Can you hear yourself? That's you in stereo, you're here.'

The pizza car climbs the hill; the lighted box comes into view. Richard stands waving both arms, bringing him in the way airport guys with orange wands bring a pilot to the gate.

'I feel terrible,' the pizza guy says, rolling down his window. 'Your pie is cold.'

'Don't worry.' He gives the guy forty dollars and the pizza guy hands the box through the window.

At the same time, a small white car with yellow flashing lights pulls up; yellow light splashes over everything, washing it the color of urine.

'I hear you've got a hole,' the man in the white car says.

Richard points to the edge of the hill.

'Pizza One to base, pie has landed,' the pizza guy speaks into his radiophone.

'Pizza One, give the man some free garlic knots, a bottle of soda, and our sincere apologies.'

'Hey, mister,' the pizza guy calls out of the car, 'these are for you.' He throws a white bag through the air; it sails, landing on top of the pizza box.

'And take this too.' He hurls a liter of Coke out of the car. It lands on the grass like a missile; the top pops off, spraying caramel-colored sugar water.

'Sorry, want another?'

'That's OK. Drive carefully.'

The man from the Highway Department has cranked up a rack of roof-mounted lights and is aiming them down the hill. He flicks the switch, the engine shudders, and the hillside is awash in a flood of crisp white halogen.

'Light of my life; I built this rig, I was going half blind – all they gave us were miner's hats.'

'You got here faster than I expected. I ordered the pizza before I called you.'

'When things are falling apart, the call goes out. What kind of pie?'

Richard opens the box and peers in. 'Mushroom, sausage, broccoli.'

'I hate broccoli. The only reason I voted for George Bush was because he hated his vegetables as much as I do.'

'Have a garlic knot.' He hands the man the bag.

'Thanks,' the government man says. 'Nice up here,' he says. 'Not like down there – nothing to be afraid of up here.'

Together the men look over the edge.

'They've been doing some work up the hill, built a bulkhead, put in a putting green and a sprinkler system. I was wondering if that might have done it,' Richard says.

The man shakes his head. 'Doubt they're taking water out – more likely they're putting water in, which would give you the opposite effect. Los Angeles is still all about water – we're either flooded or all dried up.' He looks down into the hole. 'Things like this happen when you pull something out – a water main breaks, or they're pumping oil too close by. Sometimes it's structural – there are caves underground that just collapse. Do you have many coyotes around here?'

'No.'

'Any animals or street people who could be living in a cave?'

'You mean cavemen?'

'Cave people, they come in, set up house. We've

83

got people living everywhere – you wouldn't believe it.'

'I haven't seen anyone.'

'That's what they all say. I don't want to keep you from your dinner.' He nods towards the pizza. 'But could you give me a hand?' He opens his hatchback and starts unloading – high boots, like Parliament-Funkadelic platform shoes. 'I hate this part. Snakes, lots of snakes everywhere. I hate snakes. They live out here because they like the weather.' Boots on, he steps into an old leather harness, clips on some ropes, a long metal measuring tape, something that looks like a microphone, plastic containers. He prepares to descend.

'All you have to do is hold the rope. Just don't let go.'

Together they go to the edge; the hill is drenched in the hot white of a movie set. It reminds Richard of *Capricorn One*, the movie about the moonwalk that never was.

The government man takes strange steps, tentative. 'At least it's not liquidy; that always makes me nervous. I once saw a man swallowed by a hole, never got over it.'

Richard holds the rope. His stomach growls. He watches the man measure the diameter, log the information into a pocket calculator, and then insert some sort of instrument into the earth.

'Is that an air pump? Are you going to pump it back up?'

'It's a coring instrument; I'm drilling to get a

sample. This thing only goes in about six feet, which is nothing when you think about the earth's surface, but it's what we can do. And this' – he holds up a small white probe – 'is a monitor, sends info back to the office. The Tampax, my wife calls it, "Did you get the Tampax in OK?"'

'How far will it go, how big will it get?'

'Best-case scenario, it stops tomorrow. I'm going to put flags around the edges as markers, just so we'll have a visual. I don't think you're in danger, but you might want to make sure your home-owner's policy is in good shape . . .'

Coming out of the hole, the government man hands Richard a card. 'I'm the night man; there are four of us and six day men. If you think she's really starting to move, call this number.'

Richard takes the cold pizza into the house and eats two slices while reading his homeowner's policy. The cheese is gelatinous, the sausage rubbery, the mushrooms are limp, but all of it, lying on a cold wet crust, comes to life in a delicious room-temperature combination.

The policy seems complete, though there's some language referring to damage that's a result of an act of God.

He goes to sleep, bloated, belching, the sausage replaying itself. He dreams of falling through a vortex to middle earth, a journey deep into the center of Los Angeles, sliding down a riveted, twisting titanium slide, sloshing through tar pits, roaming a desert-grass landscape fearing the saber-toothed tiger. He dreams of a tall, windowless cement building, a series of rooms, of time folding in on itself like origami. He wakes up in the middle of the night with the flavor of pizza in his mouth. He brushes his teeth and goes back to bed.

He is the wake-up call. By four-forty-five, he has double-bagged the evidence – the leftover pizza, the cold salmon dinner – has taken the trash out, and is on the treadmill. Stiff from the accident, his leg is throbbing, but he is trying to keep everything loose. He will start again. Every day he will begin again. He is on the treadmill, on the computer, working. He has to get something done before he can go back to Anhil.

Riding the wave of the market, catching it on the up, betting on the down. He thinks about what he knows, his base of information, this world of possibilities, futures, narratives, histories.

He places his bets – that's how he thinks of them – walks three miles, takes a fast shower, pours some of his special cereal into a Ziploc bag, throws in a couple of the herbal-tea sachets, and goes to the car. It's 5:30 a.m., almost exactly the same time as yesterday. It is still dark, the day/the night in a dream state, suspended.

Backing out of the garage, he feels like he's sneaking out, like he's trying not to be noticed. It is not too early to be up, but it is definitely too early to be out.

He coasts downhill – he will bring his breakfast

to Anhil, they will talk, Anhil will see his car, it will be a good day.

Where is the donut shop? He makes a left, makes a right, driving down and down, as though the city is built on a slant, an invisible mountain. He has trouble finding the place. He drives back to Cedars-Sinai, makes a three-point turn at the emergency room door, and goes from there. He passes a new park, a green grassy hill, a knoll where homeless people are sleeping under a pergola. He is going over the route, thinking about how, every time you go down a road, depending on how you do it, fast or slow, by car, bus, or on foot, you notice something different. He is thinking about the route, about the park where people are sleeping, and for some reason he starts thinking about the Kennedy assassination – routes and motorcades, cars speeding off, the futile urgency of the situation.

He was in school. The world had come to an end, an apocalypse had been announced. Why weren't the air-raid sirens going off? Why weren't they ducking under their desks? Why wasn't anyone doing anything? Instead, they sat mute in front of television sets and listened to Walter Cronkite. Because he could talk, because he could dab a tear from his eye, Walter Cronkite seemed like the only person who had survived.

He remembers being sent home, surprised there was anyone home, surprised there was dinner that night, surprised things continued on.

'I knew a fellow who worked for Kennedy, made his suits, knew his measurements,' his father said, trying to connect himself to the situation, to touch the life of someone who had touched the life of . . .

Why is he thinking about this?

And then there it is, up there on the right – glowing. He parks at the curb. The store is empty; he imagines something has happened: Anhil has been shot in a holdup, he will find him in the kitchen, bleeding.

Like a puppet, Anhil pops up from behind the counter. 'Good morning.'

Holding his Ziploc of cereal and tea and feeling slightly ridiculous, Richard stands at the counter. 'Have you got a cup of hot water?'

Is Anhil surprised that he's back? Yesterday, when he said, 'See you tomorrow,' did he mean it euphemistically, like 'Have a good day'?

Anhil brings him the hot water. 'How is your heart this morning?'

'Good,' Richard says. 'Very busy.' He drops the sachet in the water.

Anhil stares at it, like it should foam or fizzle. Finally he looks up. 'I'm glad you're back.'

While the tea steeps, Richard tells Anhil about the martini, the crying woman, the lost pizza man, the sinkhole.

'Maybe you have visitors?' He looks up at the ceiling. 'From above. Late at night I watch television, they talk about all kinds of things. At three in the morning, it's hard not to believe them.'

'You're not taking me seriously,' Richard says.

'Yes, I am, but do you expect the earth to stand still while we run all over it? Did you bring your car?'

Richard nods. Excited, Anhil runs out of the store. The car is at the curb – it is big and black and looks like a tank that would belong to a hotel, or to someone who is accustomed to being driven. Richard is not sure why he has such a big car. He got it because it was reliable, because, like any New Yorker driving in this town, he wanted some protection. He got it because ten years ago, when he went into the dealership looking for something, small, compact, the guy convinced him that he needed a tank. Black is not the color of Los Angeles, it's the color of New York. Los Angeles is champagne, cream, white, silver, gold – things that have no color, things that blend into the landscape.

'It's not really mine,' he says, apologetically, 'it's leased.'

'Of course it is. No one can just buy one of these. You have to be a king to own a Mercedes.'

It's leased because he can deduct the entire cost as a business expense, because if the car ever needs to be repaired the dealer comes and gets it, leaves a loaner, and delivers the car back when it's ready. It's leased because all he has to do is say yes and every other year a brand-new big black car, the latest-model tank, arrives in his driveway, thick with the sweet, pungent new-car smell.

Anhil caresses the metal, running his hands over every curve like it is a human body, like he is a blind man reading the most luscious Braille. He opens the doors and touches everything: the lighter, the seat controls, the rearview mirror.

'She is the *African Queen*,' Anhil says. 'If she was mine I would polish her every day, I would clean her with Q-tips.' He rubs his hands over the seats. 'The leather – it is like the most beautiful woman. If I didn't think my wife would worry, I would make love to your car.' He opens and closes the trunk several times. He moves as if to try and lift the car up from the bumper; is he testing the car, testing his own strength? 'This is my dream. I do not want too many personal things, but a good car is my dream. I'm going to drive your car. Yes? Will you watch the store?'

Richard nods. How can he say no? How can he not let this guy drive his car?

Will you watch the store? What does that mean, tell anyone who comes that Anhil has stepped out and he'll be right back, close the door and flip the 'Open' sign to 'Closed'?

He goes inside and stands waiting. A guy comes in; Richard feels obligated to go behind the counter, as if guarding the place. 'It's not my shop,' he confesses.

'Does that mean I can't get a donut?'

He can't lose business for Anhil. 'What kind would you like?'

'Glazed, and a coffee with milk and sugar.'

He puts the donut on a plate and puts the plate down in front of the man and pours him a cup of coffee. It feels strange, like he's pretending. And while the man is eating another guy comes in and sits at the counter.

'Orange juice, some tea, and a toasted bagel.'

'No bagels, just donuts.'

'Really? There are usually bagels in the back.'

He walks into the back and, sure enough, on the counter are a bag of bagels and a toaster. He toasts the bagel, pours the man a glass of juice, finds the tea bags, and serves the man.

'What do I owe you?' the first man asks.

Richard looks around; there are no prices anywhere. Very funny. Very Anhil. 'I have no idea. How about three dollars? Is that more or less than what you usually pay?'

'More or less,' the guy says, leaving the money, plus a fifty-cent tip.

Richard doesn't know how to open the register and so just puts the money on the side, tip included.

A homeless man comes in, asking for spare change. Richard gives him a donut. He takes a dollar out of his own pocket and puts it next to the register to cover the donut. It is hard work selling donuts, and he's not as good at it as Anhil. Where is Anhil? He checks his watch: seven-fifteen. His plan was to get home before Cecelia arrives.

Another guy comes in – Anhil was right, it's all men in the donut kingdom.

'Hi ya, bud, I'll have the usual.'

'And what would that be?'

By the time Anhil comes back, twenty minutes later, Richard is livid.

Anhil bounces in, literally beaming, and Richard can't hold on to the anger. 'She drives like whipped cream, Chantilly lace. She holds the road so good you don't even need pavement: that car would be good on rubble, on a dirt road, with a cloud of dust rising up in back announcing that you have been there. You could take her anywhere.' Anhil hands the keys back to Richard. 'How was it for you to be me, the donut man?'

'There are no prices,' Richard says, handing Anhil the four dollars. 'Two customers came in, also a homeless man – I gave him a donut.'

'Are you crazy? You can't give them donuts. They come back for more, they bring their friends; they're not made to give away.'

'I paid for it – it's one of those dollars.'

'That doesn't matter. I give them donut holes, spare parts – I put them outside, and they come like scavenger pigeons. It's not that I don't care, but you can't give away the whole donut. You think I don't have the disease too? I didn't come to America to be a poor philosopher.'

Something about Anhil is frustrating. He's less perfect today, less understanding. There are limits, things he misses, doesn't understand.

'You are a funny man,' Anhil says. 'You met me yesterday, and you want me to be like your mother and tell you that you are a good boy. All I can tell you is that you are a grown man with a good heart and a really nice car.' Anhil puts together a box of donuts and gives them to Richard. 'Thanks for taking care of the store. Come again soon; come tomorrow, and I'll drive your car.'

'Do you want breakfast, or did you eat already?' Cecelia asks when he comes in, box of donuts in hand.

'I'm starving,' he says, putting the donuts down, realizing that he left his uneaten bag of cereal at Anhil's. He sits at the table; his place is set, his papers are out.

'Please don't throw the donuts out.'

'Whatever you say, but I don't work for fat people.'

'What's the problem with fat people?'

'They smell and they have health issues.'

'Did you notice the hole out front?' he asks as he is eating breakfast, reading his papers, scanning the ticker on the screen in the kitchen.

'What hole?'

'Look out the window, over there. There's a hole, a big dent, like the kind of place a UFO might have landed, if you believe in that kind of thing.'

'The only things I believe in are God and a clean house. Are you going to put your headphones on, or do I have to talk to you all day?'

'I'm not putting them on, but you don't have to talk to me.'

Cecelia takes her dust cloth and can of Endust over to the window and looks out. 'Not only is there a hole,' Cecelia says. 'There's a horse in the hole.'

He stops eating and goes to the glass.

There is a horse in the center of the hole, eating grass. Again, he thinks of the perfection of the circle, the signs on the telephone poles at the bottom of the hill. 'UFO? You Are Not Alone . . .'

'Don't just stare at it,' Cecelia says.

He calls the number the government man gave him last night. 'A fellow was out last night to look at a hole, a depression. He put in a monitor and some flags around the perimeter.'

'Ummm,' the man says.

'The hole is getting deeper, and now there's a horse in it.'

'Did he give you a reference number, anything written on the back of the card?'

He turns it over. 'Yes, it looks like 9EZPIECES. Is that a joke?

'It's a code,' the man says, clicking on his computer keys. 'I've got your number in the system. Ummm, yep, there's been movement.'

'Yes, and now there's a horse in the hole.'

'OK, I'll send another man out.'

At this point they ought to send a truck, a car full of men, a load of fill dirt, or something a little more substantial, because the hole is sinking fast.

Richard goes outside, stands with his feet on the edge of the hole – it is definitely deeper than it was two hours ago, the little pink flags are several feet farther down. The horse looks up, nods as if acknowledging him, and goes back to eating grass.

'Are you stuck?' Richard asks the horse. 'Can you climb out? Come out, while it's not so deep.'

The horse doesn't move. Richard goes into the house, grabs a jelly donut, and goes back to the horse. Richard holds the donut out; the horse sniffs the air in his direction, takes a half step towards the donut, and then won't put his foot down. Richard throws the donut into the hole. The horse snorts.

'He doesn't want to come out,' Richard says to Cecelia.

'A horse in a hole is like a salt shaker in a coffee cup,' Cecelia says. 'It makes no sense.'

The horse got into the hole, he must know how to get out of the hole. Richard can't call 911 again – they'll think he's a freak. He goes back to the window. Now there's a coyote standing at the edge of the hole, or at least he thinks it's a coyote. It's standing at the edge of the hole, menacing the horse, and the horse is frightened.

Richard looks around for Cecelia; she's vacuuming in the living room. He picks up his noise-canceling headphones, takes two metal pot lids from the kitchen, and goes back outside, banging the lids together like cymbals, yelling, 'Scram. Go away and be gone.' The coyote runs.

The horse sighs, flares his lips, blinks at Richard.

'Are you trapped? Can't get yourself out? I'm

going to look in the garage and see if there's anything we can use; be right back.'

There's a young girl walking down the street, her mouth open. She is in the middle of the street calling out something – he hears only a muffled version. He takes off his headphones.

'Lucky, Lucky?' she is shouting. 'Lucky?'

'Are you looking for your dog?'

'My horse.'

'I've got him.'

'I'm not going in your house.'

'He's just over the edge, in a sinkhole.'

The horse recognizes the girl; his tale swishes.

'I was just going into the garage to look for something.'

'I'm not going into your garage,' the girl says, climbing down the hill.

'Well, I don't think you should go down there.'

'It's my horse.'

In the garage there's a garden hose, a lounge chair, a bag of sand, and a pair of skis – too narrow to use as planks for the horse to walk up. And while he imagines putting the horse on skis and pulling the horse up the hill with a rope, like an old-fashioned toy horse on wheels, he doesn't really think that'll work. There's a tall wooden door he bought for something and then decided not to use. He carries the door out – they can use it as a ramp. His shoulder and leg are throbbing, reminding him of the pain. He wonders, what's the point of having the trainer if, when you need

96

to do something, you can't do anything? He carries the door to the edge of the hole and, with the girl's help, positions it on the ground.

A school bus drives by. 'That was my ride,' she says.

'How old are you?' he asks.

'None of your business,' she says.

He figures she's about eleven – going on twenty-seven.

The girl tries to guide the horse up the door and out of the hole. He won't go. She runs up and down the wooden door, trying to show him that the ramp is safe. The horse is suspicious. Richard goes back into the house, gives Cecelia his headphones, and asks if they have any rope. She finds him a piece of thin nylon rope, and he takes it out to the girl. The girl makes a loop around the horse's neck and tries to lead him out. The horse wants to come out, he starts to come out, but something keeps him in the hole. And he's catching on to the fact that he's trapped, and is looking at the girl and at Richard, wanting someone to explain it in horse terms.

'Does your horse have a trainer, or a friend we could call?'

'Maybe we should call 911.'

'They're not always helpful. This is a weird idea, but I think we should ask the guy at the house up the hill.'

'The movie star?' the girl says. 'You can't just go and ring his bell.'

'Why not?'

'Like he's going to answer. Fine, you go, I'm not allowed into anyone's house.'

Richard walks up the hill, rings the buzzer on the gate. There's a long pause.

'Yes?'

'Hi, it's your neighbor; we've never met, but there's a horse out here stuck in a ditch. He got himself in, but can't get out. I was wondering if you could help us.'

'Hang on.'

The automatic gate peels back, the front door opens, and there he is in jeans and a white T-shirt, looking a little rumpled, a little worn. He's startlingly sexy. Richard is thrown off guard, staring. The movie star is pulling on cowboy boots with no socks. He picks up one boot and slides it onto his foot, effortlessly, no wrestling. As he bends, his T-shirt rides up, showing off muscle, skin, a small tattoo. Everything about him is better than average.

'Sorry to bother you,' Richard says. 'But the horse is in the hole, the little girl is about to cry, and, well, are you busy?'

'Just doing some reading. Let's go.' Together they walk down the hill. By now the fog has burned off; it's a beautiful day. He's walking with the movie star, the sky is blue and clear, the air crisp. It is as though the movie star has changed the lighting, changed the mood.

The girl is still trying to get the horse to walk up the plank.

'No luck?' the movie star asks.

The girl shakes her head. 'Do you think you can get him out?' she asks, tearfully.

'Sure,' he says. 'That's what I do.'

The movie star climbs down; he's in the hole, with the girl and the horse, when the government man pulls up in a plain white sedan. 'I'm Bob, one of the day men,' he says, introducing himself to the group.

Richard can't tell if Bob, the government man, recognizes the movie star, but he's acting so incredibly cool that Richard is pretty sure Bob has no idea who the movie star is.

'I'm going to have to ask you all to come on out of the hole so I can get some measurements, an accurate reading.'

The movie star and the girl climb up the door and out of the hole. Richard is thinking it looks deeper still – the pink flags are now about halfway down. Bob radios in to the office.

'I'm at the Shadow Hill site; give me whatever you've got.'

'Nothing,' comes back. 'We've got nothing.'

'The horse has something in his mouth,' the movie star says.

The horse has something in his mouth, and he's working it back and forth, moving it from side to side.

'The horse has the probe,' Richard says.

'What the hell,' Bob says.

The movie star slides down the hill and opens

the horse's mouth, and the probe falls into his hand. 'Thanks,' he says, petting the horse. He climbs out of the hole, hands the slobbery probe to Bob, and spanks himself to get the dust off. The movie star moves with something extra, a kind of physical grace and confidence that is mesmerizing.

'That's not going to get a lot of information now. We're flying blind.'

The movie star pulls the girl aside. 'What's your horse's name?'

'Lucky.'

'Do you know the name of Lucky's doctor? We need to have him give Lucky some medicine to keep him calm. We're going to get him out, but it's going to take a little work.'

The movie star pulls a cell phone out of his back pocket and hands it to the girl.

'I have my own,' she says, taking an even smaller one out of her pocket.

'While you're at it,' Richard says, 'call your mother and tell her where you are.'

While the girl is on the phone, the movie star talks to Richard. 'I don't trust this hole, and I don't trust this guy called Bob. We have to get the horse out. We need a helicopter to lift the horse out of the hole – how does that sound?'

'Good; do you have a helicopter?'

'I do, but I don't have a harness to pick up the horse. Give me a half-hour,' the movie star says. 'Make sure the vet shows up.' The movie star runs up the street, head high, chest back. Minutes later, he zooms by on his motorcycle.

'Next time you see me, I'll be up there,' he says, pointing up. He throws Richard a walkie-talkie. 'We're on channel 12.'

'Roger,' Richard says, pushing the button and speaking into the walkie-talkie.

'We need a few things – old socks, to use as ear plugs for the horse, and something to use as a blindfold,' the movie star says over his headset. 'Can you get those?'

'Roger,' Richard says, walking back towards the house.

'My assistant is working on the harness. It's not an easy item. But don't worry, my team is on it, and they work magic.'

Richard goes inside, raids his sock drawer for what he thinks look like decent horse ear plugs, goes into the bathroom, takes the belt from his bathrobe, and hurries out, walkie-talkie in hand.

A police car on a routine patrol stops in front of the house. 'Why didn't you call us? We like to know what's going on. What is going on?'

'Do you know who lives in that house?' Bob points downhill, not at the swimmer's house, but at the one right next door, just down the hill.

'I have no idea,' Richard says.

'Well, that's something the police can do.' He waves the cop over. 'Find out who lives in that house. If this hill goes, it's going to run right into that house.'

People driving by lean out of their car windows. 'Is it a movie shoot?'

'No, a horse in a sinkhole.'

'Cool.'

'My mom is coming,' the girl says. 'She called the vet, they should all be here soon.'

News leaks. Before the movie star is back, a television truck pulls up. Richard isn't sure if this is something that the movie star's assistant also arranged, or if when the cops radioed in that there was a horse in a hole, someone picked up the information. The street is filling with people.

'There's a law against gatherings of more than thirty people without a permit,' the cop tells Richard. 'Some of them have to go home – there's no permit in place. I'm counting heads: duck, duck, goose.'

'I didn't invite them,' Richard says. 'I'm not responsible for people spontaneously gathering.'

The vet arrives, and the cops won't let him through.

'Veteran or not, you can't come in.'

'I'm the horse doctor,' he says, pushing through.

'Why don't you actually do something?' the little girl says to the cops.

The horse is spooked. He can't see over the hill, but there's a lot of noise. The vet listens to Lucky with a stethoscope. 'He's fine – worried, that's all. Now, what's the proposal?'

'The helicopter is going to come and pick him up with a special sling. Have you ever used one?'

'I've only seen it on TV.'

'I think they're borrowing it from a movie studio.'

Richard hands the vet the stuffed socks and terry-cloth belt.

'What are these?'

'Ear plugs and a blindfold.'

'How're you doing down there?' the walkie-talkie squalks.

'Getting quite a crowd. And you?'

'We're just about to come over the ridge. Is the vet there?'

'Roger.'

'Can he give the horse a sedative and put the ear plugs in? Also, have the police clear the road above the hill. Once we pick the horse up, we need to put him down somewhere.'

'Roger.'

Just as the helicopter comes over the edge of the hill, the vet stuffs the socks in Lucky's ears and gives him a shot. Lucky doesn't like any of it, including the sound of the helicopter; he does a lot of stomping. 'It's going to take a few minutes to kick in,' the vet says.

'Pull back, pull back, the horse isn't ready yet.'

Richard isn't ready either; he's nervous, excited, almost overwhelmed, it's too much stimulation – maybe the vet should give *him* a little shot as well.

The chopper pulls back, and a few minutes later they come in again and lower the harness. The girl is the only one that Lucky will let in close enough.

'OK, honey, I'm going to talk you through it.' The movie star has the stunt coordinator from Paramount with him in the chopper.

'I'm not your honey,' the girl says to the stunt man.

The horse is settling down, looking glassy-eyed, stoned. The harness is a huge canvas sling, like a strait jacket. As soon as it's on and the cable is attached, the girl scrambles out of the hole. On the top of the hill, the television cameras are rolling – there's a line of TV trucks, satellite dishes up, antennas extended. The movie star manages to look directly at the cameras and give a big wave, just before the signal goes out to lift the horse.

It happens quickly: the harness pulls taut, the horse's feet are off the ground, and he's rising out of the hole. He's free and he's flying. Everyone cheers. Richard bursts into tears. Will he cry every day now? And is this something to be concerned about? Lucky is flying. The sight of a horse hovering overhead, a horse in a sling, tethered to a helicopter, is something you'd never imagine.

'This is the dicey part,' the stunt director says over the walkie-talkie. 'We have to land him gently. The second the horse has all four legs on the ground, he's going to want to bolt. You have to get the cable off so he doesn't drag us. You have to get the cable.'

Richard talks Lucky down, fifty feet, fifteen, ten, seven, three, two; the vet has a hand on him. Lucky's feet are on the ground, the vet detaches the cable, the harness goes slack.

'Go, go, go,' Richard shouts into the walkie-talkie, and the chopper pulls back. The movie star makes a salutory dip in the chopper and flies over the hill.

'Over and out,' he calls.

The harness falls to the ground like an enormous canvas dropcloth. Lucky shakes his head, trying to get the ear-plug socks out.

The girl and the vet lead Lucky up the hill towards home – feet stomping as if in protest at the indignity of it all.

The camera crews lower their antennas, and the crowd begins to dissolve.

'Is everything all right?' the girl's mother asks, arriving after the fact. 'I was in the Valley, the traffic was horrible.'

'Fine,' Richard says, wiping his eyes. 'Everything is fine.'

'Well,' Bob says, 'there's really not much I can do at this point. We don't repair sinkholes, we just track them. We stand back and let nature take its course.'

'Do you know who that was in the helicopter?' Richard asks, bending to look at what is growing on the ground.

Bob shrugs. 'Not really.'

Richard whispers the movie star's name. He plucks some of the greenery and rubs it between his fingers. Mint. It's deliciously mint.

'You're kidding; I had no idea.'

'Who did you think it was?' he asks once again,

bringing his fingers to his nose, breathing the scent.

'I figured he was your boyfriend and maybe the girl was your daughter.'

'We're neighbors, we're all neighbors.'

'That's nice,' Bob says, getting back into his white government sedan. 'You don't see much of that.'

Richard goes into the house. Cecelia is in the kitchen, wearing his headphones, making lunch.

'Did you see it?'

'What?' She takes the headphones off. 'I can't hear you.'

'You missed the whole thing?'

'Missed what?'

He turns on the television. They're showing the footage of Lucky being lifted up into the air with the red 'Breaking News' headline just beneath.

'Is that right?' Cecelia says, putting the head-phones back on. 'I love these.' She yells in the way that people yell when they can't hear how loud they're talking. 'I'm going to get a pair for myself. Can't hear anything.'

An hour later, there's a knock on the door. 'That was really great,' the movie star says, standing in the doorway. 'Thanks for thinking of me.'

'Well, I just thought the part might appeal to you; it seemed like your kind of role.'

'Maybe I'll even get a nomination.'

'It wasn't really a movie,' Richard says, worried that the guy doesn't know the difference.

'I was thinking of good citizenship – I always used to win that one. By the way, I didn't get your name?'

'Novak, Richard Novak,' he says, extending his hand.

'Pleasure to meet you. And, really, thanks for ringing my bell; it doesn't happen every day.'

'It's been all over the TV,' Richard says, leading him in, pointing to the screen. 'You looked pretty good in that helicopter.'

The movie star laughs. 'I'll tell you a secret,' he says. 'But you have to swear not to tell anyone.'

Richard nods.

'I don't own a TV.'

He is standing at the glass, looking out. The hole is deeper still. Between the footprints, the crime-scene tape, the heavy traffic, the hill is a disaster. He looks out the window at the distant palm trees like the spines of an ancient fan. Just below are yellow and orange wildflowers, the purple ice plants, the scruffy brown-and-green scrub, chaparral, mint, and flowers he can't name. While he's watching, the coyote returns, sniffs the ground tentatively, then goes into the hole and scurries out with something in his mouth – the jelly donut.

It is noon, and everything has come to an end.

The day is bright, the sky blue, the sun shining. Up the hill, the one-hole golf course is complete, a perfectly groomed twenty-by-forty-foot rectangle of phosphorescent green. The bougainvillea is in bloom.

Exhausted, Richard breaks yet another of his rules and lies down on his bed. His clothing smells like mint. He smiles, imagines dipping himself in iced tea, imagines himself in a pool with the woman in the red bathing suit. She is swimming; he is drifting, dreaming.

He sleeps. It is the sleep of exhaustion, of enormous change. He is sleeping so soundly that when the masseur comes, he and Cecelia decide not to wake Richard. They turn off the television and tiptoe out of his room. He sleeps so soundly that when Sylvia the nutritionist comes, Cecelia and Sylvia stand in the bedroom doorway, their heads bobbing to the rhythm of his sonorous snoring.

'Is he all right?' Sylvia whispers.

'It's been a hard week.'

Sylvia leaves his meals, his cereal, his sachets, his supplements, and her cell-phone number. She tells Cecelia to get some cranberries, apricots, and blueberries, and more tomatoes, more cancer protection. She leaves an extra supply of low-carb vegan brownies.

'He'll like that,' Cecelia whispers, 'he's got a sweet tooth.'

He sleeps so soundly that when Cecelia is done for the day, she lays a nice blanket over him and locks the door behind her.

★　　★　　★

He dreams of falling through space. He dreams he is pulled towards a spherical surface, a horizon, a boundary. He realizes that once you cross the boundary there is no escape: it is destiny, there is no way out.

A crack of lightning wakes him up. It is night. It is raining. He hears it on the skylight in the bathroom, the plinkety-plink of raindrops. He walks around the house to make sure everything is OK. The kitchen clock says 4:00 a.m. Seven a.m. in New York; he automatically does the math. He always does the math. He always imagines what they are doing. Ben – still sleeping. Her – on the treadmill or in bed editing. She always used to edit in bed. She would prop herself up, leaning back against an enormous teddy-bearish pillow – she called it her husband – manuscript in hand.

He dials Ben. 'I dreamed I fell into a black hole,' he blurts. 'I was about to be ripped in half when I woke up. I slept all day. That's so strange. I lay down yesterday afternoon and just woke up. We're having a storm, that's what woke me – the lightning.'

'Dad?'

'What's the weather like there?' Richard asks, recovering himself.

'Fine, perfectly fine, I guess. It's still pretty early.'

'Good. Things here are a little up in the air. I got hit by a car last night as I was coming out of a bookstore. I went in looking for something to read, something that would inspire me, and when I came out this woman ran me down.'

109

'Are you in the hospital again?'

'No, I'm home. I iced it, and then, this morning, there was a horse in a hole right outside my house. So I went up the street to Tad Ford's house and knocked on his door, and he came out, got in his helicopter, and plucked the horse right out of the hole. I'm not telling it exactly right, but that's basically the order of events.'

'This is all what you dreamed?'

'No, I dreamed I was falling into a hole; the rest happened. It's been strange. When did I talk to you – yesterday morning?'

'Yeah, you'd been in the emergency room for some kind of chest pain. Is it gone now?'

'I can't tell. Is it really four in the morning?'

'Well, it's seven here.'

'Look, Ben, I guess the reason I'm calling is because I don't want things to be bad between us, I never wanted that. A person never knows how much time they've got. I know it sounds corny. You have no idea what I'm talking about.'

'Is it cancer?'

'It's the future, Ben. I want the future to be different.'

'Is it, like, an emergency? Can I think about it?'

He wants to say yes, yes, it is an emergency, but he doesn't. He says, 'Yes, think about it.' And then there is silence. They need a change of subject. 'Your mother mentioned that you're taking a trip this summer.'

'We were supposed to leave yesterday, but Barth's train broke down, so he got here late.'

'Wow, so you're all set, you know where you're going?' He's overwhelmed with the idea that Ben would be coming to L.A. without telling him, that Ben has a whole life that doesn't include him, doesn't need his consent, approval, or even knowledge. 'Are you coming straight out, or stopping along the way, taking scenic detours?'

'I don't know if there's a specific plan. It was Barth's idea, he calls it a document for the future. I'm riding shotgun as cameraman. He wanted to make a movie so that one day he can show his kids an old-fashioned cross-country expedition. We're doing it as a kind of covered-wagon thing.'

'A Volvo is hardly a covered wagon.'

'We debated hiring a Central Park carriage horse, but we thought it would be bad for the horse.'

'Will you be staying with friends along the way?'

'I'm seventeen, I don't have "friends along the way." We're going to Cleveland, because that's where Barth's aunt lives. She's expecting us.'

'Well, you know, when you get out here, you've got a place.'

'Yeah, I know, I just, well, Barth and I haven't really talked about that.'

A document for the future. When Richard was growing up, he wasn't sure there would be a future – the air-raid siren would go off, they'd duck under their desks and frantically pray, even the atheists,

111

especially the atheists. A document for the future – it sounds so healthy, normal, youthful, filled with aunts and uncles and hope.

'And sometimes we'll sleep in the car – that's the part I'm looking forward to. Under the stars, or under the moon roof, looking up at the sky. My only fear is bears. I heard that there are these really aggressive national-park bears that have no compunction about coming right up to people and stealing from them.'

'Compunction' – the kid even has a vocabulary.

'Be careful: parking in remote places is how you get kidnapped. Park in big parking lots where you can see lights.'

'The car has an alarm; if you touch the outside, the horn beeps, the lights flash, and it says in a really loud voice: "Burglar, burglar, step away from the car."'

'Park someplace where someone will hear the car saying "Burglar." And if you're carrying something illegal, like drugs, keep them in the trunk. That's the most difficult place for them to search. It's considered private space – they'd need a warrant. Whenever you're carrying something that you don't want anyone to know about, put it in the trunk.'

'It's a station wagon – there is no trunk.'

'OK, then, put it in the wheel well, under the back part.' He's trying to be helpful, to a make a connection.

'What makes you think I'm traveling with drugs?'

'I'm not saying you are, I'm just telling you what I learned – it was on the *Today* show.'

'Weird information I'm not sure I needed to hear.' There is a pause. 'Do prescription drugs count?'

'I don't think so. Is anyone else you know doing something like this?'

'A few people are going on European exchange programs; I did that last year. I lived with a veterinarian's family just outside Paris.'

'Did I know?' There's a pause, a beat. 'When you get out here, I'm hoping you'll stay with me.'

Ben says nothing.

'Is Barth there now?'

'Yes.'

'Is he listening to this conversation?'

'I'm not sure he's listening, but he's sitting here.'

'And what are you planning to do when you get here?'

'Work for The Agency.'

'What agency?'

'The Agency, that's what it's called, it's a talent group.'

'What do they do, manage animal acts?' He can't believe he said that – he sounds just like his own father. 'Sorry. I'm sorry I said that. That's great. The Agency sounds great.'

'Whatever.'

Again there is silence. He goes to the window and sees the yellow lights of the government man's car. 'I'm here, Ben. I'm waiting. Call me if you need anything.'

The night man is outside. He's wearing a yellow slicker with white reflective tape in strips, like stripes, across his back. The yellow lights are flashing. 'I saw the rescue on television, but I wanted to take a look for myself. I wasn't going to bother you.'

'I was up.'

'The rain's not helping. If it keeps up, she's going to go.'

'Where?'

'Down.'

Down and down, like in his dream. 'Anyone ever fallen to the center of the earth?'

'Not on my watch. I saw the actor with the helicopter. Where do you know him from?'

'Lives up the street. Want a cup of coffee?'

'I'm on duty.'

'You can stand by the window and keep an eye out.'

He leaves the engine running. As soon as they're in the house, Richard regrets having invited him in. The guy is dripping, tracking his muddy footprints across the floor, and he can't bring himself to tell the guy to take his boots off.

'Vegan brownie? Donut?' He opens the fridge to see what else there is, and his dinner stares back at him. He'd forgotten about dinner.

'Donut would be great.'

Richard looks around. 'I'm trying to think – where are the parts for the coffeemaker? I'm not usually the one who . . .'

'Tea is good enough; in fact, I like it better.'

Richard makes tea.

'What are you doing up? You don't seem like a night rider.'

'I was on the phone with my son; he lives in New York.' It's probably the first time he's ever said that.

'So how'd that happen, with the movie star? He just did it – no agent, lawyer, or business manager stopped him? They don't like those people to work for free.'

'I don't think he thought it was work.'

'I'm an actor, an actor/writer. Bet you didn't know that; I came out here to become a star, and look at me.'

Richard doesn't say anything.

'Grew up in Minnesota, had a big rock collection as a kid – one of those rock-tumbling machines. I knew my stones – that's how I got into geology-related work – but I came out here to be in the movies.'

Richard nods.

'I've got a script; do you think you could get it to him?'

'Is that why you came back – to give me your screenplay?'

He nods. 'And I wanted to see if the horse was OK.'

'Lucky horse. Horse named Lucky.'

'The horse ate the probe?'

'No, he just pulled it out.'

'I'd better be getting back out there; I am the night man, after all. Thanks for the snack.'

'No problem.'

'You know, I hate to be the one who tells you this, but you should be thinking about where you're going to go.'

'What do you mean?'

'When the hill goes it's going to take something with it. Probably won't take your whole house, nothing that dramatic. But it'll need work, and it's best not to be cheap about it – that's something you'll end up regretting. Night-night.'

In the early morning it rains, a hard, soaking rain, a rain of no rain for months, a pouring, drenching rain. The soil, as if newly allergic, rejects the rain, the water sits on top. There's a surface tension that won't be easily broken. Rain splashes down onto the dirt and bounces off, running over the soil, down the street, pouring into the storm drains.

He's up early, despite having been up in the night. The rain is still coming down. He does his exercises, his homework, looking at the overnights; fingers flying, he types, trades, this is the clickety-clack of the cash keys. He reads the market, the smell of its breath, the timbre of its snore; he anticipates what will come next. Head and shoulders, top and bottom – he thinks of all the catchy phrases they used to use to describe the shape of things.

Seven a.m. He's poring over his date book, trying to piece it all together. Cecelia said he hadn't left the house for weeks. If anyone had asked him, he would have sworn that he'd been out.

Before the trip to the hospital – he marks the date of the trip to the hospital in his book with a big 'X' – when had he last left the house? A few days before? Maybe it was the week before? Maybe he went to the dentist? He looks at his date book – the dentist's appointment was on January 22. He flips through the pages. On March 27 he had dinner with an old friend from New York who called at the last minute. On April 15 he had tickets to a play – he'd ordered them just after the dinner on the 27th in a fraction of a second when he felt human again. When April 15 rolled around, he couldn't think of anyone to invite – so he went alone and kept his jacket on the seat next to him.

After that he can't come up with much. He looks in his computer; every day he saves a chart of his performance. According to the charts, nothing looks out of the ordinary, except that when he wasn't online he apparently didn't exist.

He goes to the window. The depression is a muddy pit; the footprints that were so clear yesterday, the bite of the sole of each shoe, are melting. He thinks the hole might even be filling, gathering water, becoming a cistern.

He is standing at the glass, watching the woman

in the red suit – swimming in the rain. How long has he been watching her? How long has she been in the red suit? There were others: blue with a pattern, fluorescent orange, he remembered that one, it made him nervous, made him think of hunting season, the fluorescence of hazard, caution. And before that something yellow. The red is his favorite; the red is perfect, vibrant, the color of the life force, coursing through. Would a person in the water worry about getting wet?

Lusardi. He needs to see Lusardi again, to ask him what it means to not know anything. He can't stay home. He checks the computer once more, and then he's off down the hill, towards Anhil. The radio is filled with warnings and road closings, flash floods, slide conditions; everything is about impermanence.

He parks, and runs into the donut shop holding a newspaper over his head.

'In California they pretend it is never going to rain, like it is not possible; no one keeps an umbrella.' Anhil laughs. Richard puts his wet paper on the counter and sits. 'You left your cereal; I've been eating it. It's good, like cardboard but fruity.'

'It's kiln-dried hand-pressed high-fiber flakes with fruit juices – berry extracts.'

'Maybe I could sell it?'

'Maybe.'

Anhil leans forward and looks at Richard more seriously. 'You look worse.'

'I was up most of the night.'

'How is your heart?'

Before he can answer, the homeless man comes in. He looks at both men – Anhil is about to shoo him out and Richard is patting the empty stool next to him.

'Sit down,' Richard says. 'I'll buy you a donut – don't beg.'

'Do you work here?'

'Just visiting.'

'Me too,' the man says.

As soon as the man sits, Richard is reminded that these things are not as easy as one hoped they would be. The man smells. Anhil is giving Richard a dirty look.

'What do you want?' Richard asks. 'What are you hungry for?'

'Whatever you want.'

'I want you to have what you want. Order whatever you like.'

'Don't tease me,' the man says. 'I'll take whatever you're giving.'

Anhil gives the man a donut, on a plain white plate.

'Coffee, tea, orange juice, milk?' Richard asks.

'That sounds good.'

'All of them?' Anhil wants to know.

'Whatever you like,' Richard tells the man.

'OK,' the man says.

There is a pause. 'One of each,' Richard says.

Anhil isn't saying anything, but you can tell he's

annoyed. The man eats the donut, dipping it into his coffee, and then wipes his hands on a napkin, drinks his orange juice, and gracefully sips his tea. 'Good tea,' he says. He is not without manners. He eats looking down, trying not to make much of himself. When he's finished, he climbs off the stool and heads out the door – not lingering.

'Have a nice day,' Richard calls after him, annoyed that the guy didn't say thank you.

The man turns around. 'Have a nice day. I'm homeless. What does that mean, 'Have a nice day'? Go fuck yourself.'

'You can't change the rules overnight,' Anhil says. 'Sorry.'

'It's fine; in fact, it's better – he won't be back.'

Richard watches Anhil in the kitchen. There's grace to what he does, how he runs the big mixer, frosts the donuts. He's got a dancer's athleticism – his body is long and lean, nothing extra.

'Do you go to a gym?'

'I hate exercise. Eight meals, that's how I keep my shape. I eat one thing at each: a potato, a piece of meat, some cheese. The only thing I like too much – my wife's chicken stew, prunes, olives – but you never see a man fat from chicken stew. Why are we talking like this, about nothing, when I know you come here to talk about important things?'

'My son is driving out to California with my nephew; they're leaving today.'

'Jack Korea?'

'Who is Jack Korea?'

'The poet with the beaters . . . "I have seen the finest minds of my generation . . ."'

'Jack Kerouac and Allen Ginsberg; how do you know who they are?'

'I am from another country, not another planet. My cousin taught me – he was Mr Revolutionary. Unfortunately, he's no longer with us.' He crosses himself.

'Are you Catholic?'

'No; why?'

'Because that's what that is, the crossing, it's Catholic.'

'I saw it in a movie. After someone died, the man did that, and I thought that's what people did – it looked good.'

'It's the sign of the cross.'

There is a pause.

'May I drive your car?'

'It's raining.'

'The car has a good roof.'

'OK, fine.' Richard hands Anhil the keys and goes behind the counter.

Anhil is gone, and a few minutes later a man comes in who looks just like Anhil.

'Mr Mercedes?' he asks. Richard doesn't say anything; he's not sure this is not some sort of a joke.

The man puts out his hand. 'I'm George, the brother.'

'Anhil mentioned a brother, but he didn't say you were twins.'

George laughs. 'He likes to pretend he is the only one, but then I pop up to remind him he is not alone. Even my mother didn't know. She was at the hospital. She had my Anhil, and was trying to get up out of bed, when they said, Wait, there's more. It wasn't like it is today, where they can look ahead and take inventory. I have heard about your car.'

'Anhil is out with it now.'

'You permitted him to drive in the rain?'

Richard nods.

'Brave man. In our country it never rains, I don't think he's ever driven on water.'

'How many more of you are there?'

'Two more brothers and three sisters. Anhil and I drive the same kind of car, Toyota Corolla; we got them used, two for one. Do you have brothers?'

'One.'

George smiles. 'Do you like the name George? It was the first thing I learned about America. George Washington, his face is on every one-dollar bill. And he had wooden teeth – every time one gave out, they put a new one in. When I came to America, I changed my name.'

A customer comes in and Richard gets the man a half-dozen donuts to go.

'I bet that man eats all the donuts, one after another,' George says. 'If one donut is good, why not have two? If two are good, four are even better. I love America. It will make everybody rich.'

Anhil returns. He puts his arms around his

brother; they are mirror images of each other. 'I hope he didn't scare you. He is my secret weapon,' Anhil says. 'When we make our movie, *Super Donut Man*, he will be the cruller ball in the end.'

'The curve ball?'

'The cruller, the twist.'

Sylvia and Cecelia are sitting at the dining-room table, waiting. 'What a surprise. I just want to put these shirts in the bedroom,' he says as he ducks into the bedroom, hiding his box of donuts. 'I'm sorry about yesterday,' he says, 'I was zonked out.'

They're looking at him like it's something serious. His dinner from last night is still in the fridge, and he's sure that Cecelia has seen it.

'I was on my way to another appointment, but I wanted to stop in and see how you were doing,' Sylvia says.

'Did you eat anything last night?' Cecelia asks.

He shakes his head.

'And this morning?'

'A cup of coffee.'

'Real coffee?' Sylvia asks.

He nods.

'With regular milk?'

Sylvia is stricken. 'All the good work we do and you drank that? Couldn't you have at least asked for soy milk? Even Starbucks has soy milk.'

He's staring at Cecelia, who obviously knows

about the donuts but also knows enough not to say anything. 'I was with a friend.'

'I know it's difficult for you right now – I'm not really sure why – but try and stay with the program. You're adding stress to your body at a time when it's already stressed. If you're bored, just tell me and we'll give you a few new things. What would you like that you're not getting?'

'What do you eat?' he asks her.

'Almost nothing.'

'Steamed vegetables, brown rice?'

'I take a lot of supplements.'

'Seaweed? A little bit of protein?'

'I'm not a good example. This is all I do – my life is about my food.'

At the moment, he's starving. His regular breakfast is on the table in front of him.

'I put some dried organic berries on top,' Sylvia says, 'and I think you need a little of this.'

She pulls a plastic bag from her pocket, opens it, and sprinkles some sort of powder onto his cereal.

'What is it, fairy dust?'

'Flax. I buy flax seed and grind it.'

He begins to eat.

Sylvia watches him carefully, reaching out to touch the skin on his face. 'Maybe we should add an egg? How about two mornings a week we give you some eggs? Do you like them poached on a bed of spinach? With maybe a broiled tomato?'

'The man needs to eat,' Cecelia says. 'He's starving himself. That might be what brought this on.'

'It's an anti-aging diet,' says Sylvia.

'He can't live on seafood, all that salmon. He's going to start growing gills or get a goiter or something.'

'What if I stopped eating this way, what if I just ate like a regular person?' He pushes his cereal bowl away.

'You would die,' Sylvia says.

'Do you want some eggs now?' Cecelia asks.

He shakes his head. 'Quickly, would I die quickly?'

'Over time.'

'But I am already dying.'

'Exactly – and the purpose of eating the anti-oxidants, the good oils, is to help you stay healthy as long as possible. Do you want to die a good death of old age, or do you want to die of rotting disease?'

'How about I make you some nice sunny-side-up eggs or an omelet?'

'I'm OK for now,' he says.

Who did he get Sylvia from? You get to people from other people, but who gave him Sylvia? A woman he dated? She was beautiful and blonde and blank. He dated her for two weeks – wanting to stop after the second date, but not wanting to hurt her feelings. And then she dumped him. Sylvia was her nutritionist?

'By the way,' he asks, 'do you still see – what's-her-name?'

'Who?' Sylvia asks.

'You, know who, the woman who recommended me to you, you to me? What's her name?'

Sylvia shakes her head. 'I don't remember who that was.'

Richard shrugs, changes the subject: 'What does food mean to you?'

'Everything. It means everything – love, sustenance, comfort, good care. Maybe the question is, what does it mean to you?'

'When we started, it was about running an efficient, lean, clean machine. And now it's habit, regime, structure.'

'Not just eggs,' Cecelia says. 'But bacon and eggs – I could get that nice turkey bacon, and maybe some cinnamon-raisin toast?'

'Have you ever thought of marketing your cereal?' Richard asks. 'A friend of mine has a store downtown, he really likes it.'

'Oh, really? I could make a batch for him.'

'That would be great.'

Sylvia gets up to go. 'See you next week at the regular time. Meanwhile, if there's something you're craving, have it, treat yourself. This is not the military, it's not supposed to make you miserable; you have to live.'

'Are you sure I can't make you some eggs or some French toast?' Cecelia asks.

'Tomorrow,' he says. 'Tomorrow is fine.'

While he's been having breakfast, there's been movement below. The pillar holding up the corner of the carport of the house next door has snapped, the carport is down, the broken pillar jutting out like a bent knee.

He calls Lusardi's office. 'I need to come back sooner than expected.'

'You got validated last time, right?' the receptionist asks.

'Yes.'

'And you're still hurting?'

'Yes.'

'How about two-thirty?'

He calls his insurance company – 'Something is about to happen, a kind of a sinking situation, I thought I ought to ask how these things go, what the procedure is . . .'

'Before I say anything, let's make sure your policy is up to date – name, address, Social?'

There is the clicking of keys and then a pause and what Richard is pretty sure is the flick of a lighter, the suck of a cigarette.

'Should you really be doing that – an insurance agent and all?'

'I'm addicted,' the agent says. 'Can't live without it.'

'Don't you worry about lung cancer?'

'Oh,' he says. 'It's not tobacco, it's marijuana, homegrown. Looking at your policy – you're a lucky man, you have very little to worry about.'

Richard can't tell if the man is reading his

insurance policy or telling his fortune. 'How can you be addicted? Marijuana is not addictive.'

'Trust me, I am. You must have really hit it off with the insurance agent.'

'It was a very long time ago,' Richard says. 'They let you smoke in the office?'

'I'm the only one here until noon. My name is Paul. Well, she sold you the store, and at a very good price; we don't even sell this kind of policy now – too expensive for us.'

'Lucky me,' he says, joking with Paul the pothead.

'You need to keep a record of everything, get estimates, take photos.'

'And if I have to relocate?'

'Be ready, pack a bag, when it happens go quickly. Call us when you're on terra firma. Your policy covers the cost of housing while the damage is being assessed and repaired.'

'For how long?'

'Reasonable and customary, which basically means as long it takes; that's why we don't write this policy anymore, people were moving to Europe.'

He hangs up, takes an overnight bag out of the closet, and packs a few things. He leaves the bag open on the bed and dials the real-estate agent who sold him the house, Billy Collins.

'Richard Novak – now, that's a name. I never forget anyone. Never forget a name or address.

You're on Shadow Hill. You want me to sell it for you – find you something bigger, something better?'

'I'm having a problem with the house . . .'

'It's been over ten years, it's not like we give refunds.'

'It's thirteen years, and I still like the house.'

'I could show you a few new things; times have changed.'

'We had some damage, maybe structural trouble. I don't know the extent of it yet, but I may have to relocate temporarily.'

'Would you even entertain an offer? I've sold houses for people who didn't even know they wanted to sell. They don't see it coming. Sometimes you're driving a client around and they see what they want and you have to go and get it for them, that's the job, finding out what it would take.'

'Ideas. I'm looking for ideas about what to do, what comes next.'

'Remarried?'

'Nope.'

'Well, then, take advantage of the situation, try something new. It's all about life-style. It's all about who you want to be, how you see yourself, setting a course for the future.'

'I may need a short-term rental.'

'In this town everything is short-term. Pets?'

'No pets.'

Billy, the agent, is the kind of man who at sixty is still called Billy.

A Los Angeles native, he brags about how well he knows the turf.

Just after Richard bought the house from Billy, he took Billy on as a client. Billy had made some money buying houses and renovating them, flipping them at a profit, and then Richard made Billy even more money, quickly, at the height of things, and then Billy decided to put it back into real estate – the market made him nervous.

'How's all that worked out for you?' Richard asks out of politeness.

'I could have done better.'

'You did very well. You can't always get every last drop – knowing when to quit is part of it.'

'What do you think of those tech companies now?' Billy asks him.

'I'm not really involved anymore.' He can't tell Billy that, despite everything he knew, he never thought the Internet would catch on, he never thought people like his parents would be pulling computers out of the box – living online. He thought e-mail was a fad. It was a strange limitation in his own thinking, an inability to think forward. The closest he got was childhood daydreams of Dick Tracy communicator watches and Morse-code rings, not Wi-Fi beaming information all over the world, PSAs, Palms, and people writing notes to themselves in New Age hieroglyphic code.

'So you called me and I appreciate that,' Billy says. 'I'm sure we can find you something. When do you need it – why am I asking? Now! You need it now or you wouldn't be calling.'

Billy calls back in twenty minutes. 'Don't say I don't care about you. It's all set. I got you a place in Malibu, very special.'

'Should I go and see it?'

'I think you're missing the point. I'm doing you a favor – it's not like this guy wants to rent the place. It's a house I sold to this . . . person, who's going to tear it down and build something "signature" as soon as the permits are in place, but at the moment it's furnished, it's on the ocean. Sound appealing?'

'Yes, that's why I said I'd like to take a look.'

'Well, if it was good enough for him, I can't imagine it wouldn't work for you – short-term, of course. I can try to get you in. Are you free this morning? Can you leave now? It's not like I don't have other things to do today.'

The house is four bedrooms, three bathrooms, and all of it white – white sofa, white walls, white shag carpet, white gone slightly yellow.

'It was used in the movie *Shampoo*.'

'And never rinsed.'

'You're funny. I can probably get them to clean the rug and put a coat of fresh paint in the living room, but they're not interested in doing a lot of work. But the ocean is right out there, at high tide; you can jump in off the deck. It's a different world. I've got great carpet people, they clean up crime scenes, it's like Heloise meets *Murder, She Wrote*, they can clean anything. They come in, very discreet, put on hazard suits, masks, and do what needs to be done. The hotels use them a lot: housekeepers won't put up with certain things anymore. Why am I telling you this? You tell me something. What have you been doing?' He makes the sound of a cash register: 'Kaching. That's how I think of you.'

The house is white like a cloud, a pleasant dream, brighter than bright, reflected light bouncing off all the white walls, the sea shimmering right outside. It feels hopeful, weirdly promising. Everything is white – white cabinets, white dishes, white silverware; frying pans are cast-iron with white enamel; there are white chairs on the deck, white bean-bag chairs in the living room. He goes upstairs, from room to room, white, more white, more more white. He lies on one of the beds – it sloshes. He drags himself aboard, lies back, feeling the water beneath him and dreaming of the summer to come.

He imagines this being the summer that never was, the summer that should have been. Ben comes to Los Angeles, they do all the things they should have done before. They go to ball games, they watch television, they do whatever it is that fathers and sons do.

'I'll take it.'

'Don't you want to see the rest?' Billy throws open a door. What was formerly a home office has been converted into an adult playroom/fantasy chamber, in the same way that a person might take a spare bedroom and make it into a gym. There's a harness – white, of course – mounted in the ceiling, a mattress on the floor, and a lot of pillows and extension cords – all white.

'Do I want to know?'

'The "recipient" goes in there and she hangs, antigravity. I've heard it's great. Not my cup of tea, I only know what it is because I saw it once at a convention. The downside of this house,' Billy says, closing the door, 'no pool. Everyone wants a pool, even on the ocean; a pool, a panic room – way too Houdini for me. A life raft, that's what I would want in one of these places. By the by, I'm sure we can get them to take the thingy down; I just wanted you to know it was there.'

'How much?'

'Twenty-five.'

'Hundred?' Richard asks, even he knows enough to think that's a little low for a whole house on the ocean.

'Thousand.'

'Fifteen. I'll pay fifteen thousand a month for three months, in cash, up front.'

Billy whips out his cell phone, calls the mysterious owner, and turns away from Richard. 'I have a qualified client interested in taking the house for three months – forty thousand for the three months, plus he'll pay five thousand to have the

133

carpet cleaned and everything polished up.' There is a pause. 'Right away.'

When he gets off, Richard asks, 'How come you quoted him forty?'

'I've been doing this for twenty-seven years, I know how people think. If you say, "He'll pay forty-five, but you have to spend five to fix it up," they'll say no. If you say, "Forty, and he'll pay an extra five to fix it up," they'll say yes. Everyone wants to think they're getting a deal. Here's the complication. You can have it, but not until next week – he's promised it to someone for the next five days. And then I'll need a couple of days to get it cleaned up. Could you stay in a hotel if you had to?'

He can take a long weekend and go visit his brother in Boston. 'Sold,' he says. 'Now tell me, whose is it?'

'You don't want to know.'

'Yes, I do.'

'Let's just say, you'd recognize the name; 'nuff said.'

'I'm going to be living in some guy's house and I don't even get to know who it is?'

'You're not living in his house, you're living in a house he owns – it's very different. He's never spent a night here.'

Driving back into town, he is dizzy with the vibrancy of life – or maybe it's his new diet or lack of a diet. He is about to pass out. A donut

– that would fix him for the moment; he brought a few along, thinking he'd give them to Billy, but when he saw Billy thought, No donut.

He reaches into the bag, bites into one; raspberry jelly explodes onto his face. Using his tongue, his fingers, he attempts to lick himself clean while at the wheel, like an animal grooming, licking until he is not sticky anymore.

'Always happy to see you,' Lusardi's receptionist says when he steps into the office.

Richard hands her his parking ticket.

'My kind of man – validate in advance, that way you don't forget. How is the pain?'

'I don't know. I've been busy, got hit by a car, my house is about to fall into a sinkhole, and you know that horse they evacuated – I helped.'

'So – it's a bit better?'

He pauses. 'Not really; I think that's why I called.'

Lusardi acts as though he's never seen him before – no hi, hello, good to see you again. 'What brings you in?'

'The same,' Richard says.

'Let's take a listen.'

Richard takes off his shirt. 'I don't know anything anymore. Is that normal? Is it normal to notice the enormity of everything and just go blank?' His shirt is off; he's covered in goose bumps. As Lusardi is listening to his heart, he's trying to remember how he ended up in L.A. He was still living with his wife when the company said they might need someone on the West Coast. Richard asked her if she thought he should go, and she said it was late and she didn't care, just as long as she could get some work done before she went to sleep.

He remembers her not having an opinion – was that a neutral or a negative? He remembers feeling like he had become invisible. He moved out two weeks later.

Lusardi is looking into his eyes with the light. Richard is thinking of how angry he was, and obviously still is, at his wife for letting him go so easily – and at himself for leaving without a fight.

'I dreamed I was falling in a black hole,' he tells Lusardi.

'You know what happens in a black hole,' Lusardi says as he's flipping through the chart. 'You're pulled from both ends until finally you rip apart. How are your eating habits, good? Stick out your tongue.'

Lusardi looks at his tongue. 'Did you eat a jelly donut?'

'Yes, how do you know?'

'Your breath is sugary, your tongue is coated, and you've got some on your shirt.'

'My diet has been way off. Usually it's good, but the last couple of days . . .'

Lusardi opens the chart again and flips through the pages. 'We got your labs back, your PSA – prostate-specific antigen – was a little high.

Minimally, I should do a rectal to see if I can feel anything.'

Richard drops his pants. Lusardi slips on a glove and wiggles his finger up Richard's ass. 'When men get prostate cancer at your age, it's usually worse than when they get it later. We all die with prostate cancer, did you know that? Strange but true. It's usually not the thing that kills us, but it's there. Do you ejaculate often? Are you sexually active?' he asks with his finger still up Richard's ass.

'Not much.' Richard says.

'Try and ejaculate more often; there's some mythology out there that, the more you do, the less cancer you get, it keeps everything moving. I can't say there's any proof, but why not.' He pulls his finger out. 'I didn't feel anything. Do you have trouble getting an erection?'

'No, I don't have much trouble.'

'Much trouble meaning occasional trouble? I could give you some Viagra.'

'Much, meaning I haven't been in a situation where I would know. I have no feelings except the pain, which is why I am here. I'm dead – dead men don't ejaculate.'

'Well, you wouldn't be in pain if you were a dead man. So perhaps the pain is a good sign in this case? In terms of the prostate, we can pursue it, or wait and repeat the test in six months.' He smears his shitty finger on a cardboard colon-cancer card and then snaps the glove off, as though it's all in a day's work. 'Is it still raining out? It was when I came in.'

'No . . . not really.'

'How much does it hurt?'

Richard shrugs.

'Pain management – that's what addicts do. We could just hook you up to a morphine pump and you could play the mother in *Long Day's Journey*.'

Richard says nothing.

'It's delicate – this process of waking up, coming in from the cold – you can't do it overnight.'

'Why not?'

'You'd die.' Lusardi sits at his desk. 'You don't know how to feel – or, more accurately, what to do with what you feel. When a person comes in from the cold, it's not like they immediately feel warm. If they've been out for a while, they come in and everything hurts, and the warmer they get the more pain they're in. It's excruciatingly painful. For, as much as you want to feel nothing, you feel everything, you feel too much to bear, like you'd explode, or go crazy, if you knew how much you felt.'

'I'm numb,' Richard says, flatly.

'You have some sensation.'

'Yes, something like an insect bite, an itch or irritation, like poison ivy that won't quit. The other day, after all this happened, I called my ex-wife, my son, my parents, my brother. I talked to everyone, and I felt worse.'

'Who were you growing up – back of the class, athlete, goody-goody?'

'I blended – unremarkable, neither here nor there.'

Richard is on the table with his shirt off, his pants down, feeling more than naked – small, nervous. And there's Lusardi, tapping his fingers on a prescription pad.

'Did you ever have anxiety attacks before – would you like to have something for them?'

'Is that what this is – anxiety?'

'To some degree, sure. You're mortal, you've failed, you're not the person you wanted to become, your mother doesn't love you, your father doesn't know who you are, everyone has it better than you.'

'It's not like I'm a loser. I did something. I made money. I made enough money to make a lot of people happy. In fact, I've probably made more money than my brother.'

Lusardi feigns shock in an exaggerated way. 'And now that you've done that – what? It sounds like you finished that part of things a while ago.'

'I'm uncomfortable,' Richard confesses, putting his shirt back on.

'Climb a wall.'

'What?'

'You have hit a wall, now climb it – literally.' Lusardi opens his Palm Pilot, looks something up, and writes down a couple of phone numbers. 'They'll teach you.'

'Very funny.'

'I'm a hundred percent serious. Make the mental

physical, and the physical mental, and things will improve. I can't make you feel better. It's not within my power.'

'If I were your relative, what would you tell me?'

'I would tell you that you need to do something – I would tell you to try everything. You need to be brought back to life. Don't even wait until tomorrow, begin again right now, begin again every moment. Do you believe in anything?'

'I don't know,' Richard says.

'Do you pray?' Lusardi asks, and Richard says nothing. 'Think about it.' Lusardi hands him the piece of paper with the numbers of rock-climbing schools and leaves the room.

The sadness Richard feels is so deep, so whole, it is as though he himself is sadness – that's what he held on to, that's what he kept for himself. He feels his failings, each like a claw digging in. He feels the limits of his personality, of his fear, of his ability to know himself, to know what he already knows.

And his butt is sore; the soreness seeps through his bones. Maybe he does have cancer, maybe he should let them biopsy his nut, but at the moment he's had enough.

As he leaves, the receptionist calls after him: 'Don't forget, you've been validated. Have a nice day.'

He wants to turn around and correct her, he wants to say 'violated,' he wants to say, 'I'm a dead man, dead men don't have nice days.' He wants to say something.

140

'Do you need a follow-up?' she asks.

'I'll call,' Richard says.

When he gets home, Cecelia is standing in the driveway, behind a rope of yellow plastic CRIME SCENE tape.

'We're not allowed in.'

'It's our house.'

'There's a man in there who told me to go outside.'

'That's crazy.' Richard walks into the house.

'Sorry, sir, you'll have to stay outside.'

'Who are you?'

'One of the day men,' he says, like it's a 1960s singing group, The Day Men, like The Highwaymen, and The Journeymen.

'It's my house.'

'The first thing I'm going to have you do is take your car out of the garage.'

'Is this a hijacking, are you holding us hostage? No one said you could come in.'

'Your garage is the closest thing to the hill; it could go in at any moment, and that looks like a very heavy car.'

Richard goes outside, pulls the car out of the garage, parks at the curb, and goes back into the house.

'I feel better now,' the man says. 'A lot of cars go over the edge. Sorry about the CRIME SCENE tape. I didn't mean to scare you, but I ran out of CAUTION tape and had to take what I could get.

Look, it's your house, I can't stop you from being in it, but I can tell you that it's not over yet. I was just stopping by to check. It's not like I have nothing better to do: with all the rain, I'm sure I've got some mud slides. By the way, I like your pictures. I thought they only had paintings like that in museums. Guess I was wrong.'

Cecelia comes into the house while the man is still talking.

'What I'm trying to tell you is that it's time for you to go.' And with that, the man leaves.

Cecelia starts to pack. She takes out her vacuum, her mop and bucket and fills the bucket with her favorite supplies, as though they can't be replaced – her rubber gloves and her extra pair of work shoes.

Richard picks up the phone and calls the Four Seasons. 'I was hoping to make a last-minute reservation,' he says. 'The name is Novak. Arriving in about an hour and staying, well, I'm not sure, a few days, maybe a week.'

'The usual suite?'

'That would be fine.' He knows what they're getting at – they think he is his ex-wife's assistant. It's fine, he'll get good service and they'll keep an eye out, waiting for her to show up.

'Bill it to the company?'

'Let me give you another card – personal.'

When the ex-wife comes to L.A., she's usually too busy to see him. They always make a plan; 90 percent of the time she cancels before she even arrives, and the other 10 percent she cancels at the last minute – but she always calls.

Richard begins going through the house, rushing in a progressive panic, taking things he decides he can't live without: his laptop, and his flat-screen monitor, his cordless mouse, the bag that he started packing last night. He stuffs a few more things into the bag: a tie – just in case – a sport jacket – for the same unknown reason – a better pair of shoes.

Cecelia has her head in the refrigerator, pulling out the perishables, pulling out his food for the week, packing it in ice. She drops something – the salmon that is supposed to be for dinner tonight – it lands on the floor and rolls. It rolls across the floor, rolls downhill, rolls flipping over and over, like it is swimming downstream. There is no reason why the salmon should be rolling except that the house, which was previously on an even plane, is now off kilter.

Cecelia and Richard watch the salmon roll over and over all the way across the floor, until it gets stuck on the leg of a chair. While they are watching, the phone rings – Cecelia picks it up and hands it to Richard. 'It's for you,' she says without saying hello.

'Was that your wife?'

'My housekeeper.'

The crying woman is on the phone; she sounds terrible.

'What happened, did something happen? You sound horrible.'

'I was thinking of taking you up on your offer, if only for a little bit.'

'My house is falling down. It's a disaster. Did you see the thing about the flying horse on TV? That was me, my house, it's falling into a sinkhole.'

'Does that mean I can't come over?'

He pauses. 'No, of course not,' he says. 'It just means that you probably shouldn't come here. I'm packing up and going to the Four Seasons; do you want to meet me there?'

She doesn't say anything for a minute. 'I'll meet you in the lobby,' she says.

'Give me an hour.' He hangs up.

'You really are something,' Cecelia says. 'Phone calls from women and everything, almost like a human being. Do you want me to go down there with you and get you set up?'

'I'll be fine.'

'Now, you know, I can't make your breakfast or clean up after you at a hotel, they have their own people.'

'I know.'

Richard realizes that he has no idea how Cecelia gets to and from work: she just appears and disappears.

'Are you all right to get yourself home, do you want a ride somewhere?'

'Oh, I'm not going home. I'm going to enjoy myself. Maybe I'll go shopping, maybe I'll go down to the Farmers Market and get myself a lemon-meringue pie.'

'I didn't get a chance to tell you, but while I was out I found us a place; we can't get in for a week, but it's on the ocean in Malibu.'

The doorbell rings; it's the FedEx man delivering the Bose noise-canceling headset that he ordered for Cecelia.

'You didn't have to do that – now you won't have anything to get me for Christmas.'

'It's a long way to Christmas; I'm sure you'll think of something else.'

'We can both wear them and not talk to each other,' Cecelia says, opening the box.

'And you can play music through them,' Richard says. 'And if you go on a plane it's great for cutting down the engine noise – that's how I discovered them.'

Richard loads the car. The movie star comes walking down the street. 'Is this a bad time? I was going to call, but I didn't have your number.'

'I'm just heading out,' Richard says. 'Temporarily relocating.'

'Listen,' the movie star says. 'My sister is starting a group, a kind of a reading group, about religious thought, I think she wants to start her own religion – would you like to join?'

'Thanks for thinking of me,' Richard says. 'It sounds interesting.'

'We're starting tonight, with the Jews – understanding the Jews.'

'Are you Jewish?' Richard asks the movie star.

'Of course not,' he says. 'But my parents are.'

145

Richard doesn't know quite what to do with that.

'Think about it,' the movie star says, 'give me a call; I'm in the phone book under Edward Albee.'

'Do you get many calls about the real Edward Albee?'

'He's dead, isn't he?'

'No.'

'Really? Wow, maybe I should pick someone else. What about Holden Caulfield – is he still living?'

'I'm not sure,' Richard says, not wanting to pop the bubble.

'What about the pictures?' Cecelia asks, coming out with the last bag. 'You can't just leave them in there, can you?'

He completely forgot about the paintings. He goes back, takes the paintings off the walls, wraps them in sheets, and carefully puts them into the car – seat-belting the de Kooning into the back-seat and easing the Rothko into the trunk, closing with caution. There are others he could take, but these are the two key pieces.

Cecelia toots the horn. 'I'm not going to be able to enjoy my day off if it doesn't start soon.'

'Where to?' he asks, starting up.

'You can just drop me at Fairfax.'

'You should take tomorrow,' he says, 'the whole rest of the week, really – paid, of course. There's not much to do at the moment. I'll check on the house again tomorrow.'

Cecelia nods. 'I appreciate that . . . and the headphones. If you need something, or you get yourself into trouble; call me. It's not so far. I can come.'

'Have a good afternoon,' he says when she gets out of the car. Have a good afternoon, why did he say that? It's not exactly warm and friendly. It's something you say to the guy at the gas station after you sign your credit-card slip. It's something you say to someone you care nothing about – have a good afternoon. He's known Cecelia for as long as he's been in L.A. – she was recommended by a business connection who could see that, as a newly single fellow and a greenie in town, he was going to need some special attention. She started off working two days a week, and within a couple of months was full-time. It wasn't that he needed so much looking after, it was that he liked having her around.

He pulls into the driveway of the Four Seasons.
  'Luggage, sir?'
  'Just what's in the car.'
  'The suitcase, sir?'
  'Yes, the suitcase, the laptop, the grocery bags, everything, everything in the car is coming up with me. There's a painting in the trunk; you'll need an extra man – someone very careful, if you don't mind.'
  Richard takes the de Kooning under his arm.
  She is in the lobby, waiting. 'You're not going to rape me, are you?'
  'I wasn't planning on it. I've got a lot of fish

147

with me and I need to make sure that it goes into a refrigerator.' He motions towards the luggage trolley that's coming through the front door with the contents of his car piled onto it. Behind the trolley, a bellhop carries the Rothko painting – holding it out in front like a shield.

'I've never met a man at a hotel,' she says.

'Do you have any luggage?' he asks.

'Just this bag,' she says, patting her purse, which is enormous. It could double as a file cabinet, a walk-in closet.

'Car, sir?'

'Yes,' he says. 'I left it with the man outside.'

'I'll just get someone to show you to the room.'

'How's your leg?' she asks in the elevator.

'Fine,' he says. 'There's a bruise, a big green bruise.'

He feels like Ben in the film *The Graduate*, checking into a hotel, riding up in an elevator with a woman he hardly knows.

'It's so strange,' he says. 'We named our son Ben after Ben in *The Graduate*. "Plastics. There's a great future in plastics. Think about it,"' Richard quotes the film. 'My ex-wife was my own personal Elaine. I was crazy about her.'

The bellman opens the door and leads them into a two-bedroom suite. Is this his wife's usual room – or have they given him/her an upgrade of sorts? Does she travel with an assistant, or is the second room in case Ben wants to come at the last minute?

'It's nicer than my house, nicer than where we went on our honeymoon.'

'Where do you live?'

'Hancock Park – it's perfectly fine, totally normal except for me.'

'Will you be needing the treadmill, sir?'

'Not this time, thanks.'

Richard sits the de Kooning on a chair and props the Rothko against the wall.

'Are you sure about the treadmill? We usually deliver it ahead, it goes in the second bedroom, but there was very little time to prepare.'

'All right, fine, put it in the bedroom. And a fridge – I'll need a fridge.'

'There's one in the kitchen. Shall I put the groceries away?'

'Shall I' – where is this guy from? Most people can't speak English at all, and not only does he speak it, but he 'shall I's.

'Yes, that would be lovely.'

'Is everything satisfactory?' the man asks while he's putting the groceries away.

'Yes.' Richard has never said yes so many times.

'How much is this room?' she asks.

'The rate card is posted in the closet, along with information about the hotel, fire and earthquake safety, and your in-room safe.'

The crying woman looks in the closet. 'Sixteen hundred ninety-four dollars a night,' she whispers.

'I'm sure I'm not really paying that,' he says.

'Is there anything else I can do?' the bellman asks.

'No, thank you, you're wonderful, we're fine,'

Richard says, validating everyone and handing the man some money.

It's late afternoon. The day is nearly over and he's spent most of it adjusting, transiting, transitioning. He feels out of order. Richard goes to the window; the view is of a particular kind of L.A. stillness, smog, haze, a timeless, frozen quality. You can't tell what time of day it is by looking out; you have to look at your watch.

He and the crying woman sit on the sofa, facing the television, which is tuned to *Headline News* – sound off. When you look at it carefully the room is ugly, faux fancy but boring. Everything is sturdy, durable, banal, bland, no personality, no character – it just is. All of the furniture has rounded edges – is that a safety issue, so sleep-walkers don't stab themselves, or would you call it a style point? He wants there to be something annoying about the room – some jarring chintz, vibrating striped wallpaper, a clash between bedspread and carpet – he wants something to be annoyed about.

The doorbell rings; a plate of fruit and some bottles of still water, 'compliments of the manager.'

'Do you stay here often?' she asks.

'No,' he says, 'never. My wife, my ex-wife, stays here; that's why they're trying so hard. She eats fruit and drinks a lot of water.'

'The first time I stayed in a hotel it was with a man I worked for – my boss. We shared a room. I couldn't decide if I could put my hair in curlers, the way I usually did, or what. So I put my hair up, covered it with a shower cap, and went to sleep with the shower cap on. In the middle of the night, I got up to pee and fell into the toilet – he'd left the seat up. He called out, 'Honey, you all right?' I said, 'I'm fine, dear, go back to sleep,' and in the morning there was no mention of it. Can you imagine me with my hair up in curlers?'

He looks at her – he can. He says nothing; it's not the kind of question you're supposed to answer. 'So what happened?'

'When?'

'Now, today.'

'Do I have to tell you?'

'No.'

'I started wishing I was dead. Yesterday I spent five hours in the car, picking them up, dropping them off, driving in circles, making sure I had their water, snacks, their sports equipment, circling home to wash their clothes, to walk the dog. I got in at six, cooked dinner, and they said, "We don't like meatloaf," and I said, "It's chicken," and they said, "We don't like chicken." It's like I'm their servant. No one says thank you or puts their dishes in the dishwasher or lifts a finger.'

'And why don't you say anything?'

'I'm afraid. If I say something, I won't just say something – I'll explode. I'll pick up my son's base-ball bat, which is under the kitchen table, where he left it, and I'll start smashing them in the head, I'll club them to death. I don't trust myself.'

He looks up at the clock on the television. 'Excuse me for one minute. I need to make a couple of calls.'

'I hope I didn't scare you,' she says.

'Scare me? No, you didn't scare me, I just have to call the insurance company and let them know where I am.'

'I was wrong,' Paul the stoner says. 'I don't know what I was thinking – a sinkhole is not covered, no coverage at all; earthquake, you're all set. Frankly, I would never have known there was a difference, but after you called I looked it up; I'm quite sure now that despite everything, you are not covered in any way, shape, or form.'

'Not covered at all?'

'That's right.'

'Absolutely no coverage for relocation expenses, engineers' reports, any work that needs to be done?'

'Correct.'

She is sitting on the sofa. 'Oh,' she says. 'Am I in your way?'

'Not in my way,' he says, being polite.

She picks up a magazine, flipping through the pages like she's at the hairdresser's, or a doctor's office.

'So,' he continues with the insurance agent, 'it's more like I'm uncovered, exposed.'

'Blowing in the wind.'

'That's interesting,' he says. That's not what he expected. After paying premiums for thirteen years, after never having had a claim, after what Paul told him this morning about how the agent got him a good deal, something that they don't even sell anymore, he expected more.

He hangs up and looks for his travel agent's number. He is going to go to Boston. He's not going to deal with this right now. Covered or uncovered, he's going to go to Boston and visit his brother. That's what he was thinking before this happened, and that's what he's going to do.

He calls his travel agent.

'He's no longer with us.'

'Do you know where he is?'

'He died. It wasn't travel-related; they tell us to tell you that. Is there something I could help you with?'

'I wanted to book a ticket to go to Boston tomorrow.'

'Roundtrip?'

'Yes.'

'Thirteen hundred dollars,' the man says without a pause.

'It doesn't need to be first class.'

'That's coach.'

'That's your best fare?'

'I can put you on a flight in the morning for three hundred seventy-five dollars.'

'That sounds better.'

'Will you be needing a hotel or rental car?'

'A car would be good.'

He calls one of the auction houses he used to

deal with and asks if they might take the paintings for a couple of weeks.

'We're not a boarding facility,' the head of the twentieth-century division says.

'I just assumed you might know what could be done,' Richard says. 'I'm sure there have been other emergency situations over the years.'

'Well, I suppose we could take them in if you're considering putting them up for sale.'

'Well, it's certainly something that I could consider for the next couple of weeks. I assume that I am permitted to change my mind.'

'Yes, people are always changing their minds. And where are the paintings now?'

'At the Four Seasons.'

'I opened the nuts,' she says when he is off the phone. 'I couldn't help myself. I needed to crunch.'

'I'm starving,' Richard says, digging in with her. 'I didn't have lunch, and I don't think I had dinner last night.'

'Do you want me to make you something, a snack?'

'I don't want you to make me anything.'

'All that food in the kitchen, you should eat it.'

'I have to call my brother. If I'm going to Boston to see him, I'd better let him know, right?'

'You're a freak.'

'Tomorrow,' he tells his sister-in-law. 'Sooner rather than later.'

'Great,' his sister-in-law says. 'Do you remember where the house is?'

'Chestnut Street – Brookline.'

'The key is under the mat.'

'Room service or restaurant?' he asks the crying woman.

'What do you want?' she asks back.

'I'm asking what you want,' he says.

'I don't know – you pick. I'm out of practice.'

There is silence. 'Let's just go downstairs,' he says.

At the hotel restaurant, the same woman who showed him a table the other day is there; does she know that he's the bread thief, that he took four rolls before walking out? He whispers to the crying woman, 'We should go out, to a real restaurant.'

'I feel almost human,' she says, an hour later, when they're at Orso.

'Sometimes people just need a break.'

'Sorry I called you a freak. I've never met anyone like you.'

'I'm trying to be something new.'

'It's good.'

'I don't really know what I'm doing, I'm making it up. You're welcome to stay at the hotel,' he says. 'You can either stay in my big room, or if you want I'll get you your own room.'

'Who wants to stay alone in a hotel room? That's very kill-yourself. I'm buzzed,' she says. 'Between the wine, the pasta, and this.' She gestures towards the tiramisù.

'I feel like the Goodyear Blimp. I don't usually eat carbohydrates,' he says.

'You're very fit for a man your age.'

The check arrives.

'Can you afford to be this nice?' she asks.

'Maybe not permanently, but for the moment. Come, let's waddle back to the car.'

'Are you trying to seduce me?'

'No,' he says.

'Should I be insulted?'

'No.'

'Am I that complicated?'

'No, but I might be. And, besides, that's not the point of this.'

'I am insulted, just a little. I mean I'm relieved, because I don't know what I would do, but also insulted. Do you have "problems"?'

'You're the second person today who's asked me that – do I seem like I have problems?'

'I wouldn't know.'

'What does that mean?'

'Not only are you the first person I've had a conversation with in years, you're the first man I've spoken to other than to say, "Fill 'er up," or "The boiler's in the basement," or "It's the toilet in the middle bathroom," in about twenty years.'

When they get back to the hotel, the beds have been turned down, the curtains pulled, the lights dimmed; there's a bottle of water on each of the nightstands, chocolates on the pillows, and a form for ordering morning papers and pancakes for breakfast. She excuses herself to take a bath.

He makes a list of what he needs for Boston: money, credit cards, socks, underwear . . .

'This is incredible,' she yells from the bathroom. 'It's a Jacuzzi. And you can aim it however you want. It's fantastic. It's heaven. Oh God,' she says, a little too expressively, and then she is quiet.

He packs his cereal, his powders, his vitamins. He probably can't take the salmon.

Forty-five minutes later, she comes out, wrapped in a thick robe, glowing.

'Do you need to call your family?' he asks.

'Am I making you nervous?' She makes a provocative turn.

He notices her feet as she pirouettes. She has nice feet, good strong, narrow ankles, pretty toes. 'They must be looking for you. Shouldn't you let them know you're safe?'

'Where would they look? Would they go to the grocery store and yell, "Mom, Mom, Mom," up and down the aisles? Every head would turn; the sound would be deafening. "What?" every woman would say. Would they call Triple A and ask how many ladies with minivans had flat tires today? Would they call hospitals and ask if any house-wives wandered in off the street? When will they catch on, when I'm not there for car-pool, when

157

they come home and there is no dinner? Let's see how long it takes before they really notice.'

'Do you feel guilty?'

She shakes her head. 'I feel high, like I'm floating, like none of this is real, like if I blink it will be over and I'll be right back where I was.'

'Are you afraid?'

'Only a little – I know I'm not supposed to leave my children. Men do it all the time, but women don't leave.'

There's a knock at the door.

'Maybe we're making too much noise,' she whispers.

Again, the knock. Richard opens the door. A bellhop enters with an enormous vase of flowers. 'For you, Mrs Novak.' He smiles.

'I'm not Mrs Novak.'

'I'm sorry.' He puts the flowers on the table.

'It's fine,' Richard says. 'It's not what you think. This is my . . .' He starts to say 'sister.'

'Terribly sorry,' the man says, backing out of the room.

'Do I even know your name?' Richard asks the crying woman.

'Cynthia,' she says.

And he remembers that she told him her name the other day in the grocery store. It seems like so long ago.

'Do you even have a sister?' she asks.

He shakes his head. 'Look,' he says, 'stay as long as you like, don't check out until you're ready to go home. And here' – he writes down his brother's phone number – 'this is where I'll be. Call me if you need to. I have to get up early, so I might not see you in the morning.'

She folds the paper with the number and puts it in the pocket of her robe. 'Thanks.' They retreat to their rooms.

His mind races. He's thinking about his ex-wife and this hotel, about the crying woman, about how strange it is to be in his ex-wife's regular hotel room in the city where he lives, with a woman who is basically a stranger.

He thinks of Ben on the road: Where is Ben right now? Driving? He didn't even know Ben had a driver's license. With Barth's aunt in Cleveland? In a motel? Sleeping in the car under the anti-crime lights in a truck stop?

He falls asleep, has a horrible dream, the kind that is so awful that while you are having it you're sure that you'll never forget it, a dream that is terrifyingly clear – except that when Richard wakes up he can't remember anything. He wakes up and has no idea where he is – his brother's house, his ex-wife's apartment? Everything looks different. He hears voices, people talking. Cold air blows through the room; the curtains are billowing. He wraps himself in a robe and goes into the living room.

She is there, in front of the television. 'I hope I didn't wake you.'

'I had a dream,' he says.

The two of them in their heavy robes look like marshmallows, like the latest arrivals in a spa called Heaven. He takes a bottle of apple juice from the minibar, opens it, sips. 'Too sweet,' he says, putting it down.

'You're not going to drink that?'

'I'm used to fresh-pressed, unsweetened.'

'Well, you can't just waste it; give it to me.'

He hands her the juice, goes back to the minibar, and gets a bottle of water for himself. 'There's microwave popcorn,' he says.

'How much?'

'Only five dollars,' he says.

She stands in the kitchen watching the popcorn turn in the microwave. 'This is so decadent,' she says. 'When we check into a hotel, we ask them to empty the minibar – we buy sodas from a gas station.'

'Exactly my point,' he says, popping the top on the Pringles. 'Let's be real Americans and do the gorge and gouge.'

They have the popcorn, the chips, the caramel-coated walnuts, the seven-dollar cookie. They drink the beer, the white wine, and the champagne.

In the middle of the night they have a party, eating and drinking themselves into a stupor. He gets up to go to the bathroom, and when he comes back, she's asleep on the sofa. He covers her with a blanket and sits in the chair, finishing the champagne.

He watches her sleeping. He thinks of his ex-wife,

of leaving his ex-wife. There was a crippling stillness, an absence of oxygen; he lived with it until
there was nothing left, not another minute. It wasn't
like he had the whole thing worked out; he just had
to go.

He stood at the door of Ben's room, waving bye-
bye, knowing he was not coming back. He stood
at Ben's door, etching the stuffed animals, cars,
small shoes, pale-blue walls, the sweaty, slightly
sour scent of an unwashed boy into his mind's
eye.

'Bye-bye,' Ben said, looking up.

'Bye-bye,' Richard said, and he didn't say
anything more.

He went to a hotel, checked in, lay down on the
bed. He didn't feel high or like he'd escaped, he
felt like he'd left his life behind, like he'd become
a ghost. In the morning he got up and went to
work. Someone asked if he was all right. 'Flu,' he
said, and no one asked more.

And his wife? His wife didn't say anything, didn't
call him at the office, didn't yell or scream, didn't
even check to make sure he was all right. After a
week, he called her.

'You forgot your pillow,' she said. 'It's hard for
me to take you seriously with your pillow still here
– do you want me to leave it with the doorman?'
She paused. 'What do you want, do you want me
to tell you to come back? You're the one who
decided to leave; no one told you to go.'

He couldn't go back – just the sound of her

voice was enough to ensure that. He hung up and didn't call again.

In the pocket of his jacket he had Ben's small stuffed lion. He didn't discover it until later. He couldn't bear how bad he felt about Ben – couldn't bear that he couldn't bear – and so he froze. He did nothing. He rubbed the lion's head and hated himself.

At first he saw Ben a couple of times a week – he'd call the nanny and ask her to bring Ben down, and the nanny would put him in the stroller and push him to the park. And they would play – swings, slide, sandbox. While they were playing, Richard would ask the nanny how Ben was doing, was he going to classes, seeing friends, eating, sleeping, and so on.

No matter what he asked, the nanny always said, 'He do good. He do good.'

And winter came, and it got colder and more difficult, and Richard saw him less often, and soon it had been six months since he'd left and he called his wife.

'I'm moving to Los Angeles and I want to see Ben before I go.'

'Whenever you want, any afternoon after school; I'm never there,' she said, as though they had just spoken the day before.

He went back. He walked into the building, past the doorman, rode up the elevator, and went into the apartment, the whole time feeling like he was the creep, he had done something wrong,

162

like no one knew the truth, and either way it didn't matter – truth was irrelevant.

And there was Ben. Bigger Ben.

'Hi.'

Ben ran towards him, and then, before he even got close – ran away. Ben ran and Richard ran after, half chasing him. It was a game and it wasn't a game. Ben stopped in front of Richard, Richard got down on his knees, and Ben hit him hard, laughed, and then ran away again.

When it was time to leave, Richard hugged the boy. 'Bye-bye,' Richard said, and Ben began to cry.

All peril. His mind leapt to insurance. He had the homeowner's policy with him somewhere; was he really not covered?

All peril, pencils, peppermints, Pepcid; it was like the game *$20,000 Dollar Pyramid* – things an insurance agent keeps in his drawer?

'What are you doing,' the crying woman says, startling him, 'watching me sleep?'

'I was thinking.'

'You were staring; I was watching you.'

'How could you have been watching me? Your eyes were closed. Did you call your family?'

She shakes her head.

'Don't just leave,' he says, out of the blue. 'They may not appreciate you, but you have to try. Make rules. Dinner is at six-thirty. You do the cooking,

163

they do the cleaning. Be tough.' By telling her what to do, he is telling himself what to do. 'Got it?'

She nods.

'Early flight; sleep well,' he says, heading towards the bedroom.

'If it's OK, I'll stay on the sofa; I haven't slept alone in almost twenty-five years.'

'Wherever you're most comfortable.'

Perspective. In the morning he drives back to the house, thinking he's going to check the progress of the hole, go inside, and take a look around. From the outside his house is a box, a box with windows and a view. He drives up, slows down as he passes, and then steps on the gas. At the top of the hill, he turns the car around and zooms down, past the house with the horse, past the movie star, past his own house, all the way down – to see Anhil.

'I will drive you to the airport.'

'Who'll watch the store?'

'I will call my brother; he will come, and I will drive you, and I will take your car while you are gone. I will give it good exercise.'

While they are waiting for the brother to arrive, Anhil serves Richard breakfast – the cereal, the Lactaid milk, and a cup of hot water with lemon – good decongestant for the plane.

'Thank you for the car,' Anhil says, leaving him at the airport.

'I'm not giving it to you, I'm loaning it.'

'I understand,' Anhil says. 'It is too much to give.'

Flying coach, he settles into his seat and puts on his headset, and he's fine, on the verge of enjoying himself, thinking he's escaped, gotten out. He drinks his complementary water and eats his complementary pretzel sticks. He's fine until the plane lands, until he gets in his rental car, until he pulls up at the brother's house, and then it's as though he's been getting smaller and smaller ever since he woke up that morning, shrinking as he brushed his teeth, as he zipped his suitcase, as he left the hotel, as he went through the X-ray machine at the airport, shriveling on the plane as he put his bag in the overhead, as he buckled the belt, even smaller still in the rental car, pulling the seat forward, amazed he could reach the pedals or see over the wheel. Smaller and smaller, so that by the time he arrives at the brother's house, he is less than four feet, a child again.

He pulls up, uses the snow scraper that's in the car to dust off pretzel crumbs, and goes in. The dog barks at him. 'Stop barking,' he says, and the dog stops. He goes into the kitchen, gets a glass of water, stands at the sink drinking it, then rinses the glass, dries it, puts it back in the cupboard, goes into the den, and sits. He sits on the edge of the sofa, like it is a waiting room, a way station, as though he has arrived here en route to someplace else. He thinks of leaving. If he gets

165

up and goes, if he doesn't touch anything, no one will know that he was there, that he came and went. If he does it right, he could leave without ever having been noticed. He could put his bag back in the car, the key back under the mat, and check into a hotel, designed for exactly this purpose – dealing with the discomfort of the un-familiar. The dog jumps onto the sofa, spins a circle, lies down with his head on Richard's thigh, and swallows. Richard sits for a few minutes and then lies down next to the dog, resting his head on the nubbly plaid sofa filled with crumbs, with dog hair, the meaty scent of life. He sleeps.

One of the children comes home. A girl who looks just like her mother, brainy, open-faced. She is a thing about to bloom, not yet self-conscious, not yet self-editing.

'What's wrong with you?' she asks.

'What do you mean?'

'They said if you were coming here something was wrong – otherwise why would you come. Are you dying? Broke? Are you going through that thing?'

'What thing?'

'Men-o-pause?'

'Men don't go through menopause.'

'Then why is it called *men*opause?'

'I don't know.'

'So why are you here?'

'I don't know, I felt like I needed to come, like I needed to see everyone. Do you ever feel like you need to see someone, just to make sure they still exist?'

'Are you having a nervous breakdown? That's what people talk about when they're having a nervous breakdown. Does having the nervous breakdown makes you wonder about that, or does wondering about it give you the nervous breakdown?'

'That's always the question. How old are you?'

'Almost twelve.'

It is Thursday night; Meredith's mother is there, the two girls, and a six-year-old boy Richard didn't know existed. Dinner is a well-orchestrated production, out of the fridge, into the oven, and onto the table; everyone helps.

After dinner they pile into the family car, a beige minivan; he's in the second row, in a thick captain's seat that reminds him of the one time he went deep-sea fishing.

'All aboard?' his brother asks.

The mother-in-law is having an opening at a local coffee shop, paintings she's done since her stroke. After a lifetime of doing everything with her right hand, she is now reliant on the left, dragging the right side of her body around like a deflated Siamese twin.

Friends of the family come to the Bean N' Brew. They take the mother-in-law's paintings seriously. They ask questions: How long have you been painting? Do you paint every day? Have you ever tried gouache? Everyone is proud. No one mentions that the paintings look like paint-by-number. They give compliments: I love your use of color, your brush strokes are so lush.

'I have always had a passion for color,' the mother-in-law says, her speech slurred. 'Anyone can paint,' she tells him, 'even you.'

Equally enthusiastically, they introduce Richard to their friends.

'My brother,' his brother says, slapping him on the back.

'I always thought you were an only child.'

'Older or younger?'

By virtue of getting a Ph.D., marrying first, and having a baby first, his brother and Richard long ago traded places: Richard went from being the older to the younger, losing whatever early advantage he might have had.

'Older,' Ted says, handing the title back.

'So – what brings you to Boston – business?' the brother asks, when they are back at the house.

Silence. He forgot to make up a story.

'Everything all right?' the brother asks.

'I think so,' Richard says. 'And you?'

'Good. Everything is good. At least I think it's good; I've had a lot on my mind.'

His brother, Ted, is a physicist, an inventor, a visionary who is not stopped by anything. When Richard was younger, people used to ask, 'What did your brother invent?' and Richard would say, 'The world.'

'Let's get you set for the night,' the brother says, leading Richard upstairs to Barth's room.

'I have no memory of being a child,' Richard says looking around the room, which is stuffed with the memorabilia of a boy's life.

'You were serious.'

'And what were you – not serious?'

'I was a builder, always making things with balsa wood.'

'That's what I remember – the smell of airplane glue. Did we have toys?'

'I think you had a cash register . . . a red Tom Thumb.'

His brother goes to the linen closet for sheets, towels, and a pillow. There's something about his brother carrying the bedding that is so sweet, domesticated, not what you'd expect the great inventor to be doing.

'That's funny. I think I remember carrying around a red metal cash box like it was my friend, but I'm never sure if what I'm remembering was real,' Richard says.

'You loved money; nothing made you feel better than to have money in your pocket.'

'I have no memory of that,' Richard says.

'You were a very good salesman. You went up and down the street, door to door, selling seeds you ordered from the back of a comic book. You even managed to sell seeds to people who didn't have gardens; that impressed everyone.'

'They must have felt sorry for me.'

'You made Dad take you to the bank to open your own account. And you used the points you got from selling seeds to get "prizes," and then you sold the prizes – don't you remember you got me my microscope?'

'Vaguely. Did the microscope work?'

'It worked great. We stabbed our fingers to get blood and we made slides . . .'

'It's all a little blurry.'

'You were man about town until someone with no teeth asked, "Do you sharpen knives?" and you got scared and quit. That, and Dad hated you going door to door.'

'He thought I was begging.'

'He called you a peddler. And then we had a news-paper route and we were jealous of the guy who had the *New York Times* route and got to go around collecting money and giving people little yellow receipts. We rolled our papers with advertisements, tied them with a rubber band, and then went building to building and left them on everyone's door.'

'Why do I not remember this?'

Ted shrugs. 'You were always forgetful; it was like you could only hold so much information and then you'd short-circuit.'

'And Dad – what was he like?'

'He wasn't like much – tried not to stand out, that was his goal, to not be noticed. He used to tell us that, whatever we did, we should be careful not to attract attention.'

'Now that you're telling me, it sounds sort of familiar. What else did we do?'

'We sat outside, watching people. I made things. You counted your money.'

'What do you mean?'

'Literally, if you had a pile of pennies, you counted them, put them in order, and wrote down how much.'

'How old was I?'

'Maybe nine? That was your idea of fun. Other kids played with marbles or soldiers, and you played with loose change, arranging your pennies, nickels, and dimes into brigades, and moving them across the Oriental rug as part of some kind of war game where quarters could take over, some sort of strategy for winning all the money. I never really understood the rules.'

'And what did you do?'

'Marbles. I liked playing on that rug also. It used to drive Mom crazy, the two of us in the living room. She used to make you wash your coins with soap and water because she didn't want you to get her carpet dirty.'

'She kept the furniture wrapped in plastic – a blue sofa wrapped in clear plastic, and when it rained, she'd unroll a long plastic pebbly runner that we had to walk on.'

'She was very proud of her living room. She was going to take it to Florida, but when someone finally sat on the sofa, the silk cracked – too many

171

years under plastic, and somehow it got brittle. Do you remember cutting off my finger?'

'I didn't cut off your finger. I had a saw from a children's toolbox, and I asked you to hold something while I cut it. I missed, and a little piece of your finger came off.'

'I had to get stitches.'

'It wasn't a real saw anyway.'

'Yeah, but it was a real finger.' The brother holds up his hand, and, sure enough, his third finger is a little shorter than it otherwise might have been.

'I said I was sorry about a thousand times. I practically had a breakdown over the guilt. I can't believe you're bringing it up again now.'

'I haven't seen you in a long time.'

'Would it be better if I went to a hotel?'

'I'm half teasing – it's good you're here. See you in the morning.'

Richard lies back on the bed. The room is spilling with stuff: books, a baseball glove with a ball packed into the center, pennants, prizes, model cars, flying birds dangling from the ceiling. A reading light shines through the Visible Man, an anatomical model that stands, arms spread, legs spread, offering up the meaty red view of the stuff of man, organs and arteries in a clear plastic shell.

He lies on his nephew's bed trying to remember his own life as a boy. What did he think about? Baseball, bomb shelters, air raids, the end of the world. He lies back feeling a peculiar hollow. If

172

he called his brother's name, Theodore, Ted, Teddy, Thermador, his brother would likely come back down the hall, sit at the edge of his bed, and talk to him. The brother would be like a father, because the brother is a father and he knows how to do that. And at some point his wife, Meredith, would tap on the door and ask if everything was all right, and it would all be deeply embarrassing.

He lies back, looking at the ceiling – the sticky remains of a galaxy of glow in the dark stars.

In the morning, the house smells of toast and coffee. He dresses as though he's got a meeting to get to. Truth is, he can't imagine spending the day sitting alone in his brother's house, a passive prisoner, waiting for everyone to come home. He catches a ride into town with his sister-in-law, a New England native with little use for the rest of the world.

'It's been a hard year,' Meredith says. 'We thought your brother was going to get a Nobel; it was close, and then it didn't happen.'

'That would be nice,' Richard says, not sure if the brother is really Nobel material; it had certainly never occurred to him. 'Maybe next year.'

She shakes her head. 'You don't come that close and then get it the next year; it's like a comet, it passes that close only once in a lifetime.'

'Well, even that must feel good: how many people actually think they have a chance of winning a Nobel Prize?'

'Your brother did. Two of his close friends already have them.'

'You'd have to go to Stockholm to collect it.'

'Oh, we've been to Sweden. That's what we do – every summer we take a house in Italy, Greece, Spain, France.'

'I didn't realize.'

'Ben has come with us a few times. Ben, and sometimes you-know-who, if she can get away for a few days.'

'Really? I never knew.'

'Where shall I drop you?'

'Anywhere is fine.'

'The Public Gardens? You can say hello to the swan boats?'

'That would be great.'

Nothing is open – it's too early. He walks around the park a couple of times, and then he takes himself out for a second breakfast. Finally the stores open, and Richard goes up and down Boylston Street shopping because he doesn't know what else to do, because he never shops, because every time he buys something he has a nice conversation with the salesperson. He buys something for everyone – for the kids, his brother, the sister-in-law, the mother-in-law, the dog, the house.

After lunch, he takes a taxi back to Brookline, puts the gifts in everyone's rooms, and falls asleep on the sofa, exhausted.

★   ★   ★

'Are you sure you're all right?' the brother asks that evening. 'I know you had a scare, but now you're scaring me; is there something you're not telling me?'

'He got us a mixer,' one of the children says.

'I noticed you didn't have one,' Richard says.

At dinner, Richard hands out even more presents. The brother and his wife look at Richard like they feel sorry for him.

'How come we're not having cake?' the little boy says.

'Because it's not really a party,' one of the adults says.

'If it's not a holiday, then why are we getting presents?'

'Because Uncle Richard came to visit.'

'Are you coming back again soon?' the little boy asks.

The phone rings – 'It's Barth and Ben!' one of the girls announces. 'They're in Ohio.' They put the phone in the middle of the kitchen and push the speaker button, and everyone stands around.

'Is the car running well? Are you getting good mileage?' the brother wants to know.

'What did you have for lunch?' one of the little girls asks.

'Are you enjoying yourselves?' the mother asks.

'I sent you some video. It should be in your e-mail.'

'Uncle Richard is here,' the little boy says.

'Really? Hold on, let me get Ben.'

'That's weird, really weird. Dad – what are you doing there?'

'Just came for a visit.'

'Does Mom know where you are?'

'No, I didn't think I had to tell her.'

'She knows,' Meredith says. 'We talk, I hope that's OK.'

'Fine,' Richard says, 'it's fine.' He had no idea that they talked, that everyone was so in touch.

He picks up the receiver, turning off the speaker, and presses the phone to his ear. 'So how are you?' he asks, trying to sound chipper and not terrified, because suddenly he is terrified. He's talking to Ben in front of an audience, they're standing there watching, and Richard is worried he's not going to do it well enough.

'Good,' Ben says. 'How long are you staying there?'

'Just the weekend. I had to get out of the house – it was going downhill. So how's it going? Any big adventures so far? Sleeping under the stars?' There is silence. 'You still there?' Richard asks.

'Yeah, uh, Dad, can we just talk when I get to L.A.? I mean, it's like I never talk to you and now you want to talk all the time.'

'I want to hear about the trip. I like knowing that you're OK.'

'I'll tell you about it when I see you. I'm OK, I'm always OK.'

'All right, then,' Richard says. 'I won't keep you.'

Richard hands the phone back to Meredith. 'All done?' she asks.

'Apparently.'

Meredith and the children each talk to Barth and then pass the phone to their father. Richard stands listening; he hears the ease with which his brother and nephew speak, the ease with which his brother addresses Ben; he feels the full weight of the years he missed, the gap between how he is and how he wishes he could be.

When they are done, the entire family stands over the father's computer. The movie begins. There's Barth standing outside the apartment building in New York, holding up a cardboard sign with Magic Marker lettering: 'My Big American Adventure.'

'I bet Ben made that; he's really good at art,' the sister-in-law says.

'Welcome to our magical mystery tour,' Barth says. 'This is our tour bus, the trusty 2002 Volvo Cross Country wagon, with all-wheel drive, rear-window defrost, a global-positioning system, and we're off to see the wizard.'

And then Ben steps into the picture; it's like seeing someone you only ever dreamed about. The images are jerky, like footage from an early moonwalk. But it's Ben, Ben all grown up. Ben as a man/boy with facial hair and muscles, Ben on the cusp of something larger – Big Ben. It hadn't occurred to Richard that Ben would look different, older. Barth and Ben are talking, but Richard isn't listening, he's just looking, studying, mesmerized. He'd never thought that Ben would look so much like him.

Ben looks like Richard, like Richard and the ex-wife. He's the kind of combination that only DNA can make – a little bit of this, a little bit of that. He can hear himself in Ben's voice, but he sees her in Ben's mouth – Ben has her mouth. Richard bites the inside of his cheek to keep from crying.

'When did you last see him?' Meredith asks.

'Not since September,' Richard says. 'Nine months.'

They are standing around the computer watching, and the phone rings. His sister-in-law answers and hands it to him.

'Me?'

She nods.

Who would be calling? Ben, to say he's sorry – that, yes, he does want to talk to Richard every day, twice a day even?

'Hello?' Richard says.

'You're going to hate me,' the crying woman says. 'I did a really bad thing.' He doesn't say anything. 'Sorry to bother you,' she says.

'It's fine,' he says. He can't imagine what she could have done.

'I don't know what I was thinking,' she says. 'I invited my family to come to the hotel. The room was so big and luxurious – it felt strange to be here by myself, and I thought it would be a way of making up. I was feeling a little bit better, more hopeful. After the kids went to sleep I tried to be romantic; my husband couldn't have been less interested. He said there was no way you were letting me stay here without wanting something, and what was it? I told him it wasn't sex and he got paranoid and said you were going to try and get money from him. I said you had enough money and he said there's no such thing and in the morning he made us check out but only after they raided the minibar, had room service, and ate like pigs. I'm so sorry.' She starts to cry. 'They were like a herd of elephants.'

'Don't cry,' he says. 'It's not worth crying about.' He walks out of the room, taking the phone with him. 'It's only money.'

'I packed your salmon, thinking it shouldn't go to waste, and I got in the car with them. And then, a few blocks down, at a red light, I opened the door and jumped out. I ran all the way to Santa Monica, walked into the emergency room at St John's, and said, I think I'm going crazy. They thought I was a homeless person. I'd tripped at one point and sort of fell off the road into some dirt, and so I looked gross. When I tried to explain that a man I'd met in the grocery store had put me up at the Four Seasons and that I'd invited my husband and kids to come for the weekend and it hadn't gone well, they asked if I had a history of psychotic episodes. Was I hearing voices or seeing anything out of the ordinary? And when

I tried to leave, they said they weren't sure it was advisable. I signed out against medical advice. As I was leaving, a nurse said I should enroll in something called day treatment – apparently it's like being in a mental hospital during the day but you're home in time for dinner. She said it helped her son. I told her that being home in time for dinner never helped any woman with children and got the hell out of there.'

'Where are you now?'

'Standing outside Ralph's, on the pay phone.'

'Do you want to go back to the hotel?'

'I don't think that would work. When are you coming home?'

'I could come tomorrow,' he says.

'That would be good.'

'Are you going to be all right? I can make you a reservation somewhere else.'

'I can take care of myself. Ralph's is open late – they know me here.'

'Talk to you tomorrow,' he says, hanging up.

'It's nice that you've got someone,' Meredith says when he hangs up.

'It's not what you think; it's a crying woman that I met in the produce section.'

'I should get the kids ready for bed,' she says.

He is still thinking about the crying woman, still holding the phone in his hand. He calls his ex-wife. 'What's the name of that place you go to in Los Angeles, the spa?'

'Which one?'

'Where you don't bring anything and they feed you based on your age and weight.'

'Golden Door? It's about a hundred and fifty miles outside of L.A.'

'It's a long story, but I have a friend who needs to get away.'

'Call and pretend you're from my office – why are you whispering?'

'They've all gone to bed. I saw pictures of Ben, he's so big.'

'He looks like you,' she says.

'He has your mouth,' he says.

'I should go,' she says.

He calls the Golden Door.

'It's serendipitous. Normally I wouldn't know if there was space – I'm not the reservationist – but we just got a cancellation, someone who's afraid to fly. Can your friend get here by Sunday? Does she fly?'

'She drives. Can you put it on my credit card?'

'What's the guest's name – last name?'

'I'm going to have to call you back with that; her first name is Cynthia.'

'Usually we send out a welcome packet a couple of weeks in advance, with health questionnaires, luggage tags, info on what to pack.'

'That's OK, she's really healthy and doesn't have a lot of luggage. Is there anything special she needs to bring?'

'Whatever she likes to sleep in, a few days' worth of underwear, and a sports bra. We provide the rest.'

'Great. Hold the spot, and I'll call you back with the rest of her information.'

He is pleased with himself for doing something, taking action. He gets the number for Ralph's and asks if they can page a shopper in the store.

'Is it an emergency?'

'I wouldn't be calling otherwise.'

'What's her name.'

'Cynthia.'

'One moment.'

'Would shopper in the store Cynthia please come to the manager's desk at the front of the store. Cynthia, please report to the front of the store.'

'That's funny,' she says. 'They must have said it three times before I realized it was me. I was just finishing a cake.'

'Eating a cake?'

'Decorating – they were letting me try the icing bag. It's fun here at night; they set up a huge buffet from the day's mistakes – deli meats sliced wrong, bags of chips "accidentally" opened. Everyone munches. Nice people, a lot of them have other day jobs. I think I could work here; I mean, I do know a lot about food.'

'I got you into a place called the Golden Door; it's a spa – hiking, healthy eating, massages. It's in Escondido. Can you get yourself there Sunday morning? Fly to San Diego, or take a bus?'

'I know what it is – that's where super-fancy people go, like Gwyneth Paltrow. Oh no, I can't go there, I don't have any clothes.'

'You don't need clothing – three pairs of under-wear and something to sleep in.' He can't bring himself to say 'sports bra.' 'They provide every-thing. Just go down the aisle at Ralph's and put together a little bag for yourself.' He gives her the address. 'It's better than being in a mental hospital.'

'And what about you?'

'I'll come home tomorrow and start again. By the way, what's your last name?'

The pain returns. He is lying in the twin bed of his brother's son, hoping it is the same pain, and *not* the IT pain. In the morning the pain is still there; he says good-bye and thank you and drives to the airport.

The house is where he left it – stabilized. His answering machine is blinking. One message – Lusardi.

'I saw something that prompted me to think of you – a workshop, "Transcending Suffering." Here's the number. Let me know if you have any questions.'

The pain is so intense that he'll try anything. 'Hi, I'm calling about "Transcending Suffering"?'

'Starts tomorrow.'

'And what exactly is it?'

'This is what it says in the catalogue.' She reads in a rapid monotone. '""Transcending Suffering' – a seven-day intensive working with the complex-ity of our relationships to pain, grief, and loss.

Conducted in silence. There will be daily teaching talks and private interviews scheduled at the discretion of the instructor. Geared towards those with previous meditative practice, but open to all. The fee is eight hundred and fifty dollars and includes dormitory-style housing and meals." All other services are extra.' She stops for breath. 'Joseph, the instructor, is very inspiring, older, very in touch. Check-in is one to three p.m., and the retreat begins at three p.m.'

'Sign me up; why not, right?'

'Have you ever been on a silent retreat?'

'No, but I live in silence. I wear these headsets . . .'

'You may want to try a weekend retreat first.'

'This sounds fine, perfect, my doctor recommended it.'

'It's nonrefundable. So, if you can't take it and have to leave, you lose; is that clear?'

'Nonrefundable,' he says, and reads her the digits of his credit card.

He leaves a message for Cynthia with the receptionist at the Golden Door. 'Tell her that Richard from the produce department called. Tell her he's going on a silent retreat starting tomorrow and wanted her to know where he was. In an emergency she can call him at . . . He'll be out by the weekend. He hopes all is going well and that she's enjoying herself.'

He calls Lusardi. 'Got your message, took your advice, I'm going.'

'Bring your own toilet paper,' Lusardi says.

'What does that mean?'

'Theirs is very Zen – one-ply. Also bring snacks – nuts, protein bars, things that you can consume inconspicuously to keep your energy up – and if you're a caffeine person, get some NoDoz; it can be very difficult going cold turkey.'

'I'm not a caffeine person.'

'One less thing to worry about.'

He phones Cecelia: 'I'm back from Boston, but am going away again until the end of the week. How're you faring?'

'I got my teeth cleaned, my mammogram, and if you take a real vacation, I could get my hip replaced.'

'I didn't know you needed a new hip.'

'Have you ever noticed how I walk?'

'I guess so.'

'Well, it's not exactly comfortable-looking, is it?'

'Go ahead and take care of it – if there ever was a good time, this would be it.'

'I'll look into it; I'm not sure they have hips just sitting around.'

'Do you need me to send you a check?'

'I'll get it next time I see you.'

'Well, if there's anything you need . . .'

'You sure you're all right? You know if anything happens you can call Cecelia. Just because I get paid to work doesn't mean I don't care.'

The movie star stops by. 'I was wondering where you were. I keep ringing your bell – nobody home.'

'Visiting my brother in Boston.'

'How come you're packing again?'

'I'm going on silent meditation starting tomorrow.'

'Really? I played the Dalai Lama once. I met him to get a feel for things – his gestures, his walk. You know how he's supposed to be kind of permeable, letting things pass through, no attachment? But, frankly, I was a little disappointed.' He pauses. 'I never would have pictured you as a cushion kisser.'

Richard shrugs.

'Are you bringing your own zafu or zabuton?'

'My what?'

'I'll lend you mine – the ones they have at those places are really beat up. I've got a nice cushion, buckwheat, that you put on top of the zabuton – helps your ass if you're going to be on it for a while. Also, bring your own pillow; the pillows in those places suck. Bring sheets, a pillow, and a blanket.'

'It's not supposed to be about comfort.'

'The goal isn't to make yourself miserable either.'

The movie star goes home to get the cushion, and Richard rolls up his bedding and ties it with a shoelace, like a hobo. He puts sweatpants, socks, T-shirts, and a cozy sweater into his bag, along with a notebook, a pen, and a little Booklight. He feels like he's getting ready for sleepaway camp.

The movie star returns. 'Maybe, when you're done, we can have dinner or something?'

'Yeah, that would be great.'

'I'm a really good cook. That's what I do – when I'm not making a movie I cook. They wanted me to do a cookbook, but my manager said it was a bad idea. It's not an up-and-coming kind of a thing, it's more like a save-a-sinking-ship. Is there anything that you especially like?'

'I'm pretty easy.'

'I do a marinated swordfish with a kind of avocado-citrus salsa and a wheatberry-nut salad; it's a nice lunch.'

'Sounds fantastic.'

'When are you back?'

'Sunday, I'm not sure what time.'

'So come for late lunch; bring a friend if you want.'

The crying woman, he'll bring the crying woman to the movie star's house; it makes no sense. 'Can I bring anything?'

'You won't have anything; you'll be empty from meditating.'

He calls the Golden Door again. 'I need to add something to my message. Tell her to come to Richard's house for lunch next Sunday.'

Hunger. He realizes he hasn't eaten anything all day. The fridge is empty: Cecelia cleaned it out before they left. The freezer. The Carvel cake from the night he met Cynthia is still in the freezer. He takes a spoon to it – the spoon bends. He takes a fork, spearing the chocolate.

His nephew's voice echoes in his head: 'How come we're not having cake?'

There is the sound of a party in the distance. The swimmer's backyard is strung with colored paper lights, filled with people milling. Would he recognize her up close?

When she's doing her laps, he imagines throwing something – a flower, a pebble, something to let her know that he's there. He imagines going to the edge of the hill, calling out, 'Good morning. Hi there.'

He imagines trying to break the ice. And now she is having a party – a good excuse. It makes sense until he gets there, until he goes in and realizes that he doesn't know a single person. 'Can I get you a drink?' someone asks. 'Wine,' he says, 'a spritzer.' He looks around; his eye catches a ham. He can't remember when he last had ham. He cuts himself a slice, puts on some mustard, and pops it in his mouth – delicious. He makes another slice and tops it with cheese.

'So,' he says to a blonde woman standing next to him, 'do you know all these people?'

'Most of them. Who do you know?'

'No one. I'm the neighbor up the hill – I'm crashing.'

He eats his way around the table – ham, cheese, carrots, zucchini, dip, chips, nuts. He eats in a circle, going around and around, realizing how hungry he is. He munches, listening to conversations, amusing himself – this is his idea of wild.

Finally he spots a familiar gesture, the turn of her head, the flicking of her hair.

He goes to her. 'I just wanted to say hello.'

The minute she turns towards him he wishes he hadn't come; she's different in person – her eyes are brown when he was expecting blue, and there's a harshness that leaves him with a sinking sensation. She's not who he thought she would be. He feels out of place, and he's got a cashew stuck in his throat. He coughs. 'I'm your neighbor, up the hill.'

'Are we being too loud?' she asks.

'No, no. I heard the party and I just wanted to say hello. I see you swimming every morning. I'm up early.'

'Which house?'

He points up the hill – from here his house looks good. 'The one with the sinkhole. Last week a horse fell in and Tad Ford came and got him with a helicopter – that was a big adventure. Maybe you saw it on TV?' She shakes her head no. 'Well, hopefully, the house won't slide down the hill; then we'd really be neighbors.' He laughs. She doesn't. 'Anyway, I just wanted to say hello, to introduce myself.' He's talking as he's backing towards the door. 'I'm Richard. I see you every morning, I stand at the glass, I watch you doing your laps.' He meant it as a compliment: she was his inspiration, his muse, his mermaid. He goes home wishing he'd left it as it was – in his mind's eye.

★   ★   ★

In the morning, he takes a taxi to Anhil's.

'Why didn't you call? I would have picked you up from the airport.'

'I came home yesterday.'

'Even better – a very slow day in donuts. Did you know that Fudgie the Whale is also Santa Claus? The famous ice-cream cake – if you turn it around, the whale becomes Santa Claus; that's genius. Right now all I can do is add green to the donuts on St Patrick's Day, pink on Valentine's; I can't make a man into a whale.' He shakes his head. 'I am not your stereotropical man who comes to America with poor ideas.'

Richard has no idea what Anhil is saying, he's trying to decipher: 'Do you mean "stereotypical"?'

'Yes, that's what I just said. How was your brother?'

'Fine. Right now, my son, Ben, is driving to Los Angeles.'

'You couldn't send him a plane ticket?'

'He wanted to drive. And this afternoon I am leaving for a silent retreat.'

Anhil shakes his head. 'Americans try on the spiritual life of others like they don't have any of their own.'

'I'm actually looking forward to it. And then, when I come back, I go to Malibu. I rented a house on the ocean – absolutely everything in it is white.'

'I know the house.'

'How could you know the house?'

'I saw it on television. White carpet, white pots

and pans. It's owned by the mayor. He's going to tear it down and build something bigger.'

'I'm not sure it's the same house,' Richard says, assuming there's more than one white house on the beach in Malibu.

'He bought it for his girlfriends; then he got elected and can't have any girlfriends. So now he's going to tear it down and build something for his wife. America has two kinds of politicians – one has sex, the other has war – which do you like?'

Richard doesn't answer.

'I can drive you to your silence.'

'That's OK, I'll take a taxi.'

'Take my Toyota; no one will think anything of you. And I will take care of your car, I will use it like my own.'

'OK, great. I will.'

Anhil laughs. 'You're a funny man – going to meditation, moving to Malibu.'

'What are you getting at?'

'You're stuck.'

Checking in. He cannot wait to not talk. He imagines that the silence will be easy, that it is a fantastic way to be with people, low-pressure, no need to make conversation.

The lobby smells of incense and steamed broccoli. There are signs everywhere: 'Be mindful of the quiet.' 'Pay phone accepts quarters only.' 'Receptionist has limited ability to make change.'

The people are speaking too calmly. They are speaking in hushed, practiced voices. He looks around; it is like a communal mental hospital, a low-rent cooperative insane asylum. It is as though he is going under, submitting himself for some sort of procedure, a small surgery that requires general anesthesia – that's how he thinks of the silence, anesthetic. He is simultaneously holding on, trying to prepare himself for something terrifying, and wanting to let go of everything.

They are asking him questions, handing him various-colored forms to read and sign: 'Name. Address. Emergency contact. Any medications? Under a physician's treatment? Underlying medical conditions? Blood sugar or blood pressure issues? Anything we should know about you? Religious or spiritual background? Meditation history? Are you interested in bodywork while you're here?

'Please read and initial the following: We are a sex, drug, and alcohol free institution – any violation of that and you will be asked to leave. We ask that you wear no perfumes, or scents of any kind, and that while here you use an unscented soap. No shoes in the meditation hall. We ask that you not bring reading or writing materials, part of respecting the silent retreat is a commitment to not practicing those things during the period of the retreat.'

The woman checking him in hands him a map and takes out a yellow highlighter. 'We are here.' She makes an 'X.' 'The meditation hall is here.' Another 'X.'

He overhears another retreatant checking in; it's a little like seeing who's going to be on the trip with you, like boarding the *Titanic*. 'A single room,' she says. 'I asked for a single room. I have a history of abuse; there should be a letter from my doctor on file. I can't sleep in a room with a stranger.'

'The dining room is there,' his person says, speaking a little louder, 'and bathrooms are here and here. Your room is called Citrus and is down this hall. Your roommate is Wayne, and he has not yet arrived.'

She hands him information sheets filled with mealtimes, lists of ingredients, for those with food allergies, wake-up times, a list of the talks and various activities. 'If you have any questions please leave us a written note on the bulletin board and we will respond in kind. Welcome,' she says. 'Have a good retreat.'

Map in one hand, suitcase in the other, he takes himself on a tour. The meditation building looks like a cross between the all-purpose room he remembers from elementary school and a lodge made out of Lincoln Logs. He finds the men's dormitory, the room marked 'Citrus,' and opens the door. It is a small, narrow room with two twin mattresses on plain wood frames, two nightstands, two straight-back chairs, and two metal lockers for closets. Utilitarian, not entirely clean, it is like a minimum-security prison, a detox facility. He makes his bed, puts away his clothing, and sits down with his welcome packet.

Does he still have Valium in his toilet kit? He's not going to be able to do this, not going to be able to get suddenly quiet. Already he's amazed at how loud the quiet is.

During dinner they make announcements: 'Welcome. We're glad to have you with us, and while this meal is not held in strict silence, we ask that you limit your conversation, you begin to prepare yourself for the days ahead, to acclimate to the quiet. Feel free to introduce yourselves to each other – first names only. After dinner, we'll gather in the meditation hall for our first talk – if you have a cushion, bring it with you.'

He is looking at everyone and trying not to look. He watches, scouting out the people who have clearly been here before, mesmerized by the woman who drizzles honey over everything on her plate. 'I eat no sugar after today,' she says, swirling the golden syrup in thick, ropy lines over her brown rice, her steamed broccoli, her tempeh. There is a man with a shaved head who seems to know everyone. He is either a leader or a super-smug advanced pupil who thinks everything is below him. He seems peaceful to the point of arrogance. His attitude is both alluring and annoying. The people around Richard eat in silence, so Richard eats in silence. He watches others talking, wishes he'd sat somewhere else, but focuses on what's before him, dry rice.

After dinner, he goes back to the room and gets the cushion Tad Ford gave him – if only they knew,

194

he thinks, and then corrects himself. It doesn't matter if they know or not, it doesn't matter where the cushion came from, it is just a cushion, and the movie star is just a man, and Richard is just about to start five days in the deep-freeze.

'Find a spot, everyone find a spot. There are dots on the floor, just pick a dot, any dot will do.
  'Let us begin.'
They bang the gong, light the incense, and sit quietly. The gong rings again, and they sit – waiting.

Joseph speaks.
  'Suffering is normal. Pain is normal, it is part of life. So why are we here? Why are we afraid of suffering? Why do we try and avoid suffering? Why do we think it is wrong to suffer? We medicate, we meditate, we are desperate not to suffer. What is suffering? What does suffering express – the depth of our feeling, our attachment, or desire for things we cannot possess, our ego, all that can drag us down? This week, at the beginning of our journey, we ask ourselves to be willing, able, to feel what it is we feel, not to push the feeling away, not to be overwhelmed by it, but to take note of it, to turn it over, to know it. What is its texture, the weight of our suffering? What is its meaning? Begin by touching it, by coming close to it, accepting it: Hello, suffering, I am here with you. I am beside you, one with you. I am you. I am suffering. Acknowledge what is – right now.'

Joseph talks with an evangelical lilt to his voice. He talks, and they sit in silence, finding their pain, soaking it up. They sit until they are actually in pain from the sitting, and then there are more gongs, and slowly they bow, rise, and go off to bed.

The roommate is puffy, pale, pasty – Wayne. He does not talk, does nothing except unzip his duffel bag and take off his clothes, flashing his hairy bright-white ass in Richard's face. Richard turns out the light and sleeps face-to-the-wall. He's too old for this.

In the middle of the night, he wakes, not knowing if he is in Los Angeles in a hotel, in Brookline at his brother's house, or in a hospital somewhere. The sound of Wayne snoring is deep, sonorous, and Richard cannot get back to sleep. At 4:30 a.m., someone is up and down the hall, jingling bells. They rise, descend upon the bathroom – cold water, cold showers, rough towels – and then head into the meditation hall.

Someone has moved his cushion. This morning it is on the other side of the room; the shaved-head man, Mr Happy Arrogance, is on his dot. Was it his dot? Is anything any of ours? If it was not his dot, then why did the man take it? Why did he covet the dot? Is Richard being punished, picked on? He takes it personally and vows revenge: he spends half the morning meditation mulling it over, trying to transform the movement of the cushion into something smaller, trying to make it not matter. Maybe whoever moved it thought it was someone else's? Maybe they thought they were doing him a favor, maybe they had no idea that it would matter to him? Maybe he should just go over there and shove the guy off his dot? The guy would have to know why, would have to feel bad about it. Maybe the guy is just so evolved that he doesn't care about anything, maybe all of this was a setup to prove to Richard how badly he needs to be doing this? Maybe it's just something to prove that anything can drive you crazy if you let it? He will not let it, he will not let it, and in not letting it he cannot let it go. Go, go go, he tells the thoughts, this is not helping me; like a hot potato, it goes back and forth.

If you sit with discomfort it will change.

Halfway into the session, he craves a donut. Not Anhil's donut, but an earlier donut, a donut from his youth. He remembers it perfectly, an orange cruller. A glazed frosting with flecks of orange rind in it – crisp, curled, but softly sweet. He is tasting the donut. Is it a coincidence that he remembers a donut, one of the few perfect moments from his childhood, and that he met Anhil – the old donut and the new donut?

He is starving. They break for breakfast. He eats a huge bowl of yogurt with a lot of honey on it, and raisins. It's delicious. So good, as though he hadn't eaten in a very long time.

Back in the meditation hall. He fixates on the other people; some of them are beautiful. He watches one woman's arms for a very long time, another man's back. He is watching how they hold themselves, graceful, elegant. And then something changes, he has no idea what, and he's looking around and everyone appears needy, pathetic, deformed. He suddenly hates Lusardi, thinking there's something malicious in his recommending this retreat. He closes his eyes.

If you sit with the discomfort it will change.

Into what?

There is a person somewhere in the room with a tickle in his throat, a person who half coughs, trying to clear his throat quietly, but it never works, and he half coughs again, and then, a few minutes later, again, and at a certain point Richard wants to scream, Fucking really cough, will you?

His legs are hurting, his ass from sitting, from being in one position. Last night Joseph said that, before giving in and changing your position, you should go inside the discomfort and ask yourself, Can you let go of it, can you get past it and stay where you are?

What will he do when he gets out of here? Will he be a better person? He didn't tell his family that he was going away, he didn't change his outgoing message. Should he call? Should he leave word?

All this is before lunch.

In the afternoon, there is a walking meditation. They walk in a circle, round and round, very slowly. He is glad to be outside, to be in the air. The sunlight is very bright, glary. He squints;

sometimes he closes his eyes for a few steps. It's like a bad prison movie where all the inmates are walking, shuffling chained together; if one falls, they all fall; if one falls, he is shot by the guards. He looks around; some of the people are in really bad shape, muttering, chanting to themselves.

Transforming suffering – maybe this makes it worse, wallowing in it, how do you transform anything, you tolerate it, you accept it, but what if it is intolerable?

He walks a little faster and then, knocking into someone, catches himself and slows down.

The third evening talk is 'The Talk About the Dog.' It has to be to some degree a play on words, 'dog'/'God.' It is a talk about joy, about pleasure, about the irritation of the flea, the pleasure of scratching, the lure of the bone, the compulsion to bury it, the tug of the collar, the master's pull, the freedom to run, to fetch the ball and bring it back to the master. Joseph speaks of the relationship between master and disciple, between student and teacher, which culminates with the teacher's withdrawing his attention, causing the student – the dog – to suffer from separation/abandonment, a kind of crisis of parenthood, that wears him down so that he is able to experience what is the aloneness that is reality and then transcend the limits of his ego, his need/desire to become one with the master.

The story of the dog is hopeful, but the story

of the master and disciple feels like a manipulation, a head game, something Richard wants none of. He feels himself bracing, tightening, holding himself against it.

'What can you give someone without their seeing?' Joseph asks. 'How do you give to someone next to you – without their knowing? Do you make yourself smaller on your cushion so that they have more room? Do you try and breathe happily, gently, so that they are not offended? Do you try to smell pleasant? Do you give off the feeling that you are glad to have been seated next to them?'

Richard farts. At every meal, he's been eating brown rice and lentils; he's convinced himself that it tastes meaty, like beef. He eats the brown rice and the raw vegetables, and yogurt for dessert, and he is farting all the time, uncontrollably. Because it's otherwise silent, everyone can hear; because they're meditating, they can't move away; and because of the silence, he can't apologize. It happens again while Joseph is speaking.

'When you feel yourself frustrated or angry, ask what the other person wants or needs, direct positive thought outward,' Joseph says.

After the evening talk, Richard passes a man mopping the halls. Is he a person on retreat, working for room and board – on scholarship, they call it – or is he just a regular worker, a janitor? He nods at the man, the man nods back. 'Joints for sale,' the man says softly. 'I've got joints.'

He lies in bed thinking of Ben – Ben on his journey, his adventure. What would Ben think of him here? What would Ben think of joints for sale?

The fourth day, he is exhausted from sitting, from getting up early, from the bad food. He feels the weight of his chest with every breath, he feels his lungs, his ribs, his skin lifting up and sinking down. He thinks of his brother: how nice it was to see him, but why would the brother and his wife invite the ex-wife on a vacation? Maybe it was the brother who turned Ben against him. Maybe not, maybe they were just trying to be nice, to be there when Richard wasn't? He thinks of his parents. He thinks of the night he was in the hospital, wondering if he would die. He tells himself that if he lives through the retreat he will make better plans. He will make funeral arrangements for himself, so that no one ever has to do it. If he died right now what would they do? Someone would call someone, and arrangements would be made. His parents would bring him home to Brooklyn, to the cemetery in Queens where his grandparents are buried, or maybe they would bring him to Florida and have him interred in a Boca mausoleum. His father's family used to talk about their plots – how many plots they had. Whatever it was, it was never enough. Richard will buy a place out here, a plot for himself. He will buy a plot for himself, and a couple of extras as well, in case anyone wants to join him.

Why is his mind doing this? His mind is a bottomless pit, a deep dark cavern, an open throat with fibers like cilia, like tentacles, like an octopus's arms, strong, dangerous, voiceless.

'I don't want to die,' he screams.

Did he really scream, or just imagine the scream?

In the afternoon it rains, it pours out of season. The sky is black, there is no light, they light candles in the meditation hall, they do a walking meditation inside. And they sit – for hours. Richard falls asleep while he is sitting; the sound of his snoring wakes him up.

The rain continues into the night. Richard is awake – his schedule is upside down. He wanders the halls; the scent of French fries pulls him to the reception area. The security guard, a young girl, is there with a cheeseburger and fries.

'I'm not one of them,' she says when he walks up. 'You can talk to me.'

'Those smell good,' he says.

'Have some.'

He sits in the office with her, watching a small black-and-white television with the sound turned off. 'I'm not perfect,' she says. 'I don't even try. What do they expect me to do at three in the morning, read a book?'

He nods.

'Are you doing all right?' she asks.

'My first retreat,' he says.

'You seem like you're doing fine. Sometimes people come apart – they don't know who they are, why they're here. We have a special blanket we use, like a straitjacket, but more comforting. It's called a binding blanket. We put them in that and try and talk them down. There's a special number for me to call and a team of people come and help. I've only had it happen once. Kind of dramatic – a woman thought a spaceship was coming to pick her up. Do you want a cup of tea?'

'No thanks. I think I'll try and go back to bed. Nice meeting you.'

'Sleep well,' she says.

And he does.

There is a man who cries every day, who begins to weep during the morning meditation and doesn't quit. His weep turns to a wail, and escalates. Richard knows he's supposed to be compassionate, to care about the crying man, but the man is ruining it for all of them. Why doesn't he stop, why doesn't someone stop him, why doesn't he get up and leave the room, why is it so upsetting, why does it make him hate the man?

And why does no one get up and attempt to comfort the man? Is it against the rules? Why don't they all stop what they're doing and go to the man? Would they hate him less if they could comfort him, if they knew what was wrong with him? Does his crying embarrass them because they know it could happen to them, because they know how deep the pain is, because they are all afraid that they could start crying and never stop too?

And finally the man, gasping, practically retching, chokes back the crying.

At lunch there's a sign up on the dining-room door – 'If you're having stomach trouble, look here for help.' Below it a basket of remedies – Pepto-Bismol, Kaopectate, Imodium, various herbal remedies, teas . . .

A virulent virus has let loose in the community – there are signs everywhere: 'Practice good hygiene.' 'Be mindful and wash your hands frequently.' 'We have ordered softer toilet paper.'

By midafternoon there are lots of comments scribbled on the sign – 'Free colonic.' 'Do you meditate while you go?' 'Meditation causes disease.' 'Joseph goes poop too.' 'Are the squirts part of the practice?' Who writes this stuff and when do they do it? Does anyone see them? And where are they getting their pencils and pens?

His roommate, Wayne, has left early without a word. When Richard goes back to the room to change his shirt, Wayne is gone, the bed stripped. Richard checks to be sure his wallet and personal goods are still there.

Bodywork.

When he checked in, Richard signed up for a massage on the fifth afternoon.

The masseuse shakes his hand, holding it for a minute too long. 'Make yourself comfortable,' she says, welcoming him into her den. 'Anything special I should know?'

'I'm fine,' he says. 'I mean, I have a back ache, a leg ache, a shoulder-and-neck ache.'

'That's why I'm here,' she says. 'Go ahead and get ready, faceup under the sheet, and we'll begin.' She steps outside to let him undress.

'Come in,' he says, adjusting the sheet over himself.

'You can talk if you need to – it's soundproofed,' she says. 'Some people talk the whole time, they're so glad to be able to . . .'

'I'm fine,' he says.

It is such a relief to be touched, he didn't know how much he missed it; the warm oil, her touch, it feels fantastic. He closes his eyes and takes a deep breath.

'Is the pressure OK?'

The pressure is firm but female. 'Perfect.'

She slides her fingers up into the base of his skull; it's like she's kneading his brain, draining the complicated parts.

'I can keep going if you want,' she says at a certain point, when he is facedown, his sinuses pressed into the donut-hole headrest.

'What do you mean?'

'Someone canceled for the hour after you, so I have more time, if you want it.'

'Sure, that would be great.'

'It's another ninety dollars.'

'Fine,' he says, speaking into the face holder.

'You've got a lot of tension on your gluteus; do you want me to try and release that, maybe do some internal massage?'

'Yeah, sure,' he says.

And then her finger is sliding up his ass, and he's shocked and kind of clamps down on it.

'I'm sorry, I should have warned you . . . What I'm doing now is internal massage; is that all right?'

'I guess,' he says, embarrassed at how tightly his ass is clutching her finger.

'Try and relax and don't judge,' she says, gliding her finger back and forth, rubbing him where he's never been touched before. He feels himself getting hard.

'Not to worry, that's all part of it.' There is a seriousness with which this woman is rubbing the inside of his ass. She's really working on something.

'Not everyone will allow themselves to go here,' she says. 'It's very deep.'

'It's fantastic,' he says.

'Thank you,' she says. He can hear her blushing.

The massage makes him think of the crying woman. He imagines what she is doing right now – yoga. She is standing like a tree while he is lying like a corpse – savasana.

After the talk on the fifth night, he has his interview with Joseph. Each retreatant is granted a brief interview, a chance to ask questions, to talk privately for a few minutes. He is sitting on a chair in the hallway outside Joseph's office. Even spiritual guides have offices.

There is a couple before him; they sit in the hallway, whispering, hissing – fighting. The door abruptly pops open, they are ushered in, and the door closes. He feels like he's in fourth grade and waiting to be called into the principal's office. What will the interview consist of? Will Joseph ask him questions? Will it be like a test? Whatever it is, he wants to pass, to seem smart, he wants to win.

When it is his turn, he goes in, sits in a chair opposite Joseph, and waits.

Joseph looks at him.

Everything seems trivial. He thinks of mentioning the man who moved his cushion, Mr Happy Arrogant, but decides to keep it to himself. 'I guess what I'm most amazed by is how my mind moves, how something can seem so important in one moment and then, a moment later, I don't remember what that was that I was so sure I would never forget.'

Joseph nods. 'And your practice?'

'I'm practicing,' Richard says. 'I left myself a long time ago. I hope this will remind me of who I am. Free me, open me, change me.'

'It is just a practice, it doesn't do anything,' Joseph says.

'Yes, I know.' Richard says, looking down, knowing that the moment he looks down the interview is over. He has ended it before it began.

Joseph sits. He waits. How is he able to just sit, to just wait?

Richard stands to leave.

'Take care,' Joseph says.

The sixth day of silence. Today is all about violence. Incredible violence welling up, the urge to smash, to hit, to lash out. He can feel how it happens, how rage erupts. He thinks about children who bring guns to school thinking of getting even, expressing themselves, not being ignored. He thinks of men who wander into convenience stores and point guns at the clerks' heads. What would he do if he was in a store and someone came in with a gun? Would he attempt to strike up a conversation? What brought you here? Did you feel it building? How do you feel now? Have you ever killed someone? Did it feel good? Was there a rush of power, a release a thousand times better than sex? Is it ecstasy, making someone suffer as you have suffered? He spends the day soaking in rage, worrying that when he leaves here he will go and do something – what?

Instead of killing someone, he writes on the bathroom stall with a pen he finds on the floor. 'Meditating is for people who just want to sit around. Navel contemplation is not novel. Stop the Silence!'

During the afternoon session, he realizes that he's angry because he's going to have to leave here; he's found comfort in the structure, the constant presence of other warm bodies, the wake-up bells at 4:30 a.m., the same lousy food every day, the opportunities for expressing hostility – stealing someone's spot, failing to replace the empty roll of toilet paper, eating the last of the rice.

The next morning, he's up and packed before the bells even ring. At the morning meeting, Joseph speaks briefly: 'Let's take some time to prepare to re-enter, to talk about what we take with us from this experience. Life isn't ruminating, replaying your past; stay in the moment, notice your feelings, the passing states of feeling, and let them go. Embrace the fluctuation, all that happens.' As he's sitting, he's very aware of his ass; it's almost painful, but also feels kind of fantastic, alive in a way it was never alive before. He sits, smiling, sometimes rocking from side to side. Maybe the shaved-headed guy, Mr Happy Arrogant, gets his ass rubbed every day.

'Let's warm up our vocal cords with some chanting.' Joseph begins, and they all follow, a kind of call and response that makes the hair on the back of Richard's neck stand up.

After breakfast, Richard is hugging people he has never spoken to. 'You have a beautiful back,' he says to one of the women.

'I stole your spot,' Mr Happy Arrogant says. 'You thought it was yours but it was mine, I always take that spot. I'm sorry. I shouldn't need that spot, but I did, I do, I guess I have a long way to go.'

'We all do,' Richard says.

He walks out the front door and spends twenty minutes wandering around the parking lot, looking for his car. He becomes anxious, losing the calm, feeling the difference between the silence and the rest of his life. He begins thinking that the car has been stolen, and then he looks down at the key, sees the Toyota insignia, and remembers that he didn't bring his car. It's like some weird joke.

He drives to the donut shop. When Anhil sees him, Anhil's upper lip quivers, his eyes fill with tears. Richard is surprised by the emotion, that this man cares so much for him, has missed him. Richard hugs Anhil.

'I took your car to the annual Blessing of the Cars to pray for a maintenance-free ride, holy assistance in road service, and ease of locating replacement parts, and something went wrong,' Anhil confesses. 'It is so horrible, so against the spirit of the event. Someone scraped the car with a key, they cut into the paint. Your car is wounded. I do not know how to apologize. I didn't know what to do. I couldn't call you in your silence. I took her to the shop, and it can be fixed, but it is very expensive. Does assurance cover that?'

'The good thing is, it's only a car.'

'A beautiful car, and now she has a mistake.'

'It will be fine.'

'It's nice you are not angry or thinking that I mistreated the car.'

'I am not angry.' Richard smiles, a little disappointed that the show of affection wasn't for him, but happy to see Anhil regardless.

'Can I give you a donut?'

'Just some hot water and a piece of lemon, if you have it.'

'The ceremony was so beautiful, so respectful of the automobiles, people blew their horns.' Anhil pours him the hot water. 'I have your cereal.'

Richard shakes his head. 'I had a very early breakfast.'

'How was your silence, was it clarifying? Did you hear voices? That's what happens sometimes: all the great religious figures – the visionaries and prophets – heard voices. I didn't want to say anything before you left; I could have made you worry.'

Richard checks his watch. 'I should go.'

Anhil walks out with him and shows him the car. All along the passenger side is a thick scratch.

'Only a very unhappy person would do something like that.'

'It's fine,' Richard says, getting in. 'I'll see you soon.'

She is there: sitting on the doorstep looking well rested, rejuvenated, hair done, in a Golden Door sweatsuit – Our Lady of L.A.

He doesn't even open the front door. He just notes that the house is where he left it, the hole is still there too. Everything is as it was, with the exception of two orange cones by the curb and a series of marks spray-painted from the middle of the street up onto the grass.

'How was it?' he asks.

'Amazing,' she says. 'Really great. You look thin.'

'Everyone got diarrhea. It was either food poisoning, a stomach bug, or too much fiber.'

'Every morning we went for a five-mile hike,' she says, following as he walks up the hill. She is pumping her arms, making circles around him.

'Go slow,' he says. 'I spent the last five days sitting. Every day there was an hour of walking meditation, but that was it.' Richard does an imitation of a walking meditation. He looks like Marcel Marceau on a space walk.

'So where are we going?' she asks.

'Tad Ford's house.'

'No, we're not.'

'Yes, we are.'

'Why didn't you say something? I'm not dressed, I'm in a sweatsuit.'

'It's perfect.'

'I won it playing bingo. How do you know him?'

'I met him when the horse fell into the hole.'

'That's weird.'

Richard nods.

'I just came from a seven-thousand-dollar spa week, and now I'm going to a movie star's house for lunch with a man I met in the produce section. It's like one of those *Touched by an Angel* TV shows. By the way, how is your leg?'

'Better.'

'I told Andy to pick me up at four; is that workable?'

'When did you finally call him?'

'One of the women sneaked her cell phone in and let me make a call in exchange for not turning her in. When I called he said, "I've got your number on Caller ID." "It's not my number," I told him, and he said, "You have to tell us when you're coming back; the laundry is piling up, the dishes are everywhere, we're running out of food." I told him, "There's detergent in the laundry room, a scrub brush under the sink, and a grocery store just down the road." And then I said, "I have to go now."'

Richard has the sensation of being without skin. Everything he sees, smells, touches has a profound impact. He is entirely permeable, and it's not exactly a good feeling.

Tad's little sister lets them in. 'I'm Savannah.'

'Her name's Julie, but she changed it,' Tad calls from the kitchen.

'It's a free world,' Savannah says.

They walk through the movie star's living room and onto a patio that hangs cantilevered out over Los Angeles. Savannah hands each of them an icy-cold red drink.

'Pressed-pomegranate lemonade,' Tad says, coming out with an apron tied around his waist.

'It's incredible,' Cynthia says. 'Where do you get it?'

'I make it, starting with a lime-sugar base that

I cook down, and then adding fresh pressed lemon and pomegranate. I filter it, chill it, and just before serving rub in some mint from the garden.'

'Perfect combination,' Cynthia says.

'You two look alike,' Richard says, as though it might come as a surprise.

'Irish twins,' the sister says. 'He's eleven months older.'

They sit at a beautiful table set with dishes that look like they came from somewhere very far away, a very long time ago.

'Tuscany?'

'Neiman Marcus,' the sister says.

'I want to hear everything,' Tad says to Richard. 'Does your ass hurt? Do you feel different? Are you exhausted?'

'I feel good,' he says. 'I'm glad I did it. It was interesting to notice how much my moods shifted even when nothing was happening. As quiet as it was on the outside, it was very loud on the inside.'

'I knew it, man, you're on a path.'

'Either that or you should be on medication,' the sister says.

'You're going to change the world,' Tad says.

'Hey, thanks for the cushion, it made a big difference.'

A timer rings inside the house. 'That's lunch,' the movie star says, and he and the sister go inside.

'He's so cute,' Cynthia whispers.

'They have the same expression,' Richard says. 'It's disconcerting.'

'Twice-baked Chilean sea bass,' the movie star announces, carrying out the fish.

'Avocado, tomato-onion salad, salad with arugula and fennel,' Savannah says.

'You should do a cookbook,' Richard says.

'Are you also an actor?' Cynthia asks the sister.

She takes a deep breath and belts out the beginning of an aria. The sound that comes out of her mouth is otherworldly; it freezes the canyon, hangs out over the hills, fills the crevasses, holds the air for a moment, and echoes back.

Her audience applauds. 'Wow,' Cynthia says.

'She's the real star,' Tad says.

'I'm just here for a couple of weeks, and then I go back.'

'Back to?' Cynthia asks.

'The Paris Opera.'

'This is the best meal I've ever had,' Richard says. 'Talk about transformative.'

'I'm going to take that as a compliment with a grain of salt,' the movie star says. 'After all, you haven't really eaten in seven days.'

'And what about you?' they ask Cynthia.

'I've been at the Golden Door all week – just got out this morning.'

'Isn't it the best?' the movie star and his sister say simultaneously. 'We took our whole family.'

Richard sits quietly, listening as Tad and Cynthia talk. The terrace, the landscaping, the colors, the textures of everything are all amazing to him. He could almost swear that he's on drugs, that the morning good-bye tea was some sort of monkey juice. Everything on the movie star's patio is perfect, everything is the way you would want it to be.

'Are you all right?' they ask.

'Fine, I'm fine,' he says.

Cynthia is telling Tad and Savannah about her childhood adventures, crabbing with her father on the Eastern Shore, dangling raw chicken into the water from a piece of kite, watching the crabs' pincers grab the meat.

'I didn't know you were from the East Coast,' Richard says.

'Of course I am, hardly anyone is really from here – we're all imports.'

Cynthia and Tad really seem to be hitting it off. Why wouldn't a movie star have a lot in common with a depressed housewife?

'So what do you do when you're not making a movie, or pulling horses out of holes?' Cynthia asks.

'I cook,' he says, 'and I read – a book a day. Right now I'm reading a history of the West.'

'I'm reading the new Regina Ditmont in my book club.'

'I didn't know you were in a book club,' Richard says.

'Well, it's not like you have to apply to be in a book club. Anyone can be in a book club – all you have to do is read the book.'

'It's good,' Richard says. 'It gets you out and talking to people.'

'Don't overestimate this group – they picked this

book because they thought it was about two girl-friends, they didn't realize it was the Queen of England and her sister.'

'How did you two meet?' the movie star asks.

'We're just friends,' Richard says.

'In the produce section at Ralph's,' Cynthia says. 'I was crying because my life sucks, and he'd just been hit by a car and had a big bag of ice on his leg. I made him buy a Carvel cake.'

'I love Carvel cake,' Tad says.

'It's not exactly gourmet,' Richard says.

'We always had it for our birthdays,' Savannah adds.

The movie star goes into the house and comes back with a plate of cookies and big pot of tea. 'I made these for you – lime cookies and chocolate-meringue drops.'

'Sublime,' Richard says as the cookie dissolves on his tongue.

There is a warmth, a notable lack of pretense to the afternoon. Richard is not sure how it's possible – he's never met a movie star who didn't need constant attention.

They sit on the patio for a very long time, and finally Cynthia checks her watch and says, 'I really should be going.'

The movie star hugs and kisses them good-bye, and they walk back down the hill, towards Richard's house.

'I can't believe that Tad Ford cooked lunch for me. Did that really happen? Did I win the lottery?'

He nods.

'Did you have a good time?' she asks.

'As good a time as I could – everything feels a little strange, I don't know if I'm coming or going, my gyroscope is off.'

Back at the house, he sits down on the front steps again. 'I'm still not ready to go in.'

'Can I borrow your bathroom?'

'Yeah, but bring it back,' he jokes, letting her into the house.

A large minivan pulls up. 'She'll be right out,' Richard calls from the front step.

'Is this where the spaceship left you?' the husband says when Cynthia comes out.

'You don't have to go back,' Richard says softly. He's standing next to her on the step, and they're both looking at the minivan.

'Is that really an option?'

'Why not?'

'I have nowhere to live, no job, no ability to take care of myself.'

'That should be the least of it.'

The husband beeps. 'Come on already.'

'I'm not sure I can,' she shouts, keeping her distance.

'Get in the car,' the husband snaps.

She shakes her head. 'I thought I was going back, but I'm not. Thanks for coming.'

'Come on, Cyn, just get in the car and we'll talk. The kids want to say hi.'

The children sit seat-belted into the backseat,

looking perplexed. They are at a peculiar age – too big to be little children, and too little to be teenagers.

She moves close to the car.

'Why did you bring the kids?'

'I can't leave them home with no sitter.'

'They don't have a sitter anymore; they look after each other.'

'Get in the car, Cyn,' he says. 'If I have to get out it's not going to be pretty.'

'Be nice,' Richard says.

'What does that mean, be nice? Like I'm mean, like I hit her or something? Who the fuck are you anyway?' he says, getting out of the car, grabbing his wife's wrist.

Cynthia screams.

'Let go,' Richard says, coming closer.

'Don't tell me what to do,' he says, twisting his wife's arm.

'Let go,' she says.

'Get in the car,' the husband says.

'I'm not getting in the car. I'm never getting in the car, so you can either let go and drive away peacefully, or cause a scene in front of your children.'

He drops her wrist and steps back. 'What are you doing? We came to pick you up. We thought we were being nice. I was going to take everyone out for dinner. Why don't we all go out for dinner and we can talk? Then, if you don't want to come back, I won't make you.'

'You can't make me.'

'Fine.'

'He comes too,' she says, grabbing Richard's sleeve.

It is the last thing Richard wants; what he wants is to be alone, to think about everything, to make note and order of it all.

They drive in squished silence to a famous steak joint downtown and cram into a booth.

It is a whole other world; he is abruptly and intimately inserted into Cynthia's life.

'Drinks?' the waiter asks.

'Cokes all around,' the husband says.

'Just water,' Cynthia says.

'Do you have any juices?' Richard asks.

'We have cranberry, orange, and grapefruit. None are fresh-squeezed, so you don't have to bother to ask.'

'I think I'd like the chopped salad,' Cynthia says.

'Get the steak,' the husband says.

'I'm not that hungry.'

'For God's sake, we're at a steak place. She'll have steak, medium, with baked potato and broccoli.'

'Can I have French fries and a baked potato?' the boy asks.

'No,' the husband says.

'I want a hamburger but no bun,' the girl says.

'Change your order,' Richard whispers in her ear.

'I can't.'

'Yes, you can.'

'And you, sir?'

'Nothing for me; still full from lunch.'

'For Christsakes, eat something.'

'Vegetables,' Richard says. 'Any steamed vegetables?'

'It's a steak house, not a Chinese restaurant. I'll see what they can do.' The waiter walks away.

They sit playing with the rolls and butter.

'Clifford's dad had an affair with Clifford's mom's best friend, then Clifford's mom got a boob job . . . ,' Cynthia's son says.

'We're just friends,' Cynthia says, interrupting him.

Richard elbows her. 'Change your order.'

'Be right back,' she says, getting up from the table.

Richard smiles at the boy. There is something about him that Richard doesn't like – he's fluffy, like a marshmallow, and talks in a constant whine.

'Where did you meet my mom?' the little girl asks.

'In the produce section,' Richard says. 'She was crying because you don't like her cooking.'

They are silent.

Later, when Cynthia's chopped salad arrives, the husband is baffled.

'But I was going to have some of your steak.'

'You're welcome to some salad.'

'If I'd known you weren't having steak, I would have ordered something else.'

'I said I wanted salad.'

When they are done, they all pile back into the car and head up the hill. 'We'll drop you off,' Andy, the husband, says to Richard.

'Nice meeting you,' Richard says as they pull up in front of his house. 'Good luck.'

'Nice seeing you,' Cynthia says, unbuckling her seat belt as the car comes to a stop.

'Don't start this again,' the husband says. 'We had a nice dinner; didn't you think it was nice?'

Without warning, Cynthia throws the door open, jumps out, and runs across the yard. The husband takes off after her, leaving the car door open. The interior light illuminates the children's faces as they watch their parents chase each other around the front yard.

Richard hurries out after them.

'Open the front door,' Cynthia shouts, and Richard runs up the stone walk, unlocks the front door, and pushes it open. She dodges the husband, who hurls himself across the lawn in the flying leap of an attempted tackle. The front door slams with a loud percussive pop, followed by the sound of breaking glass as the large windows crumble.

She opens the door. 'Sorry,' she says, and then closes it again, more carefully.

'It's enough for one night,' Richard says to the husband.

'You're a freak,' the husband says. 'Fine, you want her, you keep her. I have no idea what you're going to use her for – can't imagine.' He climbs back into the minivan. 'She's not going to get away with this and neither are you – you little fairy shit.' The husband drives off.

'He's not really so bad, is he?' Cynthia says, coming out of the house.

'Hard to know,' Richard says.

'The minute they drove up, I knew I couldn't go back. I felt like I'd escaped, like I got lucky. I'd die if I went back. When he drove up I felt sick, and now I feel really good. Look how strong I was.' She gestures towards the house. 'I'll pay you for it as soon as I have some money. I'll take care of everything. I can't believe I broke your house.'

'The house was already broken.'

'Do you think he'll come back? Do you think he'll come and kill me?'

'We can't stay here anyway. Between your husband being on the loose and the house being broken, we should just go to Malibu. The real-estate guy left me the key.'

'I just want you to know, I'm not going to mooch off you forever. I appreciate all you've done for me, but it's not like I'm moving in permanently. I will figure this out.'

They go into the house and tape big green plastic bags over the broken windows. When they run out of plastic bags they use whatever shopping bags are in the cupboard – Hermès, Armani, Barneys, Bristol Farms. They piece together a consumer collage meant to protect the interior in case the weather turns, and to keep the wildlife out.

223

He leaves a message for his insurance agent. 'OK, so now someone visiting me managed to break two of the large plate-glass windows – is that covered?'

He puts his dirty retreat clothes into the hamper and takes clean clothes for Malibu: hats, sunglasses, a bathing suit, white pants, pale-blue sweater, a jean jacket he hasn't worn in years. He packs like he's going on a vacation, a pleasure cruise.

'I only have this,' she says, patting a small plastic bag. 'Maybe at some point I can sneak home and get some stuff. It's not like I planned on leaving; I accidentally escaped.'

Richard hurries, moving like he has to get someplace soon, like someone who's old and worries about his ability to see in the dark.

They drive all the way down Sunset, into what feels like the wilds of Los Angeles, Santa Monica, and then up the Pacific Coast Highway, stopping at the Malibu Country Store for supplies.

'Didn't we just eat?' she asks.

'When?'

'At the restaurant?'

'I didn't really eat anything, did you?' Richard asks.

'I really want to stay on my diet; I can't eat crap,' she says, circling the potato chips.

'Neither can I.' He picks up a package of donuts, reads the ingredients, and puts it down.

They get eggs, bread, butter, water.

'French toast,' she says happily. 'With fruit!'

'Do they have fruit?'

'There's a pile of bananas by the register.'

Back in the car, Richard searches for the house number in the fading light. 'I was only here once. It's a big white box.' Pulling off the highway, he practically runs over a man in a bathrobe digging through the trash.

'Are you fucking trying to kill me?'

'Sorry, I didn't see you.'

'Am I fucking invisible?'

'Sorry.' Richard fumbles with the key, the lock, the alarm code. It's like checking into a hotel late at night – something he always hated, arriving when it's too late to see where you are, too late to change your mind.

He turns on lights.

'It's nice,' she says. 'Smells like fresh paint.'

The odor dilates the inside of his brain, a cross between a high and a headache. There is a part of him that is so exhausted he could go right to sleep, some massive sense of being overwhelmed that causes a shutdown. Like squatters, they spread out their loot on the kitchen counter. He finds a pan; she cracks the eggs and dips the bread.

The smell of the French toast makes him feel better. It's nice to eat something warm, soft, sweet.

'I found some Splenda in my pocket and sprinkled it in. Good, right?'

'Fantastic.'

'Do you think that guy was homeless?' Richard asks.

'I don't know. Most people don't rummage through the trash in the dark in a robe,' she says. 'It's so white in here . . .'

'Very white.'

Is white the color of hope?

After dinner, she goes to take a bath and he takes his jean jacket outside, neatly folds it, and leaves it on top of the trash can – it's got to be better than a bathrobe.

Alone in his room, he sets up his computer and goes online, first checking to see how his accounts did while he was away. Fine, good, no better or worse than if he'd been on them every day. And then he checks his e-mail. His brother has been forwarding the daily entries from the boys. They are getting closer, wending their way across America. He is thrilled to be in on the story, but devastated that it's coming to him secondhand.

There they are buying lemonade from a little girl with a stand on the side of a rural road – 'She had a box of Free Kittens, 10 weeks old, we wanted to take them all, instead we just played with them and took pictures. Logging a lot of hours behind the wheel – CD player is great. Accidentally left the cell phone in a diner – didn't realize until late at night – located it by calling the number. It was on the floor under the booth with all the fallen French fries, saltine wrappers, and old napkins. The waitress dropped it at FedEx and we picked it up the next morning at Mail Boxes Etc., in New Mexico. We're now in a

Starbucks, it's all pretty great. I'm sending you this message from there. Have you ever had Mountain Dew? We love it and are drinking it round the clock – lots of caffeine. We're buzzed!'

Looking at the pictures of Ben, Richard is overwhelmed – it's incredible that he has a son. A boy, a man, just like him and not like him at all, except that some piece of his essential self has continued on, has a chance to get it right, to try again.

Looking at the pictures, he feels the weight of all those years, the enormity of his absence, and he begins to cry.

Cynthia sits next to him. She holds him and he cries harder.

'I missed so much,' he says.

And when he is done, she leaves him, and as grateful as he was that she held him, he is glad to be alone with his grief.

He rises early and meditates. There is a white velvet painting on the wall; at first he thinks it's an abstraction, then he realizes it's two women making love. He sits, noticing his breath, his back, his body, the sound of the water outside, the cool air blowing through. He practices, banging an imaginary gong, gently closing his eyes, finding his breath in his body, the morning sun flooding through, seeming to rise on him, in him.

He misses the sounds of other people breathing, throats clearing. He makes a note to himself – buy incense.

He sits, breathing, transforming the darkness into light, breathing, transforming anger into compassion, into forgiveness.

He sits for an hour, and by then the sun is fully risen, the room is bright, glowing, hot. Glancing out onto the ocean, he sees something – first he thinks it's a bit of debris, floating, and then realizes it's a yellow swimming cap. He watches the swimmer, stroking her way down the ocean, swimming towards Santa Monica. The fact that there is a swimmer out there, a mermaid, is incredibly uplifting – if there is a swimmer there is hope.

He tiptoes into the living room. She is on the sofa. 'Are you awake?' she asks him.

'Yes,' he says, wondering if and why she thinks he's sleepwalking.

'You're up early.'

'Always.'

'Do you want to go for a walk?' she asks. 'I got in the habit of early-morning walks.'

Together they go to the glass, they stand looking out over the Pacific.

'From the bedroom I saw a woman swimming. She was swimming like she was doing laps, swimming the ocean like it was a forty-foot pool, and at some point she'll get to the end, touch, and turn around and swim back. Look,' he says, excited. 'I just saw something else.'

'Like what?'

'Dolphins.'

And, sure enough, there is a school, a pack of

dolphins crossing, leaping through the air, coming up out of the water, as if performing an athletic dance, as if waving good morning.

'I have to go down there,' she says. 'Are you coming?'

'I think I'm going to stay. I need to make a few calls.'

Cecelia's hip has come in. 'If it's OK with you, I'll go ahead and have them put it in. I won't be able to work for six to eight weeks.'

'I'd like to send you a check,' he says.

'Are you firing me?'

'Of course not; I imagine you'll have some expenses.'

'Hold on to your money.'

'Cecelia, when you check into the hospital, get a private room. I'll pick up the difference – you should have what you need.'

'I'm fine with what they give me.'

He calls the nutritionist. 'Cecelia told me you were away,' she says.

'I was on a retreat. They had spirulina and ground flax seed.'

'Very good. So where is your new place?'

'Malibu.'

'Oh, far. I have a route that I kind of stick to, but I could meet you somewhere along the way. Maybe Santa Monica?'

'Whatever works; I'm flexible.'

'Meet me in the Fred Segal parking lot tomorrow

at two-fifteen and I'll make you a bunch of things that will get you through the week.'

'Good, and I'll need a double order – food for two.'

'You're pregnant?'

'No, I have a friend staying here.'

'A friend – congratulations.'

He calls the trainer. 'Malibu – wow, you're out of my service area. When will you be back?'

'A month, maybe two.'

'There's got to be a gym or a Shanti out there – look in the phone book under "exercise."'

He does, and finds something called Malibu Gyrotonics.

'Have you ever done Pilates, gymnastics, or other dance-based exercise?' the woman answering the phone quizzes him.

'No.'

'I can put you in with Sydney tomorrow at three.'

'Perfect.'

'It's eighty-five dollars a session.'

'Perfect.'

'Not covered by insurance, unless you have a physical-therapy prescription.'

'Perfect.'

He calls Lusardi's office.

'How was it?' the receptionist asks.

'Transforming,' he says, laughing. 'Everyone got diarrhea. I need to make a time to come in.'

'How's today at one?'

'Perfect.' Everything is suddenly perfect.

'If your stomach is still bothering you, bring a sample and we'll culture it.'

He pretends he didn't hear that.

There's a knock on the front door. It's Billy, the real-estate agent. 'Everything hunky-dory?'

Richard nods. 'Why didn't you tell me whose house this was?'

'It seemed obvious.'

'To everyone but me.'

Billy shrugs.

'Last night my windows blew out,' Richard says. 'I need someone to take a look, but I've got no idea where to begin.'

'Billy knows someone,' Billy says, pulling a little black book out of his back pocket. He scans the minuscule but deeply neat handwriting – a list of names and numbers. 'Billy's made a lot of friends over the years.'

'Thanks, Billy.'

Richard calls Billy's contractor friend. 'I'm right around the corner. Are you home now? How soon can you be there?'

'Forty minutes – an hour?'

'Fine,' the guy says. 'Call me back when you're close.'

Cynthia comes back from her walk. 'I've arranged for us to get food,' Richard says proudly. 'I'm meeting the nutritionist in Santa Monica, and she's going to make us a package of good things.'

'Great. I met someone on the beach, a woman who knew of a program started by a plastic

231

surgeon – housewife rehab. He started it because he would do all this work on people and they were still miserable, which depressed him. They have a social worker, yoga and nutrition classes, and they help you get a job, and it's free. The doctor calls it his debt to society.'

'Are you sure it's not a cult or a way he drums up business?'

'I'm so excited,' she says, 'I'm going to get a job. I haven't had a job in years.'

'That's fantastic,' he says, careful not to burst her bubble. I've got to go,' he says. 'I'm meeting a contractor. I'm late.'

'Go,' she says. 'I'll call and find out more about it.'

Richard hurries out to the car. He's there again, the guy from last night. He's wearing Richard's old jean jacket and has a noise-canceling headset on.

Richard sees the guy and taps the side of his head. 'I have those too,' he says loudly.

The guy just looks at him and then pulls the headset off one ear.

'I have those too,' Richard says again. 'I love them.'

'Are you the asshole?'

'Excuse me?'

'The asshole who bought that shit box to tear it down.'

'No, I'm the tenant.'

'Do you know the asshole?'

'No.'

'Then what are you doing here?'

'My house fell into a hole and broke; I'm renting. That's my jacket. I left it for you last night; I thought you were homeless.'

'Nope, I live here,' he says, gesturing to the house next door. 'Fits good – thanks.' He adjusts the jacket.

'I saw you going through the trash.'

'You almost ran me over.'

Richard nods.

'I had it,' the guy says, 'the perfect line. I wrote it on something and now it's in there – somewhere.' He bends over the trash can. 'Oh, my back. Do me a favor, I can't reach that one bag at the bottom, can you pull it out for me?'

The trash can stinks, the horrible, fetid smell of decay. Richard tries to pull the bag out without sticking his head in.

'You have to bend into it,' the guy says.

And so Richard bends, dipping his whole upper body in, pulling out the bag, and getting some stinky mystery juice on his shirt.

The guy rips the bag open. 'Arrggghh,' he tilts his head back and bellows like a wild man.

'OK, then,' Richard says, getting into the car, 'have a good one.'

The contractor walks in circles around the house, throwing his weight against the pilings, attempting to shake the foundation.

233

'Electric and water still on?'

Richard nods.

'You should turn them off: not worth the risk.' He bends, scooping up pieces of broken glass; they are like beach rubble, glistening, sharp. 'I've never seen glass give out like this – I'm impressed.'

'OK, so now what?' Richard asks.

'Well, you can either go the restoration route or, you know . . .' He pauses. 'A lot of people are doing it these days – just knock it down and start over. That way you can have whatever you want – take care of all the little things that always bothered you – where the bathroom sink was, the way the doors in the bedroom opened, wishing your view was better from your bed.'

'Seems like a large proposition, knocking down my house. I was thinking of something more like just getting it back to where it was last week, when it had windows and everything worked and I liked it just fine.'

'Up to you,' the guy says, handing him his card.

Richard drives back to Malibu, stops at the grocery store, goes up and down the aisles, surprised at what he's choosing – organic vegetables, soy protein, tofu cheese – piling the cart high. He wants to stay clean, to maintain whatever it is he got while he was busy transforming suffering. They sell bundles of wood in the store. He puts four in the cart and thinks it's funny, buying a bundle of wood for five dollars. Why not sell sticks for a dollar each?

In the store, he sees the guy from the trash cans, wandering, sampling greens, talking to people who seem perfectly happy to talk to him, who seem to know him. He's got flip-flops, shaggy gnarled long hair, and a peculiar, deeply masculine, but ever-so-slightly feminine physical presence, a godly stature which gives off a lot of self-confidence for someone who looks like he hasn't had a bath in weeks.

'I'm still not sure that you're not the asshole,' the guy says to him.

'What can I say to convince you?'

'Very little. Do I look bad?'

'You look . . . rough,' Richard says.

'I go in phases; right now I'm in a fight with my body. Do I smell?'

'Not from here.'

'I'm on deadline.' He dips his fingers into a bag of lettuce and puts some in his mouth. 'Greens, very good for you.' He eats them as though he craves them, as though greens are the new candy, the new Swedish Fish. 'Where have you been?' he asks.

'I met a contractor at my house, to see how bad the damage is.'

'And?'

'Bad.'

'And before that where were you?'

'On a silent retreat.'

'You a meditator?'

'Just starting.'

'I don't believe in it. Used to do it myself, but you know what I think – people have to stop just sitting there and start doing something. It's a very self-involved activity.'

Richard doesn't say anything.

'Can you give me a ride home? I walked over here; my car's in the shop.'

'Sure, yeah. Where do you live?'

'I told you – asshole – right next to you.'

'I didn't realize you lived there.'

'Where did you think I lived? What would I be doing going through the trash in the dark if I didn't live there? Looking for crumbs?'

They drive back to the house.

Cynthia is there, waiting for him. 'They said I was the ideal candidate. I start tomorrow.'

'Should I go with you? Are you sure it's for real?'

'There was an article on him in *Self* magazine.'

'And that makes it real?'

'I'm excited; can't you be excited for me?'

'I am excited for you, I just don't want you to be abducted by a psycho surgeon who puts you in a trance and performs plastic surgery on you or anything. Do you want some lunch?'

'Starving,' she says, digging into the groceries.

After lunch, he gets back into the car and drives into town to see Lusardi.

'So?' Lusardi asks.

'I liked it. It was valuable, challenging in a way that nothing has been challenging in a very long time – except that everything feels strange now, nothing fits. I'm not who I thought I was.'

'None of us are.'

'I'm not really any different, and yet nothing is the same.'

'How's the pain?'

'You know, I feel pretty good. I think I'm still in pain; I mean, I must be, right? We're all in pain, but it's not bothering me at the moment.'

Lusardi presses the stethoscope to his chest. 'You don't become a different person – you just learn to live with yourself – that's the hardest part.' And they are quiet; Lusardi listens. 'You sound fine,' he says.

Richard drives to the house and meets yet another of Billy's friends, a guy named Giovanni.

'Doesn't look like much to me,' Giovanni says. 'We get all kinds of ground movement. Glass pops, that's what we call them, glass pops. Anyway, we just need to give the roots of the house a little tug, maybe put in some anchors, and straighten her out – doesn't have to be a big thing.'

'Around how much does not a big thing go for?'

'Hard to know for sure until you do it, but I'd figure one fifty, one seventy-five.'

'So – somewhere between a hundred and fifty thousand and a hundred and seventy-five thousand dollars.'

'Sounds about right,' Giovanni says.

'Sounds like a big thing.'

'We do it all the time,' Giovanni says. 'Do you have the plans, the name of the person who built it, the original specs?'

'I think the electrician's name is on the circuit box downstairs, and maybe there's a plumber's name down there too, written on one of the pipes.'

'I'm looking for blueprints, drawings, specific information.'

As they're talking, the doorbell rings; it's the color lady, with the painter trailing behind her – ladder and drop cloths in hand. 'We're here, right on time.'

'I forgot you were coming,' he says. 'We're having some trouble with the house.'

'We won't be in the way.' She pushes past him and starts towards the guest room.

'I don't think it's a good day for painting,' he says. 'The house is falling down.'

'Well, what do you want him to do?' she says, gesturing towards the painter. 'It's not easy to get him to come – he's very busy.'

'We may have to knock it down; no point painting right now.'

'I don't understand.'

'No paint.'

'Are you just leaving the Sheetrock bare for another ten years?'

'I'm going to figure it out,' he says – trying to avoid a fight.

'Why don't I have someone come and take a look around and we'll get back to you with some hard numbers,' Giovanni says.

'Hard numbers, that would be great,' Richard says, sending him off.

'Well, if you can figure it out now,' the color lady says, 'the painter can just do his job; it won't take him long.'

'Couple of days,' the painter says. 'I could even stay over and work really late and really early and be done in eighteen hours.'

Richard is saying no, but they don't want to hear no, and at a certain point he just steps aside and they come in.

'Do you have a check for me?' the color lady asks. 'We always get the check before we start.'

'But I don't want you to start.'

'Why did you call me if you don't want me to paint?'

'When I called you the house wasn't falling down.'

'It's not my fault,' she says.

'No one said it was.'

'Then why are you yelling at me?'

And on and on with no end in sight, until Richard says, 'I have to go now,' and goes outside, gets in his car, and drives up the hill. He drives to the top of the hill and watches. He watches thinking he'll see the color lady and the painter coming out of the house, but he sees nothing. He watches and watches, and then he drives away.

Richard is on his way back to Malibu, his second round trip of the day, and he's in a bad mood. Traffic. For the first time he understands what everyone is always talking about. He's on the 10 and he's just standing there, there's no flow. The highway is old and imperfect, the road is crumbling concrete, asphalt. Why are the highways in the East blacktop and the ones in the West asphalt? Does it have to do with heat, with creating a reflective surface, an ugly America? He's worn out, thinking about hard numbers, knocking the house down, the color lady not taking no for an answer.

Everything is not perfect, it is ugly, scrubby, scruffy, beige like it was bleached but got dirty. Even though it is a car culture, all the ones around him are lousy: old, rusted, late-model. He's behind the wheel mentally writing his treatise, his exegesis on Los Angeles and the car, when he realizes that he's hearing SOS in his head. SOS in Morse code, repeating. SOS. Dot, dot, dot. Dash, dash, dash. Dot, dot, dot.

He looks at the car in front of him and could swear that the brake lights are flashing a distinct sequence – SOS, SOS.

The highway opens up, the speed picks up. The guy ahead of him changes lanes. The taillights show no signal except the continuing SOS, which never falls out of sequence, even during the lane change. SOS. SOS.

Someone is doing it. Someone is doing it and the guy doesn't know. Richard accelerates. The guy looks at him in his rearview mirror. Richard stares back. The guy glowers and changes lanes. Richard follows him. SOS. SOS.

Richard beeps at the car in the same dot-dash pattern. He beeps and then pauses and beeps again. SOS. SOS. The brake lights flash.

Richard beeps two short beeps. The lights flash two short flashes.

He is in conversation. Someone is in the trunk flashing SOS. Richard has to stop the car; he has to get the car off the road without hitting the trunk. He puts up alongside, pressing in towards the other guy. The two cars touch as if kissing and then pull apart. The guy speeds up. Richard keeps up the pace. He leans on the horn as if blowing a warning, and then veers into the guy – hard.

The guy glares at him. 'What the fuck?'

He pulls away and Richard speeds up and does it again. People are honking, trying to get out of the way. SOS. SOS.

The guy slams Richard back and then swerves onto the shoulder. Richard follows alongside, squeezing in.

'Are you fucking nuts?' the guy yells. They are so close that Richard can hear him perfectly clearly.

He might be.

What would happen if the guy stopped, if he opened the trunk, and all that was in there was a spare tire, a couple of cans of oil, and some old clothes that the guy kept forgetting to drop off at the Salvation Army? The car is talking to him, communicating, and why would the guy be trying to get away if he wasn't hiding something?

The two of them are side by side on the shoulder. The guy is stepping into the gas and heading into him, this time clipping Richard's door. Richard returns, aiming for the guy's front wheel. Both cars slide off the road, down a grassy hill, the big Mercedes creaking, crunching, complaining, but taking it like a pro. As soon as they come to a stop the guy is out of his car and running. Richard goes after him, catching him only when the guy trips, falling. Richard jumps on his back while the guy is facedown.

'What the fuck?'

Richard sits on the guy, riding him like he's a pony, actually more a bucking bronco. How long can he keep him down? Richard kicks him with his heels, digging in.

And finally there's someone at the top of the hill.

'Do you need an ambulance?'

'Hurry,' Richard yells.

'Should I call 911?'

'Help me.' The guy is about to get away. He's wiggling out from Richard. Two men come running. 'Sit on him,' Richard says, and they do, and then one of the guys says, 'Why are we sitting on him?'

And Richard tells him about the SOS signal.

'Is there someone in the trunk?' they ask the guy. He doesn't answer.

'You'd better go,' the men tell Richard.

Richard climbs back up the hill and knocks on the trunk. 'Hello?'

'Yes,' a woman says.

'I saw your SOS,' he says. 'I ran the car off the road. Everything is fine. I'm going to get you out.'

'Don't open the trunk.'

'You don't want me to let you out?'

'Are there people out there?'

'Yes.'

'I'm naked.'

'OK.' He pauses. 'I'll crack the trunk lid and hand you some clothes.'

'My hands are tied,' she says.

'All right, I'll pop the lid so you can get some air while I find some scissors.' He reaches into the front seat and pulls the trunk release. 'How's that?'

'Good,' she says. 'I can see.'

A highway cop pulls up on a motorcycle. 'Do you need help?'

'It's a hostage situation,' Richard says.

More cars have pulled off the road; the two men who were sitting on the guy have tied him up with their belts.

Someone has a pocket knife; the girl sticks her wrists out of the trunk, they cut the duct tape. Richard takes off his shirt and pushes it through the crack, and someone has some sweatpants and they stuff those in, and then she says, 'You can open it.'

Richard lifts the lid and there she is – eyes blinking, adjusting to the daylight, wet like she's been half drowned, terrorized.

'I was taking a shower; he grabbed me out of the shower.' Her hair is still wet.

'Do you know the guy?' the cop asks.

'He repaired my television a couple of weeks ago.'

By now, an ambulance has pulled up and they're helping the girl into the back, and the guy is being stuffed into the backseat of a police car, complaining that they hurt him when they sat on him.

And the cop taking the report is saying to Richard, 'I just want to get this right. You were driving behind them and the car started talking to you?'

'SOS, SOS,' Richard says, 'in Morse code.'

'And what's that, Morse code? Is that something I should know?'

'Yes,' Richard says.

'Some kind of high-tech Internet talk?'

'He was going to kill her,' one of the men who'd been sitting on him said.

'Did he tell you that?' the cop asks.

'Not in *so* many words, but once they put you in the trunk it's a bad sign,' one of the men says.

'Right,' the cop says. 'Trunk crimes have a very high lethality.'

'You saved her life,' someone tells Richard.

Police dogs are searching the area; a bystander with a video camera is filming everything. 'Off the shoulder, off the shoulder,' a cop says, directing traffic. 'No gawker accidents.'

'I need to go home,' Richard says to no one in particular. And while the cops are getting the last of his information, address, phone number, one of the men drives his car up the hill. They escort him onto the highway, and he drives off squinting into the glare of the bleached afternoon.

He drives with pieces of metal dangling, the car sounding like tin cans at a wedding.

It is only when he pulls up to the house, when he turns off the ignition, when he is safe, that he realizes what happened. It was so strange, like something you'd see on a TV movie, only worse. The trunk smelled. When the trunk was opened, an incredible smell – dark-vinegary, urine – came up out of the car, and the girl, looking beyond scared, made eye contact with him, and Richard put out his hand to help her. He put out his hand and she took it.

Richard gets out of his car and vomits, spills everything onto the edge of the road, into oncoming traffic. He throws up and feels even worse. He knocks on the door to the homeless man's house.

'Go away.'

'Do you have some Advil?' he yells, knowing the medicine cabinet in the white cube is empty.

The guy opens the door. Richard sees his arm, sees plastic tubing he's hooked up to an IV.

'Oh, sorry, I didn't realize you were sick.'

'I'm not sick, it's vitamins. What happened to you? You look' – he pauses – 'shocked.'

'Have you got any Advil?'

He shakes his head. 'Hard on the liver. But I can help you. Come in.'

The guy pours Richard a drink. 'Scotch, better for you.' He motions to a chair. Richard sits. The guy rummages through a drawer and then goes to the refrigerator, comes back with a few small bottles. 'I'm a certified homeopath,' the guy says, 'along with being a psychopath.' He laughs. 'Open your mouth.'

Richard obeys, and he squirts a few drops from each bottle into Richard's mouth.

Richard gags. 'What is that?'

'A remedy. I make it myself.'

The man hands him the scotch. 'It helps.'

Richard drinks. He could have been killed. The asshole in the car was certainly going to do something to the girl, and he could have done the same to Richard. Did he really do a good thing? Did he save someone's life, does that make a difference, did he interrupt history, fate? What came over him?

'More scotch?'

Richard nods. The guy's house is rustic, a bachelor beach cottage, exposed wooden ceiling beams, a big desk overlooking the ocean, crooked pictures, a huge bottled-water dispenser.

'Why do you take the vitamins like that?' Richard asks.

'Because I'm nuts. I want to live forever and I've got this sagging ass, this gut. Aging is the one thing that terrifies me. I can't imagine myself old.' The guy lights a cigarette. He is rugged, weathered; his hair is like a lion's mane; his eyes are the bluest of blue; his features are hard and strong.

246

'Are you an actor?'

'No – worse.'

'A producer?'

'Further down the food chain.'

Richard shrugs.

'A writer, just another shitty Hollywood writer, a hack job waiting to happen.'

'Oh yeah, that sounds like fun.'

The man squeezes the IV bag, squirting what's left through the tubing and into his arm. 'All gone,' he says, like a little kid, and then pulls the needle out.

'Isn't a nurse supposed to do that?'

There is a knock on the door.

'Is he in here?' It's Cynthia.

'Good, your wife is back; you can go home now.'

'Not his wife,' she says, coming in.

'Girlfriend, sorry.'

'Not his girlfriend.'

'Secretary.'

She shakes her head. 'Friend,' she says. 'I'm his friend.'

'Whatever.'

'And your name is?' she says, extending her hand.

'Nic,' he says.

And Richard realizes that they haven't officially met. 'Richard,' he says.

'Cynthia,' she says. 'I was out and I heard this incredible story on the radio; was that you?'

He nods. 'I don't know what came over me.'

'You didn't rob a bank or shoot someone in the post office or anything like that, did you?'

'Quite to the contrary,' Cynthia says, proudly.

'I don't know what I was thinking,' he says, and starts to tell the story: meeting the contractor at the house, the peculiarity of how one person could think it's a small job while the other thinks he should tear it down, and how he got on the highway in a bad mood, and how the car started talking to him and he knew he had to do something.

'They were interviewing people, witnesses – they said there were two men fighting, rolling down the hill like animals, they thought it was a road-rage attack. And then they announced your name: Richard Novak is the apparent hero. That's what they called you, the apparent hero.'

'Are you injured?' Nic feels him head to toe, pats him up and down. 'Any cuts or bites?'

'What kind of bites, snake by the highway?'

'No, human. Human bites are very dangerous. Dirtiest mouth there is.'

'Who knows what he was going to do to her,' Cynthia says.

'Who was this guy?'

'A TV repairman.'

'Do you think that was the first time he'd done it?'

'It's never the first time.'

Outside, there is a sound, like a cat crying. They ignore it, and when it continues, unrelenting, the three of them go outside.

Anhil is banging on the door of the white cube,

holding a box of donuts. He turns towards them. 'I am sorry to crush in on you, but I was so worried. I saw the car on television, I would know her anywhere,' Anhil says.

They walk around the car – pretty banged up, more damage than Richard would have thought. They are on the edge of the Pacific Coast Highway, circling the Mercedes, circling the vomit next to the car, and across the way someone seems to be snapping pictures.

'Let's go inside,' Nic says.

'My house,' Richard says. 'I need new clothes.'

Cynthia unlocks the door.

'It's a vanilla fantasy,' Anhil says.

'I've never been in here,' Nic says. 'All these years right next door and never inside, I was picturing some sort of sex den.'

'Well, there was some equipment in one of the rooms, but the Realtor had them take it out,' Richard says. 'Something that hung from the ceiling.'

'You didn't tell me about that,' Cynthia says.

'I didn't want to scare you.'

Richard excuses himself and goes into the bedroom to change. He takes a hot shower.

'Better?' Cynthia asks when he comes back.

'Cleaner,' he says.

'My wife is making her chicken stew tonight – I can call her and she will bring her stew,' Anhil says.

'How long will it take?' Nic asks.

'Maybe forty minutes, maybe two hours. I would like you to meet her, even though this is sudden,' he tells Richard. 'She makes very good chicken stew; I could eat a gallon of it.'

'Call her,' Nic says, 'I'm starving.'

Nic opens a bottle of wine, Cynthia finds some snacks in the fridge; they are sitting around, waiting. The phone rings.

'Is this Richard Novak?'

'Yes,' he says. And the man hangs up.

The sun is starting to go down. 'Do you have wood?' Nic asks. 'I'll build a fire; it's my specialty, fires. My oven broke two years ago and I haven't looked back.'

'You cook in the fireplace?' Cynthia asks.

'No, actually in a Weber kettle.'

'I bought wood today,' Richard says. 'It's in packages just outside the front door.'

'You bought wood? You're not supposed to buy wood – you find it on the beach.'

Anhil's brother and wife arrive with an industrial-size pot of chicken stew, a big bag of ingredients to be added, and various containers of sauce.

When Nic offers Anhil's wife some wine, she politely declines, takes out a bottle of apricot juice, and pours some for Anhil and herself.

'What is your name?' Nic asks.

'Lipi,' she says.

'That is "Manuscript of the Gods,"' Anhil tells them.

Cynthia finds a dozen white votives in one of

the drawers and they sit looking out on the ocean, with only the candle-light guiding them into the night.

Richard closes his eyes and sees bits and pieces of the afternoon all over again, his car brushing against the guy's car, the steely sound of it scraping like something in a machine shop.

'Everybody OK with coconut?' Lipi asks before she adds coconut milk to her stew.

'It's one of the secret ingredients,' Anhil says, 'but how can it stay a secret when you ask everyone if it's OK?'

A breeze blows through the house, fanning the flames of Nic's fire, brushing across the back of Richard's neck; he shivers, buttons the top of his collar. They sit at the long dining-room table.

'There is something funny about this table,' Cynthia says. 'It looks like stone but weighs nothing.'

'It's a prop,' Nic says. 'You can buy things like this all the time, discarded props. It looks like something but it's nothing.'

Cythina holds a candle under the table. 'I think it's Styrofoam,' she says.

'Be careful,' Richard says. 'It's probably flammable.'

Lipi serves the stew. 'There are condoms on the table,' she says.

Anhil and his brother laugh. 'She means things that go with the stew – tomatoes, dill sauce, in the little bowls.'

'Yes, that's what I said – condoms.'

And they laugh again. 'I'm sorry,' Anhil says, still laughing, 'but you are very funny.'

'Condiments,' Cynthia says.

'What's the difference,' Lipi says, annoyed, 'condoms, condom mints.'

'Where did you meet?' Nic asks Anhil and Lipi.

'We lived in the same town. I fell in love with Lipi when I was eight years old. I told nobody, I didn't want anyone to say no. Her family was better than mine, and then they had a fall and I got Lipi.'

'My sister's husband left her; this is very bad,' Lipi said. 'In America people leave each other everywhere and no one cares, but in our country it is a very big deal. They decided that the problem is my sister; some friends of her husband come and kill her. I was there – hiding in the closet, afraid they might kill me too. I know who they are.'

'It was my job to protect Lipi; we left in the middle of the night.'

'I cannot go back.'

'The stew is delicious,' Cynthia says. 'A perfect combination – olives, chickpeas.'

'Thank you,' Lipi says.

When the wine bottle is empty, Nic runs back to his house and comes back with more.

The telephone rings.

'Is this Richard Novak?'

'Yes, it is.'

'It's Priscilla from the *Today* show in New York

with a few questions. Have you spoken to the young woman since the incident?'

'No.'

'What were you thinking when you rescued her?'

'I wasn't really thinking, I was kind of daydreaming.'

'There are reports that you've done this sort of thing before.'

'Not really.'

'You got a horse out of a hole?'

'I don't mean to cut you off, but we're in the middle of dinner.'

'Not a problem; a producer will call you back to go over details about your appearance on the show.'

'Who is it?' Nic asks.

'*Today* show,' Richard says, covering the phone.

Nic takes the phone from Richard. 'Thanks, but no thanks,' he says, hanging up.

After dinner, Nic lights an enormous joint and passes it around. Everyone except Lipi smokes.

'I don't get it,' Richard says. 'You drink, you smoke, and you take intravenous vitamins to keep yourself healthy – seems like a contradiction.'

'Counterbalance,' Nic says, inhaling. 'It's all about balance, and in order to balance you have to have counterbalance.'

'Do you feel OK?' Cynthia asks Richard.

'I'm fine.'

'Do you feel like a Superman?' Anhil asks. 'With X-ray vision?'

Richard shakes his head. Frankly, he feels

253

fragile, broken, like he has stepped so far outside himself that he's now a little unfamiliar even to himself.

The joint comes around again. It's been years since he got stoned. His head feels like cotton candy – light, airy.

For dessert they open the box of donuts, and Anhil goes into detail explaining the essential qualities of each donut. 'This is the newest one, I call it Early Riser. It's a very high donut,' he says, laughing. 'That's funny, high donut. Right now, I am a high donut,' he says.

Lipi shakes her head. 'When you smoke you lose your intelligence.'

Richard meanwhile is licking the glaze off a donut, mesmerized by the sugar coating, like shards of glass dissolving on his tongue.

'I'm going downhill,' Nic says, 'I'm not going to be able to hold it, I'm breaking up, I'm breaking up.' He inhales.

'I'm stoned,' Cynthia announces bluntly. 'Did you grow up in L.A.?' she asks Nic.

'Schenectady.'

'How'd you end up here?'

'You really want to know?'

'Yes.'

'I was sixteen, my brother was twenty – he was in the army. I was home; it was afternoon. My mother saw a car pull up and park at the curb. She opened the door before the man even got out. 'My husband's not home,' she yelled.

'The man stood there for a moment. "May I come in?"

'"Call your father and tell him to come home," she told me. She didn't want to hear it alone.

'I went into the kitchen and called my father. By the time he got there, my mother was chatting it up with the man, telling him stories about Tom and our family, and he just listened and drank his cup of coffee and never said anything that would give it away. Why? Out of decency? Was he sparing her or making it worse? And what was I doing? Hiding in the kitchen, afraid to go in there – afraid I might cry. My father got home, breathless and pale. He sat on the sofa without taking his coat off.

'I don't remember if they cried, or if my mother was too busy thanking the man for coming, for waiting for my father, for bringing the letter. My father was asking questions about "the arrangements" and the man gave him a business card with a number to call.

'After he left, my father went outside and raked leaves for hours. Everything froze in a kind of darkness that I'd never dreamed possible. And I kept thinking that if it had happened to me they would have been fine, but because it was Tom it was worse. Behind their backs, I wore his clothes – socks, T-shirts – maybe my mother knew, maybe she didn't. I was terrified of being caught as some kind of memory thief. But I needed it – I needed to feel him, to remember him, to believe I was like him.

'When I left Schenectady, California seemed as far away as the moon, and when I got here, I couldn't go back, not until I'd made sense of it. And by the time I'd done that, a different kind of time had passed – I was no longer the same person, I was a veteran of my own life.'

They sit in silence. There is nothing to say.

Nic goes to the window. 'The ocean looks like ink, like so much spilt black ink.'

They all sit a while longer, and then Anhil, his brother, and Lipi pack up the rice cooker, the empty stew pot.

'I put the leftovers in the refrigerator, for tomorrow,' Lipi says.

'Thank you,' Richard says. 'I'm so glad you came, so glad to meet you.'

'I love you,' Cynthia says, to no one in particular.

'This was my dream,' Anhil says, 'to be invited to a famous house in Malibu and to have my wife with me. Next time everyone comes to our house – it's not as poor as you think.' Anhil hugs him. 'Take care, rescue ranger.'

'The fire can burn out without me,' Nic says, picking up the half-empty bottle of wine and heading for the door.

Richard turns around and Cynthia is asleep on the sofa. He stands listening to the waves lapping at the edge of the land, and then slowly closes the sliding glass door.

In the bedroom, he undresses. Bruises are

starting to show: large uneven areas of green and purple on his arms, his legs, his side. He puts on sweats and goes to the computer to check his accounts. It's always comforting to check the money.

He sends his brother an e-mail: 'Helped a woman taken hostage out of the trunk of a car today. Can't sleep – looking forward to the boys arriving. BTW (by the way) – did you really almost win a Nobel?' He deletes the line about the Nobel and hits 'send.' The boys are a day or two from arriving, and it occurs to Richard that no one knows where he is – Ben doesn't, his brother doesn't, his ex-wife doesn't. He calls the answering machine back at the sinking house and plays his messages.

'It's your painter, on my cell phone, calling from inside the house. I didn't have keys, so I just stayed here. I'm finished. The room is done, so I'm going, I'm leaving. I'll close the door behind me.'

'Dr Lusardi's office. The doctor wants to discuss the health of your prostate.'

'It's Cecelia – I'm in the hospital. I was coming out of anesthesia and I saw you on television. I thought I must be dreaming. You're at the bottom of a hill, the car is in a ditch. It's on CNN. They keep playing it over and over again – every ten minutes I see pictures of you trying to climb the hill. Oh Lord, I hope you're all right.'

'Hi. You don't know me, but I'm thirty-nine and looking to meet someone nice and, well, there just

257

don't seem to be any decent guys out there. So, if you're interested, we could just meet somewhere for a coffee. OK, I know it's weird.'

'Hello, Richard, it's Charlie, from *Good Morning America* . . .'

'It's Wendy from *Hello Los Angeles* . . .'

'Dick, it's Jeff, from the *Today* show . . .'

'Ah, Mr Novak, this is Sergeant Braddock. We had a Hancock Park man come into the station today claiming that you have his wife, says you kidnapped her, and, well, given the recent activity on the highway, could you give us a call.'

'It's me. I wanted to thank you. I don't know what to say; I'm really grateful, and I'm going to keep your shirt, if that's OK. I'm at my parents' house – and I'm going to stay here for a while.'

'Are you there, Richard? Pick up. I've gotten a dozen calls today from people who seem to think you've been doing things – rescuing animals, saving kidnapped women . . . I tried to tell them it couldn't be you, you're not the kind of person who does things like that, but I thought you should know, there's another Richard Novak out there on the loose. Be careful. I hope you're feeling better, by the way; it's not like I don't care, I'm just busy.'

He lies on the bed. Did anyone else see it? The brake lights flashing – how did she know to do that? What did she think when she flashed and he beeped back the same pattern? Did she think, 'I'm safe'? Can she ever feel safe again? His arms are sore – the hill, the rough brush, rolling over the hard yellow grasses, holding on to the guy. He replays it – the hollow echo of his knuckles knocking on the trunk. The girl answering, muffled – a distant girl in a distant trunk, and at the same time perfectly clear.

Richard gets out of bed and goes back into the living room; the fire is still glowing. He camps out on the other sofa, opposite Cynthia.

'Can't sleep,' he says.

'Join the crowd,' she says.

Five A.M., he is in the bedroom, sitting eyes closed in the middle of the king-sized bed, breathing, trying to follow his breath. His mind wanders, he chases it, reminding himself to stay in his body, in his breath. He's good for twenty-two minutes and then it is over.

Cynthia is up, dressed, ready for her first day at the plastic surgeon's charitable change-your-life facility. The car isn't picking her up until eight-thirty, but she's pacing. 'Did I do the right thing? I hope I did the right thing. I mean, when you think about it, I just left, I walked out on my children. I could get in trouble for that. If Andy wanted to be an ass, he could make it so I didn't see them again. It was exhausting, twenty-four hours a day cooking, cleaning, driving.'

'Do you want to go for a walk?'

'A walk would be good,' she says. 'I need to move. I shouldn't have gotten stoned last night. I always get paranoid when I get stoned. I didn't seem paranoid, did I? I mean, I didn't do anything to draw attention to myself?'

'You fell asleep,' he says.

They walk down the beach towards Santa Monica. A dog drops a ball at Richard's feet. He picks it up, throws it; the dog gets the ball and brings it back. They do it about twenty times, and then the dog follows them back to the house and up onto the deck.

'OK, friend,' Richard says. 'Go home now.' And the dog just stands there.

'You're on TV,' Cynthia calls from the living room.

'Little is known about Richard Novak; he declined an appearance on this morning's show. Neighbors in his upscale Los Angeles neighborhood say that before last week's episode, when a horse fell into a sinkhole, they'd never met him. Is he a modern-day superhero, anonymously fighting crime, or is he just an old-fashioned Good Samaritan? If you know Richard Novak, or someone like him, let us know. Good Samaritans – an investigation, starts Monday on the eleven o'clock news.'

'You're famous,' Cynthia says.

The dog is still on the porch.

'Am I famous?' Richard asks the dog. 'What does "famous" mean?'

'Can I use your computer for a minute?' Cynthia asks.

'Sure.'

She logs on and sends the kids a message. 'Mom

here – just wanted you to know I'm thinking of you. Reminder: brush your teeth – hard to keep friends if you have dragon breath. Change underwear – clean underwear is not just for special occasions.'

Outside, a horn beeps.

Richard walks Cynthia to the car. 'Do you want to give me an address or a phone number just in case?'

The woman behind the wheel hands him one of the doctor's business cards. 'Don't worry,' she says. 'I'll have her back by five.'

'Call me if you want to come home earlier,' he says.

'I'll be fine,' Cynthia says.

As the car is pulling out, Nic opens his door. 'Hey, man, sorry if I went on last night – I really shouldn't drink and smoke.'

'You're up early.'

'I'm a morning person: no matter what time I go down, I pop up at five-thirty. Can I borrow your car? Mine's in the shop. Just for a couple of hours?'

'Yeah, sure, take it.'

'Actually, better yet, can you drive me?'

'I guess; where are you going?'

'A place down on Fairfax.'

'OK. Sure. Not a problem.'

'Can we go soon?'

'Give me fifteen minutes.' Richard goes back inside. The dog is still on the deck; Richard gives him some leftovers and a bowl of water.

'You know,' he tells the dog, 'famous people don't feed dogs, they have people who do that for them – dog feeders.' The dog just looks at him. Richard gets the dog a towel so he'll have something to sit on. The dog curls up on the towel.

By the time Richard gets outside, Nic is waiting with a shopping bag full of stuff.

'Do you even have a car?' Richard asks.

'Of course I do.' He pulls a key chain out of his pocket and pushes a button, and the garage door lifts. A huge, shiny Bentley is parked in the narrow garage. 'OK, so it's not in the shop, but I can't exactly go driving around in it.'

'Why do you have a Bentley?'

'It was a gift.'

'Nice. Who gives a Bentley as a gift?'

'John Lennon. It was John's, and he gave it to me a long time ago. It's not like I can sell it or anything.'

'And why did John Lennon give you his car?'

'Actually, I paid him a dollar for it – there had to be a transaction in order to transfer the title.'

'Am I'm supposed to ask where you knew John Lennon from?'

'He read a book I wrote and called me,' Nic says, matter-of-factly.

'Really. My ex-wife is in publishing,' Richard says.

'Sorry about last night,' Nic says, changing the subject. 'I didn't mean to bring everyone down.'

'Buckle up.' Richard pulls the car out onto the highway.

They ride in silence, listening to the car rattling, groaning over potholes. Richard puts a price on each sound – some are two hundred dollars, some are closer to two thousand. He's on the 10 heading towards town. None of the cars look the same as they did yesterday, no one is innocent, everyone is suspect, menacing. Maybe he shouldn't have smoked the pot last night – maybe he's a little bit paranoid too.

'What am I looking for – store, office – what?' he asks when they're finally on Fairfax.

'Old-age home,' Nic says, 'two more blocks.'

'Are you visiting someone special?'

'Fred.' They park in front; Nic loads quarters into the meter. 'You coming in?' Nic asks, implying that he is.

'Guess so,' Richard says.

Inside, the smell is stunning: stale urine, shit and disinfectant, bad air, bad digestion, boiled vegetables. Even though it's a nice day outside, you'd never know it. The curtains are half drawn; the windows, small and never washed, look out onto a pawnshop, a car wash, a long line of low-end commercial businesses. He can't imagine who would put a relative in here.

'Where is he?' Nic asks the woman at the front desk.

'Lunchroom,' the woman says.

They go down the hall into what must be Fred's room, or Fred's half of a room. Nic unpacks the bag he brought, pulling out packs of cheap white sweat socks and boxer shorts – ripping the packages open and writing the old man's name onto the items with black waterproof ink. 'If you're wondering why I buy the cheap ones,' Nic says as he's writing, 'it's because they lose his clothes, or steal them. I had someone make him a nice hand-knit sweater. He wore it once and we never saw it again. So I buy him crap, and every month or so I replace everything – at least he has clean clothes.' He opens Fred's drawer, dumping the old socks and stained underwear into the trash.

They go down the hall into the lunchroom, waving to everyone along the way.

Fred is a pretzelized man, bent, twisted, stuffed into a wheelchair. 'How ya doing, Fred? This is my friend Richard; I borrowed his car so we can go joyriding.'

Fred smiles, a gnarled, gap-toothed grin. 'Yie,' he says, waving as best he can. Nic pushes Fred's wheelchair past the front desk, signs Fred out, lifts him into the front seat, and puts the seat belt around him.

'Do you want to drive?' Richard hands Nic the keys. He can't imagine sitting up front with Fred.

'What are we going to get today, Fred? Some pie? Some of that really good cherry pie, or should we get meringue? Remember when we got the sweet-potato pie for Darlene, that nurse, and you and I ended up eating the whole thing before we got home? Let's go to DuPar's – they make good pie.'

'Yie,' Fred says.

'The trick,' Nic says in the parking lot at the Farmers Market, and he's lifting Fred out of the car, 'is to not be afraid. What's going to happen, I'm going to drop him, or break him? Fred doesn't care – do you? – you're just glad to be out.'

'Yie.'

Nic pushes the chair, popping wheelies, encouraging Fred to use his bent, twisted hands to shoplift: 'Go ahead, take it. What are they going to do, arrest you?'

And Fred seems thrilled; he smiles. 'Yie,' he says.

'Two cafe con leches,' Nic says to a vendor.

'Is he allowed that?'

'Fred, are you allowed to drink coffee?' Nic says loudly, like maybe Fred is a little deaf.

'Yie,' Fred says, and then the coffee comes, and Nic slowly feeds the man his cup of coffee. 'Good, right?' Nic uses a napkin to wipe drool off Fred's face. 'How are you going to get the girls if you're drooling?'

Fred smiles.

'See you next week,' Nic says when they return Fred to his mom. 'And if you need me sooner, make them call me.'

Fred points to the sign that says 'Phone Nic' that's taped to the wall by his bed.

'I really liked your dad,' Richard says when they're back outside.

'He's not my dad. I visit Fred because I can't visit my dad.'

'Dead?'

There's a pause. 'Sometimes you can't do things for the people you should do things for, including yourself, but you can do them for someone else, a stranger. Fred is a stranger. He is my stranger.'

'That's nice.'

'It is what it is. You could say I'm using him to make myself feel better and that would be true.'

'How'd you find him?'

'It's a program – Adopt a Golden Oldie – they interview you and you get someone. You want an old man? I'll give you the number. I picked Fred because he's trapped, because there's still someone in there, because no one else was going to pick him – he drools, and all he can say is "Yie."'

'You're good. Are you like one of those flower guys from the airport?'

'We're all good when we want to be, otherwise we're fucking animals. There is no VIP room in reality, and there is no reality in this city. You can't Google the answers. People talk about being on the ride of your life – THIS IS YOUR LIFE.' He takes a breath. 'Whatever it is you need to know, you already know. Imagine what it is to be in another country, another landscape – heat, insects, fear. Imagine watching someone right in front of you trip a wire, step on a mine, blow their body to shreds, in mid-sentence, mid-cigarette. Imagine yourself splattered with human flesh. Imagine talking to that boy for the five minutes when he is profoundly conscious of the fact that he is not going to make it home. Imagine the difference between that and being in upstate New York, drinking beer, trying to get laid, and spending the summer as life-guard at Lake George. Imagine zipping your friends into body bags. Tell me why anyone ever thought this was a good idea. How could anyone not be angry? You'd have to be insane.'

He stops. There is silence.

'Do you mind,' Nic says, 'while we're out, could we stop and see my producer? I keep cashing the checks, but I should say hello. Nice to have a face to put with it. Just down here, onto Melrose, a little further, and then in that gate.'

'Morning,' Nic says to the guard at the gate.

'Morning, sir,' the man says, going around the outside of the car with a mirror that lets him look underneath for bombs. A dog sniffs the car.

'Could you pop the trunk for me, please?' the man asks, and Richard does.

'Who are you seeing today?' the man asks Nic.

'Evan Roberts.'

'One moment,' the guard says, going into the booth.

'I don't think I've ever been inside a movie studio before,' Richard says.

'There's nothing to see, it's just buildings; make a left,' Nic says, directing him to the bungalows at the back of the lot. He gets out, leaving Richard in the car. 'It'll just take a couple of minutes.'

A woman drives by in a golf cart. She waves. He waves back. She looks at the car. 'Hey, you're that guy from yesterday; are you taking some meetings, selling your story?'

'Just waiting for a friend.'

When she's gone, Richard gets out and runs his hand over the car; the scratches are deep, like scars, a whole new topography. He closes his eyes and reads the car as if he were a blind person. He reads the car while reviewing the 'incident' in his mind's eye. The story – what is the story? What is he doing, and would he do it again?

Nic comes bounding out, gets into the car, slamming the door. 'Thank you very much,' he says. 'I'm so glad I took care of that; they'll never hire me again.'

'Why?'

'As soon as they meet you, the shine is off.'

'Then why'd you do it?'

'Because the guy is a little shit and I don't want to work for him – there's some strange pleasure in it for me letting him think it was his decision.'

Richard glances at the clock on the dash. 'I'm late, I have to meet my nutritionist. What's the fastest way to Santa Monica? I hope you don't mind.'

'I don't mind. In fact, I'm hungry.'

Richard can't bring himself to say she doesn't make extra, she only makes enough for however many people you order for.

They pull into the parking lot, four minutes late. 'Sorry, I got stuck. Sylvia, this is Nic, my neighbor.'

'So you're a nutritionist?' Nic says, smiling. 'Can you tell me what to eat so I'll live forever?'

'I can tell you what to eat so that you'll feel good.'

'Could you feed me those things? That's what you do, right – you feed people?'

'I could feed you,' she says, 'like you're a baby bird, but I'd have to get a medicine dropper. For the moment, I could give you a warm cookie; I have some fresh cookies in the car.'

'I could eat a fresh cookie,' Nic says, and Sylvia goes into the car and pulls out a bag of her special energy cookies. 'My number is on the label,' she says. 'Call me when you're really hungry.'

'I don't get it,' Richard says when they're back in the car.

'Oh, please, we were just chatting. Don't worry, I'm not going to steal her. You know what Santa Monica needs?'

'What?'

'A Donut Depot. Your friend Anhil should open a donut-and-juice bar.'

'I'll keep that in mind.'

They drive without talking. 'Come on, it's not my fault that she liked me.'

'I just don't get it. You're thoroughly cranky and kind of mangy-looking, and yet she threw herself at you.'

'They like that, the scruffy thing – it makes them think they can polish you up. And, not to change the subject, but you'd better get your car fixed soon: it drives like shit, and the temperature light just went on. You can use the Bentley if you want – it drives like a yacht.'

'You're miserable, and yet you're not a bad guy.'

'Is that a compliment?'

Back at the house, as he's putting the food in the refrigerator, the dog appears at the sliding glass door. He gives the dog more of the chicken and rice from last night. 'Did you miss me?'

On an impulse, he picks up the phone and calls his parents. Maybe it's something about the dog, or the visit to the nursing home.

'Hi, Mom.'

'We were wondering if you'd ever call again. I don't know what you've got yourself into, some crazy life-style . . .'

'I just wanted you to know I'm fine.'

'Of course you're fine, I know you're fine, there's no reason you shouldn't be fine. You're a young man; everything is not about you – your father had a little episode.'

'What happened?'

'He forgot who he was. We were in the grocery store, he was talking to some woman, she asked him his name, and he couldn't remember, and she asked if he had a wife and he said no, and all the time I'm standing ten feet away, looking right at him. I started waving. And he still didn't see me. I took him from the grocery store right to the doctor, who said it was one of those transient attacks. I don't want you to worry – even if he doesn't know who I am, I'll take care of him. After all these years, it's not like I can walk out on him.'

'Maybe he was just picking up girls.'

'He told the woman he was never married and that he had no children.'

'Does he know who you are now?'

'Yes, he claims the incident never happened, that I made the whole thing up.'

'Well, it's good he's feeling better.' Richard smells smoke. 'I have to go,' he says.

'Of course you do – you always have to go.'

Something smells. He goes from room to room, sniffing. There is nothing, no smoke. He opens the front door – all the trash cans up and down the street, trash cans put out this morning for collection, are on fire. Some are smoldering, some have flames shooting up. How did that happen, did a pyro drive by, squirt a little butane in each can, and toss in a match? He turns on the garden hose and puts out the four cans within reach. People driving by beep their horns. Unable to tell how far in either direction the cans are burning, he goes in and dials 911.

'Police, fire, emergency.'

'Fire,' he says.

'Los Angeles Fire Department.'

'I'm calling about trash cans on the Pacific Coast Highway. I smelled smoke and opened the door, and all the trash cans are on fire. I put out the ones I could reach, but there are more.'

'Checking. Yes, I have a report of a trash-can fire in our system.'

'It's not a trash-can fire, it's fires. Is someone coming?'

'Sir, what is your name?'

In the distance he hears sirens. He hangs up and goes outside again. A fire engine is coming down the highway. Not wanting to be late for his first Gyrotonics class, he jumps in the car and takes off. A piece of metal falls to the ground.

Walking into Malibu Gyrotonics is like entering another world: the air is without temperature, neither warm nor cool, but entirely even, equal, and smells like salt.

'I'm Sydney,' a woman says, extending her hand. Sydney is curvy in a way few women are curvy – she is not a small woman, not a large woman, but a curvaceous woman in a one-piece leotard.

'Have you previously experimented with Gyrotonics?' she asks.

'I used to have a trainer; we did weights, yoga, stretching,' he says. 'And I used to get on the treadmill every morning for an hour.'

'Used to – when did you stop?'

'Very recently. My house is . . . under construction, and the treadmill isn't accessible right now.'

'Do you have any health issues, medical problems you're being treated for, back, knees, hips, any artificial parts?'

'All original hardware,' he says.

She leads him into the room and begins by having him perform a series of simple movements.

'Taken from swimming, dance, yoga, and gymnastics. The Gyrotonic method is a series of undulating circular movements. There are breathing patterns that work with the movements to release blockages and stimulate the nervous system.'

She is testing him, bending and flexing. 'The exercises begin in the sacral area of the spine and are done with rhythm and flow, moving uninterrupted through flexion and extension, contraction and expansion. Our goal is increased muscular strength, endurance, range of motion, coordination, and balance.' She pauses and repositions him. He tries not to resist. She presses against him.

'Your pelvis is very closed,' she says. 'Take a breath. It's not unusual for men to have tight hips.'

Richard is aware of her hands on his hips, aware of something giving way, a kind of crunch or crack. Later, near the end of the session, she has him facedown and works her elbows in the cheeks of his ass. The whole thing feels more personal and intimate than what he is used to. Unlike his regular shapeless trainer, this one cannot lean over him without touching him. And there is something about the tightness of her leotard, the shape of her, soft but firm, that makes him want to squeeze her. She wears her long hair back in some sort of ponytail; he wants to play horse, to ride her. And he is shocked by what he is thinking. He finishes the workout feeling energized, released, embarrassed.

Driving back, he passes a 'Falling Rock' sign and then a pile of rubble by the side of the road. He drives around it, swinging wide into the next lane.

Up ahead are the trash cans: melted molten blobs, strange sculptures, like burned aliens by the side of the road. There are smoke streaks up the telephone poles, as though they've been hit by lightning. He parks. The houses are at the edge of the highway and so close together that they actually touch. Up and down the highway someone has staple-gunned sheets of paper to the phone poles: 'Have you seen this?' Below there is a drawing of 'this,' an ovoid shape with light beaming out from the bottom, and a phone number to call.

'What smells?' Nic asks, sticking his head out a window. 'Like lightning.'

'Someone lit the trash cans on fire – how'd you miss it?'

'I was working,' Nic said.

The window frames Nic's head exactly. Richard can see that he's got the headphones around his neck, in standby position.

'Are you all right?' Richard asks.

'Oh yeah, I'm fine. I'd come out but I'm hooked up right now, and, besides, there's someone across the street again, taking pictures, and I'm not feeling photogenic.'

'Have the signs always been there?' Richard points to the signs.

'Sometimes you see a lot of them and sometimes none for months.' Does Nic mean a lot of the Xeroxed notices or the thing itself, whatever it is? 'Maybe I'll see you later,' Nic says, retreating.

According to their e-mail log, the boys are getting closer to Los Angeles. Richard is nervous. He calls his ex-wife. 'I don't know if I'm ready. I'm in this new place, it's all very unfamiliar.'

'Well, if you don't want him, send him on.'

'I didn't say I didn't want him, I said I don't know if I'm ready. I'm having memories.'

'Of what?'

'Everything: the day he was born, when we all went on vacation, me coming to New York always carrying things, the thing with the dog.'

He doesn't go into details, though he has them all in his mind's eye. Remembering. At some point the dog had a real name, like Rocket or Sparks, but they always called him Your Brother.

'Your Brother loves you,' they'd say. 'Did anyone take Your Brother out? Have you seen Your Brother? I think Your Brother's got something – a shoe.' They got Ben his brother when Ben was six months old – a Lab puppy. Later, when they had the big talk, telling Ben that things were going to change, Your Brother lay at their feet, tail wagging. 'Your mother and I have decided . . .' It was Your Brother who comforted Ben, Your Brother who was his constant companion.

Richard remembers coming home when both Ben and Your Brother were very young, finding the occasional puddle of pee on the floor, and both Ben and the dog looking a little guilty. He remembers walking the dog at night, the beauty of New York City in the early morning, the dewy air, the sleepy fog, the dog culture of knowing other people only by the names of their dogs.

At fifteen, Ben called in tears.

'What happened?'

'Brother died.'

Three thousand miles away, Richard didn't know what to say. 'How?' The father heard his son cry, and not having heard the faintest sound, the faintest squeak, out of the boy in years, Richard began to cry. He hid it at first, and then it poured out, and suddenly there was silence on the other end.

'What are you doing?' the son accused the sobbing father.

'I'm so sorry,' Richard cried.

'Stop crying, asshole,' Ben said and hung up the phone.

Outside, it is starting to rain. The beach dog is still out there, playing at the edge of the water, entertaining himself with a piece of floating wood. Richard opens the door; the dog hears it and rushes up the steps and into the house, as if to say, I've been waiting all day for you to invite me in.

'I don't have a cleaning lady,' Richard tells the dog. 'Be mindful.'

'Kibble,' Richard writes on the grocery list.

At four-thirty, Cynthia is back. 'I bought you a present. Something I didn't think you'd buy for yourself.'

He opens the bag – a cell phone.

'Next time you're rescuing someone, you can call for backup.'

'It's great. Thank you.' A pause. 'So – how was it?'

'Nice,' she says. 'Really nice.' She takes the cell phone, plugs it into the wall. 'It has to soak up the juice.'

'Tell me.'

'OK, so you get there and they offer you coffee and this woman who was a dental hygienist and went back to school and became a social worker is there. She asks a lot of questions: where'd you grow up, how long have you been married, did you go to college, do you have any work experience, where do you see yourself in one year, in five years? And then you do some tests.'

'Tests?' He imagines medical tests, painful tests.

She nods. 'According to the tests, I'm a people person, and from just looking at me she could tell I had good teeth – I think that was the hygienist part of her. And then they took my picture.'

'Just don't let them draw on it.'

'What?'

'That's what they do, they take a grease pencil and draw improvements on your face.'

She shakes her head. 'The best part is, I'm not the only one. There are five other women, and one has six kids. One woman works part-time at Saks, another works at a computer store, and then there's someone who does wildlife rescue.'

'They all left their husbands?'

'No, some stayed. There's a woman there who cut off the ends of three of her fingers while she was cooking dinner. Her family kept eating; none of them would stop to look for the fingertips – she assumes they ate them – cannibals. Why are you being so male about this? You don't have to be defensive and you don't have to protect me, I can take care of myself.'

'It's just the plastic-surgeon part that bothers me.'

'It's run by the women and has nothing to do with the doctor.'

'Except that he foots the bill.'

'Can't someone do something good without making everyone suspicious? Why don't you go and meet him, pretend you want to have something done?'

'Like what?'

'Dunno. Eyelids.'

'Do my eyelids need work?'

'Need work? Well, your eyes open and close, so,

no, your eyelids don't need work. After lunch, I went to look at an apartment, a two-bedroom in Santa Monica. I'd have a housemate, a lovely woman who's taking a little break. She lost it, and now she's on some sort of medication.'

'How long do people stay with the program?'

'As long as they need to,' she says. 'And I got moisturizer.' She flashes a handful of samples.

The phone rings.

'I'm going to take a bath,' she says, leaving the room. 'A nice long bath.'

Richard picks up the phone. 'I'm calling about the car.' It's Danny, the dealer.

'How did you find me?'

'We have our ways. I was hoping you'd call us; technically, we own the car. Do I not take good care of you? You were my first day on the job, my first deal, you made my day, you think that doesn't mean something to me?'

'Thanks, Danny.'

'Have you called your insurance agent?'

'Not about the car, no.'

'You need to call the agent; you need a copy of the accident report. The complication is going to be that it was willful.'

'It was for a good cause.'

'This type of damage violates the terms of your lease, but I want you to know that we're prepared to overlook it; we'll absorb the cost above what your insurance will cover, minus the deductible, if you write us a nice letter telling the story of how the car was damaged and how good we were about repairing it. We'll take a few pictures of you with the car, frame it, and put it up on the wall. The owner wants people to see that we are part of the community, and, frankly, we think the car performed incredibly well.'

'The trick was getting him off the road without hitting his trunk,' Richard says. 'Can I think about it?'

'The sooner we get it into the shop the better.'

Something catches Richard's eye and he goes to the front of the house – flashing lights. He looks out the window. A flatbed is already outside, loading the car onto the platform.

'I'm assuming that's your guy.'

'It is.'

'Doesn't he need a key?'

'We have a key, we always keep a key.'

'Do I get a loaner?'

'I don't have anything at the moment, but maybe something will come in tomorrow. Give a call.'

Richard steps outside.

'You're not going to try and fight me for it, are you?' the flatbed driver asks.

Richard shakes his head.

'That's a good boy,' the driver says, and Richard isn't sure if the man is talking to him or to his truck.

Without the car, there is no means of escape, there's nowhere to go. He feels the vulnerability of having something taken from him, as if he's done something wrong and is being punished.

'Have you seen this?' The sheets of paper on the phone poles are bothering him. What is it about, what does this person want? He pulls down one of the posters, goes back into the house, and dials the number given.

A man answers, says 'Yeah' and nothing more.

'Are you there?'

'Yeah.'

'I'm just trying to find out what these signs are about.'

'Did you see something?'

'Lots of pieces of paper up and down the highway.'

Keep looking,' the man says and hangs up.

Richard overhears Cynthia on the phone talking to her children. 'Write this down. Orthodontist for you three p.m. on Thursday; eye doctor for Matt Tuesday at four – make sure he brings his glasses. The camp forms are due; call Dr Pearl's office and get them filled out. Also, ask if they can send prescriptions for your allergy medicine to take with you.' She stops for air. 'How's everything going? Daddy had to buy you new clothes because you ran out of clean ones and he didn't have time to do the wash? That's OK,' she says. 'I'll talk to you again soon, bye-bye.'

'They took the car,' Richard says when she's off the phone. 'I have no way out, no means of escape.'

'We're fine,' Cynthia says. 'We can always call a

taxi or you can just rent a car.' Seeing that he's upset, she adds, 'It'll be nice; we'll make dinner, and we can play a game.'

'Like what?'

'I saw Scrabble in the cupboard.'

'We don't have to make dinner – it's here. I picked up a supply from the nutritionist this afternoon; we've got food for a week.'

'Why aren't you married?' she says, intending it as a compliment. 'Do we have to both eat the same thing?'

'Whatever you want.'

'I want us to each eat something different, I don't want to be the same, eat the same, live the same. The salmon looks good.'

'Fine, you have salmon and I'll take the turkey meatloaf,' Richard says, taking out the salmon, the meatloaf, the ginger green beans, a beet salad, and some mesclun mix. 'I don't like this business with them coming to get the car without talking to me; I feel like a kid who just borrowed it from Dad.'

'I guess that's the way it goes when you lease.'

'Well, I'm not doing that again.'

'Hopefully you won't have to run anyone off the road again either.'

He finds Scrabble. 'Do you want to play while we eat, or eat first and then play?'

'Let's be civilized; we'll eat and then play.' He pours them each a glass of wine, she lights some candles, and they sit down to dinner. The sliding glass doors to the deck are open, there is the soft crash of evening waves, and the wind carries in the delicate sounds of neighbors talking.

'How come I can't do this with my husband?' she asks.

'Did you ever?'

'I can't remember. If we did it was a long time ago. Is it strange too that you and I haven't . . .'

'We're not in a position to.'

'That doesn't stop most people.'

'I like to think we're being mature.'

'Or monkish. I haven't slept with anyone new in eighteen years,' she says. 'Do you find me . . . Forget it,' she says, interrupting herself. 'I shouldn't have asked.' Cynthia seems annoyed. 'That was the one thing with Andy that was still good; we did it all the time, even if we didn't speak all day or we got into bed hating each other, we always did it.'

'Really?' Richard is surprised. 'Did you want to?'

She nods. 'It was the only way I didn't hate him.'

'I would have thought you wouldn't want him anywhere near you.'

'As bad as he was, there was something different at night; he was like a little boy – it used to drive me crazy – he was so needy, clingy, but eventually I kind of liked it.'

Hearing this is confusing for Richard, almost exciting: the idea of Cynthia and her husband screwing. He imagines the children asleep down the hall, cool blue nightlights glowing in the electric sockets, Cynthia with her long nightgown hiked up, getting it from Andy.

She clears the dishes off the table; Richard watches her, looking at her in a different way. He thinks about his wife's body. She didn't really have much of a body: small, thin, flat-chested. He always liked her body; when he thinks about it, he remembers in detail: nipples like snow caps, the curl of her pubic hair . . . He stops.

'Tell me about your children,' Richard says, pouring the last of the wine.

'Why don't I tell you about the minivan, what I keep in the minivan: change of clothes, one full set per kid, shoes included, each in a plastic bag, and then just a few spare pairs of socks; some old sneakers; maxi-pads for the girl, who lives in fear of one day getting her period; a laundry bag – I got tired of fishing dirty jockstraps out from under the seat, or, worse, when they get caught in the seat controls and you have to cut them free; bottles of water, Gatorade, snack bars, cheese sticks, and if it's a long day, meals, whole meals, sandwiches, salads – the girl won't eat bread, fresh fruit – they're perpetually constipated except when they eat Doritos and then they get diarrhea. And not only do I have to have enough food for my kids, but if I'm carpooling, it's like Meals on Wheels, or some sort of a soup kitchen. I feed them, drop them off, and literally have to shovel debris out of the car. I rigged a curtain around the third row so they can change clothes back there if they have to. How many hours a day am I in the car? On a good day three, on a bad day could be six.

Carpooling, I'm like an airline – if I don't get them where they're going on time with all their luggage, it's my fault.'

'What are they like as people?'

She shakes her head. 'I don't know. I must have given them the wrong impression about how you treat other people. I just hope they figure it out, learn to take care of themselves, and, maybe one day, they'll notice that they're living in a world with other people and not everything is about what they want.'

'Are you going to invite them to the apartment in Santa Monica?'

'Not yet, I need to keep it for myself for a while.' Cynthia opens the Scrabble box. 'What's the story with your boy?' she asks.

Richard picks his letters. 'He doesn't want to talk to me.'

'He's coming out here but not talking to you?'

Richard nods. 'I assume it's a good thing he's coming, he wants something, some form of contact, but there's a lot to get over. I left him; parents aren't supposed to leave their children. I don't know that I can expect anything – he's a tough nut. He gets that from his mother.'

'And you.'

Richard starts the game with *cascade*.

Cynthia builds *sorrow* off of it.

Richard goes with *wince*.

Cynthia tops with *excel*. 'Will you visit me at the new apartment and bring Scrabble with you?'

'Yes. You know, you're really good. When did you last play a game?'

'I used to have to play Candy Land with the little one because no one else would. And you?'

'My wife and I would do the crossword together in bed – she'd say, "What's another word for buffet?" and I'd give her "credenza." That was one of our better moments.'

The eleven o'clock news is dominated by another in a series of sightings of what is being described as a saber-toothed cat.

'According to experts, the cat has been extinct for eleven thousand years – but in recent months there have been sightings, with some very clear descriptions. Authorities are struggling to determine if the recent increase in sightings is of significance or a form of "copycat" hysteria. In a similar case, police are investigating the apparent murder of a horse earlier in the week, and expect to know soon if it is linked to the alleged big cat. Channel 4 reporter Elizabeth Olsen spoke with experts at Los Angeles' Paige Museum.

'What is the reality – is there a saber-tooth among us?'

'Highly unlikely; if they're seeing anything, it's a mountain lion.'

'Is there such a thing as an animal coming back from extinction?'

'Any species that's been extinct for eleven thousand years would be hard-pressed to resurface.

However, there is the possibility that someone – say, an animal trafficker in South America, where a few cats have been sighted – smuggled one into the country. We've seen a lot of that in recent years: exotic animals brought in for domestic purposes and then released when the owner can't handle the animal. We've had snakes, lions and tigers, monkeys, the occasional gorilla.'

'There must not be any news,' Cynthia says.

Richard shrugs – the idea of the cat, rising again after being extinct for eleven thousand years, appeals to him. Even if it's not possible, it should be.

At eleven-thirty-five, Leno kicks off with a joke about Richard: 'Did you hear about the guy who ran that car off the road the other day – you know, the one that was blinking SOS with the girl in the trunk? Well, his was repossessed – apparently the charge of reckless driving violated the lease. Save a life, lose your car – makes sense?'

Is it better to become a crossword clue or a joke on *Leno*?

Leno continues, 'Also in the news, the Chinese president today said he was giving up fried lice for Lent – or was that Rent?'

In his bedroom, Richard goes online. He does a little after-hours work – shuffling the deck, there is something to be said for constant vigilance, everything at its price.

He checks his e-mail. The boys are twenty-four hours away. Maybe it's good that Cynthia found a place of her own – it would be hard with her here and Ben and Barth.

In the middle of the night, the dog jumps up onto the bed. Richard feels him pressing against his leg and somehow thinks it's his ex-wife, warm, reassuring. In the morning, the dog is on his back in the middle of the bed; Richard gets up without waking him.

The contractor calls at 7:00 a.m. 'When's a good time to bring over my glass man? He needs to measure in order to get the estimate.'

'I don't have a car today,' Richard says.

'Well, let's just make the appointment and you'll figure it out,' the contractor says. 'Let's call it one-thirty.'

'Do you mind if I borrow some of these?' Cynthia asks, dividing a package of Sylvia's high-fiber carob cookies into two Ziploc bags.

'Go ahead,' he says.

She puts the cookies into two brown-bag lunches she's made. 'For the kids,' she says. 'I'm going to drop them off this morning before rehab. Well, I'm not going to drop them off. Evelyn, my ride from the program, will run into the school and deliver them – a hit-and-run nutrition attack. I'm worried that they've had nothing decent to eat. Andy probably stops at the McDonald's drive-through on the way to school and gets them McNuggets to go.'

'I can't imagine they'd eat cold McNuggets.'

'Oh,' she says, 'you'd be surprised. They probably find a way to heat them – the microwave in the teachers' lounge, a Bunsen burner – they're very crafty when they want to be.'

A horn beeps – Cynthia's ride. She throws a couple of apples into the lunch bags.

'Do you need us to drop you?'

He shakes his head. 'I'll figure it out.'

'Have a nice day,' Cynthia says, and Richard is terrified – did she really say that?

Richard gets dressed and goes to see Nic about borrowing the car. He rings the bell. He knocks on the door. He pounds. And then he turns the knob. 'Hello, anybody home?'

'In here,' Nic whispers.

'I've been knocking, ringing, banging.'

'I know.'

'Why not just answer the door?'

'Come closer and I'll give you a clue.'

'Why are you whispering?' Richard goes farther into the house and finds Nic laid out on the dining-room table. 'My back. Can't get up, couldn't get down, can't talk loud.'

'How long have you been there?'

'End of the day yesterday.'

'What happened?'

'I was on a conference call; I bent to pick a piece of paper up from the floor and couldn't get up. I crawled over here, managed to roll myself up onto the table. The worst part was, the call kept going. They were on speakerphone and just went on

289

talking – blah, blah, blah. They had no idea, despite the fact that at one point I screamed and started swearing.'

'Can I get you anything? Do you want me to call someone?'

'Could you just get me a plastic bag with some ice in it – a bag inside of another plastic bag, and then maybe wrap it in a dish towel? I don't want to get water marks on the table. It was my grandmother's.'

'It's very nice,' Richard says. The table is old-fashioned, elegant, seems entirely antithetical to Nic's personality.

'My mother's mother.'

Richard brings a pillow and the ice. 'And can you bring the little vials that are in the fridge, the ones with the green tops? I'll take a little of my recipe.'

Richard follows Nic's instructions, squirting two drops of this one, four of that, and a full dropper of another into Nic's mouth.

'How long were you going to lie there?'

'I figured either it would get better or someone would show up. I wasn't worried. Do me a favor,' Nic says, 'hang up the phone, it's probably still an open line to Burbank.'

'Do you want me to try and help you stand?'

Richard is looking down at Nic laid out; images flash – everything from the table as part of an operating room, to Nic as some sort of weird Jolly Green Giant; his feet are hanging off the end.

'Why don't you just pull up a chair and sit?'

He takes a seat in one of the dining-room chairs at the top of the table, near Nic's head – it's a little like sitting at a hospital bedside, a little like analysis.

'Were you talking about a new film when your back went out?' Richard asks, making conversation.

'It didn't go "out," it went into spasm, paroxysms of misery. And, yes, we were talking about a script I wrote. They were "giving me notes," which were starting to seem like they wanted me to write an entirely different film, and I kept thinking, That's a whole other movie, and if you want me to write that one you're going to have to pay me more, a lot more, because I already wrote this movie, which is the movie you told me you wanted. Every now and then one of them gets to me; it's usually a kid who studied film theory – movies are not about theory, it's a formula for belief, for selling popcorn.'

'How many films have you written?'

'Fifteen or twenty. Can you pour me a drink?'

'It's not even nine in the morning.'

'It was a long night.'

'How about some Advil?'

'Useless.'

'OK, how about a real muscle relaxant?'

'Let's give the recipe a few minutes.'

Richard nods and they both dip into silence. He sits by Nic's head, not talking, watching Nic, who has gone deep inside himself. Richard watches Nic's breathing, conscious, deeply measured. He closes his own eyes, breathes, realizes how much he misses meditating with people, realizes how little he's been breathing. They sit – just breathing.

'All right,' Nic says, jerking Richard out of the silence. 'I hate to do it, it fucks me up, but I can't lie here forever. Bring me a couple of Percocet and a Valium – they're in the bathroom.'

'Percocet *and* Valium?'

'It's not like I haven't done this before.'

Richard brings him the drugs and some water and then sits again at Nic's head. 'So I called that number that was on the phone pole . . .'

'And?'

'A guy answered. I said that I was looking for more information. He asked if I'd seen anything, and when I said no, he said, "Keep looking," and hung up on me.'

Nic nods.

'Do you think there's something out there?'

'I believe in staying open to possibility. What is the point of not believing, closing the door? Just leave it open, see what comes in. Contact – people want contact – if they can't find it here they'll go elsewhere.'

'What about the saber-tooth, do you think he's real?'

'I like the idea of it, nature coming back and kicking our asses. And I think he's a she, a bitch for sure.'

There's a pause.

'Last night Cynthia told me that she and her husband had sex all the time. I found it weirdly exciting – I haven't had sex in years.'

'Years?'

'Is that weird? How often do you?'

'Twice last week.'

'With who?'

'Lady friends; I'm weird but I'm not dead. Maybe you need to see a doctor.'

'I did. I mean I am, I've been going.'

At a certain point Nic feels better enough to roll over and have Richard smear BenGay on his back. 'Warm it first; I'm in pain but not without feeling, you know.'

Nic's back is hairy, sweaty, thick, meaty. Richard feels odd touching him; he's never touched another man's back before. He smears the BenGay on quickly, unevenly, slapping it on like suntan lotion. He flashes on a memory of his mother putting suntan lotion on his father's hairy shoulders, on himself as a little boy at the beach, watching.

'You have to really rub it,' Nic says. 'Work it into the muscle.'

'I have the name of a good masseur,' Richard says.

'You're doing fine. That's good, right there – that's the spot.'

'Better?'

'Much, thank you.'

'My son will be here in less that twenty-four hours,' Richard blurts. 'What if he gets here and it doesn't work? I don't even know the kid.'

Nic rolls himself to sitting. 'You want in on a secret? I have a kid.' Nic says it in a way that lets Richard know that not only does he know what Richard is talking about, but also that he's not the person to turn to for good counsel. 'A little girl, Faith, I haven't seen her in a year. Her mom left me for another woman. Sandra, my ex, is black and wanted to move back into the black community and has absolutely no use for me. I became the enemy.'

'Except that the girl is your daughter.'

'That's exactly my point – and the boy is your son, and something is bringing him out here; you'll do the best you can.'

'You should see your girl.'

'Yeah,' Nic says, easing himself off the table. 'I should see my girl. In fact, I'm going to put it on my list.' He taps his head, indicating where he keeps the list. 'So what can I do for you, there's a reason you came knocking?'

'I was wondering if I could borrow your car; they took mine.'

'The keys are by the door.'

'Do I just leave you here?'

'Help me to the sofa and I'll try and sleep my way through it.'

'I asked my ex-wife what Ben is like,' Richard tells Nic as he's helping him. 'She said four years ago the shrink told her he needs parents. It's not like she ever told me – what if it's too late?'

Richard takes surface roads – Olympic to Bundy to Santa Monica, past the Beverly Hills Hotel. The Bentley is beautiful, built as if an artist put it together – the seat belt, a modest single strap lying limp across his waist, guaranteeing only that his body would be found near the scene if there were a crash.

Bentley drives with a kind of elegance that's hard to describe; the fineness of the car makes Richard drive more slowly, leisurely, as if on parade. Did John Lennon ever actually drive the car, or was he just driven in it? Richard glances over his shoulder into the back seat, picturing the long-haired Beatle in his white suit sitting with Yoko at his side.

In a city full of Beemers and Mercedes, where even modest folks drive beyond their means, Bentley is eccentric, rich, and a little freakish. People stare. Richard waves – he doesn't know what else to do.

As he winds up the hill, he sees a 'For Sale' sign on the swimmer's house. He's secretly pleased – good, someone new will come, a fresh muse.

He stops outside his house. When he looks at it through Bentley's windshield, the house looks smaller. It's all about perspective. When he bought the house, he was coming from New York, where everyone lived in an apartment, and by comparison the house seemed spacious, extravagant. Now, when he is coming from Malibu, with the full expanse of the Pacific outside, the house feels pinched, like a hamster hut but for a man. He goes in. The high, clean smell, the perpetual polish it had when Cecelia was there, is missing.

He collects his mail – catalogues, bills, an envelope from the Golden Door with Cynthia's name scrawled above the return address. It is a letter written on stationery from the Four Seasons, the Golden Door, and free postcards she picked up along the way, and on the back of a long piece of cash register receipt – each page/card is numbered.

As I write this I keep telling myself to stop, tear it up, find what I'm trying to say on a nice Hallmark card from aisle 14, something with a picture of a duck dancing in the rain – Thinking of You. I keep thinking I should rip it up but then I keep writing. I just want to thank you for giving me a chance to open my life again after it's been closed for so long. I feel like I've been let out – saved would not be too extreme. Out of nowhere there you were in the produce section, you've taken care of me and asked for nothing in return – no one has ever taken care of me like that. That's my job!

This is the person he wants to be. He wants to be able to do this for others, strangers, it doesn't matter who, and he wants to be able to do it for himself. He flashes on his father – why his father twice in one day? – his father looking at his grades, practically straight A's, and saying, 'And you think that's good enough? Did anyone else do better?'

He reads the letter again; it makes him feel good, much improved.

'Glad it worked out,' the contractor says, coming into the house without knocking.

'Car's in the shop,' Richard says, folding the letter and putting it in his pocket.

'This is Luigi, he's working with me on another house nearby. It's the obvious panels,' the contractor says, pointing out the broken windows to Luigi.

'Why do you have this kind of glass?' Luigi asks Richard.

'It was here when I bought the house.'

'This glass is no good; it doesn't surprise me that this happened. They don't even make this glass anymore – I can get it for you special, but it doesn't come like this, no one wants it. Everyone wants double-pane.'

'More expensive,' the contractor says.

'Yes, but this is not a poor man's house.'

'Fine, then, put the double-pane in,' Richard says.

The contractor shakes his head. 'You can't just put a few in. The double-panes look entirely different; you'd have to do the whole house.'

'Then don't, just make it how it was . . . That's what I really want, I want to be able to pretend this never happened.'

'So American, pretend it never happened, that's how you get into trouble – always pretending something. You should take care of it, make it better.'

'What would that involve?'

'Big windows like these, maybe seventy-five thousand. I do a good job – yes.'

'No, let's just replace the windows that are broken.'

'OK, you are the boss, I'm not going to argue with you.' He takes out his metal measuring tape, slaps it against the windows, and speaks the measurements into a little recorder he keeps with him. 'I make no mistakes,' he says, whipping the metal tape from window to window.

Should Richard go for the better windows? How much longer is he going to be in this house?

'You're thinking too hard,' the contractor says. 'It'll look great. Just relax.'

The message light on his answering machine is blinking; someone wants to come clean his chimney – he doesn't even know if he has a chimney – more TV producers, and a message from Ben – 'We'll be there tomorrow. I'll call when we're closer.'

Richard changes his outgoing message: 'If this is Ben, call me on my cell; all other callers, wait for the beep.'

As Richard is leaving, Cynthia's husband, Andy, pops out from behind a bush and rushes up into Richard's face. 'What are you doing, what the fuck are you doing with my wife?'

'I'm not doing anything. Were you hiding behind the bush?'

'You must be doing something, because she's gone. She walked out on me, on the kids – now I don't even know where the fuck she is.' The husband pushes Richard.

'Are you looking for a fight? Because I'm not going to fight you.'

'You're not going to fight me,' he says, pushing Richard again.

'Look, buddy, I'm not your problem. You and Cynthia have to work it out.'

'Don't tell me you're not fucking her,' he says.

Richard doesn't know what to say: You shouldn't be here. You should be at work. You're acting like a real bozo.

'Mr Goody-Goody, Mr Fucking Samaritan.' Bozo is now pushing Richard all over the yard, one push, two push. 'Was that girl in the trunk some other little project you picked up along the way? Put my wife in your trunk and I'll fucking kill you.'

'For the record, I was the one who got the girl out of the trunk, not the one who put her in – that's what makes me a Good Samaritan.'

'It's kind of the glass-half-empty phenomenon, isn't it?' Andy says. 'I've got my eye on you, twenty-four fucking hours a day, I'm watching you. And you can tell my wife that the free ride only lasts so long. She still has my credit cards, but all it takes is one phone call and she's dry.'

'You know what?' Richard says. 'You're bothering

me. You're a bully and you're on my property, so leave, how about that – go away, leave me alone.'

'I'm so intimidated.'

'I'm telling you to get off my property.'

The guy swats at him; Richard ducks. 'Fucking lay a hand on me, asshole, and I'll press charges; come back here again, give Cynthia a hard time, fucking do anything, and I'll know it's you,' Richard says, speaking to Bozo in his own language. 'I'll send you the fuck to jail, and your kids will end up in foster care – does that sound like the good life?' He stops and takes a breath. 'Have some grace, accept what is.'

The little white car with the yellow flashing lights pulls up – the government man.

'What's that, your personal police force, your goon squad? You're not man enough to take care of yourself?' Bozo trips over a clod of grass and cries out. 'I'll sue you, fucking my ankle.'

'Need a hand?' the government man asks from the curb.

'Fucking fuck,' Bozo says, storming off down the street.

'Was he high?'

'Grief-stricken,' Richard says.

The government man looks confused.

'Do you think he's coming back? Should we be armed?'

'There are golf clubs in the garage. So – how are you?'

'Pretty good. I got a bit part in this little play

downtown, and I'm still carrying this around.' He reaches into the car, pulls out the screenplay, and waves it at Richard, who now feels obligated to take it. 'Ground Motion.'

'Can't wait.'

'Don't mock. I just came by to give you some off-the-record information. Your hole is not as out of the blue as it initially appeared. It might well be water-related; everything in the history of Los Angeles is. You might be able to make a claim – get some money back. I don't make promises, but I suggest you have your lawyer be in touch with the Department. FYI,' the guy says. 'And you didn't hear it from me.'

Richard nods. 'Thanks.'

'My number is on the script, if you have any notes.'

Richard gets into Bentley and starts down the hill. As he's going down, the minivan comes speeding up; Richard swerves into a semicircular driveway and watches Bozo plow his minivan into a parked car. The air bag goes off, punching Bozo in the chest, knocking him out. Richard takes the cell phone out of his pocket, dials 911, asks for rescue, and says, 'A guy just smashed his minivan into a parked car. He may be injured. He's on Shadow Hill Way.'

'Is this the Good Samaritan?' the operator asks.

'It is,' Richard says.

'I thought I recognized your voice. We're on the way.'

★   ★   ★

301

He drives to Anhil's shop. The place is empty. 'Have you had lunch?'

Anhil pulls plastic containers out of the fridge. 'Lipi made lunch – would you like some?'

'How about we go out – my treat.'

'All right,' Anhil says.

'And can I borrow a phone book?'

'White or yellow?'

'Whichever is thicker.'

Anhil flips the 'Open' sign to 'Closed' and locks the door. 'Where is my beautiful queen?'

'In the shop – having a beauty treatment.'

'You want me to drive?'

'I borrowed a car,' Richard says, acting nonchalant. He leads Anhil to the Bentley.

'Oh my goodness. It is like you are the King of England, the man. Do you think I can drive it?'

'If you sit on this.' Richard hands him the phone book.

Anhil drives, bouncing up and down on the phone book, his foot on and off the gas like a New York cab driver. His excitement is difficult to contain. 'I am the man,' he says, pumping the gas.

'Do you know whose car this was?'

'Who?'

'John Lennon.'

'Not possible.'

Richard nods.

Anhil starts to sing 'Let It Be.' 'I felt very bad when he died, very bad; that is not good for any of us.'

Anhil guides the car into the drive-through at the In-and-Out Burger on Washington Boulevard. He rolls down the window. 'One four-by-four with extra mustard and . . .' He turns to Richard.

'A double-double, protein-style,' Richard says.

'What is protein-style?' Anhil asks.

'No bun; what's a four-by-four?'

'Four patties, four slices of cheese; I won't be hungry for a week.'

They go through the drive-through and then park and eat at a picnic table facing Washington Boulevard. 'We can't eat in the car,' Anhil says. 'That would be like using it as a bathroom. And don't tell Lipi. I'm not supposed to eat beef – against my beliefs – but this is so delicious, it bears no relation to a cow.'

'Ben will be here tomorrow,' Richard says – he has to tell someone.

'I am so looking forward to meeting him.'

'Thank you.'

'No – thank you. I can't believe my phone book is riding in John Lennon's car.'

On the way home, Richard stops at a party-supply store and buys a 'Welcome' sign for the front door. It's like something you'd put up for a four-year-old, or a returning hostage, but he can't help himself.

He goes from the party-supply to the grocery store – up and down the aisles, thinking that if Cynthia is going to be making lunches for her kids he'd better get some kid-friendly stuff – organic peanut butter, organic jelly, sandwich bread, soy chips, cheese sticks.

He calls his ex-wife from the store.

'She's in a meeting,' her assistant says. 'Can I take a message?'

'This is . . . Ben's father.' He can't bring himself to say 'ex-husband.' 'I'm trying to find out what Ben eats for lunch.'

'White tuna in water. I only know because sometimes I order the groceries. Avocado, bananas – very firm. Do you want me to just punch up the list I order from?'

'That would be great,' Richard says.

'Diet root beer, sliced turkey breast, turkey-noodle soup, English muffins, and I think the rest is hers; I don't think Ben is the one eating pink grapefruit and drinking Lactaid. Should I tell her you called?'

Across the street from the house there are two people taking pictures – who are they working for? He pulls off the highway, opens Nic's garage, and drives Bentley in. He's just put the car away when he sees Sylvia, the nutritionist, coming out of Nic's place.

'Oh, hi,' she says, awkwardly.

'The meatloaf was delicious,' Richard says, not knowing what else to say. 'How's his back?'

'Better. I did some trigger-point and put Tiger Balm on it.'

Richard nods. 'Are you bringing him food?'

'No, actually he's cooking for me. Steak. I'm just running out for horseradish; I have to have horseradish with steak.'

'I had no idea you ate meat.'

'Every now and then I crave it, but it has to be rare, almost bloody.'

'Tell him I said hi and that his car is back.'

'Will do,' Sylvia says, gunning her mini-SUV onto the highway.

After dinner, Richard helps Cynthia move. Considering that she has nothing, the move consists of their borrowing the Bentley again and driving to the nearest Target store.

Driving a Bentley to Target – only in L.A. does this make perfect sense.

They go up and down the aisles: toothpaste, shampoo, razor, blow-drier, deodorant – she confesses, 'I've been using yours.'

He likes the idea of his solid stick sliding over her armpits, picking up little pieces of hair, leaving her stubble stuck on his Mitchum.

'Do you think I need to buy my own sofa?' she says, half joking, when they get to the furniture aisle.

'I think you have to practice sleeping in a bed.'

Sheets, towels, pillow, coffee mug – does the apartment have a coffeemaker? Coffeemaker, alarm clock, slippers, two pairs of pants – 'Are these really OK, or do they just look OK because everything else is bad?'

'They're good.'

Richard throws in a DVD player for the Malibu house and a handful of movies so they'll have something to do when Ben comes. And toys for the dog.

'People love their pets more than their children,' Cynthia says.

At the checkout, Cynthia wants to put it all on her husband's charge card.

'Let me get it as a going-away present,' Richard insists. He imagines Bozo stalking Cynthia.

'Don't say "going-away,"' she says.

'OK, going down the road.'

'Can I still come for dinner?'

'Whenever you want.'

The apartment building is nice, modest. At the front door Richard meets the roommate. 'Are you the husband?'

'The friend,' he says.

'I don't like men,' the roommate says.

'Someone's got to carry the heavy stuff,' Richard says.

'I don't think he should come in,' the roommate says.

'He's coming in,' Cynthia says, pushing past the woman. 'I want him to see where I'm living.'

'Well, at least take off your shoes.'

He does, and then goes up and down the stairs and in and out of the building a half-dozen times with his socks on, and in the end throws the socks out, puts his shoes back on, and drives home.

Back at the house, he puts the Bentley in the garage and returns Nic's keys – dropping them through the mail slot. Sylvia's car is gone.

'I know you're out there,' Nic says, loudly. 'So you may as well come in.'

'How're you feeling?'

Nic winks.

'That happened pretty fast.'

'Get messy,' Nic says. 'Women love a man they think they can clean up.'

'Thanks for the car.'

'Nice, isn't it?'

'I felt like a prince.'

'You are a prince.'

Home alone – Richard is glad the dog is there. The night is quiet; he sleeps with the windows open, the rolling lull of the ocean outside.

The phone rings just as he's falling asleep. It's Cynthia whispering, 'In the fridge we each have our own shelf, she writes her name on everything that's HERS. And in the bathroom we have assigned towels and our own shelves in the medicine cabinet – she's got ten kinds of medication on her shelf.'

'Sleep,' Richard tells her.

'With one eye open,' she says.

In the morning, the woman with the yellow bathing cap is in the ocean again. He watches with binoculars, determined to see how far she goes and if/when she comes back. He tracks her until she is a yellow dot. A little while later, he looks again to see if she's swimming back – nothing. Is there such a thing as a one-way swim? Maybe she has it figured out, maybe she swims down and runs back – but how does she run without shoes, without clothes, without a towel? Maybe she has it set up, she swims down, climbs out of the ocean, walks to her office. She takes the elevator up, walks down the hall leaving squeaky wet footprints, goes into her office, dries her hair, and slips into her work clothes. Maybe her driver meets her at the Santa Monica Pier? Maybe she has a morning coffee date, maybe she's an Olympian in training? Maybe she. She maybe.

The car guy calls. 'You were a joke on *Leno*.'

'I heard.'

'Not funny, right? So you're going to write us the letter . . . ?'

'When will the car be ready?'

'A couple of days.'

'When you drop it off I'll give the guy the letter.'

'I take care of you, right?'

'You take care of me, right,' Richard says, hanging up.

The phone rings again. 'Is this Richard Novak?'

'How did you find me?'

'I was given your folder. I work for a debriefing company in conjunction with the Center for Healing Expression.'

'Now is not the moment, can I call you back?'

'We just wanted to find out how you've been since you spent time with us and how you would evaluate the meditation experience and services offered. Our first question is about the food – was the quality and quantity to your satisfaction?'

'Fine,' Richard says. 'All very earthy, kind of like eating dirt.'

'Was there anything that you would have liked Joseph to speak about?'

'No, not really.'

'Anything that you'd like to see more of at the center?'

'I really can't stay on the phone.'

'We also wanted to let you know that the Center for Healing Expression is a 401C nonprofit organization. Are you interested in making a donation?'

'How much do you want?'

'We make no recommendations.'

'Fine. I'll send a check. I have to go.'

Again, the phone rings. Ben. 'I've been trying to call, but the line is always busy.'

'I know, I'm sorry, where are you?'

'I'm here,' Ben says. 'Right here. We're at the Malibu Market; I was trying to surprise you.'

'You went right by; come back towards Santa Monica and I'll go outside.'

Richard stands at the edge of the road. He tries not to look at the photographers across the street. He stands facing traffic, greeting each car as it approaches. He stands randomly waving, like someone advertising a church car wash, or flagging down help. And then he sees them: he sees the boxy Volvo, the grille like a bold, toothy facial expression. He waves.

Like an air-traffic controller, he directs them off the road and into a spot.

There's a moment when the boys are still in the car, windows rolled up, and Richard is standing on the outside: a moment when Richard feels he will never be as close to Ben as he would like to be, when Richard feels Ben will never need from him what he needs from Ben.

The car doors open; Barth gets out, video camera in hand, the red 'record' light blinking – 'We're rolling tape.'

Barth is behind Ben, over his shoulder, filming.

Richard goes to hug Ben, and Ben puts out his hand – they shake. It's better than nothing.

'I'm so glad you're here,' Richard says. 'Hi, Barth, hi, camera. I guess now I'm part of your story.'

'He's going to do a lot of editing,' Ben says.

The camera captures the complexity of Ben's arrival, the physical reaction, flickers of emotion that happen so fast Richard can't tell what's what – he sees it later on tape.

'Come in,' Richard says, ushering them into the house.

Inside, Barth looks around, the camera as his eye. 'Very white, like Dairy Queen, like vanilla. This isn't really your house, right?'

'It's a rental,' Richard says. 'I don't know if you

heard, but I had some trouble with my house, a sinkhole, so I'm here temporarily.'

And then, deciding it's time to take control, he says to Barth, 'No filming inside.' To Richard's surprise, Barth puts the camera down.

'Nice place,' Ben says. 'Is there anything here that *is* yours?'

'Something in particular you're looking for?'

'No, I was just wondering if this was your stuff.'

'It's all a rental, everything came with it.'

The dog comes up from the beach and in through the sliding glass door.

'When did you get a dog?'

'I didn't, he just appeared, and I let him stay.'

Ben gets down on his knees and says hello to the dog.

'Let me show you around.' Richard takes the boys onto the deck. It is a classically beautiful Los Angeles day – high visibility. 'Down there is Santa Monica, and that's the pier, which is an amusement park – it's nice at night, when the rides are lit up. The airport is out that way. And then the mountains . . .'

'Your neighbors are right on top of you,' Barth says, looking onto Nic's deck.

'It's all about real estate, the available inches of real estate.'

'Do you know that woman?'

Richard glances onto the deck. It's Sylvia. He doesn't recognize her at first; she's lying back, eyes closed, topless. Her body is thin, more shapely than he would have imagined – her breasts, slack, half empty, with dark-wine-colored nipples, are deeply sexy. He feels excited. The idea of it, of seeing Sylvia topless, of feeling excited, of these things happening while Barth and Ben are standing there, is too much for him. The pain shoots through.

'Yep, I know her,' Richard says.

'Is that weird, to be so close to people?' Barth asks.

For the moment, Richard can't answer.

'Privacy is overrated,' Ben says. 'Nice ocean, calmer than I would have thought. Looking at water makes me have to pee. Where's the bathroom?'

'Down the hall on the right. You can drop your stuff in the last bedroom. A friend has been using the middle bedroom.'

'You're allowed to have a girlfriend, you don't have to put her in a separate room or call her your friend.'

'She's not my girlfriend. And she just got a place of her own. You'll meet her.'

'About the closeness of people,' Richard tells Barth, 'I grew up in an apartment building in Brooklyn, there were people everywhere.'

'Yes, I know,' Barth says. 'So did my father.'

And then there is silence. Ben comes out of the bathroom and Richard stands in the hall, looking at him. So this is it – the big meeting that he's been anticipating, dreading. It's a little anticlimactic.

'I have tuna for you,' Richard says.

'I'm kind of tuna'ed out,' Ben says. 'I've had it every day for about three weeks.'

'Would you like a root beer?'

'Thanks,' he says, understanding that Richard made an effort to get the things he likes.

'I thought I'd take you guys out and show you around.'

'We've been driving for days,' Barth says. 'I'm interested in a clean towel and some toilet paper that doesn't feel like sandpaper. Which way was the bathroom?'

'Down the hall.'

'I was wondering if I'd recognize you,' Ben says when Barth is gone.

'Me too you. It's been almost a year.'

'You look different,' Ben says.

'So do you.'

Pierced over one eyebrow, his eyes deep blue, his hair dark and thick, Ben is almost beautiful. When he raises his arms, the band of his underwear shows above the waist of his jeans. Richard wonders if he ever looked so self-confident, effortless.

Barth comes back from the bathroom, picks up a bag of Pirate's Booty, and walks around the house eating. There is something annoying about him, a kind of adolescent arrogance combined with an obliviousness that rings a bell. He's just like Richard's brother, only bigger and hairier.

'Let's go out for lunch,' Richard says. 'There's a place just up the road, we can walk.'

'This seems kind of crazy. Do you do it a lot?' Ben asks as they trudge up the Pacific Coast Highway.

'No. And never at night. No one can see you.'

Lunch is like being on a date. Richard feels the self-consciousness of trying to make a good impression, of being on his best behavior, and at the same time the peculiar intimacy that comes with being related. It's a kind of a dance. Does Ben even know it's a dance? Does he care? Richard feels like he's doing a fucking fox-trot – he's sweating.

At a nearby table, a group of children are having a birthday party. There are lots of screaming kids, and when the big moment comes, when the cake comes out and they all sing 'Happy Birthday,' the rest of the restaurant chimes in.

The birthday boy's mother asks, 'Willy, do you want to cut the first piece?'

The boy nods solemnly, takes the knife, and starts stabbing the cake. He repeatedly stabs the cake while everyone watches. He stabs the cake again and again, until his father grabs his wrist and wrests the knife away. All the while he's stabbing the cake, the kid is making a high-pitched, piercing howl.

'It's OK, Willy,' his father says, taking the knife. 'It's OK.'

'So, Barth, how's college life? What's your major?'

'Political science, but it's really all about becoming a documentary filmmaker.'

'Barth won a bunch of awards for his early work.'

'Early work – you mean things you did when you were twelve?'

'Eleven, actually. I made a film about a boy in my school who was dying of leukemia. It was nominated for an Academy Award and played in eight countries.'

Richard nods. 'Yes, I'm sure your mother wrote about it in her Christmas newsletter.'

Barth continues, 'When my dad was twelve he invented the glue stick.'

'Did he? I don't recall him having a job when he was twelve.'

'That's what he says.'

Why is Richard being such an ass? Something about Barth prompts him to act competitive. He doesn't like what he's doing – devolving.

Lunch arrives.

'And what about you?' he says to Ben. 'When does your position start?'

'I have to call them this afternoon.'

'That's exciting – junior agent man.' He's trying to be upbeat – too upbeat.

'I won't be an agent,' Ben says. 'It's more like mailroom boy, if they even have mailrooms anymore – I'm not sure, with everything going by e-mail.'

'So what about you, Uncle Dick – what do you do all day?' Barth asks.

'Don't call me Dick,' Richard says, abruptly. 'I've never been called Dick,' he lies. For a while a long time ago, his mother called him Dickie – he hated it. 'Where's Dickie? What did Dickie do today?'

she'd ask in a high-pitched, descending voice. When he thinks of it now, he can still hear her saying it, feel the twinge in his ear. Why did they name him Richard? What a lackluster name, Richard Nathan Novak, a big nobody. Richard Nathan Nobody – he plummets into a depression. 'What do I do all day?' he asks out loud. 'Well, this afternoon I'll have Gyrotonics.'

'Isn't that a kind of colonic?' Barth asks.

'It's a form of exercise. You two are welcome to hang out at the house, go down to the beach, or you can come with me, it's right up the road.'

'I may need a nap – it's been a very long ride,' Ben says.

He always liked his nap. Richard looks at Ben; it's hard to imagine how infant boys become men. 'You should call your mother and tell her that you arrived safely.'

Ben nods.

Walking home on the Pacific Coast Highway, Richard feels down on his luck, like a surfer or a hobo; a guy in a truck slows down and asks if they need a ride.

Back at the house, Richard sets the boys up with towels, sunscreen, water. 'It's not like the East Coast. The sun in Los Angeles is very hot – and lately it's been even hotter than usual. And there's no lifeguard down here, and there are rocks, the tide is hard to read, and every now and then we have sharks.'

'We get it,' Barth says.

★   ★   ★

At Gyrotonics, he spins, heels over head, head over heels. He has so much on his mind that every time the instructor says something she has to repeat it.

His mind keeps going to Nic, Nic and Sylvia, and how strange it is that he hasn't had sex in years and hadn't really thought about it until Cynthia brought it up and then Nic. He keeps seeing Sylvia's tits – like good red wine, he imagines drinking them.

Could he do it if he wanted to? Would he need help? A little something to get it up? He thinks he'd be fine, but suddenly everyone makes it sound like a huge problem – he's worried.

The Gyrotechnician is stretching him, lifting his legs; her head is between his legs, and suddenly he's paying attention, distracting himself from his distraction. He tries to make conversation. 'How long have you been doing this? Were you always interested in Gyrotonics?'

On the way home, he stops at the Malibu newsstand, buys *Time, Newsweek, Sophomore, Frenzy,* and *The Best of Hustler*. He hopes no one sees him – it's the first time he's bought porn in twenty years. It's funny and pathetic and he's got to know if it works.

At the house, he makes a straight line for the bedroom, tucks the bag deep under the sheets. Ben is down the hall sleeping. Barth is still out on the beach – Richard sees him from the bedroom window: blubbery, white, furry.

At six he knocks on the door and wakes Ben – 'If you sleep all day you'll be up all night.'

For dinner, the boys take everything out of the fridge and heat it. They eat all the food that Sylvia made for the entire week: the salmon, the meat-loaf, the haricots verts, the molasses cookies.

The conversation dissolves into a debate between Richard and Barth about who starred in the film *The Rain People*. Richard swears it's Shirley Knight and Barth says Shirley MacLaine. At a certain point, determined to prove he's right, Richard gets up from the table and looks it up online.

'You win,' Barth says, when Richard delivers the verdict. 'Are you happy now?'

After dinner, Barth goes for a walk. 'He needs a cigarette, but you're not supposed to know that,' Ben says.

'Are you all right sharing a room with Barth? Because, if you want, you can have the middle room.'

'The girlfriend suite?'

'She's not my girlfriend.'

'I'm fine to stay with Barth.'

'How did you two get to be such good friends?'

'We went to Camp Wigwam together every year.'

'Who arranged that?'

'Mom asked Uncle Ted and Aunt Meredith where I should go – they thought it would offer me some stability.'

'How many years?'

'I started when I was eight, and two years ago I was junior counselor in a bunk of seven-year-olds.'

Richard nods. 'I sent you care packages, right?'

'Yes.'

'Ted and I went to Wigwam.'

'I know.'

'I didn't realize it was the same place.'

Barth comes back, showers, and leaves the bathroom looking like a flood area.

Richard takes one look and bellows the boy's name. 'This is not a hotel and it's not a lake . . . We do not leave towels on the floor, we do not leave puddles of water – and I'm assuming it's water – on the floor. We put it away, bathmat up, spread the shower curtain so it doesn't get moldy, and make sure everything is clean and neat and ready for the next person.'

'I get it,' Barth says to Ben loudly when the boys are in their bedroom. 'Your father's gay.'

'I'm not gay,' Richard shouts and then hates himself for responding.

From his bedroom, he calls the ex-wife. 'Barth,' he says, exhaling. It comes out sounding like barf.

'Ignore him,' she says before he can say more.

'They ate a week's supply of food for dinner,' Richard says.

'It's about portion control. You're the adult. Ben's finally under control; don't you remember how pudgy he was at his Bar Mitzvah? I had to buy him a husky suit.'

'What's a husky suit?'

319

'It's the same as plus size – fat people's clothes.'
'Really?'
'He outgrew it.'
'The suit?'
'And the chubby phase.'

Richard remembers the Bar Mitzvah – he doesn't remember Ben being 'husky.' Richard sat with his parents, his brother, and his sister-in-law and felt like a complete outsider. He sat with his parents while she and Ben sat with their two hundred best friends, and he paid the bill. He should have been angry, and yet he felt grateful to be invited at all.

'You have to set limits.'
'I would have figured that at seventeen he would know what he wanted or needed.'
'That's why he eats all the tuna.'
'Too much tuna.'
'That's why I get turkey also.'
'He doesn't look fat.'
'He's not fat – he wants to be perfect.'
'You sent him to my old camp?'
'Yes.'
'On purpose?'
'Yes.'
'Did I like camp?'
'I don't know. Ben did. He went back every summer for eight years.'

Richard lies on the bed, exhausted. He thinks of calling his brother to ask him about camp, but is afraid he'll inadvertently say something nasty about Barth.

In the distance, he hears a dim ringing – his pants are calling him. It's Cynthia calling on the cell. 'Your regular phone has been busy for an hour.'

'I was talking to Ben's mother.'

'Did he get there? Do you like him?'

'He reminds me of myself, and the other kid, my nephew, I want to smack him. All I can say is that now I understand what you've been through. The cooking, the cleaning, the worrying. It's exhausting.'

She doesn't say anything for a minute. 'Sixteen years, twenty-four hours a day, three hundred sixty-five days a year.'

'I can only imagine,' Richard says. 'How was your day? How's the roommate?'

'I like the job program. I'm thinking something retail, something high-traffic. I like a lot of activity. The roommate is nuts, but I don't think she's dangerous.'

'Maybe one night we can go out for dinner or something – the boys ate all the food. What's that noise?' Richard says – he hears something in the background.

'It's her. Either she's banging her head against the wall, or more likely I'm not allowed to talk on the phone after ten p.m. We'll talk tomorrow. P.S. – I looked in her room – she keeps a teddy bear on her pillow.'

★　　★　　★

He locks his bedroom door and takes out his stash. He tugs at himself. Were women's breasts always that large? He closes his eyes and thinks of the women he dated when he first got to L.A.: women waiting to get married; some already had been married and were living off the profits, hoping to land someone richer the second time around. They were all very attractive in an all-too-perfect way. He remembers one in particular – the hills and curves of her ribs, her hips. He made love to her once, thinking there would be more – she made love to him once knowing that would be it. He remembers her on her knees in front of him – how he exploded into her mouth. She said he gave her butterflies, and so he did – ordering her a box of live ones sent overnight. He thinks of Cynthia, Cynthia and her husband fucking, and finds that perversely inspiring. He thinks of Cynthia on her knees, the husband behind her. He thinks of the meditation masseuse, with her finger up his ass. He thinks of his ex-wife, and suddenly everything is in gear – he comes quickly, surprising himself.

In the morning, meditating, he remembers what Joseph said – about tolerating discomfort, not feeling the need to act to relieve it. He'd like to do that again – a silent retreat. He could see himself spending one week every month just sitting.

There is a noise – the knob. And then a knock at the door. Richard lets Ben in – thankfully Ben doesn't ask about the door being locked. In his underwear, Ben climbs into Richard's bed. Despite everything, there remains a familial intimacy, a comfort level. Richard pushes the porn to the bottom.

'I feel like I walked in on something,' Ben says.

'Like what?'

'Dunno – your mid-life crisis.'

'Well, as you know, about a month ago, I woke up not feeling right, and I'm trying to get a handle on it.'

Ben nods. 'Did they find anything wrong with you?'

'Nothing out of the ordinary. At a certain point, things change, work differently. I may have to get my prostate biopsied.'

'All men have prostate cancer.'

'No, they don't.'

'That's what I heard. All men die with, but not of, prostate cancer.'

'Where'd you hear that?'

'One of Mom's friends.'

Does Ben walk around in his underwear in front of his mother? He's wearing knitted boxers; Richard has seen them in the store, but never knew how they really fit. They look good on Ben – he's well built, muscled. Richard imagines the girls go crazy for him.

'Do you want to come for a ride with me? I'm going to see Cecelia.'

'The cleaning lady.'

'She had a hip replaced.'

'I sort of forgot about her.'

'I'm going to visit; I thought you might want to join me.'

'Where's your car?'

'In the shop. I had a little accident last week – I've been borrowing from the guy next door.'

'Can I think about it?'

'Sure. Did you call The Agency yesterday?'

'I left a message.'

Barth is in the bathroom with the door open.

'Close the door,' Richard bellows.

And he does.

Richard goes to ask Nic about borrowing the car. Nic is at his desk, staring at the sea, wearing the headphones.

'I've got to see someone in Los Feliz. You need anything? You want to get out, visit Fred? Your kid?'

Nic shakes his head – 'I'll pass.'

'OK if I borrow the car?'

'Please, take the car.'

'I'll go with you, if you want company,' Ben says.

'Can you drop me at the pier?' Barth asks.

Richard is glad for the time alone with Ben. He doesn't explain about the car, doesn't tell them it belonged to John Lennon – he doesn't want Ben to think he's showing off, and for some strange reason he just doesn't want Barth to know. He also doesn't call Cecelia ahead – she'll talk him out of it. He figures he'll call from along the way – pie in hand – and she won't be able to refuse him.

They take the 10 into town, get off at Fairfax, and stop at the Farmers Market. 'She likes pie,' Richard tells Ben, getting a raspberry-peach and giving Ben a tour of the market – which used to be a place where real farmers brought their produce and goodies into town and sold them, and now it's kind of a tourist attraction.

Ben nods. He buys postcards. From a parking lot off Vermont, Richard calls Cecelia; she tells him there's no need to come.

'But I want to,' he says. 'I'm already down here on Vermont, and I brought you a pie from DuPar's.'

They're greeted by Cecelia's husband, Walter. 'It's my day off.'

'We brought pie,' Richard says, holding out the box.

'Come in.'

'This is Ben.'

'The boy from New York?'

Ben nods.

'What's that like? Dirty? Noisy?'

'It's nice,' Ben says. 'There's always something going on.'

Walter shakes his head. 'Can't imagine it. At the post office we get a lot of people from the East wanting to transfer out here – even on a rough route, the sun always shines in Los Angeles. It's all about quality of life. I've got relatives in Newark, never see them, I don't like the cold.'

'Would you like some tea?' Cecelia pushes her walker into the room.

She looks like an old woman. The top of her hair is suddenly gray; was it gray three weeks ago, did the rinse wash off, did she go gray overnight? Richard hugs her, holding tight. 'How are you feeling?' Over Cecelia's shoulder he sees her noise-canceling headset on the kitchen counter.

'Let's just say they don't exactly tell you the truth about how it's gonna be. I guess if they said it's like getting run over by a Mack truck most people wouldn't let them do it.'

'You'll feel better soon.'

'What choice do I have? It's not like you can take it back and ask for a refund.'

There's a pause.

'So this is home,' Richard says.

'This is the house you paid for,' Cecelia says.

'You worked hard for it.'

'I did not,' Cecelia says. 'I hadn't worked for you six months and you gave me twenty thousand dollars for my down payment.'

'I did?'

'And you didn't let me pay you back.'

'Frankly,' Walter says, 'I don't like the feeling of being indebted.'

Richard shrugs. 'I have no memory of it.'

'You think I've been nice to you all these years for nothing,' Cecelia teases him.

'Her hip would have lasted a lot longer if she wasn't cleaning houses,' Walter says. Cecelia shushes him. 'I guess it's a good thing they can put a new hip in,' he continues, 'they didn't use to be able to do that. Back when I was in Korea, lots of boys lost parts and they couldn't do much for them. Do you know, we black soldiers from World War II and Korea still haven't gotten our medals. I just wonder if nice white folks know that.'

'I didn't know that,' Richard says.

'Didn't think so,' Walter says.

'It's his bone,' Cecelia says. 'He chews that bone every day.'

'Well, let's put it this way,' Walter says. 'I was proud to serve my country, even if my country isn't proud . . . Hopefully, they'll come before I die. It was the integrated army – that was a big deal. Executive Order 9981, signed by President Harry Truman, July 1948. My whole life I've been a government worker. The military and the Postal Service.'

'Want pie?' Cecelia asks Walter.

'Sliver,' Walter says. 'Watching my sugar.'

'Is there anything you need?' Richard asks Cecelia.

'I've got it all,' Cecelia says. 'I'm going to physical therapy and hope to give them back this walker next week.'

'If you think of anything, let me know. I have this cell phone now, so you can call me anytime.' He writes the number down.

'How's the house?'

'They're working on it.'

'And you,' she says to Ben, 'got a summer job?'

He nods. 'Starts tomorrow.'

'You let me know how it goes.'

'I will. We'll see you soon,' Ben says as they're leaving.

'I'm counting on it,' Cecelia says.

In the car on the way home, Richard thanks Ben for going with him. 'It was good we did that. She's worked for me for more than a decade, you can't just let that go.'

'Why do you hate Barth?' Ben asks.

'I don't hate him.'

'Yes, you do.'

'I don't know.'

'The good thing is, he doesn't notice.'

Richard nods. That's part of why he hates him.

Instead of taking the highway home, Richard goes the scenic route. He takes Ben to Chinatown for lunch. He takes him to a place that a woman took him to on a date about five years ago – Hop Louie's. The restaurant is deserted except for a large group of Chinese people gathered around an enormous table.

'Are you open?'

'Open and ready to serve.'

They order a bountiful spread – hot-and-sour soup, sweet-and-sour pork, steamed dumplings, fried rice – and immediately Richard feels guilty: they've ordered too much, Ben will overeat and have to go back to the husky department.

'Are you still playing the piano?' Richard asks.

Ben nods. 'One night, I got to duet with Harry Connick. Mom and I were at some party and I asked him if he'd play with me.'

The food arrives.

'What did you do for your birthday this year?'

'Mom took me and a bunch of people from her office to a super-fancy new restaurant – the kind of place that's twenty dollars a bite – I calculated it.'

They eat until they are stuffed, and they crack their fortune cookies: 'Happiness is before you.' 'A good friend sometimes says nothing at all.'

The long way home: Richard takes Ben to the tar pits, tells him about the La Brea woman, the saber-toothed cat who may or may not be extinct. They both breathe deeply and talk about whether or not a person can get high on the smell of the asphalt.

'It's a strange city,' Richard says. 'Filled with things that are not obvious. Did you know that tar can pop up anywhere within a five-mile radius? And up in Beverly Hills, there are people with oil wells in their backyards?'

'Are we near Disneyland?'

'Disneyland?'

'Yeah, I always wanted to go to Disneyland.'

'You really want to go to Disney?'

'Yes.'

'Fine, we'll go.'

'Good.'

There is a pause as though something has happened.

'When you left, was someone having an affair?'

'No.'

'That at least would have made sense.'

And then a change of subject.

'Did your uncle really think he was going to win a Nobel Prize?'

'Apparently.'

'Must be rough.'

'According to Barth, everything he ever did was all about getting to that moment, and now he thinks it's all shit, he walks around muttering, "Not good enough, someone won, someone always wins."'

'When he was younger he used to have temper tantrums,' Richard says. 'My parents would sit in the living room and ask each other what they should do: Should we call the police? On our own child? His outbursts were impressive – he would bang on the walls, smash things. "Jews don't call the police,' my father would say. "The police are Irish and they're not interested in our problems."'

'Weird.'

Richard nods.

On the way home they stop at Anhil's – Richard introduces Ben. The boy orders a jelly donut.

'You don't need a donut,' Richard says. 'We just had lunch.'

'OK,' Ben says. 'No donut.'

'Nic called. He invited me to a wow-wow tonight on the beach. Will you be there?'

'I don't know if we're invited.'

'Of course you're invited – you just don't know it yet.'

'We've been out all day. Are you going?' Richard asks.

'For certain. I am closing early. I have a special hat.' He goes into the back and comes out with an old Shriner's hat. 'It's a wow-wow, like when Barney and Fred go to the lodge.'

Richard has no idea what Anhil is talking about and doesn't have the energy to clarify. 'All right, then,' Richard says.

Back at the house, there's a message on the machine for Ben from The Agency. 'You're scheduled to report at eight a.m. tomorrow. Any questions, please call.'

'Do you know the address?' Richard asks.

'I have it somewhere. Is there a car I can use? I want to leave the Volvo for Barth.'

'I'll call about mine; it should be ready.'

Richard brings Bentley's keys back to Nic. He's on the phone, but waves Richard closer. 'Are you coming tonight? Did you get my message?'

Richard shakes his head.

'I stapled a note to the outside of your house – didn't you see it? – "Hungry, Bored, In Search of Something – Join Us Tonight." I need to know how many dogs do I buy. Do you eat beef? I'm getting beef dogs, turkey dogs, tofu dogs. How many dogs per person, how many ears of corn?'

'What exactly is it?'

'It's whatever you want it to be. A bunch of guys, a bonfire on the beach. Bring your boys.'

'Who comes?'

'Yes, hello,' Nic says into the phone. 'I need beer, regular and nonalcoholic, Diet Coke, and those soy chips, two bags of each flavor. Can you put it on my account and I'll send someone to pick up everything? Thanks.' He hangs up. 'Guys, random guys, locals from the beach, guys from the studio, my accountant came once, went home dirty and his wife wouldn't let him come back.'

'Should I invite my movie-star friend?'

'No actors, that's the only rule.'

'I can't believe you have any rules.'

'All societies have rules.'

'What time?'

'We start the fire at eight.'

'Can I bring anything?'

'Marshmallows and sticks.'

Richard calls the car guy.

'I was hoping you wouldn't call.'

'What do you mean?'

'On the way back to you they had an accident – it's totaled.'

'You wrecked my car?'

'I didn't wreck it . . . If you hadn't moved all the way the hell out there, it probably wouldn't have happened. None of it would have happened. I don't even want to discuss it. Maybe we should just call it square, cancel the lease, you pay me five thousand dollars, and we won't even submit the first set of repair charges to your insurance.'

'You totaled my car and now you want five thousand dollars? How can you say none of it would have happened? Something worse would have happened; we would have turned on the evening news and read about some girl found in pieces.'

'Oh, right, I forgot about her. Fine,' the guy says, 'don't pay me. I'll send you a new car, a new lease, we'll start from the beginning again. Just write the letter, OK?'

'When will I get the car?'

'By the end of the week.'

'I need it sooner. Tomorrow morning.'

'Impossible. I'm not even sure I have the car on the lot.'

'End of the day.'

'I'll do my best.'

Richard, the boys, and Nic get a lift to the pow-wow. Richard dutifully carries the marshmallows and shish-kebab sticks he bought at the overpriced store up the road. The back of the van is filled with hot dogs, beer, ice. About two miles down, they park at the edge of the PCH, where the surfers are loading their boards, calling it a day. Like sherpas, they carry load after load down onto the beach, setting up electric hot-dog grills, coolers for the beer, trash cans.

'About how many people are you expecting?'

'I always lose count – fifteen, forty?'

'How often do you do this?'

'Maybe three or four times a year.'

'Do you charge admission?'

'It's my treat.'

'I'll give you some money.'

'I don't take money. Help me get this folding table up. We'll call this craft services.'

'Are we making things like ships in bottles and leather wallets?'

'On a movie set, craft services is where the food goes.'

Nic and Richard go down the beach gathering wood.

'I would think it's illegal to have a bonfire – an ember could escape and start something.'

'It is. We get a film permit. It's the one thing this town understands – the movie business.'

As people arrive, they introduce themselves – it's a lot of guys in Hawaiian shirts, Philip, Rick, Ron, Larry, Vance, Simon, Tenzi, and Pliny, but you can call me Joe. They hug each other, do some back-slapping, call each other 'man,' 'dude,' and 'brother,' and ask, 'Where's it been?' Richard is reminded of how much he doesn't like group events. He wonders how he could get home from here. Could he call a taxi? Where would he tell it to stop?

A leathery man of indeterminate age extends his hand. 'I am Tenzi,' he says. 'I have been in this water every day for twenty-five years. Three times bitten by the shark.' He shows Richard three bites, one on the arm, one on the leg, and one on the thigh. 'I have a lucky card. How do you know Nic?'

'I live next door. And you?'

'I know him from the sea. I taught him to surf a long time ago.'

'Do you know the woman with the yellow bathing cap?'

'Madeline,' he says. 'She swims every morning.'

Richard nods.

'She keeps shoes under the boardwalk.'

Richard smiles – glad to know the secret.

The hot dogs are turning. A huge cauldron of corn is boiling. Anhil arrives last with boxes of donuts: 'I put up a sign – "Closed for Private Party" – and cleaned out the cases.' He puts his hat on and does a jig in the sand. 'I am a beach bum, a caveman.'

Richard looks down and realizes that he's got his good shoes on. He takes them off, tucking them into the sand next to a pile of wood. Barefoot, he wiggles his toes – nice. Barth and Ben are playing Frisbee in the distance; the sun is setting; it's reminiscent of summers long ago, when he and his wife would take a share in a house on Long Island.

'I just changed my car insurance,' one of the guys says to Richard. 'It had gone up four hundred dollars without me noticing; I got it back down, took me twelve and a half minutes – I clocked it. How much are you paying?'

'I have no idea,' Richard says.

Someone hands him a beer. 'It's a chemical culture,' the guy says. 'My kid can't do his homework unless he takes Ritalin, and when my daughter started on an antidepressant she thought it meant she was a big girl – like going from chewables to gelcaps. It's a rite of passage, like what getting braces used to be.'

Another guy spends the whole evening alternating between talking on his cell phone – saying, 'Hello, hello, can you hear me? It's not a good signal. Hello, can you?' – and checking his BlackBerry for messages. 'I'm in the middle of something big,' he says.

An enormous hole is dug, the fire is lit. The hot dogs are roasted. Barth is filming, and, sure enough, a cop comes along and asks if they have a permit. Nic shows him the permit, and they give him some hot dogs and a couple of cans of Coke, and he hangs around for a while.

'How many dogs did you eat?' Richard asks Ben.

'Two turkey, one bun, no corn. And you?' Ben asks.

'One turkey, one tofu, no bun, half an ear of corn.'

After dark it gets chilly; Richard wraps a vinyl tablecloth around his shoulders like a blanket.

'I'm wiggly,' Anhil says. 'I had a whole beer, never have I had a whole beer. I have no tolerance for drink, I go crazy.'

'You had a fake beer,' Ben says.

'What do you mean, a fake beer? I had the whole bottle.' He holds up the empty.

'It's nonalcoholic beer.' Ben shows him the label.

'Never heard of such a thing.'

'It's for people who have a drinking problem.'

'Why not just have apple juice?'

'That's real beer.' Richard points to the surfer, who's randomly finishing off other people's beers, pretending he's cleaning up – he picks up a bottle, tilts it to his lips, and then puts it in his trash bag.

'That is not stationary,' Anhil says, meaning 'sanitary.'

'No, it's not.'

They light a sage torch and pass it in a circle. Drums begin to bang. The air is filled with scent.

'This is the wow-wow part,' Anhil says.

'Breathe deeply, listen to the beating of the drums, the crashing of the seas, and know that we are alone and we are together,' Nic says.

Richard leans over and whispers in Ben's ear, 'We can go anytime you want.'

'I'm fine,' Ben says. 'And Barth is really enjoying it.'

Richard continues whispering in Ben's ear. 'I just want to apologize, I had no idea what it would be.'

The talking stick is being passed. 'You are an eagle, a tiger walking in the forest; speak to the talking stick,' Nic says, handing the stick to the man next to him, who holds it, head bowed.

It's corny, but the hair on the back of Richard's neck is standing up.

'This goes out to my dad, who is long gone,' the man says. 'A message of forgiveness and release. In letting go of my anger, I am losing my feelings for you, but I am getting something too – freedom. For that I thank you.' He passes the stick.

'Fuck you, Frank; you know who you are, and you know what I mean.'

'Jenny, I love you.'

'Don't feel like you have to say anything,' Richard whispers.

'Thank you for having me,' Ben says when he gets the stick.

Barth is too busy filming to take the stick.

When the stick comes to Richard, he passes it on like a hot potato.

'To the great white shark who lives in the sea,' says the guy after Richard. 'I honor you, I am in awe of you. We are in a contest to see who lives the longest, but tonight I am the sea.'

The drums continue to beat; some of the men break off and go into the center of the circle and dance around the fire. Nic does it – he dances like a wild animal, throws his head back and screams. 'This is the bear in me, the wild man, the angry ass.' He rushes towards the fire and back and towards the fire and back, fanning the flames with his body.

'It's better than bowling,' Anhil says, going in to dance. He dances like he's walking on hot coals.

With a maniacal, terrifying laugh, Tenzi, the surfer, grabs a torch, runs towards the water and disappears.

Reflexively, his body acting before his brain, Richard takes off after him. He doesn't see where the water starts, just focuses on the spot where he last saw Tenzi, where he saw the flame extinguished. As soon as his feet are wet, he draws his arms long and hurls himself forward into the sea. The plunge snaps him into extreme consciousness for the second it takes to ask, What am I doing? He thinks of Tenzi, he thinks of a man hurling himself into dark waters.

He feels for the man, catches his leg, loses it, pushes up off the ocean floor, arcing out of the water like a fish, and grabs the surfer – ankle and wrist. Tenzi fights Richard. Richard loses the wrist, but hangs on to the ankle. Onshore he see white dots, flashlights, like cartoon eyeballs peering out of the black. Men are in the water, wading out; they bring Richard and Tenzi back to shore.

Ben is on the beach, screaming: 'You fuck, you fuck! You jump in to save a drunk fucking stranger and you don't give a fuck about me standing here wondering if you're drowning. What if you died? That would fucking suck. I didn't drive all the way out here to watch you die!'

'I didn't die. I'm fine. I'm wet, but I'm OK, and I helped a guy out.'

'You're not some fucking superhero, you fuck.'

'Look at me,' Richard says. 'I'm fine.'

Richard doesn't know what to do; he holds Ben against his wet body. Ben is six inches taller than Richard, more muscular – Richard holds him as tight as he can.

'Let go,' Ben says. 'You can let go now, I'm done.'

Back at the house, no one says more.

In the morning, Ben comes out in a dark suit, looking like an undertaker.

'You look great – serious, formidable.'

'Mom bought me three suits,' Ben says.

'Do you want some breakfast?' Richard shakes the bag of Sylvia's special flakes. 'It's custom-made, good stuff.' He puts a little in a bowl.

'Got milk?' Ben asks.

Nic is fast asleep. Richard slips into his house, takes the keys, and drives Ben into town. The Agency has its own building, a miniaturized marble Pentagon that flies its own flag.

'Very military,' Richard says.

'It was started by two ex-CIA guys who wanted to make action-adventure films.'

'When you're ready to come home, call me on the cell; I'll hover starting at about five-thirty.'

He drives to Anhil's; the lights are off, the door still has the 'Closed for Private Party' sign on it. He waits. Customers come and go, leaving empty-handed. At quarter of nine, Anhil shows up.

'People have been looking for you.'

'I partied all night around the fire. You missed the best parts. Someone had a guitar: "Kumbaya my lord, kumbaya," "Ninety-nine bottles of beer on the wall, ninety-nine bottles of beer.' I saw the sun come up, I learned to make my penis into a pancake.'

'What?'

'The Ron is a comic – he can make his Johnstone into a hot dog on a bun. It was very much fun. When I got home, I showed Lipi. She screamed, but she was screaming anyway. I have never been gone so long. And your brother's son?'

'Barth?'

'Yes, I invited him to come and stay with Lipi and me – did he tell you? He is going to make a movie about me, and then I will be famous.'

'He's going to stay with you?'

'Yes,' Anhil says. 'Maybe I should not have told you, maybe he was saving it as a surprise.'

'No, it's fine, it's good. You would make a good movie.'

'I thought so too: I am a movie.'

Richard Drives to Lusardi's office, pulls into the parking lot, and waits. He watches the receptionist arrive, park her bronze Nissan, and go inside. Minutes later, Lusardi pulls up in an old Jag.

Richard buzzes the office.

'You're early,' the receptionist says.

'Do you think you can squeeze me in?'

'He's got a very tight schedule,' she says, and then waves him in. 'Hurry,' she says.

Lusardi is behind his desk eating bricks of shredded wheat out of the box.

'I think maybe I tried to kill myself,' Richard says, and then explains running into the sea, the whole idea of the pow-wow, the talking stick, and how he found all of it intensely annoying.

'Why would you want to kill yourself?'

'I don't know. I'm a good swimmer – I swam in high school, I was a summer lifeguard, I used to swim in the ocean. I remember as a boy my family going to the beach – my mother sitting onshore, not wanting to get her hair wet; my father going in only up to his knees, he never learned to swim. My son, Ben, is here – visiting. Did I already say that? I came out of the water and he was yelling. He's so angry, but doesn't say anything.'

'Maybe he's afraid to.'

Silence. Richard is all the more annoyed with himself, for being so self-centered. It hadn't occurred to him that Ben would feel he was risking something.

'Does it seem strange that I was a swimmer but forgot?'

'We forget what we need to forget. Maybe you weren't trying to kill yourself, maybe you were really trying to save someone – maybe you were saving yourself.'

'My stomach is killing me,' Richard says.

'I'm sure it is; have you eaten anything this morning?' Lusardi asks, sweeping crumbs off his desk.

Richard shakes his head. 'I gave Ben some cereal but I forgot to eat.'

When he comes out of the doctor's office, the receptionist asks, 'Do you need to be validated?'

'I didn't get a ticket; the gate was up.'

'Oh,' she says sadly, shaking her head. 'That's gonna cost you, they'll charge you for a full day.'

'How can they charge me for a full day? It's not even ten-thirty.'

She shakes her head. 'They don't speak the language.'

'Is Dr Anderson ever here anymore?'

'He comes in late, his wife has Alzheimer's.'

'I didn't know.'

'Neither did he; she's only fifty-three.'

'How did they figure it out?'

'She didn't know who she was anymore.'

As he's leaving, he helps an old woman in the waiting room put on her sweater. Her legs are wrapped in bandages; when she speaks every muscle in her neck pops out.

'Are you going to be able get home OK?'

'Of course,' she says, 'I got here, didn't I?'

'I'll give you a ride.'

She shakes her head, 'I didn't live this long doing things like that.'

As soon as Richard helps her, other people in the office help her: one woman unfolds her walker and another holds the door.

'That's the point, isn't it,' Richard says to no one in particular.

He leaves, thinking about the woman, her legs, her walker, her independence.

He passes a VW dealer, a lot full of Beetles. If there ever was a car he wanted when he was Ben's age, it was the Beetle.

He pulls in. The Bug is a happy car, entirely pleasant, anti-depressed, not a family car, not a carpool car, a fun car. A salesman holding a flower makes a beeline for him. He hands Richard the flower – a gerbera daisy.

'We do a special thing here at Hollywood VW: whenever you come in, we'll give you a fresh flower for the car – forever. The car has a flower holder – but you already knew that, right? What are you driving now?' the guy asks.

'Something borrowed.'

'Well, let's take a look at it, for comparison's sake.'

'No,' Richard says, 'let's not.'

'It's nothing to be embarrassed about. You should have seen what I was driving before I got this job. My father's Datsun; he kept it in great shape, but the car was older than me.'

'You know what,' Richard says, 'I want to buy the car, so let's go from there; in fact, I think I want two. Can you do something on the price if I take two?'

'There's wiggle room.'

'Two convertibles – one in black for my son, Ben, and one in pink – do you have pink?'

'We have a really pretty bright blue.'

'OK, one in black and one in pretty blue.'

He takes out his credit card.

'You can't charge a car.'

He takes out a check.

'No personal checks.'

'Give me a clue, then,' Richard says.

'Bank check. Do you want the car in your son's name?'

'Yes, it's a gift.'

'How old is he?'

'Seventeen.'

'Then it has to be in your name unless it's farm equipment.'

'Why?'

'Do you really care why?'

He calls his ex-wife. 'Quick question: what's Ben's Social Security Number?' He doesn't tell her about the car, doesn't want to be talked out of it, doesn't want her approval or not.

He calls Cynthia, gets her license number and Social, and then he calls Paul, the stoner at the insurance agency, and asks him to add them both to his policy.

'Are you starting a business?' the stoner asks.

'I'm liberating people.'

He asks the dealer, 'Can you deliver the cars tonight?'

'We don't usually do things that quickly.'

'Make an exception,' Richard says.

'Is it a deal breaker?' the guy asks.

'Yes,' Richard says.

'Fine,' the guy says, 'we'll do it.'

Richard feels a sense of satisfaction, like he's done something – something unexpected, something nice, one for Ben and one for Cynthia.

'Deliver the cars to The Ivy in Santa Monica,' he says. 'Leave them with the valet-parking guy – it's a surprise. Here's my cell number if you need it. I'd like them there by seven. And ask your guys to drive carefully.'

It takes longer than you think. By the time the paperwork is done, there's not time for Richard to go back to Malibu before he has to pick up Ben. He drives up the hill, to his house. The broken windows have been boarded up, but other than that nothing has been done.

He goes inside, changes into exercise gear, and gets on the treadmill – nervous about having spent so much on the cars, about what the house is going to cost him. He goes online; his assets have taken a dip, the lack of constant monitoring, tweaking, is a problem. He's fine, he will always be fine, but he needs to keep an eye on it. A new regime – meditate, calculate.

While he's walking, he reads the government man's script, 'Ground Motion.' It's a disaster film combining fire, flood, earthquake, pestilence, mud slide. The film opens with a voice-over. 'What you are about to see is a work of fiction, it has not yet happened, and yet each of the elements represented are real. It was written using everything I know about the state of the world we live in – which means, it's coming soon.' He's in the middle of reading when he hears footsteps behind him. Pain spreads across his chest.

'Sorry,' the movie star says, coming into the room. 'I didn't mean to startle you. I rang the bell, you didn't answer, so I squeezed in through a hole where a window used to be. I saw the car. I used to know a screenwriter with a car like that – it used to belong to Elton John.'

'John Lennon,' Richard says, and the movie star doesn't say anything.

His chest is still crushing. He wonders if *this* is in fact IT. A major movie star breaks into his house and gives him the heart attack that kills him. He slows the treadmill, but keeps talking – no sudden changes.

'Where have you been?' the movie star asks.

'In Malibu. My son is visiting with my nephew; we went to a pow-wow on the beach last night – a bunch of guys talking to a stick.'

'Oh yeah, I went to one of those.'

Richard is starting to notice that, no matter what you tell the movie star you've done, he's done it too.

'And I think maybe my son has some sort of fungal infection on his foot,' Richard throws in – it's not even true.

'Very hard to get rid of – I had to take medicine

for a year,' the movie star says. Either he's disease-ridden, a big liar, a nine-lived cat, or deeply sympathetic.

'What are you reading?' the movie star asks.

'A script by one of the government men who was helping me with the hole.'

'Any good?'

At least he doesn't claim to have already read it. Richard hands him the script. The movie star stands next to the treadmill, reading.

At five, Richard starts back down the hill, driving in circles around The Agency. He watches. Every car coming out of the garage is a BMW – 745Li, 5 Series SUV, 3 Series convertible.

His cell phone rings.

'Are you out here?' Ben asks.

'Yes, where are you?'

'Across the street, at Johnny Rocket's.'

Ben gets into the car holding a large shake – he sucks on the straw, chocolate rises up through the clear plastic straw, the cup beads with sweat. Richard starts to say something about the shake and then stops himself. Why can't a perfectly healthy kid have a shake at the end of his first day of work? He's proud of his silence.

'I didn't have lunch,' Ben says.

'Neither did I.'

Ben offers him a sip.

'It's good,' Richard says. 'Really good. I haven't had a milkshake in a million years.'

'There's a reason people like ice cream. Where's Barth?'

'No idea, I haven't been home. How was it?'

'OK.'

'Better or worse than you expected?'

'More intense.' He sucks; the straw starts gurgling, pulling air.

'I thought we'd all go out for dinner and celebrate – you, me, Barth, my friend Cynthia.'

'The girlfriend.'

Barth is asleep on the deck, his back sunburned to the point of looking like a steamed lobster.

'What were you thinking?' Richard says.

'I saw this incredible thing – a woman swimming with the dolphins, she was like a mermaid. I stayed out here waiting for her to swim back.'

'She walks back,' Richard says, with great authority.

'And I was planning my movie in my head – the one about Anhil, Bollywood meets Hollywood, a comedy in a donut shop.'

'I thought you were making a documentary.'

'I am, but it needs a frame, a second story – don't you think?'

'I wouldn't know. Have you ever been in the sun before?' Richard asks. 'Do you have any idea of how strong it is?'

'You sound like Grandpa.'

'I'm sure I do.'

Ben brings an aloe-vera plant from the kitchen and squeezes gel out of the leaves.

'How do you know how to do that?'

'It's a nanny thing – she was always squeezing aloe vera out of everything.'

Richard puts the gel on Barth – he's meaty, it's like slathering goo onto bacon. 'We're all going out to dinner. Do you want to come?' he asks Barth.

'No, I don't feel very well.'

He gives Barth a bottle of Gatorade. 'Drink this – a lot of it – and if your back gets blistery you're going to have to go to the doctor.' He shakes his head. 'How could you just lie there frying?'

'I just kept thinking about how great the sun feels.'

Richard and Ben meet Cynthia at The Ivy. She looks good; the dress from Target fits her well.

'So – you left your family and now you're in rehab?' Ben asks.

'It's not really rehab, it's like a job-training program for women who haven't worked in a long time.'

'What do you do there?'

'Work on math and computer stuff. Right now we're running what we call the store,' it's really just a storage room, but it's stocked – we've got wooden play food; clothes for Barbie Dolls, everything in miniature. Everything has a bar code, we learn to scan, to put things on sale, keep an inventory, balance profit-and-loss statements. I haven't had a job in fifteen years. Luckily, I know all kinds of computer games, from playing with the kids. One of the women has three fingers with no fingertips – they got cut off in a food processor and she thinks her family ate them, she's relearning how to type.'

'I went to rehab when I was fourteen,' Ben says.

'You did?' Richard asks.

Ben nods. 'For three weeks. We had family therapy and everything.'

'How come I never knew?'

'Mom was so mad about the whole thing that, when she checked me in and they asked for my father's name, she told them I didn't have a father, she said that she was a single mother and had used a sperm donor; she couldn't exactly go back on it.'

'How's The Agency?' Cynthia asks Ben.

'They took us into a conference room and said, "This is THE AGENCY. These are the rules. Do not make eye contact with your superiors – we talk at you, not to you. Do not lean back in your chair – if you are leaning back you are not working. You have not earned the privilege of daydreaming. Keep yourself and your superiors well hydrated, always offer visitors something to drink. Do not leave the office before your superiors." Another guy came in – the "field nurse" – and gave us our confidentiality papers, parking passes, and a set of Agency playing cards with pictures of all the top agents, their names, backgrounds, client lists. And then I learned how to roll calls.'

'Roll calls?'

'Yes, "I have so-and-so calling for you."'

Their dinners arrive. Huge portions.

'We could have shared,' Cynthia says.

'It reminds me of The Palm,' Ben says. 'Grandma and Grandpa always take us there for special occasions; it has good lighting, and there's one in every city. The Palm in New York, The Palm in Boston.'

Cynthia excuses herself to go to the ladies' room.

'She's nice.'

'She's not my girlfriend. I met her in the produce section, I'm helping her through a difficult time. What were you doing that you had to go to rehab?'

'Everything. I looked so sick for about a month that Mom told people I had mono.'

When Cynthia comes back, she tells them how the roommate lost one of her 'pills' and kept accusing Cynthia of stealing it until she found it in the living-room carpet. 'I may have to move.'

'You could live with us,' Ben says. 'Your room is still empty.'

'Thanks, but this is your summer to be with your dad, and, besides, I need to be on my own. What's most exciting to me right now is the idea of being alone, entirely alone – no one talking to me, not sharing a bathroom with anyone.'

'Don't you think you'd get lonely?'

'No.'

Richard's cell phone rings. He politely excuses himself and steps outside. Richard signs for the cars, tips the delivery guys, and goes back to the table.

The waiter brings out a dessert with a candle in it. 'Happy Birthday,' the waiter says. 'I'm assuming you don't want me to sing.'

'Oh, it's not my birthday,' Richard says.

'Yes, it is,' Cynthia says. 'Don't be shy.'

'Blow out the candle,' the waiter says.

The three of them share the dessert – with Richard continuing to protest, 'It's not my birthday.'

'Of course it's not,' Cynthia says. 'But I told them it was your birthday because in a lot of places they give you a free dessert if it's your birthday.'

When they are done, Richard picks up the check, Ben and Cynthia thank him, and they all walk outside.

Richard is excited, but trying to act cool. They stand on the sidewalk waiting for the car. 'Can we give you a ride home?' he asks Cynthia.

'Sure,' she says.

The valet brings up the cars. Ben and Cynthia stand around, waiting for Bentley.

'I have something for each of you,' Richard says, pointing to the cars. It takes them a minute to catch on.

'Black for Ben and blue for Cynthia – I wanted pink but there is no such thing.'

'Are you serious? You leased cars for us?' Cynthia says.

'I didn't lease anything; I paid cash.'

'I haven't had my own car since I was eighteen,

and that was a green Ford Falcon that belonged to my aunt who died of breast cancer – I always worried that the car was contagious.' She kisses him and begins to cry.

'Your girlfriend,' Ben says.

The valet throws the keys to Ben, and Richard gets in on the passenger side. They take off up Ocean Avenue, yelling back and forth between the cars:

'Does yours have a flower?'

'Yes.' Cynthia turns on the radio and dances in her seat.

'Try the heated seats,' Ben says. 'Look at how the roof goes.'

'Whoopie!'

Richard feels good – good to the point of being afraid.

'You're a lucky guy,' Cynthia yells to Ben. 'You've got a great dad.'

'It's complicated,' Ben says.

Later, when they are home, Ben asks, 'How do you buy a car for someone who is not your girlfriend?'

'You do for others what you can't do for yourself.'

After Ben is asleep, he goes next door to return the Bentley keys.

'Want a drink?'

'Sure.'

Nic pours Richard a scotch.

'I should thank you for having us last night,' Richard says.

'I should thank you for going in after my friend,' Nic says, tossing back his scotch and pouring another. 'He's a perfect example of a man who should never under any circumstances drink.' With great expertise Nic rolls a cigarette and lights it.

'Do you like all the wow-wow, as Anhil calls it?'

'I like the hot dogs and the dancing around the fire. And I like to scream, and I'm kind of a pyro; you didn't stay for the part where we light a hundred sparklers.'

'What's the story with the Ron guy and his . . . ?'

'Penis puppet. Personally, I like the fruit fly.'

'I thought you said no actors.'

'He's not an actor, he's a comic and a contortionist.' Nic leans back and takes a drag; the cigarette sizzles.

'Do you remember anything about being a kid?' Richard asks.

Nic exhales. 'Let's see. Mosquito bites, high humidity, no air conditioning, no locked doors, porches, sitting outside at night, my paper route, running track, slapping the baton in someone's hand, football games, following my brother around. When you're a kid, war is 'Bang-bang, you're dead,' cap guns, snowball fights, shirts and skins in an apple orchard. About fifteen years ago the Vietnamese invited us to visit where he died. We didn't go.'

'I don't remember anything,' Richard says. 'It's not like I keep thinking, Oh, I don't remember; it's more like nothing occurs to me and then, all of a sudden, a little piece comes back and I think, That's interesting, I'd completely forgotten that.'

'We live in a time when no one wants to remember. We pretend we are where it starts. Look at the way we live – we build houses on cliffs, on fault lines, in the path of things, and when something happens, we don't learn history, we build it again, right on the same spot, bigger, better.' Nic pours. 'Fallout accumulates. What we've got now is a blend of fact and fiction that we're agreeing to call reality.'

'What was the worst thing you ever did?' Richard asks.

Nic's answer is instantaneous. 'Slept with my brother's girlfriend, after he died; for a second I felt like my brother, and that was incredibly powerful, and then it was awful. You?'

'I offered to get my father stoned.' He laughs. 'I showed him some pot. "You think you're such a big shot,"' he said, and then he wanted me to take it outside and bury it. He was afraid we'd all go to jail, as though the police were going up and down the Brooklyn streets sniffing people's pockets.' Richard laughs again.

They drink and listen to the ocean.

'There is a woman I know, a survivor from World War II,' Nic says. 'Everywhere she goes she takes a little something, she worries that when she gets to the next place there will be nothing. In her purse there's always something wrapped in a napkin, there's always something extra from the grocery store. She once told me, "It's easier when they have something free by the door, like those free AOL discs." She has hundreds of them; she slips one into her bag and is, for the moment, relieved. More scotch?'

'A little.'

'What do you think of this?' Nic says. 'I have a recurring dream of going into the ninety-nine-cent store, and there's a suicide bomber in there buying duct tape. He's standing in the aisle, wrapping duct tape around his middle, around his bomb, and I'm the only one who sees him, everyone else is shopping.'

'Are you drunk?'

'No doubt. But the dream is real; I've had it three times.' He pauses. 'Too bad your friend with the donut shop doesn't have a Santa Monica depot, I could really go for one of those sprinkled high-tops.'

On Saturday, he takes Ben to Disneyland. Barth is at Anhil's, Ben drives. He drives like a kid from the East Coast, a kid who took lessons on weekends, who only drove in the summer.

On the highway, he stays in the right lane, despite the millions of people using it to fade in and out.

'Am I doing something wrong?'

'No, not at all, nothing wrong, just maybe give it a little more gas, so they don't all have to go around you. It's difficult in this lane with everyone entering and exiting and us hovering at forty-five.'

Ben nods. He pushes it to forty-eight. His daisy in the flower holder is wilting. It takes a long time to get to Disneyland. Main Street, U.S.A.

'It looks exactly like I thought it would,' Ben says. 'It's so clean, like they want it to look brand-new every day.'

It seems wildly expensive; how do poor people or people with more than one kid afford this? Richard wonders. It's not like Rye Playland or Coney Island, where five dollars used to buy a day's entertainment.

'Isn't it amazing the old mouse is still so popular?' Ben says as he has his name embroidered on the back of a mouse hat – twenty-two dollars.

Pluto strolls over and puts an arm around him, and Richard growls. He's aware of himself being grouchy, weirdly just like his own father. When he was a kid, they would finally go and do something fun and his father would be miserable and the rest of them would spend the day baby-sitting his misery.

'No one ever took you to Disney World, not even when you were in Florida visiting Grandma and Grandpa?'

'No,' Ben tags.

'Not with your class at school?'

'We went to places like Normandy in France and to someone's family's organic farm.'

They get in line for the driving ride. You must be at least three years old and so high to go on this ride.

'Aren't we a little old?'

'How could we be too old? We never did it before,' Ben says.

'We're taller than everyone here.'

The cars are on a metal track, you're not really free, but you get the sensation of driving; there's four inches of 'wiggle room' in each direction.

'Did you love each other?' Ben asks as they take off.

'Yes.' Going around a curve, some lunatic six-year-old keeps bumping into the back of Richard's car, even though he's flooring it and there are signs everywhere that say 'No Bumping.' 'I loved your mother very much; I'm still drawn to her.'

'What happened?'

'Did you ever ask your mother?'

'Yes.'

'And what does she say?'

'She says you wanted more than she could give.'

'That's true with one modification: I wanted more than she *wanted* to give me, which is not the same – she chose not to give it.'

'Is it weird to make a person and then have the marriage fall apart and then no one wants the person?' Ben asks.

'We wanted you, there should never be a question about that. You were wanted.'

'How would I know?'

Going from ride to ride, Ben is so excited that he can't bear the slowness of walking. He runs. As jaded as the kid is, there's something about him that's untouched, something genuinely sweet that Richard really likes.

They spin in the Mad Hatter's teacups.

'So why didn't you take me with you?'

'I had no idea where I was going.'

'Didn't you know that I needed you?'

'I'd never had a kid before.'

'But you were one once, you had your own father, your own childhood.'

It feels like an interrogation, like the kid is going to spin him around and around until it all falls out, until there is nothing left, and Richard thinks, Fine, do it, I deserve it – it's the conversation they've never had.

At Space Mountain they wait in line for twenty-five minutes. The people in front and in back of them probably know them better than they know themselves by the time their turns come.

'I didn't think I was leaving you in a dangerous place; I left you with your mother.'

'You left, that's the only thing that matters.'

AWOL. Lost at sea. He didn't fight. He couldn't bear any drama. He went to a hotel. It wasn't like he had the whole thing worked out, it just happened that way. He went to a hotel, lay down, and thought he would die. There was the crippling stillness, the absence of oxygen, the physical pain. He remembers physical pain. He almost whips his cell phone out of his pocket and calls Lusardi to tell him he's made the connection, but he can't bear for everyone at Space Mountain to know more. He remembers the pain – he won't forget it now. He didn't call for a week, and when he did she said, 'What do you want, do you want me to tell you to come back? You're the one who decided to leave; no one told you to go.'

'Did we ever talk about roller coasters?' Ben asks.

'I don't think so.'

'I love roller coasters,' Ben says.

On Space Mountain, Richard feels like his body might explode, his muscle fibers are vibrating, with every up and down his stomach sinks, he feels tortured.

As soon as they are out, Ben wants to go again.

'I've got an idea,' Richard says. 'We'll get in line together, and then, when it's our turn, you go on your own and I'll run around and get in line again, and that way you can just keep going around and around.' They do that about six times, until someone catches on and gets annoyed.

Richard's feet are killing him. The only food around is hot dogs and hamburgers and weird chicken nuggets, and what they call a salad is a plastic bowl of iceberg lettuce with carrot shredded on top. He buys himself an ice-cream sandwich, and because the sun is baking his head, he gets a hat. 'What name do you want on it, Dickwad?' Did the guy say 'Dickwad' or did Richard just think it to himself – loudly?

'Blank,' he says. 'Just leave it blank.'

And now he looks like a hot, sweaty, over-whelmed mouse that's been had – just like everyone else in the park.

In one of the gift shops, Ben wants an enor-mous stuffed animal; it costs $175.

'The camel is my animal,' Ben says.

And Richard has to say yes.

On the way back to Malibu, Richard is at the wheel.

'I'm not done yet,' Ben says. 'I want to keep going.'

'What does that mean?' It means they stop in a shopping center that has an indoor game park and sign up to play Laser Tag. Again, there is a wait; there are boys everywhere, jumping, climbing, clamoring.

'Have you done this before?'

'A couple of times. There's a place in Times Square, we used to go for birthday parties.' There's a pause, a moment when they're both distracted watching two boys fight over who put quarters in the vending machine. 'You know,' Ben says, 'you never took me anywhere, never met my friends, never taught me how to be a guy, how to fix things.'

Richard listens, thinking about the trips he made to New York, carrying things, things he'd collected over the months between trips, things he'd bought at the last minute worried he didn't have enough, the time he brought a bike with him, a computer, the bones of a dinosaur.

He came carrying everything he could think of, and always it was the wrong thing. Why didn't I get you a football, a baseball glove, we could have gone to the park and tossed a few around? It's raining; we can't go to the park. It's snowing; we could go sledding. Do you have a sled? Maybe we can get one; he is on the phone calling; sold out, out of stock, next week? Snow doesn't stay on the hill for a week; maybe we could borrow one. Any of your friends have a spare? How about an empty box, a big cookie sheet, a magic carpet . . . well, at least let's get some hot chocolate.

'You never taught me to shave without slitting my throat, never helped with homework, never took me to a game, a concert, a show.'

'That's not true,' Richard says, on the defensive. 'We went to Radio City once to see the Christmas show.'

'Yeah, and I ate too much candy and threw up in the ladies' room, because when I said I didn't feel good you didn't get up, and some lady took pity me on me and brought me in there.'

'I went looking for you. I looked everywhere. I thought you were missing. I never thought of looking in the ladies' room.'

Their number is called. Richard pays and they're ushered into the Armory.

'No running, no pushing, no firing at the eye. Any violation of any of the aforementioned and you are out of the game. When you are hit, your vest will flash. It will flash for fifteen seconds;

while it is flashing, you cannot be hit again. While it is flashing, you cannot fire. Your score is kept electronically. Those are the rules.'

They put on heavy vests, like breastplates, with guns attached by coiled phone cords. A man fits Richard's vest to his body. 'First time?'

Richard nods.

'Go slow. The kids will run you down.'

Richard and Ben are on opposite teams. Richard is Red, Ben is Green.

'That way I can kill you,' Ben says, gleefully.

They go into the game room. There's a countdown, flashing lights, a fog machine, everyone hides. The game begins with a loud farting blast – an air horn. Kids rush past Richard; he is surrounded by the rat-a-tat-tat of plastic gunfire. Someone runs past – smashing him in the leg. Richard grabs the kid by the shirt and shakes him. 'No running.'

His vest starts flashing; he's hit. He didn't see it coming. Looking around, he has no idea where it came from. Richard takes cover. From his perch, he fires back, hits a big fat kid – easy target. He picks off another one, and then he's hit again. His vest is still flashing when he passes Ben on the bridge.

'You all right?' Richard asks.

'Yeah,' Ben says, heading off into the dark.

Richard works his way around the lower level, ducking in and out of corners, hideaways, learning to fire using the mounted mirrors that reflect his shot – ricochet, you're dead. He is breathing hard. His vest goes off again. He hears laughter.

'Ben?'

'Yeah.'

'Where are you?'

'I'm hiding.'

Richard waits for his vest to recover. He isn't sure exactly where Ben is – to the left or to the right. As soon as his vest goes clear, he's hit again.

'Ever wake up and think, "I blew it"?' Ben asks, speaking into the chemical fog.

'Yes.'

Richard's vest reactivates; Ben pops out and shoots him – point-blank. The boy waits, poised to kill him again.

'What fun is it if you keep shooting me right away?'

'It increases my score.'

'Don't I get another chance?' Richard asks.

'You missed your chance.'

Richard ducks around a pole, firing at someone passing by – direct hit. 'What's the point of always being angry with me?'

'You talk with your feet,' Ben says

'What does that mean?'

'Behavior. It's not what you say, it's what you do.'

Richard gets good at the game, learns how to avoid being killed, acts like a sniper, hits a few people out of the blue.

The game ends – they come out sweaty, excited.

Richard offers to go yet another round. 'Anything else you need to say to me?'

'Not right now,' Ben says.

They turn in their guns and go home.

On the way home, Richard stops at PC Greens; Ben stays in the car. Richard runs in; he's starving. He throws some of everything into his basket: every green, every vegetable, some organic turkey to make chili, some beans, some sort of soy ice cream, more root beer.

Across the aisle he sees Joseph, from the retreat. Joseph with a basket with nothing in it but chives.

'Hello,' Richard says.

Joseph nods – he seems to have no idea who Richard is. He continues talking to the young man he's walking with. Richard follows them along the next aisle, listening in. 'The disciple's love is dominant, and just at the moment when he needs the master most, the master no longer gives the disciple anything – nothing. The disciple suffers, his trust has been betrayed. But the entire purpose of the relationship is to create such incredible loss that the disciple's ego is broken, and only then can the disciple transcend the limits of his consciousness and become one with the infinite, the master. Beautiful, eh?'

'Are you a member of the club?' the woman at the register asks.

'Apparently not,' Richard says.

He piles the bags into the trunk. 'I just saw the guy who ran my meditation workshop. For seven days I stared at him ten hours a day. I spilled my guts in a private meeting with him, and he looked at me like he'd never seen me before.'

'He probably has a lot of students,' Ben says.

'That's what you'd call a big teaching on how insignificant you are.'

'It's not you personally,' Ben says. 'We're all insignificant.'

A moment later, Richard glances over – Ben is crying.

'More,' Ben says. 'I want more.'

'Of what?'

'Everything.'

Instead of driving home, Richard and Ben drive to the Santa Monica Pier. They share the pint of soy ice cream and cram themselves into the toddler teacups and onto the mild Matterhorn and then turn in wide, elegant circles on the Ferris wheel.

Later, when they're back at the house, Ben says, 'That was fun.'

Richard takes it the wrong way: 'Are you giving me shit? All day it was unrelenting; I didn't say anything, I listened, I figured I deserved it; but at a certain point it's enough.'

'No,' Ben says, earnestly. 'I really had a good time, I'm saying I had fun.'

'Yeah? Me too – I liked Disneyland.'

And they both put on their mouse hats, duck behind the sofas, and start throwing things at each other – socks, dish-towels, pillows. The dog barks.

★   ★   ★

That night, the evening news reports a run-in between the mysterious big cat and a tractor-trailer, which jackknifed when the driver swerved to avoid what he described as a 'lion.' 'One of the animal's toes was severed in the incident, and the highway was closed for over an hour while the county coroner and animal-rights activists alternately gathered evidence including the toe and blood samples and fought over possession of the items. According to veterinarians at the Los Angeles Zoo, it is likely that the animal survived the incident and has headed into the hills. Tonight, the Los Angeles hill country is alive with trackers and wildlife advocates, all searching for the wounded animal, in a race to find him first. Clearly, whoever finds him will have a lot to say about what happens next: there are those who believe the animal should be shot on sight, those who want to trap and study him, and others who believe it is humans who are standing in his path.' The camera cuts to the Natural History Museum, where 'members of the He Was Here First campaign are gathering for an all-night vigil down here at the tar pits in support of the animal.'

'Malibu hasn't touched his dinner. Are you all right?' Ben asks the dog.

'He's all right; sometimes he eats too many dead fish and gets a stomach ache.'

'Maybe you shouldn't leave the door open all the time,' Ben says.

'He's a beach dog, I don't want him to feel trapped, he has to be able to come and go. Don't let him lick you on the face.'

'Why not?'

'He rolls in dead fish, licks his balls, and then you want him to lick your face? 'Nuff said.'

Richard's cell phone rings. It's Cynthia; she went to her kid's soccer game in the new car. 'It was fantastic; I stayed, I cheered everyone on, ate a hot dog, and then said good-bye and left. The best part was, I didn't have to drive anyone home.'

'Did you see their father?'

'He's away on business – the gardener's wife is staying with the kids.'

Richard senses that there is something more, something she's not saying.

'And?'

'I went on a date?'

'With who?'

'A weatherman. I met him at the gym.'

'Really.' He's a little bit jealous.

'In a spinning class. I was saying how much I liked the Weather Channel, it's very relaxing, and he said he was a weatherman, and then we had to stop talking because the class started on the uphill, and when it was over he asked me out – breathlessly.'

'And?'

'It wasn't as strange as I expected. We went to the movies.'

'Do you think you'll see him again?'

'You're jealous.'

Richard doesn't say anything.

'Admit it.'

'OK,' he says.

She laughs. 'You don't want to sleep with me, but you don't want me to date someone either.'

'I didn't say it was healthy. Do you like the guy?'

'I have no idea,' she says. 'I just thought that since he asked I should go – it's what the girls at the rehab call practice dating. You should try it.'

Ben is still on the deck, with binoculars. He likes to watch where Malibu goes; he worries about the dog's heading up onto the highway.

'He's not interested in the highway,' Richard says. 'He's lived here a long time, you have to assume he knows what he's doing.'

'He's a dog, he doesn't know about traffic.'

Ben turns the binoculars onto Nic's house. 'Dad, Dad, come here.'

Richard rushes over. Ben hands him the binoculars. 'Do you see what I see?'

Richard takes a look, peering into Nic's living room. 'A woman with frizzy hair? I think it's his cleaning lady.'

'It's not a cleaning lady, it's Bob Dylan. Look at his nose.'

Richard takes a second look. 'He looks old.'

While Richard is looking, Dylan comes out onto the deck and stares at him from all of fifteen feet away. 'Hey, man, don't look in, look out. The performing seals are that way.' He points to the sea.

Richard lowers the binoculars and waves apologetically, 'We were looking for the dog.'

'Malibu,' Ben calls, 'Malibu.'

The dog barks, races up the steps, tail wagging, and Dylan goes back into Nic's house.

'Oh, that was good, really ripe. I was just spying on someone,' Richard says.

Ben goes to the front door – opens it.

'Now what are you doing?'

'I want to see what kind of car he came in.' They both look out; there's an impossibly long black limo parallel-parked, spanning the width of two houses, with a cord of white lights down the side that make it look like the *Queen Mary*, or the *Nimitz*.

'I wonder how Nic knows him?' Richard says.

'Do you know who Nic next door is?' Ben asks.

'You mean what he does?'

'Who he is?'

Richard looks blank. 'He's a screenwriter.'

'He's Nicholas Thompson, he wrote *My Brother Country*.'

'Was that a movie?'

'It's a book, Dad, a totally famous book.' Ben leads Richard to his computer and Googles Nicholas Thompson; fifty-seven thousand results pop up. 'That's him,' Ben says.

'Now that you mention it, the name rings a bell – vaguely.'

'Vaguely? What planet did you grow up on? He was the spokesman for your generation.'

Ben clicks, opening a picture of a beautiful young man with thick blond hair in a buckskin jacket with fringe – a cross between a football player and a god.

'Well, Nic looks nothing like that guy,' Richard says. 'That guy was fantastic-looking.'

'He was younger,' Ben says. And then Ben clicks on a link to *Rolling Stone* and there's Nic on the cover with the headline 'He Speaks for You.' And then he finds another, later article, in *Time*, 'Missing in Action,' all about how Nic has gone underground and is living as a recluse somewhere in Los Angeles.

'He's hardly missing, he's right next door, he goes to meetings at the movie studios, plenty of people know where he is.'

'Well, his fans are looking for him – he kind of ducked out on the whole fame thing.'

'I don't think he wanted to be a writer,' Richard says.

'But he is a writer. He also wrote a bunch of books under the name Michael K. Stone – *Concrete Castle, And There I Was.*'

Richard and Ben sit at the computer, reading about Nic, while Nic is next door having a beer with Bob Dylan. It's a little weird. Richard feels like a spy, a cheat.

In the morning, the limo is gone and Richard wants to knock on Nic's door, but he's embarrassed and a little intimidated. He thought Nic was his friend, he was happy to have developed a friendship with a guy his own age, a guy he had something in common with, and now he doesn't even know who Nic is or was, or if Nic was playing some kind of game with him.

Richard goes to Anhil's. 'It turns out Nic is famous.'

'Of course he is,' Anhil says. 'Everyone in America is famous. Only a famous person could toss such a great wow-wow.'

Is Anhil confusing famous with fabulous?

Barth is there, helping Anhil make the donuts. 'I told him he can't make a movie about a donut maker without knowing how donuts are made.' Anhil winks at Richard. 'Two hours of donuts equals a half-hour of movie shooting.'

'Why didn't you guys tell me about Nic?' Richard yells to Barth, who's in the back mixing donut batter.

'We couldn't believe you didn't know. I ID'ed him on the first day.'

'Have you read the book?'

'Yeah, in junior high. It's one of those young-man-goes-on-a-quest-in-search-of-himself stories.'

'Where is the other big bag of sugar?' Anhil asks, and Barth hauls a huge bag of sugar out of the storage room.

'Was this book translated into my language? I don't like to read in English – the English language does not really have much variety.'

'What is your language?'

'I read Sanskrit, French, and English, and speak English, Hindi, Urdu, Bengali, French, and a little Italian. What do you think we did growing up? We had no Direc TV.' Anhil shakes his head. 'Americans always think they are smarter. Did anyone ever tell you that your Ivy League is poison ivy, and that's why you're all so busy scratching your heads and your behinds.' Anhil laughs at his own joke.

'I had no idea,' Richard says. 'He doesn't act like he's something special. I just thought he was the fucked-up guy next door.'

'He must have money,' Anhil says, 'because at the end of the wow-wow he said we should go looking for real estate, he wants me to open a Donut Depot in Santa Monica. Maybe you and Nic will back me?'

Anhil goes into the back, and together he and Barth measure ingredients into the gigantic bowl – 'To be good at donuts, you have to learn how to do the same thing again and again with consistency. It is about getting the same donut every day. People come back because they want the same donut again, not to be part of an experiment.'

Barth turns on the mixer; flour flies everywhere.

'Too fast,' Anhil says. 'You have to go slow until all the ingredients fold in.'

'My father is a scientist,' Barth says, out of the blue. 'He almost won the Nobel Prize.'

Anhil nods. 'That's good. Lipi's sister is coming to visit. She is very beautiful; maybe you'll marry her. She is a mathematician coming to UCLA to finish her Ph.D., she is like a goddess. Before you go, I have to show you something.' Anhil takes Richard into the basement of the store. 'There is blackness creeping in,' Anhil says. 'It frightens me.'

Pungent, black, sticky, it smells like roadwork – tar.

'It can happen to anyone,' Richard says. 'I heard a story where the police caught someone they'd been looking for for years – he murdered someone and took off leaving tracks. There are yards that ooze black – it seeps up under the grass and takes over; dogs, cats get stuck in it; swimming pools crack and fill with it.'

'You are not making me feel better,' Anhil says.

'Call a plumber or a foundation man.'

On the way home, Richard drives by the house. They were supposed to start work, but so far nothing has happened. The city is, 'off the record,' taking some version of responsibility for the sink-hole: they've agreed to send a crew to fill the hole, but deny responsibility for the property damage.

Back in Malibu, he opens the fridge – empty. He calls Sylvia and leaves a message that he needs a double order of everything: high-protein, low-carb, and some extra snacks. 'I've got the kid staying with me and he eats like a horse. P.S. He really likes your cookies.'

At noon, Sylvia calls back, 'I'm coming that way this afternoon, so I can just drop it at the house.'

'Great,' he says. 'I should be here.'

'If you're not, I'll leave it with Nic.'

'Perfect,' he says. 'So you two are pretty serious?'

'Actually, no,' she says, 'but he has a good sense of humor.'

He runs into Nic while he's putting out the recycling.

'Are you avoiding me?' Nic asks.

'I don't know what to say.'

'How about you apologize for being a Peeping Tom?'

'Oh, I am sorry about that. Ben called me to come look, and I thought it was like your cleaning lady or something.'

Nic smiles. And then there is a pause and neither speaks. 'What's the problem?'

'I just don't get it.'

'What's to get?'

'I thought we were friends. I was liking having another equally fucked-up guy to hang around with.'

'And?'

'I don't know who you are. Actually, I should say I didn't know – and now I do. Why didn't you say anything? Is it some sort of a game, fun for you, deceiving the guy next door?'

Nic shakes his head. 'The opposite. I was enjoying having a friend who didn't give a shit who I was – you may have noticed I don't really have friends.'

'Bob Dylan.'

'He's not my friend, he just stopped by.'

'John Lennon.'

'You're being mean. What does it matter who I am?'

'It would have been nice to know.'

'It was nicer for me that you didn't. I'm making French toast, you want some?'

Richard shakes his head. 'I already had a cruller.'

'Well, at least come inside; I can't have this conversation with an audience.' Nic tips his head towards the photographers across the street.

'That's what they're here for? Pictures of you?'

'I used to think they were trying to catch the mayor coming out of his love nest, but when he left and they stayed, I figured it out.'

Richard follows Nic back into the house. He sits at the kitchen table, looking at everything differently. The mess has taken on new meaning. It's not just any mess, it's Nicholas Thompson's mess.

'Are you sure you don't want some?' Nic asks, cracking eggs into a bowl.

'I'm not sure of anything.' He glances at Nic's desk, his computer screen. 'What are you writing?'

'I'm working on a book.'

'And you write movies?'

'And I write movies. As you probably know, many of America's great artists have sold their souls in order to pay the rent.'

'Did you write a novel?'

'I wrote a bunch of crap under another name – if that's what you're asking about. This is a real book, something I care about.'

'What's it about?'

'Hopefully, transformation.' Nic taps the file drawer of his desk.

'Do you have more than one copy?' Richard asks.

Nic laughs. 'Nope, I use my typewriter.'

'Just knowing that makes me nervous.'

'All living is living dangerously,' Nic says, grinning. 'I can't take what I write on the computer seriously. I need to pound it but, word by word, line by line, in order for it to mean something to me. I like the hum of the machine, the way you have to really hit the keys.' Nic opens his closet; it's filled with IBM typewriters, one on top of another, and boxes and boxes of ribbons and correcting tapes. 'I've got a guy who comes to fix them – last time he was here, he'd just fixed the one at the L.A. County Morgue; it was sticking, having trouble with the toe tags.'

'Did you tell Anhil you would invest in a Donut Depot?'

'Yeah, I was thinking we should find him a spot in Santa Monica – his donuts, Sylvia's healthy snacks, a one-stop shop.'

Richard pauses. 'So what's the story? Are you a recluse? Are you missing? Are there people out there looking for you? And what makes you so special anyway? You seem, pardon me, equally fucked up as everyone else, and still they think you're a god.'

'They don't know me. Do you know the old joke? To your mother you're a captain and to your father you're a captain, but to a captain you're no captain. I don't like people expecting me to be able to fix their lives; it's not like I have special powers or know something the next guy doesn't. I'm a guy whose dad sold insurance, who got famous because my brother died and it fucked me up. Me getting famous only made things worse for my family. They'd come out in the morning and there'd be people camped out in the front yard.'

Nic puts French toast on a plate, douses it in syrup, and passes it to Richard, who digs in, despite having eaten the cruller.

'Can you imagine the burden? I could barely speak for myself. The whole thing was me trying to figure out what I thought, and then there I was being invited to testify before Congress, give commencement speeches, officiate at weddings, be at the birth of children; Kellogg's wanted to name a cereal after me. I left home because I couldn't stand it. I didn't know what to do, how to feel; I was afraid. My family lost its hero. I ran because if I didn't do something I'd burst. I walked because I didn't have a car, because I was angry and needed to pound it out mile for mile, because I wanted to see what was out there, just beyond my reach. I wanted to know what America was. Everywhere I went, someone gave me something – a pair of pants, a shirt, a little bit of their person. They gave me their stories. I typed them up on an old portable typewriter with carbon paper, I sent the carbon pages home and kept the originals with me. I was obsessed about not losing things – can you imagine? Now I could just walk to a Kinko's in every town, make a copy, e-mail it, fax it, beam it up, and store it in cyber-space.'

Nic eats his French toast and then hooks up his IV vitamins, talking all the while.

'There was a darkness in America, and I was the wandering boy – poet, prophet, flimflam man. I came to California because, compared with the cold of upstate New York, I liked the idea of the sun always shining. I walked all the way across the country to find myself, only to then lose it again, on account of people wanting me to be something I wasn't – a guru or a leader. I was just a guy. I am just a guy.'

'The guys at the pow-wow?'

'They have no idea.'

'Really?'

'Yeah, how would they know? As far as they're concerned, I'm just a lucky hack.'

'Do you really have a kid, and an ex?'

'Yep, and she really left me for another woman. I'm a freak but I'm not a liar. Do me a favor – pretend you don't know. You're agonizing, I can see it.'

Richard pretends to change the subject. 'What about the donut shop, do you think it's a good idea?'

Nic nods.

'How would it work?'

'We'd be partners, with Anhil. The three of us would sign on the lease, and then we'd take a cut of the profits.'

'What's the risk/reward ratio?'

'I have no idea. It's an investment in a man; your friend Cynthia could work there, she could run it.'

Richard smiles. 'That's a good idea, she wants something in retail.'

'Can I just ask you something?' Nic leans forward.

'Yeah, sure.'

'What were you doing back then? I mean, it was a pretty active time for most people.'

'I'm a little younger than you.'

'Not that much. Were you completely out of touch with the rest of the world?'

'I was sheltered. We went to the beach at Cape May for two weeks and thought we were fancy.'

'Weren't you afraid you were going to be drafted?'

'I'm flatfooted, wore leg braces when I was really little, metal braces, and brown orthopedic shoes.'

'What was the matter with you?'

Richard shrugs. 'I have no idea. And my brother is deaf in one ear,' he says, puzzled, the memory just coming back to him. He shakes his head. 'I didn't remember that until just now, when I said it.' Richard takes off his shoes and looks at his feet – pale, very pale, hairy toe knuckles, and absolutely no arch. 'Maybe that's why I was a swimmer and not a runner.'

'The right leg looks a little thinner than the left in the calf,' Nic says, studying his legs.

'Yeah, I know. It's always been like that.' Richard puts his shoes back on. 'What was I doing? I read a lot of books, biographies of people who invented things, men starting companies. I really liked Einstein and the guys who invented computers.'

'I thought your brother was the inventor.'

'I think I started it and then I got more interested in business. I was always setting up little companies. From the time I was about twelve, I made a profit.' He stops.

Silence. Contemplation. He is distracted, going from Nic's story back into his own.

'You can't escape yourself,' Nic says. 'Everyone has a history.'

Richard calls his parents; his mother answers.

'Do you remember the Vietnam War?'

'What, no "hi, hello, how are you"? Is this a quiz show – do I get a new car for the right answer, a hundred dollars' worth of free groceries?'

'I'm just trying to piece together something. Did you and Dad ever talk about the war when I was growing up?'

'No,' she says. 'We didn't talk about things like that in the house – we didn't want to frighten you.'

'Why would it frighten me?'

'War made your father very anxious – it was good for the insurance business, but bad for the

Jews. The whole way Roosevelt handled what they called the Jewish Question – the Nazis, he knew they were killing Jews long before he did anything to stop it. There are still people – right here in our condominium complex – who say it never happened. We don't talk to them. The Vietnamese weren't our people; we were still recovering from our war.' She pauses. 'All I can say is that it should have ended sooner – what comes out after the fact is always interesting.'

'And what about my leg and the brace? Was I born with something wrong with me?'

There is a long silence.

'You had a virus,' his mother says. 'And it went to your leg.'

'What kind of a virus?' he asks; it makes no sense.

Another pause. 'Polio. You and your brother – I was terrified that I'd lose you, both of you. I thought it was a cold, but you cried and cried like you were in a lot of pain and then had trouble with your leg. I didn't know who to blame. Your father was devastated. He wanted us to move out of the city, he said it was the city's fault for having unsanitary conditions, he wanted someone to accept responsibility. I think he felt guilty.'

'And I was never Bar Mitzvahed?'

'No. You could do it now if it means something to you – you're circumcised, and that's what counts. We had a nice party for that.'

'I don't remember it.'

'Thank God.'

'Your brother had a Bar Mitzvah,' his father says, taking the phone from his mother – clearly he's been listening in. 'A group Bar Mitzvah at the Reform Temple. There was a luncheon; a lot of people got sick from the egg salad – there was something wrong with the mayonnaise, it had turned. Since when are you so religious?'

'I'm not. I'm just trying to remember things.'

'History changes, you can't hold on to anything.'

He hangs up thinking about his parents' getting old, how much is already lost, how he'll never get it back. He thinks about how long he's kept away from them, as if protecting himself, but they're not who they were, the secrets they were keeping are already gone – they don't remember what they forgot to tell him.

In the morning he gets a call from the contractor. 'We had to quit work on the house – you've got a colony of fire ants living there; a couple of the guys got stung. I only hope they don't sue.'

'For what?'

'They could claim you knew the colony was there.'

'What colony! I don't even know what you're talking about.'

'Look, get an exterminator – that's the first thing you need to do – and then, when they say it's safe, call me back. There's no hurry.'

'There is a hurry – it's my house, it's in pieces.'

Fire ants – he imagines a colony of little ants dressed in firemen's garb, heavy coats, hard hats. He pictures red ants in native wear – kind of Hawaiian, or like tribesmen of New Guinea – dancing around a fire they made with a piece of old broken bottle glass and a dry leaf, sending smoke signals to other colonies up and down the coast, celebrating a sting.

He calls six exterminators before he finds one that deals with fire ants; he gets that guy's name from his insurance agent – Paul, the stoner, who asks, 'Are we ever going to meet in person or is this it – these random, impersonal phone calls?'

'I have no idea,' Richard says. 'Do you exist in reality?'

'Yes. Next time I suggest you stop by the office.' Paul's voice is high and thin; Richard imagines him as enormously tall and long, like a California tree.

At the end of his next session, Sydney, the Gyrotonics instructor, asks him out. They go to dinner, they go dancing. She invites him back to her place. 'If you don't like my peaches please don't shake my tree,' she sings. 'There's something I should tell you,' she says. 'I have only one breast.'

'That's OK,' he says, thinking that it's somehow genetic, in the way that a guy can have only one nut.

'I had cancer.'

He nods.

'I had surgery.'

He nods again.

'So – I have only one breast. I haven't done this in a long time.' She pauses. 'I thought you should know.'

'Neither have I,' he says.

'Not since then,' she says.

'Are you all right?' he asks.

'I'm fine.'

He holds her. They stay like that, standing, holding, for a long time. They kiss. She is a good kisser. He's not sure he ever liked kissing before, but her mouth tastes good, feels good. The wetness of her mouth, the briskness of her tongue catch him off guard. He feels a rush of blood, hot and cold, terror and desire. Enveloped in the heat of her body, her scent, foreign, unfamiliar, reminds him of how much he liked the smell of his wife. How when he left her he took her perfume, and every now and then would spray a little, getting a dose, a fix of her.

'Is this all right?' he asks.

'It's perfect,' she says.

The absence of the breast, the unevenness of her, at first makes it difficult; it is a less-than-perfect fit. First he is on top of her, unbalanced, and then she is on top of him, self-conscious, the single breast hanging like an empty udder. The scar is a single long dark line.

They find a good position, spooning; he is behind her. 'It must have been awful,' he says.

'I felt it,' she says. 'At first I thought it was nothing. I waited, and then it was something. I could have had reconstruction at the time, but I wasn't ready. I remember thinking, Why not just put something else there – a hat rack, or a plant stand – why not just hang geraniums off my chest wall? I told them I'd think about it, and then I just couldn't think about it again.'

He holds the one breast in his hand like a piece of fruit.

Later, they stand next to each other at the bathroom mirror.

'You look good,' he says. 'You're incredibly shapely.'

'Thanks, so do you,' she says. 'You're very fit.'

They stand side by side, looking.

'You're very brave,' he says.

They make love again.

He touches her scar with his tongue. She shudders. 'Does it hurt?' he asks.

'No,' she says.

He makes love to every part of her, the breast and the absent breast, the positive and the negative space. It is slow and profound, and when he comes the release is deep, astounding, like something outside of reality, something unnamable, of the gods. He embarrassingly exclaims, 'Oh yeah,' before he can stop himself.

And when they are done, they are not sure if

they are married, are bound at the soul, or will never see each other again. They have given each other a great gift. Emptied and refilled.

He rolls over. 'Are you Jewish?' he asks her.

'Half,' she says.

He goes home. It is late. The house is dark. He walks in, sees dinner on the table – untouched. There are candles burned all the way down, flickering in pools of wax. The house smells like vomit. Ben is perched on the kitchen counter, livid – drunk.

'Welcome to the party, shithead. I tried to call you and got no answer, and then I had a drink. I waited, I tried again, I kept trying to call you, and I kept drinking. I finished a bottle of wine.'

'My phone must have been in my pants.'

'That's more than I want to know.'

'Did something happen? Where's Barth? I thought you guys were going to the movies.'

'Anhil took him to a donut show or something. I thought something happened to you – maybe you wrecked the car, had a heart attack, or you just left. I made you dinner. I fucking walked down to the grocery store, bought stuff, and cooked, and you didn't come home. You didn't come home and you didn't even have the fucking courtesy to call.'

'I'm sorry,' Richard says.

There is silence.

'I drank the wine and then I drank all your

scotch. I don't know why, but I drank your scotch. What is scotch anyway, and why do people have it in the house? It tastes like shit. I drank it, every last drop, and I don't feel very well. I'm not a big drinker, that was never one of my problems. I threw up in your bathroom; it made quite the splash.' He laughs. 'I didn't clean it up yet; I'm not done. I finished the scotch, but, you know, I could go another round. I was thinking I'd dip into the Mr Clean any minute now. You fucking suck.' He slides off the counter and crumbles onto the floor as though the counter is higher than he anticipated. 'You don't care about anything other than yourself – everything is about you. It's your fault I'm gay, that I go around trying to get men to pay attention to me, to fuck me.' He is waving the empty bottle for emphasis. 'Oh, and another thing, I love you. I love you so fucking much. If anything ever happened to you, I'd go crazy. I'm already half crazy, and I hate you for it. I never really had a father; I lived my whole life with some enormous fucking hole. Oh, and speaking of which, I'd like to fuck you. I mean why not? What better way of getting to know you?' Ben pulls up to Richard, humping him like a dog.

Richard pushes him away. Malibu barks. 'You're not too big for me to hit,' Richard says.

'That's great. You want to fight? What do you want, to spank me, tie me up, and maybe whack me with your belt? Do you mind if I jerk off while you do it? Maybe that's what we should do; maybe, as a rite of passage, you should just fuck the hell out of me.' He pulls his pants down and bends over, flashing his ass at Richard. 'Or maybe I should fuck you – maybe that would be a way to rid myself of this wretched feeling. If I raped you, would I feel better? That would be a hell of a thing for a son to do to his father. Do you think that's in any of the books? Would you press charges?'

'Pull up your pants.'

'I never told anyone, but whenever I was mad at you I would go out and give an old guy a blow job; that was my way of getting back. Sometimes I did it to people you and Mom knew – it was like double word score, extra points,' Ben says. 'My whole life, I kept thinking you'd know I was miserable, you'd know I needed you, and you'd come and get me – you'd rescue me. And you didn't even fucking call.'

'The time difference,' Richard says. 'I thought you were sleeping.'

'People call home from fucking spaceships; there is no excuse.'

'You're right,' Richard says. 'It's OK to be angry.'

'It's not, it's not OK. It's not OK for you to just say "I'm sorry," like that means something. I'm fucking sick with rage – that's why I ended up in rehab. I was getting stoned to make it go away, to stop being so scared. Don't you understand – you hurt me? You're still hurting me. You call to tell me you went to the hospital with chest pain; I have fucking chest pain every day, my goddamned bone marrow hurts. There is so much I don't even know how to say to you, I could fucking kill you,' he blurts in rubbery, drunken anger, charging towards Richard, and then he pulls back and is quiet. 'Want to see what it's like not knowing if someone's ever coming back?' Ben takes off down the back steps, into the night.

Richard goes after him. At the bottom of the steps, he listens for a clue, a direction, a sound in the distance. He doesn't hear anything except the waves lapping at the shore. Did Ben go into the water? Did he go up towards the road?

'Ben? Ben, are you out here? Can you hear me? Don't do this. Ben! Come back, let's talk. I'm sorry. I'm really fucking sorry, I can't apologize enough.' He runs down the beach, towards Santa Monica, his flat fucking feet pushing off the soft sand; he is not a good runner, but he keeps going.

'Ben? Ben, please.'

Looking up at the highway, at the movement of the cars around the curve, he wonders – would Ben have run up to the road? Would he have put a thumb up to hitchhike? This is how bad things happen, this is how they become irrevocable, this is how you can lose someone forever.

'Ben,' he bellows.

The night is moist, the air hanging, dense fog. He looks again towards the road and towards the water. The amusement park is in the distance, the Ferris wheel spinning, colors pulsing as if offering happiness for half-price, barkers willing to make

391

a deal, four darts for three dollars, another dart another dollar. This cannot be happening. He thinks of the saber-tooth. What if the saber-tooth is real, what if he is out there somewhere waiting? He's probably hungry – he hasn't eaten any people yet, because there are no people on the streets, everyone is always in a car. Does he eat cars? Richard pictures punctured tires, tooth marks. He runs farther down the beach.

'Ben! Ben, where are you? I'm sorry, Ben, sorry for everything. Ben, can you hear me? Just say you can hear me. Ben!'

He trips over something – a thick, heavy thud. He falls hard onto – what? – an animal? He pats the animal's flesh – rough, dense, leathery. The animal shifts, groans. A pack of sea lions? The sea lions are resting, lined up next to each other, on top of each other. He hurries to get up, worried they will think he's an intruder and attack. He pushes off the lion, back onto the sand.

He's floundering. He's lost. He goes farther, trips over a stone or a stick, and collapses as if cleaved open. 'Marco,' he screams into the silence. 'Marco.'

'Polio,' his brother used to call back. Richard remembers his brother calling 'Polio' and starts to sob. It's all too much.

Out of the darkness, Ben appears, face dissolving as though the scotch were a solvent. He approaches Richard, his jaw drops, and he vomits, splashing Richard's ankle. Ben kicks sand over the vomit and sits next to Richard.

'You were supposed to come and then there was a blizzard and I kept thinking you'd come anyway, you'd find a way. I thought nothing would stop you, and you never showed up. There was a kid in my class at Dalton whose father came and stole him and they went to Brazil and never came back. The mom went crazy. Every day I hoped for something and there was nothing. You were the missing man.'

Richard stands up and Ben knocks him down.

'I'm so sorry,' Richard says. He gets up again and offers Ben his hand, and Ben takes him out at the knees.

Richard has no choice but to wrestle with him. They go at it, digging themselves into the sand, turning around and around in a circle of frustration, kicking, spinning, until Ben is not fighting anymore, until he's limp in his father's arms.

'I'm cold,' Ben says.

'That's the thing about L.A. – you can freeze to death under a rosebush,' Richard says.

Ben is passed out on his lap. Richard holds him, grateful just to have him, to feel his breathing, his chest moving evenly, his features flaccid, his lashes so long. Despite the fact that Ben is grown, he's still a boy, a small boy.

Even though it is not cold, Richard begins to shiver. It is his sweat evaporating, the moist night air. He gets up and half leads, half carries Ben back to the house. He undresses the boy and tucks him into bed.

Richard hangs a bunch of silverware tied with twine off Ben's doorknob, figuring if Ben wakes up, either to puke or kill him, he'll hear him.

And then he goes into bathroom. There's vomit everywhere, around the toilet, in the tub, up the wall. He gets a roll of paper towels and every cleaning product he can find and scrubs. He scrubs with everything and anything – Mr Clean, Comet, the brush made for cleaning a barbecue grill. He scrubs the tile, the grout, the shower curtain, and then finally gets in the shower and scrubs himself.

In the shower, he catches the scent of the Gyrotonics instructor, the woman with one breast. It already seems like so long ago. Her scent is on him like an animal's. She is in the hair on his chest, his cock and balls are coated with an intermingling of their juices. He lathers himself, scrubbing clean, trading the smell of sex for the smell of soap.

Out of the shower, he goes to the window, looking for lights at Nic's, wishing he had someone to tell the story to. The house is dark except for the computer screen, glowing blue, like a swimming pool.

He thinks about the woman. Was it nice, was it good, was it handicapped sex – they're both so handicapped this was the best they could do? He thinks it was good, he thinks it meant something to both of them. He wonders if it will happen again.

His mind goes back to Ben – the image of Ben pulling down his pants and flashing his ass at

Richard, Ben telling him about giving men blow jobs. What does it mean to want your father to fuck you?

He is tempted to call his ex-wife, but waits. He thinks about the single-breasted woman, the way she told him; it just about makes him cry. He takes out his pornography and jerks off – maybe it will help him sleep.

At four in the morning, 7:00 a.m. in New York, he calls his ex-wife. 'He's gay,' Richard says.

'Good morning.'

'He tried to sleep with me.'

'He needs a father.'

'He drank all the scotch, threw up everywhere, and made a pass at me. He wanted to fuck me, or me to fuck him, I'm not clear which, but, whatever it was, he meant it.'

'He meant that he feels confused, that the situation is confusing; he's testing you, that's what children do, they constantly test you. This trip means a lot to him; don't blow it.'

Richard hears a noise in the background, paper rustling, the scratch of a pencil. 'Are you editing while we're talking?'

'I've been at it since six.'

'He told me that whenever he was mad he used to give blow jobs to our friends, your friends.'

'I have no doubt. It's not easy. It's never been easy. I've been a working mother, a single parent in New York City, for thirteen years. I did the best I could. Are you calling me at seven a.m. to complain?'

'He talked about wanting to kill me.'

'Can you blame him? It makes perfect sense,' she says, siding with Ben. 'Look, Richard, he's had all of these feelings for years, they have to come out. I'm sure it's not pretty, but I doubt he's going to kill you. Lock your door if you're scared.'

'I locked his.'

'That's great, hold him captive.'

A flash of pain – Richard was trying to keep Ben safe, to protect him, not hold him hostage. 'I'm doing the best I can,' Richard says, knowing it is not enough – the situation requires more.

'If I can get a few things off my desk, I'll come out for a day or two. Maybe if we all spend some time together that will help. Be kind to him; he loves you very much, despite what he says. And set limits, make sure he knows what you will and won't tolerate.'

'I'm trying,' Richard says.

At 7:00 a.m. he scrambles a beautiful bunch of eggs for Ben and thinks of someone waking up hung over – his stomach turns. Richard gives the eggs to the dog, makes some toast for Ben, pours a glass of juice, and goes down the hall.

'Ben, time to wake up.' He puts the juice on the night table and nudges the boy's shoulder. 'Up and at 'em.' Ben stirs slightly. Richard keeps shaking him. 'OK, guy, let's go.' Ben's eyes open; he squints, looking at Richard as if to ask, Who are you?

'How're you feeling, long night?'

Ben sits up.

'You OK?'

'Yeah,' Ben says, and that's it.

Nothing more, no explanation, no elaboration, no idea if Ben even remembers what happened.

'I made you some toast,' Richard says.

Ben gets up, takes a shower, eats his toast, drinks some water.

'I think maybe I'm still drunk,' he says when he falls over trying to put his pants on. 'I feel pretty weird.'

'Are you all right to drive to work?' Richard asks.

Ben walks across the living room in a straight line, one foot in front of the other; he does it again, backwards. He closes his eyes and touches his finger to his nose.

'I think you'll be fine,' Richard says. 'Drink a lot of fluids, you need to flush everything out.'

'Did I do anything totally weird?'

The father shrugs.

'Were you ever a fuckup as a kid?'

Richard shakes his head. 'I don't think so. I didn't drink, I didn't do drugs, when I was in my twenties I smoked pot. I thought it was really radical.'

'You didn't have to clean my puke in the bathroom, I was going to do that. No one should have to clean up someone else's puke.'

'It's not like it could wait, and, besides, I didn't want the dog to eat the vomit.'

'That's nice, very dadlike.'

'I enjoyed it,' he says, telling the truth. 'I felt very dadlike, very parental.'

Ben pours himself another glass of juice. 'You got laid,' he says, speaking into the refrigerator.

'Yeah.'

'I think I sort of knew that's what you were doing, and I freaked out; I figured once you got a girlfriend you'd dump me.'

'I'm not going to dump you. Now go to work; call me later.'

Ben leaves, and Richard is sick with exhaustion. Drained but agitated, he lies down, tries to follow his breathing, but can't. He sees Madeline, the swimmer, go by and wonders why he didn't think of it sooner. A swim. At water's edge, he remembers dipping his feet into a milky-blue antiseptic bath before entering the high-school pool; his skin was perpetually chapped from the extreme chlorine. He plunges in – the act of immersing, the sand sucking at his feet, the salt stinging his eyes, is delicious. He swims towards Santa Monica, crawling, turning his head to breathe, seeing only water and sometimes a flash of beach. The resistance of the water is a strange relief. It is as though he is high from the tumult of last night – the tsuris, his mother would call it. Ocean rolling, he swims, and when he runs out of breath he lies on his back, pacing himself. He is not alone – there are surfers and dolphins – and whatever discomfort he felt earlier is replaced with a buzz, a positive charge, a sense of having survived.

He swims until he can't move his arms anymore, until he has no kick left, until he cannot lift his head, and then he lets a wave carry him back to shore. He walks down the beach back to the house, showers, dresses. It's 10:30 a.m. – what the hell do people do all day?

He calls his brother at work. 'Not interrupting, am I?' It's one-thirty on the East Coast.

'Just answering e-mail. I get seventy or eighty a day, people who would never pick up the phone are perfectly happy to e-mail. How's Ben?'

'Really screwed up.'

'He's seventeen.'

'He's gay,' Richard says.

There's a pause; clearly the brother already knew or suspected. 'It's not considered deviant anymore.'

'It's not what a father hopes for.'

'It's not an illness. Every kid is different,' his brother says. Barth turned out great, but look at Penny, she's brewing some kind of eating disorder and she's a shoplifter; twice she's been picked up for stealing eye shadow. It drives Meredith crazy – can you imagine the daughter of a feminist stealing makeup?'

'Why does she steal makeup?'

'No idea, we've never even seen her with makeup on.'

'Maybe she wears it in secret.'

'And Meredith's father almost had to do jail time for tax evasion; we bailed him out.'

'The lawyer?'

'About ten years ago, he just decided to stop paying his taxes – no real reason. When they caught up with him, we had to loan him money so he didn't go to jail, and he was disbarred, and he never repaid us – it was Meredith's inheritance from her grandmother.'

'I had no idea.'

'It's not like we go around telling people. Families are filled with shit.'

'What were we like – did we ever do anything bad?'

'You once told Dad he was mean, and I think he would have liked to have killed you – "ungrateful son-of-a-bitch," he called you.'

'Did you know we had polio?'

'I knew you had something that made your leg sick and that you impressed the doctor, who thought you might never walk without the brace. Don't you remember, your shoes?'

'We always had good shoes.'

'Well, there was a reason.'

'Don't you think it's really weird that no one told us?'

'They felt lucky we survived and didn't want the stigma of it. I think she even changed doctors so it wasn't in our records.'

'Can you do that?'

'She didn't want people to think badly of us.'

'Why was it bad? It wasn't our fault, we got a virus.'

'She associated it with poor hygiene – dirty Jews and so on.'

'Do you remember your tantrums?' Richard asks. 'You had incredible tantrums, and you'd break things, and Dad almost called the police on you, but Mom stopped him.'

'He did?'

'Yeah, it scared him; he worried you were crazy. He'd say, "Do you need to go to a hospital?"'

'I don't remember that.'

A silence – maybe he shouldn't have mentioned the tantrums. 'Meredith told me about the prize. I don't know what to say.'

'Very disappointing; it was the one thing I wanted, and now it's not going to happen, so does that make me a loser?'

'I don't think so.'

'Meredith says if one of the kids came to me crying about it I'd tell them how wonderful it was that they'd worked so hard, gotten so much recognition, and accomplished so much, and when it's a prize that only one person gets it's hard to be that person – not winning doesn't mean you lose.'

'She's right.'

'I know, but I still can't swallow it, and secretly I'm mad at myself for ever thinking I might win.' He changes the subject. 'Are you still seeing the woman from the produce section?'

'We're friends,' Richard says.

When he's done with the brother, he calls Cynthia. 'Free for lunch?'

'Yeah, sure, I guess, is everything all right?'

'Twelve-thirty. I'll pick you up?'

He takes her to a health-food place near the housewife rehab. 'What's spelt?' he asks.

'It's the new-old whole wheat.'

'And what's gluten – why do some people want it and some don't?'

'It's not good in the gut,' one of the customers says.

They sit at a small table in the corner; she sprinkles sesame seeds across her salad.

'How's the roommate?' Richard asks.

'Someone hijacked her computer – online – gave it a worm that ate everything, cored it out. In the morning there was just the shell, the box, blinking at her, couldn't read its own hard drive. It threw her over the edge. Apparently, that's how this whole thing started – identity theft. Her ex-boyfriend's new girlfriend stole her identity, ran up huge bills, and it took two years to clear her name. Anyway, I had to take her back to the hospital; she started saying the worm was in her brain, attacking her brain.'

'And the weatherman – are you still seeing the weatherman?'

'Off and on,' she says. 'He helped me get her to the hospital, but I have to end it. There's something about his hair – it's so well organized that when I run my hand through it, it doesn't budge. So – what's up with you?' Cynthia asks. 'You called the lunch.'

'Everything,' he says. 'Turns out Nic next door is some kind of culture god hiding out; the photographers across the street are there for him.'

'You're like a freak magnet,' she says. 'First me, then the movie star, and now the ghost of J. D. Salinger.'

'How do you know Salinger?'

'I'm a housewife; I'm not illiterate.'

'Anyway, Ben spotted Bob Dylan at Nic's, and now I feel like I can't talk to the guy; I don't know if I'm intimidated or pissed at him for not saying anything.' She nods. 'And then Ben . . . Well – he's gay.' Richard takes a breath. 'It gives me the creeps, the idea of him with other men – when he sees me naked, does he find that interesting?'

'No.'

'Why not?'

'You're his father.'

'Who knows what gay people think?'

'Just because someone is gay doesn't mean that they're attracted to every person of the same sex.'

'He made a pass at me – more than that really, it was violent and really scary.'

'That's sad,' Cynthia says. 'He must be really angry.'

'Of course he's angry, but it doesn't mean you try and rape your father,' Richard says loudly, and the whole restaurant falls silent.

'Are you ever going to date?' she asks him in a whisper.

'I took your advice,' he says. 'I tried it.'

'And?'

'That's what started this whole thing – I was out late at her house.'

'How was it?'

'Good, weird.' He's about to say more, but then looks at Cynthia, whose expression is pained. 'And, by the way, it turns out I had polio as a child but my mother never told me.'

'This was all this week?'

'In the last three days; I'm exhausted,' he says.

'Have the ginger-ginseng smoothie,' the person at the table behind him says. 'It's restorative.'

'Thank you,' he says, and then talks more softly. 'I feel like I'm on a roller coaster – never knowing what's going to happen next. Speaking of which, do you have any interest in donuts?'

'I just ate that whole salad,' she says.

'Anhil, Nic, and I are looking for a place in Santa Monica to open a branch of the Donut Depot; we thought you might like to manage it.'

'Would I have people working for me?'

'Yeah, I guess so, one or two.'

'Would it be my own shop, would I be the donut lady of Twenty-third Street?'

'Pretty much.'

'Are the donuts good?'

'Very good, fresh, new flavors every day – raspberry, peach, lemon.'

'What's the time frame?'

'As soon as we can find a space and get it outfitted. Anhil will cook the donuts downtown and deliver them, and the new store will also sell Sylvia's cereal and snacks. It'll be sweet.'

'Sounds good; as you know, I've been thinking retail.'

After lunch he calls Sydney, the Gyrotonic date.

Her machine picks up; he starts to leave a message. 'Hi, it's me, I just wanted to see how you were.'

She picks up halfway through. 'Sorry, I didn't hear – who's calling?'

'It's me,' he says, 'your date, the guy from last night. I just wanted to follow up.' It sounds so professional. 'See how you're doing.'

'Oh, I'm pretty good, and you?'

'I'm fine,' he says. 'I got home and my kid was really mad, but I'm all right.'

'How old is he?'

'Seventeen, but, you know, we've never really lived together, and he'd made dinner for me and then I didn't come home.'

'What about Wednesday?' she says. 'Could we get together on Wednesday?'

'Sure,' he says.

'Why don't you come here and I'll make dinner. Come early, if you like.'

'I'll be there,' Richard says, hanging up.

Anhil and Lipi throw a celebration in honor of his sister-in-law's arrival: 'Lipi has been cooking

405

for a week.' Richard is looking forward to it – looking forward to not having to deal with Ben one on one. Their house is a rented bungalow in the Hollywood flats. The surrounding homes alternate between the well-kept and others with ill-hung sheets for curtains, barking dogs, and bars on every window. At Anhil's, the ceilings are low, the rooms small and dark, but instead of feeling like a cave, it is a magical resting place, spotlessly clean, warm, the air filled with amazing spices, the heat of food steaming. Just breathing in, Richard is transported.

They are waiting for Lipi's sister to come from the airport. 'Make my words,' Anhil says, 'she is a goddess.'

And he's right, Lipi's younger sister, Lakshmi, is radiant. She is delivered from the airport by Anhil's brother, and when she comes into the house Lipi takes off her apron and hugs her.

Richard looks at the two sisters – on the one hand, they look alike, and on the other, Lakshmi is a thousand times more beautiful.

'She was born that way,' Anhil says, seeing what Richard is seeing. 'And she is very smart. She has come to America to finish her Ph.D. in mathematics and physics together.'

'How long will you stay in America?' Richard asks her.

'The rest of my life,' Lakshmi says.

Dish after dish, bowl after bowl is passed, foods filled with spice, hot and heavy, cool and creamy, chutneys, things with yogurt, chickpeas, and, incongruously, steamed lobsters. 'Lakshmi's favorite food; don't ask,' Anhil says, pinching himself with a claw.

'The rice is delicious,' Richard says. 'Everything is incredible.'

'It's just rice,' Lipi says.

'But it is perfect.'

'Everything here is much more than it is – because it has passed through Lipi's hands,' Anhil says, toasting her.

They eat until they are too full to push away from the table. And, still sitting there, plates before them, Barth stands and introduces some clips from his work in progress.

'I'm not going to say anything except thank you to Anhil and Lipi for inviting me into your life, into your home, and just that I've really had such a great time.'

The film begins with a scene of Anhil as a swashbuckler à la Errol Flynn, Anhil fighting an invisible villain, waving his sword back and forth. The background is a distant forest and blue sky; the camera pulls back to reveal that Anhil is fighting an inflatable figure – one of those men parked by the side of the road who dance on account of a fan blowing up his ass. The camera pulls farther back, and we see that the set is a painted cinder-block wall of a car wash. When Anhil's car comes out of the car wash, a bunch of guys dry it; the swashbuckler tips them and drives away. Everyone laughs.

And then there is Anhil in the donut shop, Anhil saying, 'In America you have some immigrant people who are princes in their own country, but they come here and work in a parking lot and they are happier – what is a king without a kingdom?' His brother walks in carrying supplies for the donut shop. 'I am like the lemon,' he says. 'I don't fall far from the tree.'

There is a scene with Barth and Anhil test-driving a Mercedes in Bel Air, driving past the huge gated houses. 'What do you think of these people?' Barth asks.

'They are very lucky and thin; it's cowboys and twins,' Anhil says.

Later, standing at a hot-dog stand, Anhil addresses Barth and the camera: 'I am eating this hot dog for you, to show you how American I am. This is not good for you, not something you should do at home. If you are going to eat a hot dog, make sure it's kosher.'

Anhil and Barth drive back to the Mercedes dealer, and the salesman asks what they think of the car.

'What's not to love?' Anhil says. 'How much a month?'

'On a three-year lease, we're looking at seven hundred and fifty dollars a month. Interested?'

'Thank you,' Anhil says. 'I will return your call.'

'How many donuts is that, Anhil?' Barth asks as they're leaving the dealership.

'Is this a test question – if I answer correctly, do I win the car?'

Barth laughs. 'Seriously, how many donuts do you sell a day?'

'Sometimes four hundred; it's the standing orders – the firehouse, the hairdresser, the senior center, people who buy two dozen at a time. Tomorrow I raise my prices. Up ten cents a donut. I cannot live by Toyota forever.' The film cuts back to the opening scene.

'This is my America,' Anhil says, sweeping his sword through the air, accidentally knocking the antenna off his car. 'I hate it when that happens . . .' There is laughter in the background.

'Thank you, thank you,' Anhil says, bowing at the table. They all clap and turn to applaud Barth, who of course is filming.

'How much of the film have you finished?' Richard asks.

'We're alternating between shooting the documentary parts and some fantasy stuff that Anhil and I have been developing about mythologies – cowboys, Hollywood, the promise of America, the dream.'

'It's great,' Richard says. 'It really captures something.'

On the way home, Richard goes on about the film. 'I didn't realize how talented Barth is; he managed to get the dissonance of Anhil's experience, his fantasy versus the reality, and simultaneously capture Anhil both as he sees himself and as others experience him.'

'He pays attention,' Ben says. 'He sees things.'

'It's not obvious.'

'That's what makes him good at it. People feel comfortable with him, they don't see the camera as an intrusion but as an extension of Barth himself – he's been doing it since he was a kid. At camp they hired him to make the promo video. He got everyone to help – campers, cooks, the mean nurse in the infirmary.'

'It's very good. Do you remember, when you were younger, we'd pass a pet store and you'd be really angry with me for not rescuing all the puppies?'

'Am I supposed to think there's a link between Barth's movie and my deprived childhood?'

'I'm wandering in my thoughts. You used to want to be a veterinarian when you grew up.'

'Don't anymore.'

'Why not?'

'Euthanasia. I don't like that the animals don't understand they're going to die. I used to have a job walking dogs and house-sitting; the way I looked at it, people were paying me to drink their liquor.'

'Did you really?'

'Sometimes.'

'Well, what do you want to be?'

'Something where you don't get your hands dirty.'

'Remember when I took you on vacation? We flew all the way to London, spent one night, and you wanted to go home.'

'I was eight.'

'You liked everything to always be exactly the same. It was kind of rigid.'

'It was comforting,' Ben says.

'We got home and your mother was on vacation and I stayed with you in the apartment for a week – we had a good time, we went to the Museum of Natural History, the zoo, the park.'

Ben nods. 'Why are we talking about this?'

'Just thinking about things.'

They drive in silence for a few minutes.

'Are you really gay?'

'Yes.'

'Do you think you were born gay or you became gay?'

'Are you asking because you want to know if it's your fault?'

'I suppose.'

'To one degree or another, I'm sure it's your fault. Feel better now?'

In the morning, Billy picks up Nic, Anhil, and Richard in a huge SUV and takes them looking for real estate; Barth rides shotgun with the camera.

'This is so exciting,' Anhil says, 'going shopping with my big American backings.'

'Who is watching the store?' Nic asks Anhil.

411

'My brother.'

'So – you're opening a new business?' Billy says.

'Yes, Mr Hill.' Anhil has decided that Billy's name is Mr Hill, and no one can bring themselves to correct him.

'It's actually a branch of an already existing operation,' Nic adds.

'A donut shop,' Anhil says.

'Would they be cooking donuts on site? A lot of people have problems with odors – you know, dry cleaners, bakeries.'

'No cooking – the donuts will be cooked downtown and delivered to the new location,' Richard says, definitively, when in fact he's making it up.

'Are you scouting locations?' someone on the street asks after they circle the same block three times.

'Yes.'

'For a movie?'

'No, a donut shop; do you think this would be a good spot for a Donut Depot?'

The guy shrugs. 'I'm wheat-free.'

They look at locations, with parking, without parking – one was a former bakery, another a bank with a drive-through window, and one was a store that sold 'pieces of the imagination' and went out of business quickly.

'They must have really believed they were going to make money, because they spent a lot on the renovation,' Billy says.

'It has to be easy,' Nic says. 'Everything about

it has to be easy. No one wants to think too hard about getting a donut – they'll talk themselves out of it.'

Everywhere they go, they buy cups of coffee – hot coffee, iced soy latte.

'Did you notice the napkins in there? They had really thick napkins, not the rough one-ply ones. What's more cost-effective, a lot of thin napkins or one nice thick one?' Nic asks.

They cruise like teenage boys – except with the needs of old men. 'Is there a restroom? I drank all that coffee and now I need to take a leak.' They cruise and, like all guys riding in cars, they can't help talking about women, except Billy – Billy talks about men, sometimes as though they were women, as in, 'He was such a bitch.' They talk about women who dumped them and how some-times they didn't even catch on to the idea that they were being dumped.

'When I was about fourteen, I was dumped by a girl at a party – she met another guy she liked better, and when I asked her what was so great about him she turned around and in front of everyone screamed in my face, "You're a turd!"' Nic says. 'It took me a full year to recover.'

'I crave women, it is never enough,' Anhil says, then, turning to Nic, 'When you were famous; did you get a lot of girls? Ever have two at once? Three? That's my fantasy.'

'I had a lot,' Nic says.

'Did you do anything like take photographs of

them?' Anhil has the ability to ask questions that would otherwise seem rude, but because of his intonation, the innocence with which he asks, Nic just smiles and answers.

'No photos,' Nic says.

Anhil tells the story of his cousin who came to America and opened a photo-developing booth in the parking lot of a shopping mall. 'No luck,' Anhil says. 'Everyone went digital, business was poor. And then, one day, a tractor-trailer making a delivery to the furniture store backed up into the photo booth and squashed him – he never knew what happened. He was the blind spot.'

They cruise for hours and finally find a spot on Montana Avenue. 'I purposely didn't show it to you first; it's small, but it's a good location. You can put tables outside, there's parking. It's a corner. I think corners are good for cafés.'

'I like these trees,' Nic says. 'This is a place where you could sit for a while.'

'Oh, it is very pretty. It is upstream,' Anhil says.

'Upscale,' Nic says.

'That too,' Anhil says. 'We can put an auto-rickshaw station out front – to make deliveries.'

'What is an auto rickshaw?' Billy asks.

'Bajaj auto rickshaw,' Anhil says. 'It has three wheels, one in front and two in the back; the joke is, if the rickshaw can get its front wheel into a parking space you can push the rest of the rick-shaw in . . . Good for crowded places, but here it would be for fun delivery.'

'Let's do it,' Richard says.

'Thank you,' Anhil says to everyone. 'Thank you. This is my dream come true.'

On Wednesday, at breakfast, Richard announces, 'I'm going to be out late tonight, if that's all right.'

'You can have her over here,' Ben says.

'No, I can't. I haven't dated in years – it's all too strange. At best, it's an experiment.'

'Should I call and check on you?'

'I'll be fine,' Richard says. 'I just wanted to be sure you'd be all right.'

'I'm good.'

In the afternoon, Richard goes to the liquor store, prowls up and down the aisles agonizing over what the right wine would be. Finally he picks out something overpriced – decent, but nothing spectacular.

When he gets to her house, she is working in the garden. She greets him with a kiss; he can smell her scent – spicy, like clove. She leads him into the house and directly into the bedroom, undressing him and herself quickly. Nude, he is still holding the bottle of wine. She takes it from him as they lie back on her bed. They make love. He pays special attention to the scar, the absent breast, and then, feeling like he's trying too hard, he devotes himself to the one lonely breast – which now maybe isn't so lonely, because it's getting all the attention. They make love for what feels like hours; the sun goes down, the moon rises. They

415

make love like animals, it is entirely about the body, about their most primitive needs.

In a postcoital surge of affection he accidentally blurts, 'I love you.' The phrase hangs in the air, suspended, unanswered. She reaches under the bed and pulls out her earthquake kit.

'What's in it?' he asks.

'At the moment – my joints.'

'What else?

'One hundred one-dollar bills, my makeup – I couldn't bear to be in a shelter without a little makeup, I look like hell in the morning. Bars of chocolate, solar cell-phone battery, water-purification tablets, aspirin. Should I go on?'

'How much pot do you keep in there?'

'Not a lot, maybe ten joints.' She lights one and hands it to him.

She brings dinner into bed – ripe cheeses, avocado, olives, tomatoes she's dried herself, caponata she made, pesto she crushed in a bowl she made in a pottery class. He thinks about something Joseph said at the meditation: 'There is great comfort in daily ritual, feeding yourself from the garden.' As they are eating, she tells him that when she goes hiking she eats things she finds along the way – mushrooms, ferns. She tells him her hair is the color of copper because she uses a dye she makes herself; she tells him that she studied to be a belly dancer, and that she has given names to all of her plants – Margaret, Jonas, Yvette. 'All things do better when they have a name,' she says.

He thinks again of Joseph, talking about the struggle for transcendence played out against the fact that we are 'placed' in life in a human body. Something she says cuts through his thoughts: 'You've given me great confidence; next time we make love, let's do it in a public place.'

In the morning, it hurts to pee; Richard calls to make an appointment with Dr Lusardi.

'I have nothing available,' the receptionist says.

'When might something open up?'

'Dr. Lusardi is not with this office anymore. I have to put you on hold, one moment please.' He waits, wondering what happened to Lusardi. She picks up. 'Dr. Anderson suggests that you come in and speak with him.'

'Good,' he says. 'When?'

'Two o'clock.'

'What brings you in?' Dr Anderson asks when he finally comes into the room. Richard has read every back issue of *Modern Maturity* in the office.

'I've been seeing Dr Lusardi?'

'Yes?'

'I wanted to follow up – you know, talk to him about some things.'

The doctor flips through Richard's file. 'How have you been feeling?'

'Pretty good.'

'Any more chest pain or nausea?'

'No – just that one day.'

'And your prostate – urgency, difficulty?'

'Same as it was, except that . . .'

'How about I take a listen?' the doctor inter-rupts, then presses a cold stethoscope to his chest. Dr Anderson makes Richard miss Lusardi all the more – Dr Anderson is not interested in Richard himself, he is only interested in the mechanics of him.

'I thought I heard a little something – probably just a valve. Do you have mitral-valve disease? Has anyone ever mentioned it?'

'No.'

'I'm going to repeat a few tests for my own peace of mind – also an EKG, we don't have a current one.'

'Dr Lusardi did one.'

'It's not in your file; he must have taken it with him. Don't worry – I won't charge you.' The doctor calls in the nurse.

The image of Lusardi roaming around L.A. with the rhythms of Richard's heart in his pocket is disconcerting. He wants his strip in the file, where it belongs.

'When you went to the ER, what did they do?'

'Not much – a scan to make sure I wasn't having a stroke.'

'But not an echocardiogram?'

'I don't think so.'

'We'll send you to someone.'

Richard is starting to stress. 'Relax,' the doctor says, 'the test won't be any good if you're not relaxed.' He hooks him up, talking while watching the tick-tock of Richard's heart. 'I myself had a little something earlier in the year, felt something, didn't know what, turned out I broke a string on my heart – at my age they don't even fix it, like an old car they just let run down.'

'Did Lusardi really take my EKG?'

'No,' the doctor says, 'I'm sure it's around here somewhere, probably just misfiled.'

'So where is Dr Lusardi?'

'You tell me.'

'What do you mean?'

'He's gone, vanished – turns out he wasn't really a doctor; we were on to him, which is why he ran.'

'Not a doctor?'

'He wasn't who he said he was. Yale has no program in psychological internal medicine.'

'Well, then, who was he? He wasn't stupid, he wasn't wrong.'

'No, but he didn't have a license; he was a philosophy student from the University of Chicago who dropped out.'

'He was a good talker, he listened, he understood.'

'He was crafty,' the doctor says, ripping the EKG tape out of the machine, bringing the tape up close to get a good look.

'What tipped you off?'

'The insurance companies; he wasn't in anyone's system, he claimed it was something about how they were entering his information, that they were reversing a "u" and a "z" and that it had happened before. I was feeling good about him, paternal, a young protégé, someone I could leave things to. My wife and I didn't have children. I met him at a medical conference about a year ago. As you know, I've been under a lot of stress – my wife is not well.'

'How is she doing?'

'She does best when she doesn't know what's going on. When she comes to the surface, she gets frightened. That's the hardest part – when she looks scared, it's heartbreaking. She bit the dog. Are you sleeping?' the doctor asks Richard.

'Fitfully,' Richard says, remembering Lusardi's story about growing up in Chicago, raised by his mom, earning his way through college and medical school surrounded by children of privilege who took everything for granted.

'I didn't worry until now – I'm going over all his records, his patient notes, to make sure he didn't mistreat anyone, reviewing prescriptions, tests. He was a con man, but he didn't really take anything.'

'Except my EKG.'

'Which was probably just misplaced.'

'Will you press charges?'

'I'm only hoping he didn't do any harm.'

'Just because he wasn't really a doctor, does that mean what he said was wrong?'

'I'd take it with a grain of salt.'

'Is that a prescription?'

'It's my professional advice.'

'It hurts when I pee,' Richard says. 'That's why I came in – I slept with someone and, well . . .'

'There's a moment when something comes up – your colon, diabetes, heart – and you think, So now I know what it's going to be, where it's going to end. It's always a surprise,' the doctor says, lost in his own reverie. 'It's not what you think. Even fortune-tellers never give you the bad news – if they can see it. And, knowing, what do you do? Do you make peace with it? Is there such a thing as a good life, a good death? I digress – sorry. So tell me again, you got a little nookie and now you wonder if you got something else along with it?'

Richard nods.

'We can test for all that. Don't worry, drink a lot of cranberry juice, and we'll have the result back in the morning; or, if you want, I can give you a big dose of penicillin now, a shot in the fanny.'

'Let's wait for the results.'

'Prudent,' Dr Anderson says. 'We'll call you.'

Richard leaves wanting to track Lusardi, to get the real story. He wants to tell him it's fucked up, but he's no one's dummy.

The strange days of summer. There is no here, no there, the days are incredibly still, the light is brightly muted – it's hard to know if that's the passing of the season or poor air quality. The town has dried up – everyone who can get away has gone, making tracks for islands off Canada, Europe, Maine.

Richard wakes up to hear there was a small earthquake. 'A little action in Tumble Town over night. Some of you got an early start – about three-point-six on the Richter – some broken dishes, a little cracked plaster, but not too bad.'

Midday, Ben calls from work. 'Can you come and get me?'

'Ben? Are you OK?'

'I need you to come and get me – now.'

'Did something happen? Is there a problem with the car?'

'Dad!'

'I'm on my way. I'm putting on my shoes. Where should I get you?'

'I'll call you back in a few minutes. I have to go.'

Richard goes zooming down the Pacific Coast Highway, takes Sunset the whole way into town, in and out of lanes, his foot on the gas.

Twenty minutes later, his phone rings, 'Where are you?' Richard asks.

'I'm outside, at a pay phone; how far are you?' Ben asks.

'Ten minutes.'

'I'll call you back.'

'Ben?' And the line is dead.

Richard spots him wandering on a side street near The Agency.

'What happened?' Richard asks, and Ben begins to cry.

'What happened – what is it?' Richard can't imagine.

And for a moment Ben is crying too hard to talk. 'One of the guys, the leaders, got into the elevator with me. He pinned me against the back of the elevator and grabbed me by the balls – hard. He said things and then kissed me here, near my ear. It still hurts. I went into the bathroom, and everything down there is red. Is it something I did? Did I look at him funny? No one there knows I'm gay.'

'What's the guy's name?'

Ben wipes his eyes with his sleeve.

'Hassam, Roger Hassam.' Ben says. 'And then, when the elevator opened, I did the weirdest thing: I ran down the steps to the security desk, flashed my ID, and said, "They sent me to pick up the tape, I need the elevator one – now!" And the guy popped the security video out of the deck and gave it to me. "You never saw me, never gave me anything," I said. And the guy nodded, like this stuff happens every day.' Ben hands the tape to Richard.

'Does anyone else know you have this?'

'No. My car is still in their fucking parking lot.'

'How much do you care about this job?'

'I'm not going back, if that's what you're asking me.'

'That's fine,' Richard says. 'I'm going in there – what floor?'

'The guy used to work for the CIA; he'll probably kill you. My first day there, one of the guys warned me – he said, "Never get into an elevator alone" – but I didn't know what he meant.'

Richard leaves Ben in his car, idling at the curb. 'If I'm not back in twenty minutes, call the police.' He marches into the building, takes the elevator up.

'Hassam,' he says to the receptionist. 'Which way?'

'Your name?' the girl says, picking up the phone to buzz.

'Down here?' Richard points to a hallway.

'Actually, he's in the conference room with a client,' She says.

Before anyone can do anything, Richard is in the conference room. There's an older gentleman sitting at the far end of the table who looks very familiar, and a few other men huddled around him. Richard feels like he's walked in on something – he's out of his element. It's incredibly awkward.

'Hassam,' he says, and a guy in the middle looks up.

'You're busted.'

'I don't know what you're talking about,' the man says.

'My son's balls. Earlier today you had my son by the balls in the elevator. You've got two minutes to figure out what you're going to do to make it up to him, or the LAPD will be down here confiscating your computers, all your computers, given that you are a partner in this firm, and no doubt they'll find some interesting materials.'

Hassam stands. 'I think you should leave.'

'I have the tape,' Richard says, slipping the tape into the deck behind him.

'Stop,' Hassam says, before the tape begins to roll.

Four men appear in the doorway, guns drawn. 'Stop,' Hassam says again. And the room falls silent.

'Sir, are you all right, sir?' the men with guns ask.

'Fine,' the man at the head of the table says. 'It's not about us.'

'I'll buy the tape from you,' Hassam says.

'It's not for sale.'

'Well, then, what do you want, if not money?'

'Apologize to the kid, make sure he knows it's not something he did, make sure he knows that you trespassed his person, his boundaries, his rights, and you write him a glowing recommendation on his internship with the firm.'

'And?' Hassam says, waiting for the deal breaker.

'That's all.'

'Do I get the tape?'

Richard shakes his head. 'No one gets the tape. Consider this fair warning; if it happens to anyone again – he'll testify.' Richard pushes the 'record' button on the deck and is out the door. He takes the elevator all the way down, picks up Ben's car, and drives up the ramp to street level. He is shaking when he pulls up behind Ben. He puts the VW in park and crawls into the passenger seat of the big car.

'What happened?'

'I busted him. I marched right in there and said, You're in such fucking trouble.'

'Was he in his office?'

'In the conference room, with a bunch of guys; one looked very familiar.'

'Oh God,' Ben says. 'President Ford was due in there this morning for a meeting.'

'I'm surprised there wasn't more security,' Richard says, and then realizes there were men with guns drawn, aimed at him, ready and willing to shoot him – Secret Service.

'Then what happened?'

'He asked how much I wanted for the tape – I said it wasn't for sale.'

'He must have loved that.'

'Can't sell it – that's blackmail. Anyway, you should be getting a major apology and a very nice recommendation. Are you sure it was Gerald Ford? I think maybe it was Harrison Ford.'

'That too, it was Harrison Ford meeting Gerald Ford and his son Jack; they're making a movie about the Ford presidency.'

Richard nods. 'Yes, now that you mention it, there was a younger guy. I feel sick,' Richard says. 'I need a drink. Can you drive us somewhere?'

Ben puts the car in gear and takes them to Johnny Rockets.

'And what was Ford doing there anyway?'

'They're agents with heavy government ties; that's what I've been telling you.'

At Johnny Rockets, they sit in a booth having chocolate milkshakes.

'I can't believe I did that,' Richard says. 'It's so not me.'

'It was for me,' Ben says. 'Thanks.'

'Is there any relation between Tad Ford, Harrison Ford, and President Ford?' Richard asks.

'I don't think so,' Ben says.

'It's a lot of Fords,' Richard says.

From their booth they can see the ex-president's two-car motorcade emerge from the building, a big SUV with 'US Gov't' plates and an unmarked sedan.

'It's him,' Richard says, again thinking about the guns pointing at him.

'Don't tell Mom,' Ben says.

Richard nods.

The next morning they decide to take off for a few days, drive up the coast, explore. Richard goes to see Nic, to let him know that they're leaving. He and Sylvia are on the deck, each hooked up to an IV. 'Vitamin infusion,' Sylvia says. 'The next-best thing to sex.'

'Best just after sex,' Nic says, smiling, lighting a cigarette.

'You look pale,' Sylvia tells him. 'Next week I'm going to give you liver and beets.'

Nic stands and, pulling his IV pole after him,

leads Richard into the kitchen. 'I was about to come find you. I got a call from the kid, the little girl. She wants to see me – more to the point, she wants to bring me to school for Show and Tell.'

'As what?'

'Her father. According to my ex, her classmates don't believe that she has a father and don't understand what it means that she now has two mothers, they've been giving her a hard time – "Did your daddy marry them both?"'

'You should go.'

'Do I get dressed up? I've never been to Show and Tell. I don't have a suit or anything.'

'Just pants and a shirt.' Richard slaps Nic's back. 'It's great that she called.'

Richard and Ben get in the VW, put the top down, and drive up the coast – Miles Davis on the CD player, Malibu curled up on the backseat. After a while it starts to feel like they are climbing: the road curves, and the twists and turns are sharper. There are signs for rock slides, slippery roads, inclines; the rough cliffs are more dramatic. A bird with a huge wingspan soars over them.

They drive and drive; they are going just to go, to ride, to listen to music, to feel the wind, to see where it takes them.

They call Ben's mother from the car and pass the phone back and forth between them. 'I can't hear you,' she says. 'You sound very far away. Call me later; I'm about to go into a meeting.'

They eat snacks they buy in gas stations, stop at local vineyards, let Malibu loose to chase scents. 'He's probably only ever lived on the water,' Richard says. 'This is the first time he's chased rabbits.'

Up past Santa Barbara, they find an inn that will also take the dog and have a communal dinner with the other guests – everything served is from the innkeeper's garden. Richard and Ben look at the other guests and then look at each other for clues. Something has happened between them – a bond. Now Richard really is the father and Ben the son, and together they are a team. The three of them share a king-sized bed, Malibu in the middle pushing Richard and Ben to the edges.

At dawn, father and son sit on a precipice high above the Pacific. Malibu is down below, jumping from rock to rock, chasing pelicans.

'It doesn't get better than this.'

'I don't think Malibu has ever had a vacation,' Ben says.

Coming back to L.A. is hard. There are messages on the machine: the contractor is almost finished, but has questions; the sinkhole has been filled and covered with fresh sod – the bright green stands out against the scrub and wildflowers.

Cecelia wants to come back to work – part-time. She's not allowed to 'do' anything but wants to get out of her house. Richard calls an industrial cleaning company and hires a crew of four to go through the house. It's covered in dust, in dead fire ants and pesticide – he can't give it back to her dirty.

Richard and Ben go to look at the house. In addition to everything else, they have built some sort of underground retaining wall, so now there's a kind of dirt hump that looks like an oversized mole tunnel in a ring around the house.

The movie star is there, working with the construction guys. 'Isn't it great? Really looks good, right?'

'Do you know what you're doing?' Richard asks.

'Well, yeah, the guys show me; it's not like they're just letting me randomly bang away at your house. In my next film I play a guy who was a carpenter; I thought I should get a feel for it. Hey, sorry about the fire ants. I think they came from my house – my sister bought some planters in Mexico that turned out to be infested. I read your friend's script – the G-man who was here about the hole. It's not bad; we're gonna option it. Have you ever met his wife?'

'No.'

'She works as a hotel phone operator, but she's like a starlet; I'm thinking I should put her in the film.'

The color lady shows up with the painter, who Richard has decided is also her sex slave. 'You survived,' she says.

Richard has no idea what she's talking about. 'Yes,' he says.

'What are we thinking now?' she asks.

'I don't know,' Richard says. 'You tell me. And by the way, this is my son, Ben. It's his room you've been working on.'

She stands in front of Ben, looking at him closely, and then closes her eyes and waves her hands back and forth in front of him, around him, over him. 'I'm getting a reading,' she says.

Mesmerizing though it is, Richard is distracted by the sight of the movie star rappelling off the side of his house, holding a nail gun.

'I'm seeing a desk that's "school of,"' the color lady says. 'And a chunky handmade rug from Belgium, beautiful neutral-tone walls, grayish-brown mouse.' Her eyes pop open. 'Like it?' she asks Ben.

'Flat-screen TV,' Ben says, channeling along with her. 'High-speed Internet access – wireless.'

Saturday morning, Nic pounds heavily on the front door. 'Fred's dead. The nursing home called – he took a turn yesterday, they took him to the hospital. He died overnight. I don't understand why they didn't call. I am the person they're supposed to call.'

'Can we drive you down?' Richard asks.

At the hospital Nic tells people he's Fred's son. The nurse is embarrassed. 'We weren't expecting anyone; we sent him down to the morgue. I can have someone meet you there.'

'What happened?'

431

'He'd most likely had a stroke during the night; we gave him oxygen and fluids, we supported him, but as you know he was DNR, that was a decision that he made – and then, while he was with us, he had what looked like another stroke. It was very peaceful.'

'I want to see him.'

'Yes,' she says, picking up the phone and arranging for Fred to be taken out of storage. Ben and Richard go to the basement with Nic, waiting for him on the opposite side of a pair of heavy double doors marked 'Authorized Personnel Only.' Every time someone comes or goes, they catch a glimpse of Nic bent, talking to Fred. He is with him for a long time. When he comes out, his clothing smells of formaldehyde or whatever it is they're using now.

They go to the nursing home. 'Is there a plan for a funeral?' Nic asks the director, a hard woman with a pinched face, like dried fruit.

'No funeral plans. We notified his niece in Delaware; he'll be cremated and interred at a plot shared with his wife, who predeceased him.'

'Why wasn't I called?'

'The family was called.'

'My name is on the paper that Fred signed, making his wishes clear.'

'What can I tell you?'

'I want there to be a service for his friends to have a chance to say good-bye.'

'Mr . . . ,' she says, and waits for Nic to fill in his name.

'Thompson,' Nic says.

'We try not to make a big deal out of death. Everyone here is going to die, they all know it. We don't like to stir their feelings or cause panic.'

'How about respect? How about treating them as adults who do know exactly what is going to happen to them, and make it a memorial service they can think about in a good way?'

'You are a guest here, you have friends among our residents, but you don't make the rules – I do.'

'With your permission,' Nic says, 'I would like to hold a service and invite the residents.'

'Not on the property,' she says.

'Fine, off the property. Tomorrow. I will provide transportation and assistance for anyone willing and able to join us. Is that acceptable?'

She nods.

'And what would be a good time for the residents?'

'They're morning people,' the directress says.

'How's eleven a.m.? I'll have them back in time for lunch.'

'Fine,' she says.

'And what about his belongings?'

'We usually recycle them. I can give you a few plastic bags if you'd like to clean out his room.'

Nic goes down the hall, piles Fred's belongings into his arms, and goes around the home, speaking to each of the residents.

'Fred wanted me to give you his red sweater. Tomorrow we're going to celebrate Fred's life – we're out for pie. We'll leave around ten-thirty.'

He gives away Fred's slippers, his new socks, his clean bathrobe, his cane. Nic gives Lillian – a woman who could still make Fred blush – a few of Fred's photos, the only truly personal item in his room: Fred as a young man in the army, Fred and his parents. 'He had it for you,' Nic tells her. 'But I think you knew that.'

'A lovely man,' Lillian says. 'Thank you.'

Nic gives photos to Ben – Fred's wedding, Fred and his wife on their twenty-fifth anniversary. 'Give one to Barth and keep one for yourself; whether you know it or not, you carry the past with you everywhere – it's better to know.'

Nic tucks Fred's comb into his own back pocket, and he puts Fred's radio in the arms of a man who can barely lift his head.

'Fred asked me to be sure this made its way to you – he said you loved music,' Nic lies.

The man mumbles something.

'We'll have transportation and pie, because you know how Fred felt about pie,' Nic tells everyone. The residents are excited: not only have they received gifts, they have something to look forward to – pie.

'What about drinks? Can we get a decent cup of coffee?'

'Yes, coffee, tea, whatever you want.'

Nic rents two minivans and hires a couple of off-duty aides from the nursing home. Richard calls Cynthia and asks her to come. 'We need chaperones – some of these people have a tendency to wander.'

In the morning, Nic and Richard and Barth and Ben and Cynthia and thirteen residents make the trip to the Farmers Market.

'What do you call this place?' one of them asks.

'It's the old Farmers Market,' another says.

'Look, Brussels sprouts; we used to grow those in our garden, on the stalk, just like that. Can I hold them, just for a minute?'

Richard buys the woman a stalk of Brussels sprouts for two dollars. Barth of course is filming the whole thing, the loading and unloading of the old people.

At the memorial service he sits next to Cynthia. 'Thanks for coming; how's the roommate?'

Cynthia shakes her head. 'Not good – she's still in the hospital.'

'Are you going to get a new one?'

'No. I'll keep the second bedroom open and start inviting the kids over – one at a time for overnights or weekends. I'm missing them.'

Richard nods. 'That would be nice.'

'Well, I am their mother.'

While they're talking, Richard notices one of the old people peeing on a chair.

Nic begins. 'As far as I know, all Fred had was a bowling ball, his wife's dentures, and a couple of old pairs of shoes from when they used to go dancing. He liked pie, a nice big slice of pie, and he liked people. He liked each one of you, and you could tell from the way he would just light up as soon as anyone spoke to him. Is there anything any of you want to say about Fred?'

'When Fred came to the home, he could still walk – with a walker, but, boy, he made tracks down the hall,' one of the residents says.

'I remember Fred,' another one says, and says nothing more.

'When I die, can we have Chinese food?' one of the men asks.

When they return them to the home, Lillian grips Nic's arm and pulls him towards her. 'Does this mean I'm not going to see you again?'

'No, Lillian,' Nic says. 'It means that from now on every week I am going to come and visit you.'

'Thank you,' she says.

'I'll see you on Wednesday,' he says.

'Oh, and I like lemon-meringue.'

'Good to know,' Nic says.

After Fred's funeral, Richard calls Sydney – he's craving comfort, and he got good news back from the doc, just some sort of irritation, nothing infectious. They make a plan to drive to Santa Barbara for dinner; it's neutral territory. On the way up, she gives him a blow job while he's driving, and at the big moment he nearly rear-ends a tanker truck ahead of him on the highway. In Santa Barbara, they go for a walk along the beach, and at a certain point she commands, 'Make love to me, here, now.'

Her sexuality is robust, overwhelming.

For the reason of simply wanting to try it, Richard took a Viagra before he left home – he ordered it online. He is hard as a rock and he is on top of her – thinking he's having chest pain, or maybe it's just the position.

They're screwing and screwing and he doesn't come, and at a certain point it's practically painful; she's already given a couple of really big war whoops, and he's at it all the more just trying to finish so they can stop. It's like an itch that he can't stop scratching; there's no end in sight, and he starts thinking that even if he comes now he's so overexcited, so aerobically energized, his heart will actually explode.

Finally, fear gets the better of him and he pulls out, puts it away, stiff, sopping wet, hoping it will surrender on its own.

They walk; he thinks she's starting to fall for him and feels himself backing away, and then she tells him that she doesn't know how he feels about her but that she has to be honest, she doesn't want to mislead him, and the other day, at PC Greens, she met someone.

He's a little let down but mostly feels the pressure is off, and now he feels *it* relaxing, and suddenly he has to pee like nothing else. Richard excuses himself and does it farther down on the beach, where someone sees him and yells, 'The world is not your toilet, fuckhead.'

*   *   *

She arrives without warning – his former dearly beloved. 'I'm in the car, on my way in from the airport – caught a late flight. I'll be at the hotel.'

'You're here?'

'I told you I was coming. Oh God, I'm ringing.'

'You said you'd try.'

'Well, here I am. That's the office calling, I gotta go.'

'Should we meet for breakfast?' Richard asks.

'I'm double-booked.'

'Lunch?'

'Double again.'

'Dinner?'

'I'm trying to stay on New York time. Six?'

'Fine, good, we'll see you then.'

He goes to tell Ben.

'I already know,' Ben says. 'Dinner at six.'

'I never told her I bought you a car; I didn't want her to say no.'

'I told her; she said it was the least you could do, and she didn't understand how you could buy a car for a woman you're not even sleeping with. The trick is getting Barth to give back the Volvo.'

Richard laughs. He calls the hotel and orders flowers to be sent to her room; suddenly shy, he signs only Ben's name on the card – 'Welcome to L.A.'

He flashes on the last family vacation they took: Ben was about three, they went to St Barts. He took Ben swimming every day, and she spent most of the time editing a manuscript. He remembers

Ben with water wings, Ben naked, peeing in the pool, the thin arc of yellow spreading through the clear water.

It's been almost eleven years since they were all in the same place at the same time. He's looking forward to it. When he goes to the newsstand to pick up the morning papers, he stops at the barber shop. Trimmed; the barber dusts his neck, pushing prickly shards of hair deep down into his shirt.

In the middle of the afternoon, the concierge calls him at home.

'Excuse me,' he says. 'For calling behind the back.'

'Yes,' Richard says.

'I am calling because there has been a little accident – she was bitten by a dug.'

'By a dug?'

'Yes, a dug.'

What is a dug? A person named Doug? 'A bug? She was bitten by a bug, like a bee sting?'

'No, a dug. DAWG.'

'Is she all right?'

'She is with ice; I thought you should know. This is her son, yes?'

'Yes,' Richard says, because it is easier than saying no.

'I remember you,' the voice says, and Richard wishes he hadn't heard that part.

'Yes,' he repeats. 'I'm on my way.'

It takes him an hour to get there – the traffic is horrible. He calls her from the car. She doesn't mention the dog bite, and he starts to wonder if maybe it was some sort of setup by the concierge to get Ben there. He floats an idea.

'I'll be near the hotel this afternoon; how about I stop by?'

'Oh,' she says, 'that would be nice.'

He passes through the lobby unnoticed, rings the bell to her room. 'Come in,' she calls, 'it's open.'

Does she look the same? Different? Older? He has no idea. In his anxiety he sees everything but her.

The room itself is familiar – this is where he stayed with Cynthia the night the house sank. She is in the living room, her shoes off, foot up on the coffee table wrapped in ice.

'Nice room,' he says.

'It's the same room I always have.'

'Is it?'

She nods.

'Twisted ankle?' he asks.

'I wanted to buy a present for Ben, I was walking, and they just came after me, little wild dogs like a pack of miniature wolves. 'Sit,' I yelled. 'Stop. Stay.' They heard nothing. I tried to run, but those are not running shoes.' She points to her Manolos, tossed off near the door. 'They chased me down Rodeo and into Saks. I dove into the store kicking them off; one had his teeth sunk into my ankle, and I was shaking my leg trying to get him loose. The others were hurling themselves at the glass doors, scratching, barking.

'The security guys did a wonderful job, trapping them in garment bags and turning them over to the police. Apparently it's not the first time it's happened: there's a pack roaming Beverly Hills. They would have eaten me alive.'

'And so one bit you?'

'At least one. I can't bring myself to look.'

'Did you call a doctor?'

'I spoke to Charlie's office in New York, he said I have to get a rabies shot; do you have a doctor here?'

'It's a sore point,' Richard says, lifting the ice pack to look at her leg.

Her panty hose are shredded; there are bite marks on her leg. Her calves are thin, ankles slim, but her feet are not the feet he remembers – thicker, hammer-toed, they are more like her mother's feet. He notices something on her toes – white, like fungus.

'Should you be taking that stuff I see advertised – Lamisil?'

She laughs. 'It's not fungus, it's a bad paint job. I asked for French tips and they blew it.'

He calls Dr Anderson's office.

'It's Richard Novak,' he says to the receptionist. 'I'm calling because my wife has been bitten by a dog.'

'I didn't know you were married,' the receptionist says.

'She needs a rabies shot.'

'Hold on.' She comes back on the line. 'The doctor was about to go home, but he says he'll stay, he'd love to meet your wife.'

'Charlie told me to keep my leg up,' she says.

He lifts her; he feels it in his back, but says nothing. She puts her arms around his neck. She is carrying the ice pack – cold between his shoulder blades. She leans her head against his chest; he breathes deeply. He loves her smell. He loves her; he has always loved her, that's why he had to leave.

'Nice to see you,' he says, while they are waiting for the elevator.

She smiles. 'How's Ben?'

'He's good, really good.'

In the elevator going down, a disembodied voice speaks to them: 'Can you hear me? This is a test, we are testing our system. Can you hear me?'

'Yes,' they say in unison.

'Can you say a few words so we can be sure we hear you?'

'We are riding in the elevator,' Richard says. 'We are going down. Where are you talking to us from?'

'This is a satellite transmission from Burbank. Thank you for taking the time to assist us. This completes our test.'

'Looks like they found you very appealing,' Dr Anderson says, taking a look at her leg. 'Any idea what kind they were?'

'Pointy ears, sharp faces, the kind that are in those ads for Mexican food.'

'Chihuahuas?'

She nods.

'Sure it wasn't the saber-tooth?' the doctor asks, half kidding.

'Do you have saber-tooths on Rodeo Drive?'

'We've got everything,' the doctor says.

'It was dogs,' she says, 'little dogs.'

'Are you up to date on tetanus?'

'I'm up to date on nothing,' she says.

'Have you seen this kind of thing before?' Richard asks the doctor.

'Can't say I've seen it, but I have heard about them, packs of untamed dogs. Have you ever had a rabies shot?' he asks the ex-wife.

'A shot in the stomach; isn't that what rabies is?'

'Actually, now it's in the arm.'

'I wouldn't have thought it was something you kept in the office.'

'I keep one of everything; I like to be prepared for all eventualities,' he says. 'Do you have any allergies, sensitivities – eggs, shellfish, nuts?'

She shakes her head. 'Once some makeup remover gave me a rash, but that was years ago.'

'OK, so we're going to give you two shots today, tetanus and a rabies, and then you'll have to have five more rabies shots over the next four weeks. It's very important that you get the full series of shots; rabies is fatal, but the shots are not.'

Richard is looking at her – the planes of her face, the texture of her skin, the way she wears the passage of time – it all looks softer, warmer than he remembers.

'By the way, we found your EKG,' the doctor

says to him. 'It was in a pile on Lusardi's desk.' He steps out of the room to prepare the vaccines.

'I want to leave,' she says, suddenly. 'I don't like shots.'

'It's not an option,' Richard says.

'I don't care.'

'We need to stay,' he says, taking her hand, squeezing.

'Since when are you like this?'

'Like what?'

'So kind?'

'I don't know,' he says. And then, to fill the silence, he says, 'Did you know I had polio?' – as though this is a good change of subject – but it's on his mind.

'You didn't have polio.'

'I did, only I never knew. Why would you say I didn't?'

'Because you didn't. You weren't in an iron lung and you aren't in a wheelchair.'

'There are a variety of forms.'

The doctor comes back into the room. 'We had a little bit of an earthquake this morning – did you feel it?'

'I felt nothing,' Richard says.

He gives her the shots. 'I'll have you sit in the waiting room for about twenty minutes, just to be sure there's no allergic reaction, and then you'll need the second shot in, say, three days. Your regular doctors can get it for you, but if you're still here, give a call and I'll do it.'

'Thank you,' she says. 'Thank you very much.'

'A pleasure to meet you.'

Richard helps her off the table and into the waiting area.

'My plane was late getting in,' she says. 'We lost an engine over Ohio and had to go all the way back to JFK to get a new one.'

Richard remembers the last time they made love; he did it knowing he was leaving, he kissed her cheek, her neck, her hair knowing it was the last time. 'What were you thinking when we got married?' he asks her.

'I had high hopes.'

'Do you remember what happened on our honeymoon?'

'The volcano erupted and we had to leave; there was ash, molten lava,' she says; it was a game they used to play, always retelling the story of their relationship.

'The first time in more than a hundred and fifty years – we got out just in time – we went to Paris,' he says.

She is quiet for a while. 'What are you thinking?' he asks, assuming she will say something about him, something about Ben.

'I've been crazed,' she says. 'There's someone at the office who just does nothing; everyone else works like a dog, and this one guy does nothing, and I haven't had the nerve to say anything.'

Like a kick in the stomach – same as it always

was – it confirms what he felt long ago, what he knew. 'Do you ever stop?'

'Why would I want to?'

'Do you love it – is it satisfying?'

'I don't have time to think about it.'

'Is that why you do it, so you don't have to think?'

She doesn't answer.

'Do you?'

'I like to be active.'

In the waiting room, the television is tuned to a local news station. 'An Orange County mother is a hero. In a grocery-store parking lot, her car rolled on top of her toddler, pinning the child's arm. Maria Santiago lifted the car, and the child was able to crawl out with only a broken arm – the incident was caught on the store's external surveillance camera. "What were you thinking when the car ran over your daughter's arm?" "I just knew I had to get my baby out. I prayed to God to give me strength."'

Richard changes the subject. 'The other day, I saw a squirrel that had just been hit by a car; it wasn't dead, it was lying there, kicking frantically.'

'Did you roll over it?'

'What do you mean?'

'Did you drive your car over it and put it out of its misery?'

'No; why?'

'Well, wouldn't you want someone to do that to you if you were on the side of the road – to put you out of your misery?'

'No,' he says, horrified; it would never occur to him. 'No,' he says again, making it perfectly clear. 'Talk to me, hold my hand, but don't run me over.'

The doctor returns, checks her blood pressure, pronounces her good to go. 'Take Tylenol, keep it elevated, and if you run a temperature above a hundred and two, call me.'

Promptly at six, Ben arrives. He sees the ice pack, the gauze bandage around his mother's leg. 'What happened?'

'Feral Chihuahuas,' she says.

'Are you all right?'

'I'm fine,' she says. 'All cleaned up, vaccinated.'

'You're sure you're OK?' he asks again.

'Yes,' she says. 'And you? How's the job?'

'Uh, let's just say I'm not going to be the next superagent.'

'Everything is an experience,' Richard says.

The three have not been in a room together since Ben's Bar Mitzvah, and then they were with a hundred other people. Richard half wishes someone would appear, a facilitator or someone who could fix it so it all made sense.

They are there – each entirely separate – like characters on a stage, blocked for dramatic effect, the two men standing, the woman seated on the sofa – with everything between them.

'So – what now?' Ben asks.

'My assistant made a reservation at Orso,' she says.

'You're supposed to keep your leg up,' Richard says.

'Well, there are three of us at a table for four; that's what the extra chair is for.'

Ben keeps looking back and forth between them, moving his head, shifting.

'Are you looking for something in particular?' Richard asks Ben.

Ben leads them into the bedroom and has the three of them sit on the edge of the bed facing a large mirror – Ben in the middle.

'Do you see it?' Ben asks.

'Not sure what I'm looking for,' Richard says.

'The mattress is hard,' she says. 'It must be new.'

'My face,' Ben says. 'Look at my face. The hairline is yours,' he says to his father. 'And my eyes, my eyes are exactly the same as yours,' he says to his mother. 'And my chin . . .'

'That's your grandfather's chin,' Richard says.

'You can see where it all comes from, who it belongs to.'

And so they sit, the three of them looking into the mirror, looking at Ben, looking at themselves. They sit, and then there is a shudder, the lights dim and then brighten, and a few seconds later the room goes dark, the air stops.

The emergency lights click on – the room fills with a stale orange glow.

'What do you think it is?' she asks.

'It's been hot,' Richard says. 'We've had high electrical demand.'

Ben goes to the window. 'The good news is –

the lights are on out there.' He points twenty floors down.

'We should go to dinner,' she says. 'Even if we just go somewhere nearby, it's stifling to just sit here.'

'If there's no power, there's no elevator, and you have rabies,' Richard says.

'I forgot.'

He wants to turn on the TV, wants to see what happened, wants pictures, information, instant-aneous everything. Richard picks up the phone, dialing 0.

'It's not us personally, it is this side of the street,' the man at the front desk says. 'It is the grid, the grid has gone bad.'

'Any idea when the power will go back on?' Richard asks.

'When the grid is good,' he says. 'Meanwhile, I can send something up to you, a bottle of white wine, some pasta – we still have gas and are boiling water on the stove.'

Security guards with flashlights go up and down the hall, knocking on the doors, counting how many people are in-house and passing out flash-lights. 'Please stay in your rooms until lights are restored. If you have to leave, use the fire stairs at the far end of the hall and take your flashlight. The fire stairs are staffed and secure.'

'Why don't I go down and pick something up?' Ben says. 'I can take the stairs. What do you want – pizza, sushi, Chinese?'

'Do you have a menu?' she asks. 'It's hard to order without a menu.'

'Think of what you like and then name it,' Richard says.

'Ginger shrimp,' she says, 'and if they don't have that, some other spicy shrimp, just not in tomato sauce.'

'And?'

'Steamed vegetables with chicken, the sauce on the side,' she says. 'Brown rice, and some spare ribs.'

'And you?' Ben asks his father.

'Oh, steamed vegetable dumplings, and maybe, if they have it, soft-shelled crabs.'

'You're still eating soft-shelled crabs from Chinese restaurants?' she asks.

'Yes, why?'

'That's what you ate twenty years ago.'

'I still like it,' he says, giving Ben a wad of cash.

'And some Tylenol,' she says. 'Can you get me some Tylenol?'

'He's a good kid,' she says when he's gone.

'He's great.'

They are alone. Self-conscious, he goes to the window. He stands at the glass, looking out; it is not a luminous city, but, like all American cities, it glows in the dark. There are enormous billboards like beacons that light automatically at dusk, drawing all eyes to movie-star faces forty feet tall. 'Coming Soon.' 'Opens Friday.'

He steps away from the window and looks at her. 'You seem agitated.'

'It's been a strange day.'

'Breathe,' he says.

'What?'

He goes to her, puts one of her hands on her chest, the other on her belly. 'Close your eyes and breathe into this hand, fill your back, your belly; then slowly let the air out; and when you are ready, breathe in again.'

'I must have a fever,' she says.

There is a knock at the door; a red-faced porter hands Richard a bottle of wine – 'From the concierge. I carried it against my heart, I hope I did not make it too hot.' The hallway is humming, the emergency lights, the red 'Exit' signs, all of it seeming to stir the swirling pattern on the carpet. Richard gives the man twenty dollars.

Ben returns with two huge shopping bags of food and a bunch of outdoor candles he bought at the ninety-nine-cent store. They spread the food out on the coffee table. The candles are lit; Richard pours a glass of wine for everyone.

'A feast,' she says, propping her leg up on the sofa.

'An indoor picnic,' Richard says, bringing a pillow for under her leg.

The room is filled with a warm, buttery glow.

'This is delicious; where is it from?' she asks.

'If you saw the place you wouldn't be happy,' Ben says.

'Is that what it's called?'

'No, but I figured it was OK – it had a Health

451

Department 'A' rating and there were a lot of people in there eating.'

She takes a couple of Tylenol, washing them down with the wine. Richard refills their glasses, and slowly the whole family gets stoned from the lack of light, of air, the MSG, the wine.

And although there is a great and likely unbridgeable divide between the three of them, there is also a sense they are together, there for each other as much as they can bear to be, and though it might not be the fullness that one wants, and though it might not be enough, it is something, it is more than nothing.

'Do you ever think about how things might have been different, how my life might have been if you didn't get divorced?' Ben asks no one in particular.

'Did we ever actually get divorced?' Richard asks his ex-wife.

'What are you talking about?' She sits up, splashing wine.

'I can't remember if we ever signed divorce papers.'

'I signed divorce papers years ago,' she says.

'At whose request?'

'Mine,' she says. 'I like things organized – dot the "i"s, cross the "t"s.'

'I was asking about me,' Ben says. 'Do you ever think about how it would have been different for me?'

'Yes,' Richard says. 'I think about it a lot.'

'If this was the end of the world, the last conversation we'd ever have – what would we say?' Ben asks.

'Is it something you think about?' Richard asks. 'How things would have been – the end of the world? It's all very fragile, isn't it – our time here.'

'I don't like games like this,' she says.

'Well, I just want to say that if this was the end of the world, right now, it would be OK with me,' Ben says.

'If this was the end of the world, I personally would wonder what was going to happen next – the world as we know it is not all that there is; there is more, something larger than any of us,' Richard says.

'If this was the end of the world,' she says, interrupting, 'I would stay up talking to you, but it's not, so I'm going to lie down.' Richard helps her off the sofa. 'It's been a very long day, I have to get up early, and if I don't go to sleep now, everything will be ruined.'

Richard and Ben follow her into the bedroom and lie on the beds, while she goes into the bathroom.

'We should stay the night,' Richard says to Ben. 'What about Malibu?'

'He'll be OK – he has food and water, and the door is cracked open so he can go out.'

'I think I should go home with her,' Ben says softly from his bed. 'Summer's almost over, the stuff for the donut shop has all been ordered, and I can always fly out and help with the installation.'

'I want more,' Richard says, from the other bed. 'I want to go to Disneyland again, and I want to go to Knotts Berry Farm; I heard they have a really good roller coaster. I want to go all kinds of places with you, maybe take one of those bike trips across France – do you like riding a bike?'

'I guess.'

'We can train – if we start now, we'll be ready by next spring.'

'OK.'

'Do you want to take Malibu back to New York with you?'

'I don't think he'd like being alone in the apartment all day, and, besides, you need him.'

She comes out of the bathroom in a T-shirt and climbs into the bed where Richard is. 'Night,' she says.

Ben says nothing more, and Richard realizes that the boy has fallen asleep.

Richard thinks of leaving, of getting up and going, but instead he climbs under the covers next to her – her body bends to accommodate him.

At 6:00 a.m. she is on the treadmill in the second bedroom in her bra and underwear. 'I wasn't expecting company,' she says, gesturing to her outfit.

'It's cute,' Richard says.

'The power's back on,' she says, increasing the incline. She has already eaten her half a grapefruit and her decaf cappuccino. Ben is still asleep in the other room.

'It's nine a.m. in New York. I'm late.'

'Where are you going?' Richard asks.

'I have two breakfasts – seven-thirty and a nine – and then a meeting at ten-thirty and lunch at one.'

'How's your leg?'

'Fine, but my arm is sore from the shots,' she says.

Back in the bedroom, he watches her dress; he always thought it was incredibly sexy, the way she would sit at the edge of the bed and roll her panty hose up her legs, stand, reach behind herself, and zip her skirt. He watches, overcome with longing.

'I may have to head back to New York tonight – a production crisis – but I'll call you later,' she says, leaving – the two discreet Band-Aids at her ankle the only mark of her attack.

Overnight, a fire has started in the hills: the flick of a match, a lightning strike, a smoldering ember. It spreads quickly; dry chaparral bursts into flame; fire skirts the ground, hopping from stick to stick. It starts small, intimately, but spreads with enthusiasm.

As Richard and Ben drive from Beverly Hills into Santa Monica, they see the smoke high up, far away, fire on the hill.

'When she goes, are you going with her?' Richard asks.

Ben nods. 'I'll be back. You believe me, right?'

'Flat screen, high-speed Internet,' Richard says, reminding Ben of what will be in his new room.

'A bicycle ride across France,' Ben says.

'I'm going to hold you to it,' Richard says, dropping Ben at the new donut shop – the painters are there, the counter guy is coming, it is a work in progress.

'I can't say good-bye,' Ben says.

'Call me,' Richard says.

Ben holds his fingers to his ear, making the sign of the telephone. 'Will call,' he says.

Nic is outside the house in Malibu, digging through the garbage. 'I think I threw away something.'

'What?' Richard asks.

'I don't know. As I was emptying the can I had the feeling I was throwing away something I shouldn't. I bought a shredder,' he says, dumping an enormous pile of shredded paper back into the trash can.

'You look like you haven't slept in days – everything OK?'

'Working like a dog.'

'Script?'

'Novel. It's like I'm on fire,' Nic says.

Richard follows Nic into the house – it's a mess, coffee cups, half-eaten sandwiches, wads of crumpled paper all over the floor, two typewriters set up, motors humming.

'Just waiting for the last page to firm up,' Nic says. He feeds paper into the shredder, which spits confetti. 'Rough drafts. So I called my folks,' he says.

'Oh?'

'Yeah; you know, the whole Fred thing spooked me. "When are you coming home?" was the first thing my father said. "First flight out," I said. It was the only thing I could say. It was like they'd been sitting by the phone for years. "Do you have a jacket?" my mother asked. "It gets chilly in the evenings, it's not like it is out there." While I was talking to them, I couldn't remember why I'd stayed away for so long.'

'It'll come back to you as soon as you get there,' Richard says with confidence.

Nic looks worried. 'Did I ever mention how much I hate to fly?'

'No.'

'Petrified. I have a recurring image of the small plane that crashed in New Jersey a couple of years ago, hurling people still strapped in their seats into the parking lot of a Kentucky Fried Chicken.'

'Do you want me to go with you? I'll fly to Albany, check into a hotel for a few days, and, when you're ready, fly back.'

'That's probably the nicest offer I've ever had.'

'It's not just an offer.'

'How about you just drive me to the airport?'

'Just say when.'
'Give me a couple of hours.'

The dog is glad to see Richard; he gives him an enormous greeting, complete with a full series of licks to the face and ears. Richard feeds him and takes him for a long walk. The tide is high: waves lap at the timbers under the houses; seaweed wraps around Richard's ankle, tickling him, trapping him. Richard thinks about Ben, Ben back in New York, a senior in high school, Ben taking the SATs, applying to colleges – what does he want to be? Richard thinks of the house on the hill, of moving back, of being alone. He cannot bear the idea of going back to what was, spending the days home doing nothing. He can't do nothing, but what can he do? He has a good car; he will be the man who picks up the donuts from Anhil and delivers them to the new location; he will outfit the trunks with racks, they will slide the trays of warm donuts in, and he will drive them to Santa Monica twice a day. And after he drives the donuts – then what? It will only be 6:30 a.m. He will meditate. He will sign up for a yoga class in Santa Monica – that's perfect, he likes it there, likes the feeling of the place – and then, at 8:00 a.m. he'll go to the gym, eat breakfast at the donut shop, and then – he'll go visiting. Not just one person, but a dozen people. He will visit door to door delivering donuts to the elderly, the infirm – OK, not delivering donuts, it's not like old people want to be eating donuts – he will deliver Meals on Wheels to old people. He'll arrange for Meals on Wheels to have Sylvia cook for old people on special diets, people who need good nutrition. It will be his gift; he will pay for it and he will deliver the food and visit the old people. He sees himself knocking on doors, ringing bells. 'Mrs Donziger, it's Richard from Meals on Wheels.' If they want to talk, he will sit down and talk. If not, he will simply bring them food and good wishes. He's thrilled, he's finally figured it out, he has something to do – he is useful. He imagines calling his parents in Florida and telling them the good news.

'What do they need you for?' his mother will say. 'Don't they have children of their own who can take care of them?'

'Sometimes you can do things for others that you can't do for yourself.'

Just after noon, Nic calls. 'It's now or never.'

Richard goes to help with his bags. The house has been transformed: everything is clean, in order, the dishes washed and put away; it is as though even the air itself is changed. The last couple of bags of trash are by the door.

'My inner maid rose up and burst forth,' Nic says.

'Did you wash the floors?'

'Aye,' he says. 'I swabbed the deck, and I swabbed myself as well.' He's showered, shaved; there's a fresh scratch on his neck. His hair is combed back – he looks different, older, worn. 'I finished the book,' he says.

'Where is it?'

Nic kicks the lowest drawer of the file cabinet. 'Twenty years in the making.'

'Do you have a copy?'

'Nope. How long does it take to get to the airport – can we make it in an hour?'

'You have everything: clothing, toothbrush, medication in case your back goes out, vitamins?'

'They don't travel well.' He pulls a pint of scotch out of his jacket. 'Road food.' His suitcase is a small duffel, a sausage.

'How long will you be gone?'

'A few days. Do me a favor?'

'Yeah, sure.'

'Visit Lillian. I told her I would – she likes lemon-meringue.'

In the car, Nic sweats. He takes off his jacket and untucks his shirt. He gets sticky, pale.

'Are you nauseated?'

'No. Ten bucks says when I get to Security they pull me aside. I didn't bring presents – is that OK?'

'Get a box of See's candy at the airport – mothers love that.'

Nic nods.

'What are you most afraid of?' Richard asks.

'Dying,' Nic says.

'In a plane crash?'

'Yes, either on the plane or at my parents' house.

I can't tell which is worse.' He pauses. 'Look, if I'm not back in a week, come get me.' He writes the address and phone number on a piece of paper.

'You know you can call me anytime.'

'If I die, you're in charge of the book.'

'You're not going to die.'

'Bottom drawer.'

Coming back from the airport, Richard finds the roads crowded, people leaving, not running but flocking, their cars piled high with stuff, the air is charged with drama and smells like barbecue. The fire is burning closer to Malibu.

When Richard gets back to the beach, Ben is gone. He knows it right away – the presence of absence. There's no note, no message on the machine. He calls the other house, checks the messages: the exterminator; the painter; Patty, the 911 operator, 'checking in.' 'We haven't heard from you in a while, so I'm assuming you're feeling better – which is a good thing. If I remember right, you're living in Malibu. I heard things down there are really bad with the fire and they're expecting some wave activity – from storms offshore. As a 911 worker, I'm supposed to be cool, detached, but shit like this makes me really nervous.'

Nothing from Ben.

Richard can't stay there – he can't just sit, it's too awful. He drives to Anhil's. The air is better there.

'I met your wife,' Anhil says, eyes twinkling.

'Ex-wife,' he says.

'Very nice,' Anhil says.

'Did Ben tell you he was leaving?' Richard asks Barth.

'Before today? No,' Barth says. 'You shouldn't take it personally, it's just the way he had to do it. He had a really good summer, he could have stayed with you forever.'

'I followed Ben up to your house; the little Bug, she is in the garage,' Anhil says. 'He let me drive her – she is a happy, smiling car. I laughed the whole time I was driving. I took the flower from the dash.' He points to a gerbera daisy in a juice glass on the counter. 'I did not want her to wilt.'

'Don't be mad,' Barth says.

'I'm not mad,' Richard says, angrily, 'I'm hurt.'

'Have a donut,' Anhil says. 'It will make you comfortable.'

The idea of the donut reminds him of Lillian – visiting Lillian will make him feel better. Not thinking about how bad he feels will make him feel better.

From the car, en route to DuPar's at the Farmers Market, he calls Cynthia.

'Want to have lunch?' she asks. 'The weather guy just blew me off. He had to prepare a special report on the wildfire and the offshore storms – it's a weather extravaganza.'

'I'm all the way downtown. How about dinner?'

'I wish I could,' she says. 'But Meagan's coming;

it's our first mother-daughter sleepover. I'm really excited, I bought stuff to bake cookies. I'm going to be a mom again. I'll call you later,' she says.

At DuPar's he buys a lemon-meringue pie, and then goes to the home. Lillian is alone in her room.

'Hello, Lillian,' he says.

'Who are you?'

'I'm a friend of Fred's – we met the other day at the memorial service.'

'I thought the other guy was coming, the cute one.'

'He had to go out of town.'

'Are you two lovers?'

He's surprised.

'No.' He laughs. 'I'm divorced.'

'You'd make a good couple.'

'I brought you pie,' he says.

'Well, let's have it already,' she says.

All he's got for serving it is a plastic knife and some forks, and a couple of Styrofoam plates. He starts to cut a slice. 'Bigger,' she says, and he moves the knife. Richard looks at Lillian, who gives him the eye that she wants it bigger still.

'Okey-dokey,' he says, slicing the pie.

'Delicious,' she says, 'absolutely delicious.' She savors each bite: the meringue is perfect crispy brown on top, melts in the mouth; the lemon tart, custardy; the crust breaks away. 'I'll tell you a secret,' she says, picking up crumbs with a bony finger. 'I'm diabetic, so it's not like I can eat like this every day.'

'Lillian, how could you do this? Why did you say you liked pie if you're not allowed to eat it?'

'So what if I die? I can't live with nothing to enjoy, nothing to look forward to. Don't tell anyone.'

'What if you have a problem? I have to tell someone.' He wants to run out of the room. He wants someone to come and make her throw up what she's eaten. He grabs the box right out of her hands as she's going back for more.

'I'm not going to have a problem. I managed to live perfectly well for eighty-nine years before any of you came along and, with my luck, I'll probably live eighty-nine more.'

'Well, if you do you'll be the first.'

On her television he sees footage of the wildfire. 'In the effort to contain the fire, one helicopter took an unusual step, landing in a Westwood parking lot, hooking up to a hydrant, filling up, and taking off again. These guys are fearless. Another crew made a water drop on a woman driving down the high canyon road who'd become surrounded by a wall of fire.'

'I should get going,' he says.

'Does that mean you're not coming back? I never should have told you.'

'Oh no,' he says, 'I'm coming back, but I'm not bringing pie.'

'Fine. Bring me some of that candy for diabetics; it's all right except that it gives me the runs if I eat too much.'

'Fine,' he says, 'I'll bring you a little bit of the candy.'

On the way out of the home, holding the rest of the pie, Richard runs into the director. He confesses.

'That's why we don't like them to have visitors,' she says. 'I'll have the nurses check her sugar tonight.'

'Thank you.'

He has trouble getting home: the traffic is heavy, roads are closed because of the fire. It takes him an hour and a half, crawling.

The air is a yellowy acrid haze – the wind blows particles that stick in the throat.

He is cranky, thinking about Ben. What prompted him to go? Was he ready, or did she make him? Will Richard see him again? When?

'Earlier today, in some areas, canyon residents hid in their swimming pools, breathing through snorkels, while the fire blew over them,' the radio reporter says.

'The thermal intensity is amazing, like something out of the Bible,' a man adds. 'A vacuum of flame, sucking things up, a fire tornado – I saw fire a hundred feet high.'

'What's hard for even the most experienced of us to comprehend,' the reporter continues, 'is how rapidly this fire has spread. There are now thousands of acres involved, dozens of homes already lost. Will all of Los Angeles burn? I've got one of our county commissioners on the line.'

'The good news,' the commissioner says, 'is that there's a natural extinguishing point – the Pacific Ocean.'

'We'll be back with you shortly; meanwhile, if you want to donate bottles of water or sandwiches for the firefighters, please bring them to your local L.A. county fire department. The effort will be ongoing throughout the night.'

Richard eats the dinner that Sylvia delivered a couple of days ago while watching the news channel. 'Night is settling on Los Angeles, and firefighters hope that means that the wild-fire which has been raging all afternoon will slow its fury. Earlier today, firefighters got themselves into a tight squeeze when a hill they were standing on shifted, opening a crevasse estimated to be a hundred and fifty feet long and twenty feet deep and four feet wide. Several of the men lost their footing, fell in, and were later rescued. And, in a strange twist, about half an hour ago firefighters working on a Topanga Canyon ridge spotted what they're describing as the infamous mystery cat – a large animal some believe may be the sole surviving saber-toothed cat. The company reported seeing the animal at the top of a hill; the hill then burst into flame – which is what this very dry brush will do – trees exploding before their eyes, and then the cat was gone. No one knows if it was some sort of visual phenomenon or the real thing. So, tonight, up in the hills, everyone is wondering. And, given the danger of both the fire and the animal at large, officials are urging people to stay put.'

Malibu keeps going to the front door – scratching. Richard's not sure if it's because he's missing Ben or he senses something's up.

'That's not our door,' Richard tells the dog. 'That door goes to the highway; we go out the other door, to the beach. Do you want to go out?'

From the beach, looking back, the sky is glowing yellow, like the end of the world. The air smells like burned toast. Far down the road, at the inter-section, he sees mobile news trucks parked, their satellites fully extended. He sees the amusement park at the pier – the Ferris wheel is stopped – everything is stopped. The winds shift, the smoke gets heavier.

He goes back into the house, rummages; on the floor of the closet he finds a gym bag that must have been the mayor's, it's got a red necktie in it, a thing of deodorant, and some glow-in-the-dark condoms – and an emblem on the outside says ROSE BOWL 2002 VIP. He packs a few things in case they have to evacuate: a leash, a plastic bag filled with kibble, chocolate bars, and a change of clothes. He puts the cell phone into the all-weather case Cynthia gave him and slips it into the bag.

Richard goes into Nic's. He opens the file cabinet and takes the manuscript – if he has to go, he's going to take it with him. He's stealing the man's book in an effort to protect it. He puts rubber bands around it in both directions, slips it into a plastic bag. He takes a deep breath – his lungs fill with smoke.

Far up the hill, embers glow like fireflies, waves of fire caress the hillside, flames jump and roll back. The wind shifts, pushing the fire forward.

It happens in the middle of the night. At first he thinks a truck went off the road and crashed into the house. A roaring rumble, the walls shake, the floor is like Jell-O, the house shifts. He hears the front door burst open, breaking the frame. He stuffs Nic's novel into his shirt, grabs the bag, runs into the living room. The hill is rolling in; there's the splintering crack of wood giving way, the deep bellowing of walls caving in, rubble crashing through, propelling him out of the house, over the deck, along with everything that was the dining room. Richard is spilled into blackness. He is thinking this is the end, this is it, this is all there is. He is dumped into the ocean, splashing and sputtering. Something is coming towards him, bumping against him – the dining-room table. He grabs it, hoists himself up. Malibu, dog-paddling, scratches his way on board. The table floats. Richard remembers Billy telling him not to put anything hot on the table – it was a prop made for a movie – a prop made of Styrofoam.

He plucks a piece of the wooden deck out of the water, and uses it as a pole to push debris away from his raft.

He remembers Nic telling him, 'It's not the

wildfires that are going to get you; it's the secret of Malibu – the septic tanks. The hills are filled with leaking septic tanks dumping "water" into the ground and at some point it's gonna give. It's a river of piss and shit that'll wash us all away,' Nic had said. 'Malibu is the last of the Wild West: it's every man for himself and then some.'

Richard lies on the table, taking a kind of inventory: arms, legs, everything is intact. He lies on the table, rolling with the waves, thinking of the story Joseph told about a man whose house was taken by a flood and he was left floating down his street, which had become a river – on top of a door – and all the man wanted to do was open the door. What did he think he would see, where did he think it would lead? Finally, the man couldn't stand it anymore; he positioned himself on the frame, pulled the knob – the door opened, he fell in and drowned.

Was there some larger meaning – was it a parable, an allegory, or just a story?

He is floating, drifting, and he is breathing and watching his breath and watching the sky. The orange-yellow of the wildfire is giving way to the orange-yellow of dawn. The sun is rising, the air straightening up, pulling tight.

He takes the cell phone out of the weatherproof case and pushes the 'power' button. The phone lights up, shows good signal and a decent charge. Richard unzips the mayor's gym bag, opens a condom, rolls it over the phone, and ties it off.

He floats.

There are surfers in the water – tiny and far away. He is out farther than he thought. The ocean, which was so stirred last night, is glassy, calm. He gives the dog breakfast, eats some chocolate, blows air into the Ziploc with Nic's manuscript just in case, and they wait. Richard tells himself not to fight it; for the moment he is safe and should accept what is. The sun is bright on the water, a golden streak; dolphins jump nearby. He is going out to sea.

Just after dawn, his cell phone rings – muffled, distant. He puts the condom phone to his ear. 'Hello,' he shouts.

'Don't be mad,' Ben says. 'I told you I couldn't say good-bye.'

'Is your mother there?' Richard says.

'She's here.'

'How's her leg?'

'It's OK. Are you sure you're not angry?'

'Can you find her for me?'

She picks up the phone. 'Richard, I'm on my way out, I have to go and get another damned rabies shot on my way to work.'

'Turn on your television.'

'I can hardly hear you. What channel?'

'I don't know, try CNN.'

'Wow, that's impressive – is that near your house?'

'That *is* my house.'

'Where are you calling from?'

'I'm floating,' he says. 'I'm out in the middle of the ocean.'

'You should try to swim back to shore.'

'There's a helicopter coming, it's just above me now, there's a man with a camera – I'm waving. Can you see me? Can anyone see me?'

She is watching him live from New York; he is on the dining-room table, at sea. 'Are you OK?' she asks.

'Fantastic, never better,' he says, and he's not lying. 'I'm just floating, waiting to see what happens next.'

A man leans out of the chopper with a megaphone. 'Hello down there, can you hear me?'

'YES,' he screams.

'We have you in our sights,' the man says. 'Hold on.'

Somewhere deep in the ground below the tectonic plates once again shift. And far in the distance, something catches his eye: Richard watches as the enormous Ferris wheel rolls gracefully off the Santa Monica Pier and into the water.

'We will not forget you,' the man says as the chopper banks to the left, pulling away, flying back towards the pier.

'Dad, are you still there?' Ben asks, panicked.

'Yeah, I'm here.'

'I can't see you anymore.'

'I'm here,' he says, 'I'll always be here, even when you can't see me, I'm still here.'

ACKNOWLEDGMENTS

For their inspiration, good care, and strong advice, the author would like to thank: Tracy Glaser, Amy Hempel, Marc H. Glick, Sara Holloway, Patricia McCormick, Dan Menaker, Anne Philbin, Marie Sanford, Paul Slovak, Cynthia Wornham, Andrew Wylie, Sarah Chalfant, Jin Auh, The Writers Room NYC, Andre Balazs, Philip Pavel and the staff at the Chateau Marmont, the Dorothy and Lewis B. Cullman Center for Scholars and Writers at The New York Public Library, Elaina Richardson, and the Corporation of Yaddo.